Praise for LEGACY OF THE ANCIENTS

"Ron Sarti single-handedly revitalizes the post-apocalypse subgenre . . . This is one series I don't want to see end."

Robert J. Sawyer, Nebula Award-winning author of *The Terminal Experiment* and *Frameshift*

"LEGACY OF THE ANCIENTS gives us real people, throws them into hard circumstances, then threads them through a story that compels our attention. Buy this book!"

William Barton, author of *Acts of Conscience* and *The Transmigration of Souls*

"An absolute pleasure to read . . . Thought-provoking examinations of problems with real world analogs . . . should move LEGACY to the top of everyone's to-be-read pile."

Michael Stackpole, *New York Times* bestselling author of *Star Wars® X-wing: Rogue Squadron*

"LEGACY OF THE ANCIENTS shines with intrigue, humor, and well-crafted, believable characters."

Lynn Flewelling, author of *Stalking Darkness*

Other AvoNova Books by
Ron Sarti

THE CHRONICLES OF SCAR

LEGACY OF THE ANCIENTS

Book Two of
THE CHRONICLES OF SCAR

RON SARTI

AVON BOOKS • NEW YORK

This is a work of fiction. Names, characters, places, and incidents either are the product of the author's imagination or are used fictitiously. Any resemblance to actual events, locales, organizations, or persons, living or dead, is entirely coincidental and beyond the intent of either the author or the publisher.

AVON BOOKS
A division of
The Hearst Corporation
1350 Avenue of the Americas
New York, New York 10019

Cover art by Greg Call
Published by arrangement with the author
Visit our website at **http://AvonBooks.com**
Library of Congress Catalog Card Number: 96-95169
ISBN: 0-380-73025-1

First Avon Books Printing: June 1997

Printed in the U.S.A.

WCD 10 9 8 7 6 5 4 3 2 1

In memory of my parents,
Remo Mario and Lucille Ann Sarti,
and my brother, Robert Francis Sarti

And for Mark and Erica

Contents

PART II
ARKAN

PART III
TEXAN

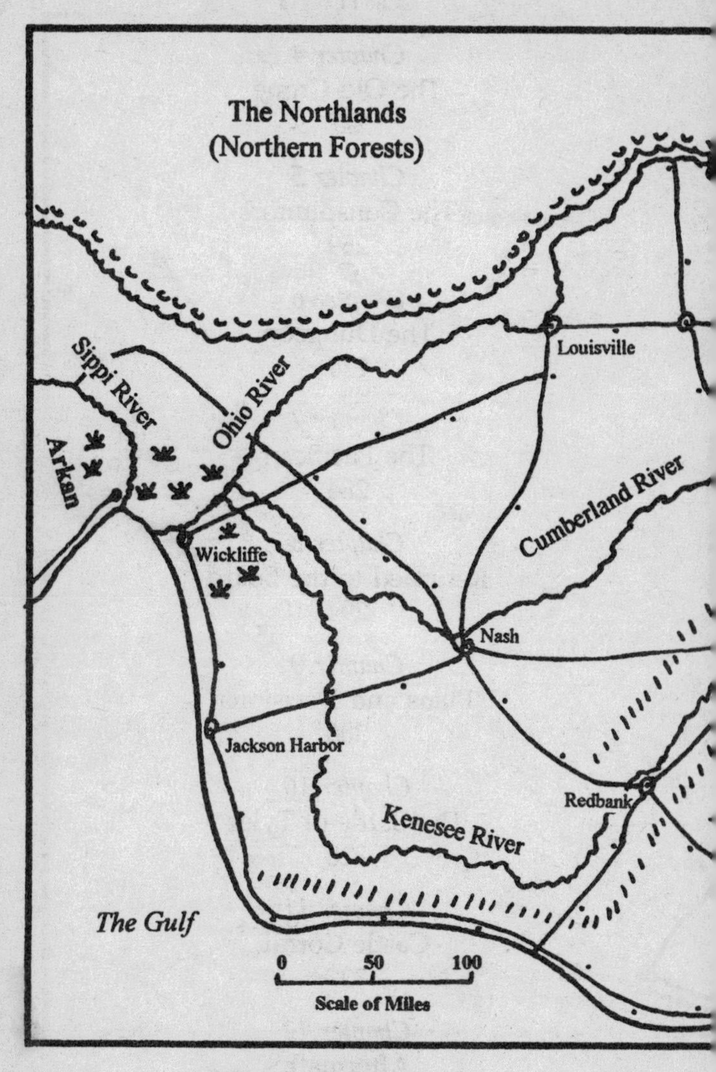

Map of Kenesee 2653 A.D.

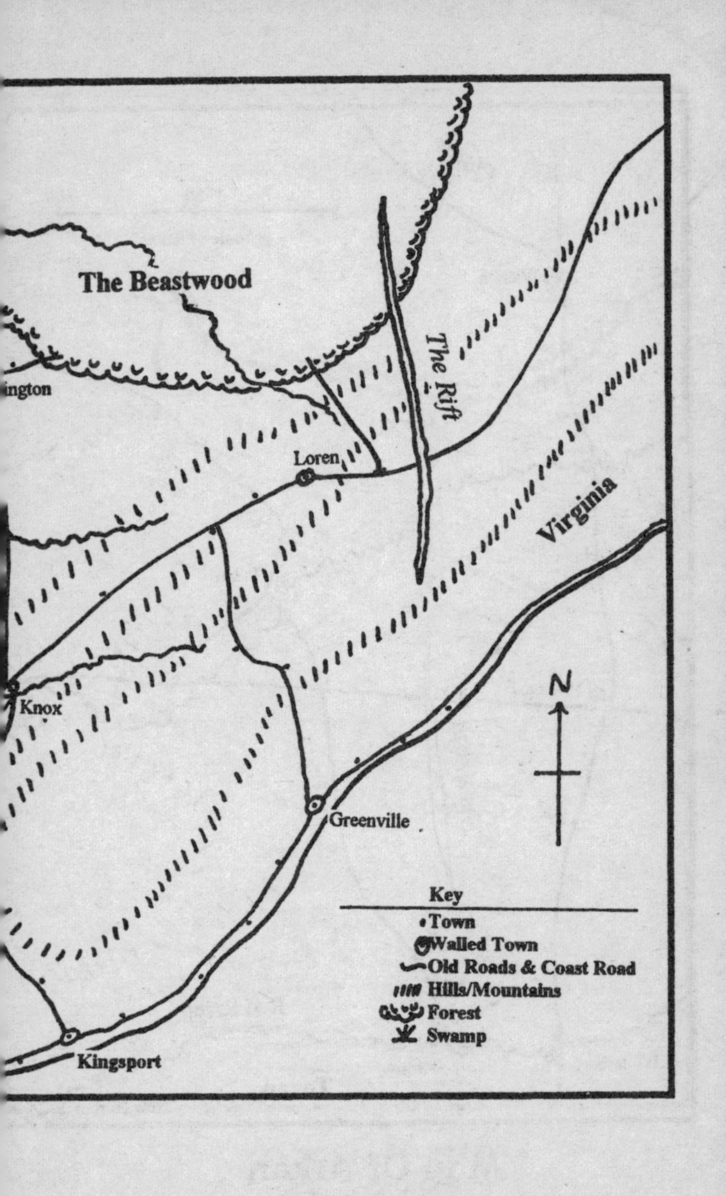

The Beastwood
ington
The Rift
Loren
Virginia
Knox
Greenville
Kingsport
N
Key
Town
Walled Town
Old Roads & Coast Road
Hills/Mountains
Forest
Swamp

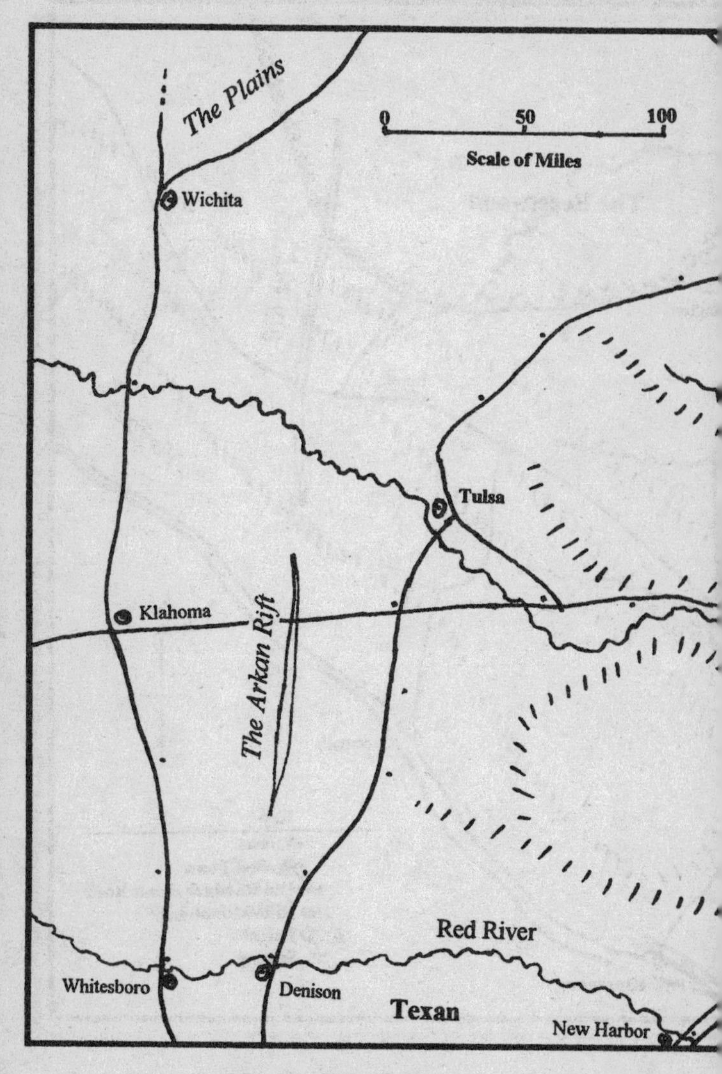
The Plains
0
50
100
Scale of Miles
Wichita
Tulsa
Klahoma
The Arkan Rift
Red River
Whitesboro
Denison
Texan
New Harbor

Map Of Arkan

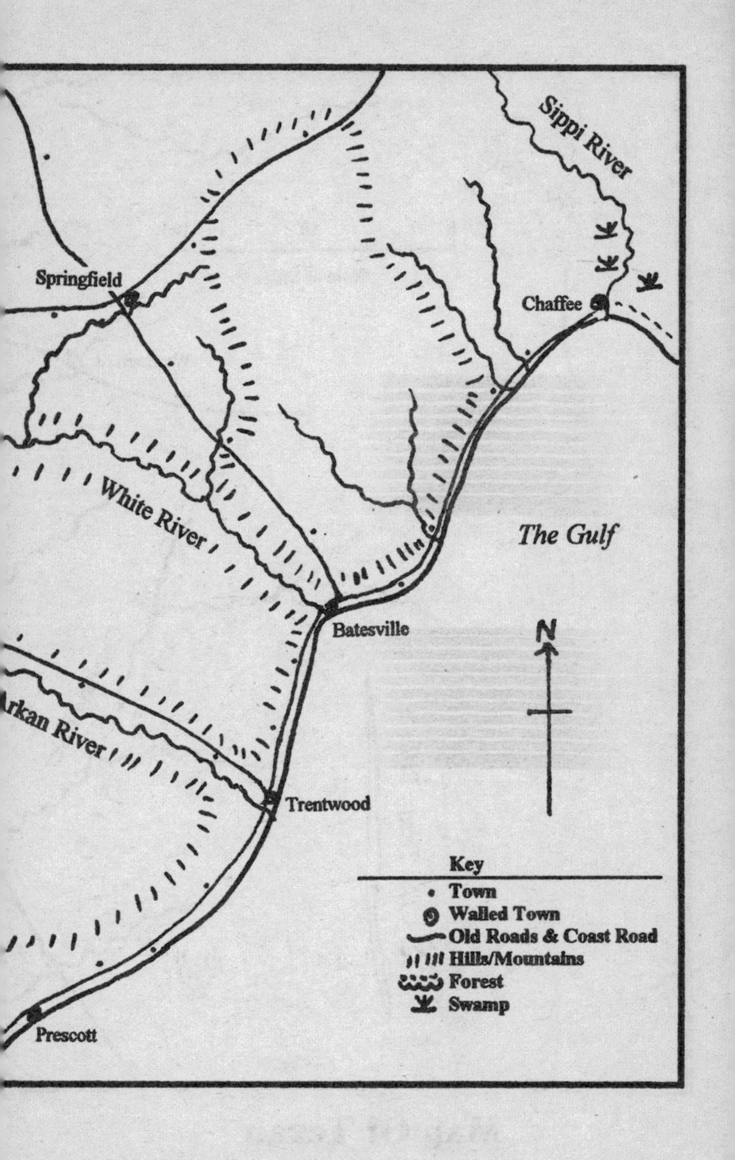

Sippi River
Springfield
Chaffee
White River
The Gulf
Batesville
N
rkan River
Trentwood
Prescott
Key
Town
Walled Town
Old Roads & Coast Road
Hills/Mountains
Forest
Swamp

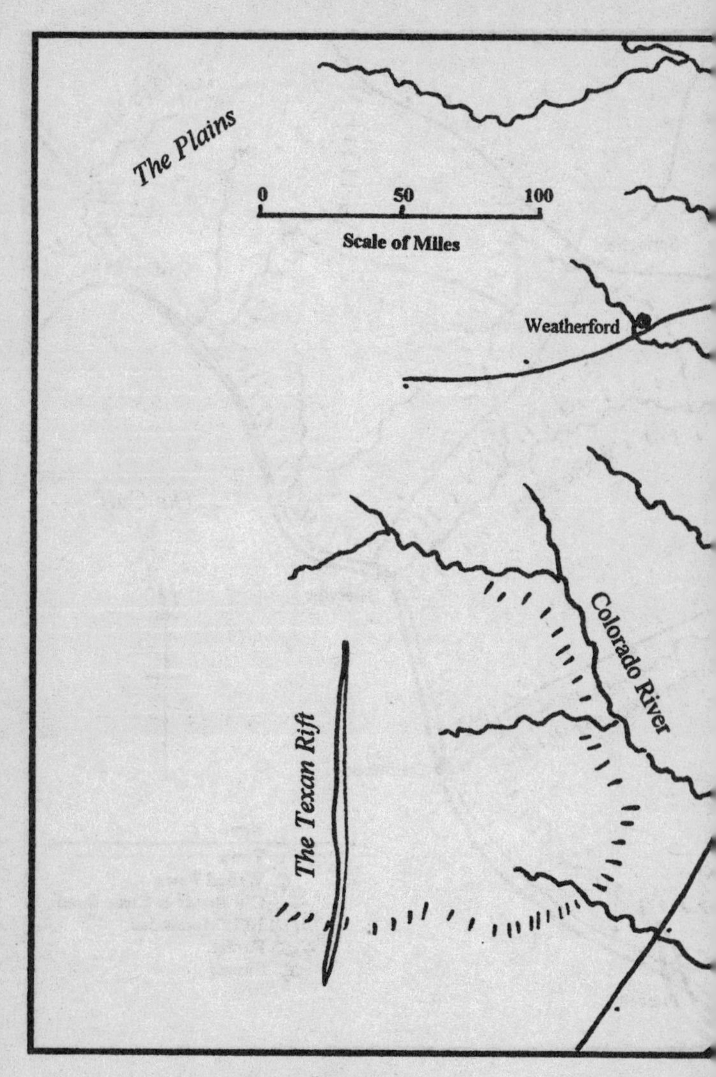
The Plains
0
50
100
Scale of Miles
Weatherford
Colorado River
The Texan Rift

Map Of Texan

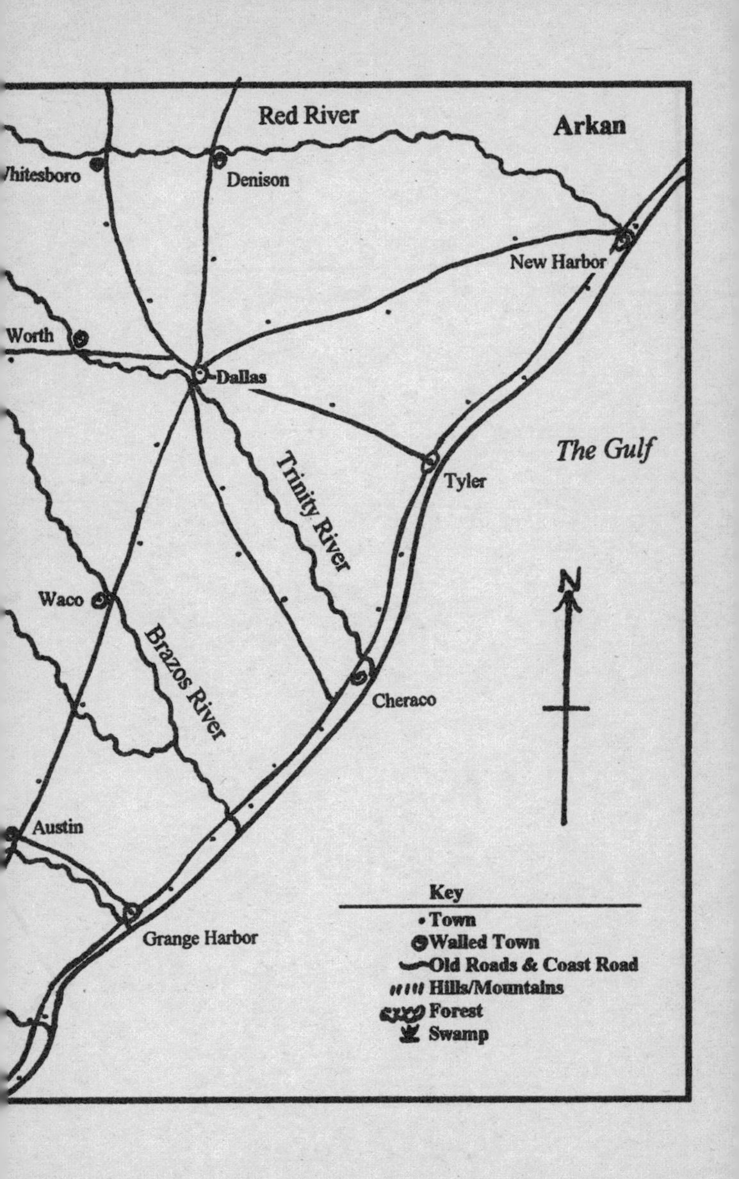
Red River
Arkan
/hitesboro
Denison
New Harbor
Worth
Dallas
Trinity River
The Gulf
Tyler
N
Waco
Brazos River
Cheraco
Austin
Grange Harbor
Key
Town
Walled Town
Old Roads & Coast Road
Hills/Mountains
Forest
Swamp

KENESEE

1

The Museum

"And this device," Professor Wagner continued, laying his hand proudly on the pitted and worn metal of the museum exhibit, "is what the Old World called a 'Toaster.' "

The royal party, more than a dozen of us arranged casually but politely by rank, clustered in front of the table upon which the object sat. Around the toaster were a half dozen other devices from the same era.

Apprentice Wizard Lorich brushed thin strands of blond hair back from his face and leaned forward to look more closely at the boxlike object, his awkward form dominated by the hump on one shoulder, his large nose protruding at the object. He gasped when he inferred its purpose. "*A toaster*? Good Lord, such a weapon! Flames must have shot out of those two openings to incinerate whoever—" He stopped, his face twisted in dismay, appalled at the image in his mind. "It's barbaric!"

The professor sighed.

Wizard Murdock jabbed a discreet elbow into Lorich's ribs. "I believe it was used to cook bread."

"Every morning they barbarically made toast for breakfast," said Dr. Amani, the royal physician.

Lorich rubbed his side and smiled weakly. "I see."

"*This* room is devoted to Old World domestic items," Wagner explained impatiently, and then pointed beyond the archway. "*That* room displays their weapons. We'll get there soon enough."

I would have to make sure we steered Wizard Lorich past the item labeled "Flame Thrower" when we changed rooms. Barbaric, indeed.

Lorich's confusion was understandable. The School of Magic certainly provided a solid grounding in the basic academic subjects as well as in the magical arts. The school turned out good and loyal wizards with the skills and wisdom to serve their kingdom with honor. But extensive study in Old World history was not a priority. Only university scholars such as Professor Wagner, or those with the benefit of a royal education, such as Robert and I had received, could be expected to be familiar with the Old World. And even then, our knowledge was not complete by any means.

A guardsman appeared at an entrance to the room and nodded at Sergeant Major Nakasone. The sergeant major went over to him and they spoke quietly. Perhaps it was a message of great import, and we would have to cancel the tour of the museum. Then I could go up to my room, have Walter stoke up the fireplace, and settle into my padded chair with a warm drink. I listened to the whispers with great hope.

Robert glanced at Nakasone and then ignored the incident; everything in due time. "Please, Professor, continue your tour. It's been most interesting so far."

Relieved, Wagner elaborated upon the function and utility of toasters, and then moved on with enthusiasm. "And here, we are most fortunate to have one of the few remaining examples of a 'Vacuum Cleaner.' "

The royal party listened respectfully. Robert and I were in front, of course, the due place for the king and his brother. The royal advisors, Bishop Thomas and Mr. Kendall, followed immediately behind. With them was the newest advisor, Wizard O'Dowd, who would on the morrow be officially appointed High Wizard of Kenesee. To either side of the advisors were clustered the beastmen Kren and Sokol, Wizard Desjardins Murdock, Apprentice Wizard Lorich, Royal Physician Amani, and a half dozen other professors of the university. Sergeant Major Nakasone, commander of the King's Royal Guards, had no set position, but hovered on the outer edge of the group and inspected each room before we entered it.

The sergeant major needn't have worried, though I certainly would never discourage his thoroughness since it helped ensure my safety. The Royal Museum had been closed all day in preparation for our visit, and then royal guards had swept through the building, ensuring that all doors and windows were sealed and no one remained within. Two squads waited at the front door to escort us back to the castle.

It had been a while since I'd entered the museum. It was just down the street from the castle, and I had been a frequent visitor as a young prince, coming to know the longstanding exhibits too well and growing bored when they did not change. After the climactic events of the last year, the university faculty had decided to update the museum and create a proper display on the War Against the Alliance. We were officially approving the new exhibits with this tour. Professor Wagner, however, could not resist the opportunity to cover everything, old and new.

We left the Old World domestic life room and moved on through Old World weaponry, past early models of powder guns, one called a "flintlock musket" and another a "percussion cap musket," to more formidable devices in use at the time of the Cataclysm. As Wagner surveyed the instruments of death, there were sighs of regret from our companions for the lost glories of mass destruction.

"Look, Arn," whispered the beastman Major Kren, stroking the slightly-bent barrel of an ominous-looking weapon entitled "machine gun." "Just think what we could have done at the Rift Gates with one of these."

I pointed to an antitank rocket. "And just think what that would have done to us."

He nodded regretfully.

Lorich was not the only member of the party seeing this part of the museum for the first time. The rooms devoted to the Old World were normally closed off, and only a select few were allowed through the locked doors to study the wonders of the ancients. Oh, certainly any commoner could find information about such things in the Royal Library, if so inclined. It was estimated that over half our population now had the ability to read—somewhat. But reading about something and seeing it before you are two different things. No use giving anyone ideas.

Dazed by the weapons, Lorich stumbled after the party as we moved on through rooms devoted to the Cataclysm (including two really well-done paintings of a city drowning) and the Dark Centuries, and thence to the wing devoted to Kenesee history. Professor Wagner expounded upon our heritage with vast sweeps of word and hand, waxing eloquent upon the greatness of our kings, the endurance of our people, the glories of our traditions, and similar myths that nations concoct when reality is not quite so becoming.

We came to the rooms devoted to current and royal history. Each of the old kings had a display cabinet holding a somber portrait, around which lay the remains of his life—scraps of cloth and paper and metal that marked the brief time before he became history. There was even a cabinet holding the rags I had worn when I was first brought to King Reuel. The exhibit also included a painting with two portraits of me as a boy, one lad dirty and unkempt in the rags of the gutter, and the other clean and groomed, adorned in the finery of the royal family.

Actually, I thought I was much better looking than the artist had made me appear, but that tended to be a regular problem. Painters never seemed to capture my features in quite the right light, though the scar slashing my left cheek from ear to chin did nothing to help the cause. Perhaps a right profile might produce better results.

Mine was the only recent display in the museum devoted to a member of the royal family who had not been elevated to king. Other princes had surely had displays in their time, but with their passing the display items had been relegated to the moldy shelves of the cellar, forgotten by all. Doubtless, mine would join them eventually.

The display cabinets for the old kings had been placed closer together, making room for new exhibits that caught the attention of the party. There were appreciative noises as we approached the cabinets devoted to the events of the last year. Professor Wagner and the faculty beamed with pleasure. The center of attention was a forest of banners, pennants, standards, and flags hiding one wall. Nearest the wall were dozens of the national flags of Virginia, Arkan, Texan, Mexico, and the Isles, while in front of them clustered the colorful regimental banners from each nation. They hung limp on their poles, silent testimony to the disaster that had overtaken the Army of the Alliance. Suspended from the ceiling, dominant over the trophies below, were spread the red flag of Kenesee and the banner of the Beastwood, the beastmen's flag a field of white except for the cluster of green trees that filled its center. The women of Lexington had done a beautiful job of sewing.

Forgetting protocol, Ambassador Sokol strode forward until he stood beneath the flag of the Beastwood and stared up at it, the gray hair of his pelt flowing almost to the shoulders of his coat. He turned, his jaw clenched with emotion. He bowed to Robert, and then the rest of us, before speaking.

"Following our emissary, Major Kren, I have come to Kenesee and been ambassador for almost four months. You have welcomed me with warmth and hospitality, opening the innermost halls of power to me. Yet not since the Battle of Lexington have I felt as touched by the courage and generosity of your people. You have shared the glory, and honored my country in a way I had not expected. May your people see this display, and realize that our nations share much, and have yet much to share."

There was applause. Kren sought out Wagner and pumped his hand. "A generous thought, Professor. You have my gratitude, and the gratitude of all beastmen."

Wagner bowed his head in humble acceptance. He'd better be humble. Robert and I had forced him to add the Beastwood banner to the display.

The party broke into small groups examining the cabinets and flags, leaving Robert next to me in the middle of the room. He shifted his stance, putting a hand upon my shoulder for support and balancing between me and his cane.

"Getting a bit tired?" I asked.

"Not at all," he reassured me. "Well, perhaps just a bit. No matter. Let's take a look at the displays."

Sergeant Major Nakasone lifted a questioning eyebrow at the king, but a shake of Robert's head told the sergeant major to wait.

Robert let go of me and we walked over to the cabinets slowly. It was hard to remember that he was just twenty-one, less than a year older than I. He had been crushed by a mammoth at the Battle of Yellow Fields, and come close to death. Good care and an iron will had seen him through a painful recovery during the last five months. His bones had mended well enough, but the socket of one leg could not be wholly cured. He would never be the warrior he had been. He would always limp, find horseback riding awkward, and feel the nagging discomfort of pain. But he was still a man, he could walk with his cane, and he was the king, with the strength of mind and force of character to guide Kenesee through a difficult recovery.

For the nation had been sorely wounded, too.

The others politely drifted away as we approached, leaving us to view the displays in regal isolation. There was a cabinet for King Reuel containing his portrait and one of his battle uniforms, as well as the broken shaft of the lance which he had carried on his last day. At the bottom of the case, identified by a little white card, was a leather envelope containing wrinkled and worn sheets of paper covered with writing. These were letters of guidance and instruction written by King Reuel himself.

There was a cabinet for General John Black, too, with a charcoal rendering of him standing defiant at the Battle of Yellow Fields. We had no general's uniform for him, for his had been lost during the retreat. The uniform in the cabinet was the one he wore while in the royal guards, the three yellow sergeant stripes upon each sleeve resplendent against the black cloth. And at the bottom of the cabinet, carefully lain before the uniform, were his pipe and tobacco pouch.

His cabinet was close to mine. I think he would have liked that.

There was another cabinet, too, for High Wizard Graven. The great wizard had allowed himself to be taken captive by the Alliance in order to mislead them, and had been slain during the Battle of Lexington. His robes were on display, and from his portrait hard eyes peeked out suspiciously as he brooded upon whatever plots his mind might be imagining.

Robert had suggested the last display was only fitting, and I had been unable to dissuade him. Perhaps Graven was entitled to a bit of remembrance before being relegated to the waiting shelves in the cellar. Perhaps.

Lorich stood alone before Graven's cabinet with bowed head, and sniffled. He took out a kerchief and, with a loud honk, blew his nose.

Robert studied the displays. "They've done a very nice job on these, don't you think?"

"Very nice," I agreed.

He shifted his weight onto the cane. "I still miss them. Reuel, Graven, Black. All of them. I'd gladly give up the throne to have them back. And all those other men we lost at the Yellow Fields.''

I didn't like it when Robert mentioned Yellow Fields. He dwelled too often upon it. ''Perhaps we should hear what message Nakasone brings us,'' I suggested.

Robert grew thoughtful, unaware that I had spoken. ''King Reuel knew how to put mistakes behind him. Even after the failure of the Beastwood Campaign, he went forward, learning from defeat but never dwelling on past error. He made it look so easy.''

Robert's confidence had once been unshakable. And it still was, except for one fact that gnawed at him. He had made the decision to fight at the Yellow Fields, and the defeat of our army followed. He had made the wrong decision—not a foolish decision, given the information we had, but merely one that turned out to be incorrect. Yet he held himself guilty, and would not let go.

Now if you wanted to talk guilt, some of us might have more to account for. But it wasn't worth losing sleep over. At least, I told myself that.

Robert put both hands on the head of his cane and stared at the floor thoughtfully. ''You know, Arn, you've been invaluable to me these last months. You've never questioned any of my decisions, and you've been following all the details, ensuring that my instructions were carried out properly. I appreciate that. You can't know how much.''

Well, that was nice to hear. He certainly should be appreciative. The last months had been less than enjoyable, with an endless parade of nobles and mayors and regimental commanders and midlevel officials to see. Under Robert's direction, I'd had to administer, consult, mediate, organize, and promulgate to officials uncertain of what to do in their new positions. I'd been forced to chastise, console, encourage, explain, inspire, praise, promise, threaten, and relieve men still suffering from the tragic cost of the war. I ended up with headaches by the end of each day, my stomach slowly churning forth new and delightful varieties of indigestion. I was not made for such duties, training or no training.

It almost made me long for the uncomfortable days of campaigning, when John Black and Murdock handled everything for me, and all I had to do was nod in agreement when they proposed a course of action.

And yet, I had been pinned in place by duty more securely than any butterfly in a collection. The sad truth was that I had been needed. No, not Arn Brant, not that illegitimate, lazy, cowardly, and morose son struggling with matters beyond his abilities, who depended upon others to hide his incompetence; but rather, Prince Arn of Kenesee, Prince Scar, the Hanging Prince, the Silent Prince, The Scourge of the Alliance who had held the Rift Gates against the Easterners, defeated the Arkans at the Battle of the Crossroads, and destroyed the Army of the Alliance at the Battle of Lexington.

Well, if they wanted to think of me as hero, so be it. More the fools, they.

Strange how mankind needs to mold the world into simplistic images in order to soothe the frantic inner search for meaning, each individual creating a different version of reality. Man conceptualizes a world according to his preference, to give some meaning to the harsh reality that exists in gutter and grave, some comfort for the fear that haunts his soul. That was why the people embraced Prince Scar. That hero, who existed only in the minds of the people, was needed as a voice of authority to help restore order in the land.

Kenesee had lost over 21,000 of its finest men in the war, including half the nobility and many officers who also held important civil positions in towns and villages. The country could have fallen into chaos if steps were not taken. Robert had performed brilliantly as a leader and administrator, meeting every problem and concern with the practical and necessary solution, even when those solutions were neither quick nor easy.

Our first concern had been famine, since there had been no spring planting and many farmers would never be returning to their land. And with over twenty thousand prisoners of war to guard, it was necessary to keep hundreds of men in uniform who would otherwise return to their farms. Robert's solution was a special parole to prisoners of war willing to take an oath and work rather than wait in prison camps. Thousands had accepted the offer and been sent to the farms of Kenesee, allowing us to put in a late spring planting and reap a decent harvest. The fishing fleet had also been augmented with paroled prisoners, and a major portion of each catch was smoked or salted for the winter months. It looked as if we would make it through the winter without anyone starving.

Town commerce had also been affected, but the manpower shortage had been met by allowing women to continue working in the shops and trades as they had during the war, supplemented now by more of the oathbound prisoners. Thus, the nation was recovering better than might have been expected—if you didn't count the fact that almost every woman had lost a father, or son, or husband, or brother. Many had lost more than one.

Robert tapped his cane on the floor. "Arn, are you listening?"

"Hmm? Oh, sorry. Just thinking. I'm tired, too. I need . . . a rest."

"It's been difficult for you, hasn't it? Well, things have been put in order now, and I think we might spare you for a—Yes, Wizard O'Dowd?"

The wizard stood a respectful distance away, a slightly built man of deferential manner, with spectacles and short, graying hair. He stepped forward reluctantly. "I'm sorry to catch you now, sir, but I know how busy you are. I just wanted to ask you one last time to reconsider this whole matter of the High Wizard."

The royal solitude broken, Murdock felt free to stroll up, his dark face scowling in mock indignation. "O'Dowd, my dear friend, are you trying to shirk your duty?"

Robert forced a laugh, trying to be festive. "The pot has called the kettle black. The answer to your question, Wizard Murdock, is yes. Wizard O'Dowd is asking me to reconsider the decision."

"Alas, he does not realize that a royal decision is not easily changed," Murdock commiserated. "He will learn, my King, he will learn."

O'Dowd clasped his hands in consternation. "But sir, Wizard Murdock was my superior at the School of Magic. The number and power of his psychic talents are greater than any magician in Kenesee. The position of high wizard should rightfully be his."

Murdock shook his head regretfully. "We've gone over this all before. I'm not made for court life. Nor would I enjoy commanding obstinate wizards like yourself. Nor, most importantly, do I have any talent for premonition. Now, let us take you, in contrast. You served bravely in the war as a regimental wizard, and are respected by our fellow magicians as one of the most powerful wizards in Kenesee. I know your abilities as an organizer, and I'm confident you can get as much out of us as High Wizard Graven did. And there is the one essential talent. Weren't you and Graven the first to raise concern about the Rift Gates? You have the ability to foretell, and it is fitting that King Robert have you at his side. I can be more valuable in other ways."

"Yes," said O'Dowd, frowning. "You want to go off adventuring."

Murdock tried to keep a straight face. "I must admit that I am content with the occasional journey in service of my country."

An idea brightened O'Dowd's features. "Well, if I'm to be High Wizard, then you must obey my directions. What if I order you to stay at my side here at the castle? What then?"

Murdock paused in dismay. "Would you do that?"

O'Dowd smiled. "No, Wizard Murdock, I would not. You're safe, for I will give you no order you don't think wise. You are subject only to the King and the Prince. But I warn you. One day you, too, will have to accept responsibility."

"I fear you are right," Murdock mumbled. That any should hear was not, I think, his intent.

Robert watched all this in bemused silence. "Is Wizard Murdock always this much trouble?"

"Much more," I replied. "Of course, he is of some use now and then."

"Now and then?" Murdock interjected.

"When he isn't getting wounded," Kren added as he came up with Sokol. "He's a terrible drain on the medical resources of your kingdom. Jason the Healer could have made an entire career treating this man."

Murdock looked the beastman up and down. "Alas, all make fun of me, whose poor body is covered with the scars of devoted service."

Lorich, who had been listening, came to the wizard's defense. "Major Kren, you're a fine one to point out such things.

Who took an arrow in the shoulder hurling buckets of oil at the Rift Gates?''

Ambassador Sokol's eyes narrowed at the words.

Murdock gave Lorich another elbow in the ribs.

The elder beastman turned to his dark-pelted countryman and spoke gruffly. ''What is this about you, our neutral emissary to Kenesee, fighting Easterners at the Rift Gates?''

Kren smiled weakly. ''I didn't engage in personal combat, sir. But there was this siege tower, and, well. . . .''

''The Gates might have fallen if it weren't for Major Kren,'' Murdock offered. Whether his words corrected the mistake or worsened Kren's plight was debatable.

''And this is how you keep a low profile?'' Sokol admonished with a somber tone. ''This is how you obey orders?''

''Sometimes orders have to be ignored for the good of all,'' Kren pleaded. ''Don't you think so, General Sokol?''

The elder beastman harumphed as he searched for words. He had disobeyed his own instructions from the beastman senior council to defend the Beastwood when he marched into Kenesee and attacked the Alliance at Lexington.

Robert turned to the beastman. ''Ambassador Sokol, you see why Murdock is such a danger to have at court. His impunity is like a disease. It infects all those around him, until royalty and commoners are bantering words like old battle comrades. No, I shall leave him to his school and his adventures, free to assist Prince Arn, and they will be my strong right arm.''

Murdock bowed. ''As you wish, King Robert.''

Robert snorted. ''Notice how humbly he complies with orders to his liking. Wizard Murdock, Graven warned us about you when we visited the School of Magic.''

''He did?'' Murdock asked with a pleased look. ''What did he say?''

Robert had him now. ''That information is for the ears of the High Wizard only.''

Lorich came around to Kren and pulled him aside. ''I'm sorry, Major Kren. I've gotten you in trouble. For some reason it seems lately that every time I open my mouth the wrong thing comes out.''

''That goes with your age,'' Kren said. ''Besides, you didn't reveal any secret. The ambassador learned about my exploits at the Gates from gossip soon after he arrived in Kingsport. Your comment simply forced him to officially recognize it. Just formal protocol. It will go no further—I hope."

The party fell silent for a moment, and Robert took the opportunity. "If we may, Arn and I would like to discuss a matter with the sergeant major." The members of the party took their cue and drifted off about the room while Robert and I went with Nakasone to a corner.

Nakasone was a short man with a bald head, still lean and hard-muscled in spite of having served in the royal guards for over three decades. He spoke with the crisp confidence of one who does his job supremely well. "Sir, I've just been informed by Sergeant Nielson that two men were questioned by the dock patrol and then taken prisoner as they disembarked from a merchant ship. They were brought to the castle."

"And why were they brought to the castle instead of the town prison?" Robert asked patiently.

"They asked to see the King. They would not identify themselves, but stated that they were emissaries with urgent business to conduct. Nielson had them held and searched. They claim they have left an item with the ship's captain that we must see, though they won't say what it is. I've sent a man to the docks to bring the item to the castle."

"Good. Anything else to report?" Robert asked.

"There was one thing . . ." Nakasone paused, enjoying the brief moment of drama. "They both had Texan accents."

We completed the tour of the museum, much to the joy of Professor Wagner and his colleagues, who had feared an interruption. The scholars need not have worried. There was no love lost between Kenesee and Texan, and the emissaries could wait and contemplate their future for a few hours.

Outside a crowd had gathered—many to wait for the museum to open to the public so that they too could see the new exhibits, but most for the chance to see royalty. The people broke into cheers as we stepped out the door, so Robert and I waved with the proper royal decorum. A woman with a little girl in her arms stepped forward, the little girl holding a bouquet of dried flowers for Robert. He took them from the child with a gentle smile and warm graciousness.

I gave my attention to the mother, an attractive, raven-haired young woman only a few years older than I.

"Where is your father?" asked Robert, perhaps reluctantly, of the child.

The girl was silent, but her mother shifted the child, so that Robert could see the small red and black ribbon pinned to her coat. Many women of Kenesee wore the ribbon now. The red for Kenesee, and the black for the fallen.

"Dead in the war," the girl's mother confirmed.

Robert nodded, teetered on his cane as he leaned over to hug the child, then straightened and bestowed a kiss upon the hand of the woman. The crowd roared.

"He does that very well," I observed quietly to Murdock, who stood next to me.

"He does," the Wizard affirmed. "And she is quite pretty, no?"

"The thought never entered my mind." Well, perhaps a thought. Whether I dared do anything besides *look* demanded careful consideration. My dear Angela was in Kingsport, and staying at the castle. She was quite tolerant of my looking, within reason. Her smile faded when my attention lingered where it shouldn't. How long I might live after dallying with another, I couldn't say. Not long, I suspected. Fortunately, her determination to keep me content—accomplished with amazing enthusiasm, I must admit—left me with little energy for other women.

"Besides," I added, "You're the one bringing joy and comfort to the women of Kingsport."

"Murdock!" the king called. "Take this woman's name and place. She's a veteran's widow. See to it that she is taken care of."

"Yes, King Robert," he responded, and the crowd applauded.

The wizard caught up a moment later and took a place behind me. "Yes, quite the attractive woman. I'll visit her tomorrow. Duty can be hard, but we must face it bravely. We must look it in the eye. We must—"

"—Get moving," I concluded as we took position between the double row of guards and headed back to the castle.

Kingsport had suffered no damage in the war, and the appearance of the town was unchanged. We proceeded down

King's Way, past the Silver Spur Inn and the stables where the horses of the royal guards were kept, and came to the castle. Flags and pennants were flying in the chill November wind, and the gates stood open awaiting our return. The only difference from previous years were the many guards who waited on the walls and at the gates. The royal guard reserves had not been demobilized yet, for prisoners of war were scattered at worksites throughout the town, and the threat of foreign assassins could not be discounted until we concluded peace treaties with Virginia and Texan.

The Alliance had fallen apart with the destruction of its field army. King Herrick of Arkan had declared, upon receipt of the news, that his oath to the Alliance ended with the defeat of his allies at Lexington.

With Prime Minister Billy Bay dead at Lexington, the Isles had sued for peace and sent emissaries. They brought an offer of reparation and requests for prisoner exchanges. We had accepted their money, and the Islanders in our hands had been sent back before the winter gulf storms.

Patron Carlos Esteves of Mexico, taken prisoner at Lexington, had already signed a treaty with us. Unfortunately, his country wouldn't honor it. The Mexicans didn't want him back after the disaster he'd led them into. The new Mexican government declared it would pay reparations and a ransom for their countrymen in our hands on one condition: we had to execute their ex-leader. I thought this a good arrangement, but Robert did not. We finally convinced the Mexicans to sign a treaty that didn't force us to hang Esteves, who instead hung around the castle making a nuisance of himself. He would not stop trying to give the king advice.

Governor John Rodes had escaped and returned to Virginia after our victory. He'd sent a rather stiff note through an emissary requesting a prisoner of war exchange, but refusing to discuss terms of peace. There were reports he had formed a new army of green troops, but he might have had a legitimate need for those. The northern tribes were taking advantage of the bloodletting to raid the upper borders of Virginia. Whether the Plains Tribes were similarly threatening Arkan and Texan was not yet known.

From Texan there had been no communication at all. General Jack Murphy, President of Texan, had also escaped our efforts to capture him. He'd returned to Texan and retained control of the country, thanks to his trusted subordinates. Since the Texans had seized four or five hundred of our citizens and hauled them off to their slave pens, we'd quickly sent a young messenger requesting their immediate release. A spy reported that the messenger went into Murphy's Castle Corral in Dallas—but never came out.

Virginia's reluctance and the Texan silence were understandable. Unfortunately, they knew that we were but little stronger than they. Yes, a third of our army had survived, leaving us a core of battle-hardened veterans ready to meet any threat. Yet dared we send this small force away from the soil of Kenesee to impose our will? Unlikely.

In spite of making them wait, I knew Robert wanted to meet with these Texans. The king was not one to waste the moment.

Still, he'd waited long enough to complete the museum tour; he could at least have waited till after dinner.

Robert summoned his advisors straight to the council room, where hot cider and cooled wine were served. During the war the room had been crowded with maps and stacks of books as King Reuel and Graven analyzed strategy. Now, most of the maps and books had been returned to the castle library, but the map mural of Kenesee remained, filling a wall and adorned with small painted banners and flags marking the battles and skirmishes of the conflict. Robert sat in his chair at one end of the table. Bishop Thomas and Murdock sat on one side, with Wizard O'Dowd, Kendall, and Sergeant Major Nakasone on the other.

Only Sir Meredith was absent, as he had been since the summer, the matter of rebuilding Lexington taking his attention. The task had also seemed to energize his father, the grumbling old Duke Gregory, who was reported to be hurrying around in a carriage and supervising the reconstruction. The two had promised to rebuild the town and make it even more beautiful than before. The cost was a blow to the national treasury, but the reparations expected from the other nations would help.

I took the end seat opposite the king. The rest waited expectantly, uncertain of the reason for this meeting. Robert told them of the Texans, and then had the two emissaries, as they called themselves, summoned. We turned our chairs and assumed the proper degree of somber rectitude.

The first to enter was a tall middle-aged man, well-built and distinguished-looking, the touch of gray in his hair lending authority to his chiseled features. The second was younger, shorter, and much heavier, with a fringe of black hair and a wisp still dressing the pate of his head. He did not look happy to be there.

They stood before us, the one calmly looking us over with a stoic eye, the other glancing about shyly, fidgeting on one foot and then the other. Both were dressed in the common cloth of traders.

Murdock eyed their clothing and smiled at me.

Merchant disguise. How original.

Nakasone looked the two men up and down, and then dismissed the guards. I knew the two had been searched thrice over, once by the sergeant major himself, or he would never have allowed them in the presence of the king. Even so, Nakasone positioned himself between the emissaries and Robert.

O'Dowd dipped his pen into the ink bottle, prepared a few sheets for note taking, and waited in readiness.

Robert gestured to the chairs behind the emissaries, and the two sat. "I am Robert Brant, King of Kenesee, and this is my brother, Arn Brant, Prince of Kenesee. And these are our advisors." He introduced each of the rest.

When Robert was done, the distinguished-looking man rose with an easy flourish and gave a correct bow. "Our thanks for giving us audience so quickly," he said without irony.

Well, it was quick, all things considered. They'd only arrived a few hours ago.

"We come as emissaries of the Texan nation," he continued. "I am Peter Mason, Great Landholder for the region around Dallas. My companion"—Was there the faintest hint of disdain slipping out as he introduced the other?—"is Scott Chalmers, Senior Aide to General Jack Murphy. We have grave matters to discuss."

"Indeed?" Murdock observed. "And what of the young messenger that was sent to you? The mayor of Greenville is pleading for news of his son."

The landholder was silent, eyeing his companion with an accusing look. The short man spoke up reluctantly. "General

Murphy tore up your message in a fit of rage and had your messenger imprisoned. I'm afraid that during his imprisonment the boy attempted to escape . . . and was killed."

The faces around the table hardened.

Chalmers swallowed. "I had nothing to do with it, I assure you."

Bishop Thomas could restrain himself no longer. "So, you come to make peace after killing thousands of our soldiers and enslaving our people. And now you announce the death of our messenger. You have audacity, I will give you that."

Kendall waited until the bishop was done. "What does Jack Murphy offer?"

"Oh, no," the nervous Chalmers corrected. "We're not here to represent General Murphy."

The council's faces turned from anger to puzzlement as Chalmers concluded his message.

"We're here to oppose him."

2

The Emissaries

"You are here to oppose General Murphy as President of Texan," Murdock restated, pondering the words.

We looked at each other with surprise. Rats leaving a sinking ship? Now here was an unexpected development.

Wizard O'Dowd pointed his pen at Chalmers. "Are you saying that you don't represent General Murphy or Texan?"

Chalmers shifted uneasily at the sharp tone of the question. His discomfort was understandable to me, even if I lacked sympathy for the Texans. It was little more than a year since I had sat as an emissary before the rulers of the Beastwood, wondering what fate they planned for me.

The little man leaned forward in his seat and opened his mouth, but Landholder Mason—now that their unpleasant news about our messenger had been delivered without bloodshed—gestured to his companion for silence.

"Your question is not altogether correct," the landholder noted. "As Aide Chalmers has indicated, we do not represent General Murphy. But we do represent Texan, or at least many in Texan who are weary of Jack Murphy's blundering regime. Please be aware: he has no knowledge that we are here. If our visit to you were made known, our lives would be forfeit, and our families sold into slavery."

Kendall spoke up, suspicion clear upon his homely features. "So. Is this *weariness* limited to leaders and landholders, or do the common people feel as you do?

"Yes," Bishop Thomas agreed. "Do you represent a palace revolt, or a popular uprising?" Popular uprising? Palace revolt? The bishop must have been reading again.

"There is grumbling at all levels—"

"Grumbling?" the bishop responded. "That's all?"

Mason did not seem like a man who endured interruption well, yet he did so now, replying patiently. "In Texan, to grumble in private might bring a warning visit from the local deputy. To grumble in public is to risk imprisonment. Now, the complaints are spoken aloud in the marketplace, and the deputies do nothing—to the commoner. Please, if I may, I will explain."

Mason looked at each of us in turn, ending with the king.

Robert nodded.

The landholder nodded back. "Thank you, King Robert. Texan is a nation no different from any other—"

"Except for slavery," Murdock murmured aloud.

Robert gave the wizard a look.

Mason forced a smile. "I might remind you that Kenesee enjoyed a lucrative trade in slaves only a generation or two ago, as did several other nations."

"Granted," Murdock replied amiably. "But we did away with that institution fifty years ago. Is Texan about to do the same?"

"No, we are not," the landholder said evenly. "But the issue here is not slavery. It is about removing General Jack Murphy from power. General Murphy has his loyal followers.

He appeals to the national pride, our churches back him as the legitimate ruler, and our economy, if not prosperous, has at least enjoyed stability under his regime."

Murdock opened his mouth to speak, saw Robert's glare, and shut it.

The door opened and closed, Sergeant Jenkins entering to stand patiently at the back of the room. In his hands he held a long, loosely-wrapped burlap bundle.

Mason eyed the sergeant and his bundle, but bore on without hesitation. "There are fewer now who believe in him. He presented himself as the central leader of the Alliance, and thus couldn't escape blame for the disaster to our army. You destroyed our first-line units, so that General Murphy escaped to Texan with only a few members of his staff, such as Senior Aide Chalmers. For a short time we thought General Murphy might abdicate, but we were proven wrong. He'd left most of his elite guards—he calls them Presidential *Guardos*—in Texan to foil any usurper, and they remained loyal. He returned to his castle, frightened the gullible with talk of an invasion from Kenesee, and grasped the reins of power even more tightly than before. He let people grumble, the better to identify his enemies and thus turn necessity to his advantage. Those who are not blindly loyal to the General are fearful of him. None dare act alone."

Mason waited while we absorbed his words.

Robert sat with his arms folded across his chest and studied the papers upon the table. Without looking up, he spoke. "And?"

Mason bowed. "King Robert, you perceive my words before they are spoken. Even in a land of fear, there *are* a few who will trust each other and speak out amongst themselves, a few brave enough to risk all. Senior Aide Chalmers is one of these, and he holds an invaluable position within the General's castle itself. Our ranks include mayors, landholders, and regimental commanders. There are more who share our feelings, but dare not join us. Not until we have help."

"Now we come to it," Murdock warned.

I finished my cider and took a cup of wine. I didn't like what I was hearing.

Mason gestured with a sweep of his hand. "With the proper encouragement, I believe fully half the regimental commanders and their men would join us, and as many mayors. Perhaps a third of the landholders would also. They need only know that Kenesee had pledged its support, and they would rally to our cause."

Nakasone looked at the Texan warily. As head of security within Kenesee as well as commander of the kingdom's royal guards, he had the right to speak in council. "You ask us to split our forces, to send our men across the Gulf to help you rid yourselves of a villain. And once we have disposed of Murphy, our army would be invited to leave and you could put in another tyrant of whom you are not so weary. General Murphy has done well for us. His pride and overconfidence helped us defeat him. Why should we want someone more capable in charge of Texan?"

Good thinking. Why not let the Texans fester in their own greed and cruelty? We no longer had anything to fear from them. Why risk troops far away from Kenesee just to overthrow one man?

Nakasone's words gave the council pause. Things were looking better. I'd been getting worried for a moment.

The landholder seemed to expect the argument. He nodded in understanding and took a step closer. "I cannot deny the merit of this man's words. Unfortunately, there is another factor. The nations have for two hundred years lived by the Codes. Our religions adopted them, our people respected them, our leaders followed them. There have been occasions when one side or another has winked at some rule. Why, the entrenchments you built at Lexington were a violation of the Codes. Yet that violation was a minor one. On the other hand, General Murphy has not lost his taste for conquest, and is seeking ways to overcome the destruction of our army. His solution will prove devastating to all the nations. We believe, God help us, that he is planning to repudiate and violate the Codes."

Kendall grimaced. "And the nature of this violation?"

The Texan held out a hand for the package held by Jenkins. "If we may . . . ?"

Jenkins pointedly ignored Mason's hand and gave the package to Nakasone, who unwrapped the item. The cloth fell away, and the dull metal was revealed. He raised it for all to see.

In his hands, he held a musket.

There was silence in the room for a long moment. Bishop Thomas shook his head doubtfully. "An artifact from the Old World, certainly."

Nakasone was examining it carefully. "No, sir. Doesn't look old to me. The metalwork looks new."

Robert drummed his fingers on the table once, twice. "Mr. Mason—you're claiming General Murphy is manufacturing powder weapons."

"Yes, King Robert. To my utter regret, I am. There is a shame upon Texan, and General Murphy has brought it upon us."

Nakasone passed the weapon to Robert, and it made its way around the table, each of us examining the thing.

The sergeant major commented upon the mechanism as it passed from hand to hand. He'd always had an interest in Old World weaponry. "It's not loaded. Looks like a version of the old flintlock. We've got one in the museum. Professor Wagner pointed it out today. Muskets were museum pieces by the time of the Cataclysm, a primitive single-shot powder weapon capable of firing a ball of lead. It required reloading with loose powder. Not very accurate beyond fifty yards, but deadly if it struck. Line up two or three ranks of men with these against you, and you'd have real problems."

The chilly atmosphere toward our visitors had disappeared with the appearance of the weapon, replaced by somber consideration. Robert made a gesture at the wine bottle, and Murdock immediately filled two glasses and handed them to the emissaries.

Chalmers took his with thanks and gulped half down in relief before pausing to consider the vintage. "Quite good."

"From Lexington," I explained.

"Oh? Ohhhh . . ." He stared at it glumly.

Mason took a sip, nodded in approval, and had more while he waited for our response.

The king obliged him. "So, you would like us to voice our support. Will that be all that is required?"

Mason grinned. "You know it will not."

Robert took in the expressions around the table before again gazing at the landholder. "And do you have specific proposals?"

"Yes, King Robert. We have two. For one, we ask that when the time is ripe, Kenesee provide forces to help us in our struggle against General Murphy. Even a few regiments may tip the balance."

Robert's handsome face remained impassive. "And the second proposal?"

Chalmers could stand it no more. He bounced up and looked around the table, his glance finally settling upon me with hopeful eyes.

My stomach rumbled loudly and began to churn.

"If," he said, "a representative of Kenesee were to come to Texan and meet with the undecided, many would be swayed to our side."

I rubbed my forehead.

"Are you all right, Prince Arn?" whispered O'Dowd.

"Headache starting," I mumbled back.

Robert sat erect in his chair. "And that is all you require?"

The landholder nodded. "That is all, King Robert. Without your help, General Murphy will remain in power. With it, he will be removed. With Murphy gone, much can be accomplished. We will return those Kenesee citizens taken from your shores. You will unburden yourself of Texan prisoners. Reasonable reparations will be paid to Kenesee. And cordial relations between our nations can be reestablished." He pointed at the flintlock. "Perhaps most important, this sacrilege can be stopped, and the Codes restored."

Robert remained stonefaced. "Are there any questions for the emissaries?"

Wizard O'Dowd reviewed his notes, chewing on the upper tip of the feather pen. "And when might the time be 'ripe'?"

Mason shrugged. "After your representative has met with our countrymen and we organize a plan of action. The exact timing will be your decision, though we do have some recommendations."

Kendall shifted in his chair. "Senior Aide Chalmers, you are on General Murphy's staff. Gregor Pi-Ling is Murphy's advisor from Pacifica. I saw Pi-Ling at the Battle of Lexington, but he escaped with the General. Is he still advising Murphy?"

Chalmers nodded. "Yes, Mr. Kendall. He is."

"And does he support this violation of the Codes?"

Chalmers shrugged. "Yes sir, I presume so. Though as an aide, I'm not one of General Murphy's inner circle of decision makers. Mr. Pi-Ling is, along with the Chief Sheriff of Texan, Matthew Bartholomew. Neither is inclined to idle conversation. Secrecy is a prime virtue in the Castle Corral, and each of us knows only what is needed to do his own work. I avoid talking to Matthew Bartholomew. He is a dangerous, cruel man, and an idle or misspoken word in his hearing can mean the dungeon.

"I have had only occasional discussion with Pi-Ling. I have never heard him say a word against the General. And yet, who knows? He's a likable man, but since we escaped from Kenesee he has seemed quieter, more moody, even gloomy. But then, who in our nation hasn't had reason for gloom?"

There were more questions of this sort for the Texans before we knew as much as could reasonably be expected.

"I will consider your request," Robert assured the two men. "In the meanwhile, you will be restricted to your quarters and kept under guard. Your presence here will be kept a secret. You will be informed when we have come to a decision."

The Texans stood and bowed, Chalmers clearly relieved to have avoided any disagreeable consequences.

The emissaries retired under the care of Sergeant Jenkins and we turned our chairs back to the table.

"Your thoughts," Robert asked; it wasn't a request but a command.

O'Dowd waited for others to speak. When no one did, he cleared his throat for attention. "To review the situation, these emissaries are requesting that we help them depose Jack Murphy. They want two things—" He ticked the items off on his fingers. "First, someone to go to Texan to rally support. Second, a number of regiments to aid their cause."

He looked around for agreement. Finding it, Wizard O'Dowd continued. "I recommend that before dealing with either of these requests, we first determine two other matters: whether we can trust these rebel emissaries, and just as important, whether the elimination of Jack Murphy as President of Texan is a goal we wish to adopt."

Murdock beamed at O'Dowd with a proud smile. "Did you hear that?" he whispered to me. "A clear and concise analysis of the situation. Couldn't have done better myself.''

''And perhaps a good deal worse,'' I whispered back.

''By God's Light, I would not trust them,'' Bishop Thomas declared. ''Anyone who would betray his ruler is without honor.''

''And yet,'' Robert said reasonably, ''if a ruler is an enemy of God, then his followers may abandon him for God's Will. Could that not be the case here?''

Bishop Thomas was brought up short. It always turned out that his pronouncements fell apart during such discussions, and the king would have to point out the inconsistencies without humiliating the religious leader of Kenesee. ''Ummm. That could be,'' the bishop granted reluctantly

''Nevertheless, your suspicions are well founded. If we bestow our trust upon these men, it will be a watchful trust. Mr. Kendall, have you any light to shed on this matter?''

Kendall shrugged. ''My intelligence sources report that there is discontent within Texan, just as these two have indicated. And Murphy has retained control of the government. Little more is known, and I have heard nothing about new violations of the Codes, although there have been rumors of forbidden research since last winter. One spy was lost trying to discover more about such violations. Their security is very tight. I would not doubt that Murphy might try something like this.

''As to the two emissaries, I have met them before, but know little more of them than what they told us of themselves. Mason is a proud man, with very extensive ownership of land. Chalmers is competent, obedient, and subservient—all qualities of the good functionary or clerk. His participation surprises me, but perhaps he possesses a conscience and courage in greater measure than his appearance indicates.'' Kendall paused for a moment, then hurried on. ''Can we trust them? I don't know. There is always a risk in such ventures. Yet, it's not unreasonable to expect such action as these two have taken. Possibly, we should have anticipated and encouraged it, letting internal dissent neutralize our enemies.''

''Anyone else?'' Robert asked. ''All right, we assume they speak the truth as they know it, and their rebellion is legitimate. Then we face the question: do we wish to depose General Murphy?'' Robert looked around the table expectantly.

I definitely did not like where this was heading. The idea would have to be quashed now, or not all. It was important to appear uninvolved and objective as I spoke. "As Sergeant Major Nakasone has pointed out, Kenesee has little to fear from Murphy anymore, and Texan is far away. Our losses have been heavy. Perhaps we should not be too . . . hasty."

Robert pondered my words, got up and crossed the room to the maps. He glanced briefly at the mural of Kenesee, and then focused upon a map of the continent that stood on an easel. Kenesee occupied the center of the map, with the Gulf to the south, Virginia and the Beastwood east and northeast, respectively, and the Northern Forests at the top. West and southwest on the Gulf coast lay Arkan, separated from Kenesee by the Ohio and Sippi Rivers. Further down the coast lay Texan, its border with Arkan formed by the Red River.

In Texan, the road net was like a grasping octopus, tentacles radiating from Dallas. Only the Coast Road ignored the political imperative, wending its way from the Red River south, following the coast until the road crossed the Colorado River and entered Mexico. From Kingsport to Dallas, it had to be over a thousand miles by land. Even as the gull flies, the distance couldn't be less than seven hundred miles. And yet, across those many miles the Texans had come.

I mentioned the distances to buttress my argument, and then added a thought. "The Gulf winds are easterly. Our troop ships will sail before the winds without difficulty. Only a few days at sea, good weather permitting, and the regiments will arrive. Yet, should those units be needed in Kenesee, the trip back will not be so easy. Tacking against the wind will lengthen the voyage greatly. The enemy on our borders could do much in that time."

I was quite proud of myself. I'd actually considered military factors, just as John Black would have done. Of course, I used the arguments to my personal advantage, but—

"Does anyone disagree with Prince Arn?" Robert asked.

The others had been studying the map too. Kendall spoke up. "I can't disagree with the facts that have been presented. The dangers that Prince Arn has mentioned are real. And yet, it's my duty to point out that this threat to the Codes must be eliminated. We must assume the worst from Jack Murphy. He will not be content to rest with such weapons at his command, but will look to conquer again. The introduction of powder weapons will start us on a path that we have avoided for two hundred years. As terrible as our wars have been, destruction will be far worse once we start down that path.''

Robert sat down again and rubbed his chin thoughtfully. ''Anyone else?''

''General Murphy has caused us irreparable harm,'' stated Bishop Thomas.

''Slavery flourishes under him,'' Murdock reminded.

''He has our people,'' Nakasone intoned.

''So,'' Robert summarized. ''You think we should depose him?''

''AYE!'' rang out a chorus of voices.

Amid the clamor I was unnoticed, silent.

Robert spoke grimly. ''Such is my feeling too. Our soldiers from the coastal villages have returned home only to find their wives and children snatched away. I won't have citizens of Kenesee held as slaves in Texan, and this alone would give us cause to act. Further, as long as he holds power, General Murphy will be a threat to other nations and to the Codes by which we have lived these two hundred years. We must remove him. At the appropriate time, we will determine our strategic position and how much force we might send the Texan rebels to aid their cause. Which leaves only the matter of choosing a representative, a recognized figure of Kenesee to rally the undecided Texans. Who knows? If we choose wisely the Texans may do the job themselves and our regiments won't be necessary.''

I could see it coming now. There was no way out.

Taking his cue from Robert, Wizard O'Dowd spoke up again. I was coming to dread his logical analysis. ''The mission will be one of great secrecy, and the one chosen will be going into great danger. He will have to deal with intrigue, bribery, and deceit. He will have to be cunning—''

''—And sly—'' added the bishop.

''—Devious—'' agreed the sergeant major.

''—Ruthless—'' chimed in Kendall.

''Someone skilled at lying, cheating, and stealing,'' Murdock agreed.

''Well, then,'' concluded O'Dowd. ''Do we have such a man?''

I looked up from my wine cup. All eyes were upon me, faces bright with anticipation.

"Thank you for your confidence," I answered with a scowl, and laughter filled the room.

When all was quiet again, Robert cast me a smile. "Though we lighten the moment, none can miss its import. This is a grave matter we undertake, and while the kingdom is not at stake, we risk much, including the lives of those involved. There is danger, and men must consent to take such extraordinary risk.

"Arn, by birthmark and wound, you are marked twice over as Prince of Kenesee and can prove your identity to the Texans. There is value to that, though dubious if you are captured. Of greater worth is your reputation. None is held in higher esteem among our people, nor greater respect among our enemies. Finally, you are a proven commander who can lead any force that might be sent you. As King Reuel risked you for great cause in the Beastwood, so will I risk you in Texan. Do you consent to undertake this mission?"

They had done it to me again. Lay a great task before a man when he is with his companions, spell out its importance to all, and then ask him if he will accept it. Well, what was I to say? Only the most craven would refuse the task, content to live with dishonor.

Still, maybe dishonor wouldn't be too bad. . . .

Murdock kicked me under the table.

"Uhhhh . . . yes, I will go."

Murdock had a satisfied look about him. "Sir, I think Arn should not go alone, and I ask to accompany him."

"I had planned as much," Robert replied. "Sergeant Jenkins might also be a worthy addition to your party, if he will consent to it."

Consent to it? The problem would be holding Jenkins back. The fiery little sergeant had led the guards protecting me during the campaign. In spite of his size, he was a formidable opponent and liked nothing better than a good fight. Another fearless warrior to get me into trouble.

"And how would you plan to go?"

Good question. I hadn't the slightest notion.

The bishop gestured at the map of the continent. "The Gulf

is the fastest way to get to Texan. A fast trading schooner would have them there in less than a week."

Memories thrust themselves up in my mind. Bad memories. I got up and went to the small window which the room enjoyed, and stared out. We faced the west, and the sun was a red globe descending below the outer battlements. Beyond them I could see the tops of masts, marking the location of ships at the river docks. Although the battlements blocked my view, I knew the docks well, and remembered the long pier upon which I first set foot when arriving at Kingsport more than a decade ago. The arrival had been a relief, an end to three days of misery aboard the river schooner which had carried me from the mouth of the Ohio to Kingsport, tacking back and forth against the brisk winds from the east, surging through waves, rising and falling and rocking back and forth with a motion that left me green-gilled and wanting to die. Three days of misery, unable to eat a bite. At the pier I'd bought a loaf of bread, the first food I'd eaten since we'd left the port of Wickliffe, and with the shrinking loaf in hand I'd wandered up and down the dock, gazing at the bannered walls of the town and the fluttering pennants adorning the turrets of the King's castle.

Safe on dry land. And now, they were suggesting I cross open water all the way to Texan.

"No," I objected. "Not by sea—I can't take sea travel."

"It's only for a week, Prince Arn," Bishop Thomas reasoned.

"Have you ever been seasick?" I countered.

"Arn has a point," Murdock mused. "Perhaps a direct entry into Texan is not the wisest. An overland route might have benefits, but there is no need to travel entirely by land. We could ship from Kingsport or some other port on the west coast, and debark in Arkan. That would only be two or three days by ship, Arn. Entry into Texan could be made at the Arkan border. Since Arkan and Texan were recent allies, entry through their common border might be easier than coming straight into a Texan port. It would take longer, depending upon our disguise, but if we left in the early spring, past the worst winter storms. . . ."

"So be it," Robert decided. "To Arkan by ship, and then the land route for Arn, and the troops could later sail directly to Texan. Arn, I presume your party will travel as merchants again?''

Why not? I opened my mouth to speak, but Murdock was too quick.

''Actually, sir, a different guise might be more appropriate.''

''Oh?'' Robert commented. ''And what might that be?''

''One idea comes to mind. I read it in an Old World book, and it has always held some appeal. Now, here's the opportunity. Why shouldn't we go as entertainers in a traveling road show?''

I gawked at him in disbelief. ''A road show?''

''A traveling theater. Or whatever else you'd like to call it. Just like those troupes invited to perform at the castle when they visit Kingsport. We'll work up a few entertainments, travel by day and present a show each night. I have a few ideas—''

Poor Murdock. The man had gone crazy.

I put a comforting hand on the wizard's shoulder. ''Your pardon, my King. Murdock must be overcome with fatigue—''

''No, I'm fine. The idea will work.''

Bishop Thomas was beside himself. ''King Robert, with all due respect for Wizard Murdock, that is the most idiotic idea I have ever heard.''

Robert was troubled. ''I don't like it either. Such a thing involves wagons, I presume''—Murdock nodded affirmatively—''which will slow your progress. Your draft horses won't be able to outrun mounted pursuit, and you won't be able to take saddle horses without arousing suspicion. Instead of keeping a low profile, you'll be putting yourselves on display at every stop. Every deputy and constable and sheriff and petty official between here and Dallas will want to check your papers. And Arn is not an unknown figure. Nor are you, for that matter. Have you considered these facts, Wizard Murdock?''

Murdock grinned at us. ''I have, King Robert. Before the war, merchants might have been the most sensible guise for such a mission. Now, it's different. Sergeant Major Nakasone, as head of security for Kenesee, what do you think?''

The sergeant major stared at his hands for a long moment,

deep in thought, and then looked up. "I'm surprised to say it, but Murdock is correct." Oh no, not Nakasone too! "Sheriffs and border guards will be looking for certain characteristics; a profile, we call it. Merchants and peddlers with foreign accents would be the first ones stopped. Look at the Texan emissaries who were seized at the docks. A theater troupe might be watched to prevent stealing, but its slowness and visibility rule out other suspicion. I wouldn't give a theater troupe more than a passing glance. For a quick mission in and out, to one location in Texan, I would say no. But for extensive travels throughout the country as Prince Arn will have to do, the idea has merit. The one condition is that the party members play their roles well—on and off stage."

Murdock looked positively smug with Nakasone's support, and launched yet another persuasive offensive. "As for Prince Arn's appearance, that can be dealt with quite simply. Arn might be recognized in his current state, with long hair and a shaven face. Let him grow a beard to cover that scar, crop his hair short, and who's to recognize him? Putting him in plain clothes and short hair worked last year even amongst his own citizens. I can grow a beard too, and dye my hair black again. Few Texans have ever seen us. The danger is minimized. Is that not so, Sergeant Major?"

Nakasone considered Murdock and me, and addressed the king. "I can't blame the good bishop for thinking the scheme crazy, for it certainly appears so at first glance. But I think Wizard Murdock has the truth of it."

The king sought further opinion. "Wizard O'Dowd? Any concerns?"

The future high wizard stopped nibbling the feather top. "Concerns? Yes. I have many. As do we all. But I foresee no disaster, no dark futures, if that is your question. At least, not yet. I would need to sleep on it for a few weeks to be sure."

"So," Robert sighed, weighing the possibilities against the risks. "It might be done as Murdock recommends. It might be."

I surrendered to the inevitable. One way or another, I would have to go to Texan. That was clear. They were merely arguing method, not course. I did not relish the idea of wandering down the coast road for months, and I did not look forward to being within reach of the enemy without a means of flight. But if Murdock felt that was the best way to proceed, then I would go along with his opinion. He had been right too often in the past—guided me past error too many times—for me to spurn his advice.

"I agree to the plan," I said reluctantly. I consoled myself that at least the wagons would provide a bunk and some shelter from the elements. I hated sleeping on the ground.

Robert looked pleased despite himself. "So that's settled. You'll go as a theater troupe. When will you leave?"

Murdock rubbed his chin. "A military campaign should properly wait for spring, when we can move troops with less danger from winter storms. There is a goodly ways to go by road, but even then, I'd say we still have a month or more before we should leave. We'll need to learn our stories and develop some acts. Wagons will have to be bought and prepared. But we'll transform into actors only when we're far from Kingsport. We should assume there are spies in town, Sergeant Major?"

"Aye, that would be wise," Nakasone affirmed.

"Our departure, then, must seem natural, and we must have an explanation for being absent so many months."

O'Dowd pointed at the wall map of Kenesee. "Perhaps if Prince Arn were appointed special ambassador to the Beastwood for negotiations. . . ."

"Yes, that has merit," agreed Murdock. "But then, why will we be traveling west by the coast road when the Beastwood is to the northeast?"

"Well," O'Dowd continued, "if you were to first go to the Great Swamps to do a little hunting. . . ."

"A dinosaur hunt!" Bishop Thomas exclaimed. "There hasn't been a royal hunt since the Rites of Manhood."

"Very well then. I ask that you work out the details amongst yourselves in the next few days, and present the plan at our next meeting. Are there any questions? If not, then we will inform the emissaries of their success."

The two Texans returned, and Robert waved them to their seats. "My brother and I have consulted with our advisors, and a decision has been reached. Prince Arn will journey to Texan by spring."

Chalmers nodded with relief, and even Mason seemed to

lose a bit of his stiff-necked demeanor at the words. Nice to know you'll live.

"Details of his travel you need not know. In regard to military force, units will be sent when and if he makes such a request. You have gained what you came for."

Mason took a step forward, ready to make a grandiose speech of acceptance and gratitude, no doubt, but Robert held up his hand and stopped him.

"I must make one thing clear to you both," Robert stated gravely, his eyes boring into the two of them.

Ah, good. He'd warn them what would result if anything happened to me.

"Arn is the last member of my family. My only brother. Many might think him a valuable bargaining chip, a sure way to compromise my decisions, could they hold him hostage. Yet, I am not so easily swayed. I serve as King, and Arn as Prince. Our lives are devoted to our country. It is so with our advisors, and all the men of Kenesee. If there is treachery, if Arn should fall into the hands of enemies, they will have gained no advantage. There will be no ransom, no backing from our course, no change in policy. Arn will accept his fate, as I will accept his fate. The welfare of Kenesee, and the good of all men, will be my only concerns. Is that understood?"

I listened to his words with dismay. No threats? No warnings of vengeance? I swallowed and remained silent.

Mason gave a brief, respectful bow. "We have heard, and understand. We respect your courage. I cannot guarantee Prince Arn's safety. We cannot even be sure of our own. But there will be no treachery."

The formal meeting was ended, although we took dinner in the council chamber, eating with the Texans and questioning them about General Murphy and Texan. They would leave in a day or two aboard the same ship they'd arrived on.

Late in the evening the Texans were shown to a guest chamber, two guards outside their door. The rest of us retired to our own rooms, although Robert beckoned to Murdock before he left. I had not been asked to stay. I moved off down the hall slowly, leaving the door open and listening carefully.

Robert sounded weary after our long day. "Murdock, in regard to Lorich. Am I correct in my understanding that he will be your apprentice rather than Wizard O'Dowd's?"

"You are correct, sir," Murdock stated. "Wizard O'Dowd would be happy to have the boy, since he was Lorich's teacher at the School of Magic. But High Wizard Graven requested that if anything should happen to him, he wanted me to take the boy. He was quite proud of Lorich, as am I."

"Very good. And will Lorich be accompanying you on your journey?"

"I had not planned on taking him. I thought he might learn more here."

The danger of the journey went unstated.

"I would prefer that Lorich be with you," Robert countered. "Certainly, his instruction will be no less for being with Murdock the Magnificent."

The title was rendered with respect.

"The honor is appreciated, my King. But may I ask why Lorich should go with me, rather than remain here? Has he committed some fault? I know he is still a bit clumsy in manner and word, but—"

"No, the fault is not with him." There was a pause, and I had to strain to catch the words. "The fault is with me. On occasion, I am a bit—uncomfortable, shall we say?—with him around."

"Would you like me to talk to him? Tell him to behave differently?"

"No," Robert objected sternly. "It is nothing he's done." His voice lost its sharp edge. "One cripple in the court is a tragedy. Two, a farce."

Well. Another crack in Robert's armor. First, guilt over the Yellow Fields. And now? Self-consciousness, as our old tutor in psychology would have said. Shall I admit I felt a twinge of—satisfaction, I suppose it should be called? Robert was human after all, with a foible or two of his own to bring him a step down, a step closer to the rest of us wallowing in our faults. The moment of satisfaction faded, and I looked at my boots in embarrassment—embarrassed for Robert, and for myself. At moments, we are all unworthy. It's just that some of us have so many more moments than others.

A door closed, and Murdock came down the hall. I stood and waited for him. We continued down the passage together, and I did not have to ask him about his brief meeting with the king.

Murdock spoke softly. "Poor Robert has taken two wounds, one to his body and the other to his spirit. The wound to his body was great, but not as great as he fears. The wound to his spirit came when he guessed wrong at Yellow Fields. It was not his fault, and yet he cannot escape the guilt. It eats at him like a poison, and I do not know the antidote. I will tell O'Dowd. Perhaps he can provide comfort while we are away."

"Comfort?" I asked, unsure how to seriously discuss my brother's foibles and trying to cloak my uneasiness with humor. A discussion of emotions was difficult for me. Sex was different. "The comfort Robert needs can only be found in the arms of a woman."

"Perhaps you are right," the wizard mused, missing the joke.

And that started one part of me thinking even while we chatted. "It looks," I said, changing the subject, "as if we'll be traveling again."

Murdock roused himself from his thoughts. "Indeed. Well, I hadn't expected to go back to Texan in my time, but life is full of surprises."

"Are you sure about this traveling theater?"

He grinned. "Remember, magicians are taught to give performances. I must admit, my own act was acclaimed one of the finest in the land. I'll work with Lorich, and we'll come up with a fine bit of magic. He can also give soliloquies. Perhaps something from *King Richard the Third*, or the *Hunchback of Notre Dame*."

"The hunchback from where?"

"Never mind."

"And what shall I do? You know I can't act. Words will fail me on stage."

We proceeded down the hall to our wing, where the bachelor chambers were clustered. "Well, Arn, perhaps you might be a jester or clown. A whole act without a word. Or, how about some display of martial skills? A bit of swordplay, perhaps, or knife throwing. You were pretty good with the one John gave you."

"Ummm. That I can do."

"There you are. Now, don't worry about a thing, except pleasing your young woman friend."

I stopped. "Angela. She won't like it. What do I tell her about the journey?"

"Why, do what any sensible man would when dealing with an anxious woman."

I waited expectantly.

"Lie."

3

Arrangements

As we walked, I asked Murdock if he was interested in a nightcap.

"Well, Arn, if you insist, I mustn't disappoint you. But I have more to do tonight. I need to talk to O'Dowd, and Lorich, too."

"So, Lorich will be your apprentice?"

"I suppose," the wizard speculated. "I've never had an apprentice before. After I was done with my youthful travels, I began teaching at the School of Magic. In a sense, all the students were my apprentices, and O'Dowd's too. We lost a goodly number of them in the war. Regimental wizards. A handful were mere boys, you know."

I knew.

We nodded to the two guards standing at the entrance to the bachelor wing and passed through. There were four rooms in the wing, as well as an alcove at the end of the hall. Robert had moved out of the wing into the king's chambers, and Murdock had taken his old room. The Wizard O'Dowd had taken Graven's room, while Kendall and I each kept ours. Kendall and Megan had exchanged promises during the summer, but Kenesee law required a year and a day between formal betrothal and marriage, so he was still in the bachelor wing. Lorich remained in the alcove, pleased as ever to have a tiny space which he could call his own.

His curtain was pulled back and he was seated on his bunk polishing boots by the light of an oil lamp. I couldn't tell if the boots were his own, O'Dowd's, or Murdock's. Though the boy had gone through a war and served at the side of the high wizard in storm and battle, he was still an apprentice, and the tradition of boot polishing was not forgotten. It was supposed to teach humility. I could think of a few public officials who could have used a month or two of such duty.

We greeted Lorich, who stood and smiled weakly, as if embarrassed by his mistakes of the day. I would have to tell him some time of the humiliating blunders I had made as prince, but for now we left him to his work and went into my chamber. I was pleased to see our servant, Walter, stoking the fire into a cheerful blaze.

"Prince Arn! Wizard Murdock! Just a moment and I'll have the fire going nicely for you. Marta turned your beds down earlier. The fire will take the damp out of the air in a moment. I'll do yours next, Wizard Murdock." He puttered about the hearth, adjusting the logs with a poker, his head bobbing at the fire. On the mantelpiece above were various knickknacks I had collected over the years, including the broken pieces of a small carved boat. Walter often asked if he could repair the boat for me, to which he always received a firm no.

I poured a bit of sweet liqueur into three glasses. It had become a bit of a ritual over the past months between us. Marta knew her husband's weakness, and he had little opportunity for a taste of anything stronger than hot cider. He never touched the bottle in my room—that I knew of—but could look forward to our little ritual before bed. It was the old man's only real pleasure, other than the talk of the castle. And it gave me a chance to keep up with the gossip.

"Thank you, sir, that is kind of you." He sipped the amber liquid and smacked his lips. "Ah, that does go down nicely on a chilly evening. Well, I've heard that you've had a busy day, good sirs, both of you. Some strange visitors occupying the King and his advisors. I hope everything is all right?"

"Most assuredly," I told him. "Have you heard anything else about the visitors?"

"Well, there are rumors that they're from Texan, but I don't know that for sure. I hear everything is quite hushed about them."

"It's supposed to be." It was impossible to keep a secret within the castle. Arrivals, departures, plans, all seemed to form the basis for chatter. But nothing could be done about that, unless we wanted to cut out some tongues. I didn't think Robert would let me do that.

"I have a question for you."

"A question?" Walter brightened with pleasure. "Yes, sir. I'll try to answer it if I can."

"It's in regard to King Robert . . . and rather sensitive." He looked at me expectantly. "Has he had any visitors . . . that is, has he had any . . . uh, companionship since taking his wound?"

Murdock cocked an eyebrow at me, but kept his peace.

Walter ran a hand through the thin white strands of hair on his head. "Oh. I see your meaning. Well, now, Prince Arn. You know I don't handle the royal chambers. Alfred and his wife take care of that wing. He would be the one to ask. We have talked at times, you know, and various things do get mentioned, but Alfred is very discreet and loyal to the King."

I stared at him.

"But, well, if you don't mind my saying so—no sir. He hasn't."

That's what I'd thought. Well, I couldn't solve every problem, now could I? The king had just saddled me with another mission. I had to look forward to an uncomfortable winter traveling strange lands with the daily risk of capture. And imprisonment. And worse. I resented it.

Yet for all that, I knew there was something I could do for Robert. Something that might give him confidence and lift his spirits. Why, perhaps he might even see things differently, and decide that it was better to leave Texan alone.

"Thank you, Walter. You've been most helpful. Please call Sergeant Jenkins for me when you're done."

He caught the note of dismissal, swallowed the last of his drink with another expression of gratitude, and was out the door. Walter didn't move as fast as he used to, and it would take him time to get out of the king's house and across the court to the barracks.

I took the time to light my pipe.

Murdock sipped his drink. "Arn, you have something on your mind. Other than our coming journey, that is."

"You've been with me too long."

"Not *too* long. Now, what are you plotting?"

I extended my feet toward the fire and let the heat soak into the soles of my boots. "I'm going to help Robert."

"Oh? And how do you plan to do that?"

"The same way I helped Lorich."

"Ahhh. I've heard about that. Your concern is certainly appropriate, but your action may be unwise. Robert is no inexperienced boy. He may resent your interference in his private affairs."

I shrugged. "We'll see."

Walter must have outdone himself, for it was only a few minutes before there was a knock on the door. Sergeant Jenkins strode through in full uniform, snapped to attention, and then went immediately to rest position, a fine picture of cocky arrogance.

"Good evening, Prince Arn. Good evening, Wizard Murdock. How may I help you fine gentlemen this evening?" Under the surface formality, he spoke with a tone of confident familiarity that few would have dared in my presence. Well, after what we had been through, he'd earned the privilege.

And Murdock really *was* a terrible influence.

I pointed at the bottle of liqueur. "Help yourself, and then take a seat."

"Yes, sir. Thank you." Jenkins poured a good measure and sat on the bed.

I puffed on my pipe, the room filling with the pleasant aroma of tobacco. "Sergeant Jenkins, the King has recovered and is able to enjoy—uh—companionship again."

Jenkins grinned. "Yes, sir. I get your meaning."

"However, it seems that due to his condition, he is somewhat reluctant to renew acquaintances. Once before we faced a problem of this sort—"

"Aye, sir," he interrupted. "That we did. Beth took care of that matter as she promised. She didn't care at all about Lorich's hump or appearance at all. That's how my Beth is. Course, she wasn't 'mine' back then. And look at Lorich now. He's had more experience since, but it's the first time that's important. Beth told me about it later, you know. What she found most interesting—''

''We know,'' I interrupted him in turn. ''She has a certain expertise in such matters. I thought that perhaps she might be willing to repeat her performance with the King. Her discretion in the past has been excellent, and we'd expect that again. Tell her she'll be generously compensated. Very generously.''

Jenkins sat up in surprise. ''Uhh—yes, sir. I'm sure she'll appreciate your offer. But, well, things are different now, sir. You see, we sort of hit it off together, and we've given our promises to each other.''

Now this was news to me. If they'd given promises, then they might be married in less than a year. And that would mean Sergeant Jenkins would have to leave active service with the royal guards. While reserve guardsmen were free to marry, the regulars had to be single. I would have to think about Jenkins's revelation. It would be strange without the confident little guardsman around to take care of matters. Which brought my thoughts back to the matter at hand.

''She's stopped working,'' he continued without pause. ''She has enough money, since she's a thrifty sort with a good head on her shoulders. Been investing her savings with the lenders. A girl can make a fortune if she—''

''I'm sure. If Beth isn't available, is there anyone else you might get for us?''

Jenkins scratched his head. ''There's a handful of girls who are really quite pretty. Problem is, I don't know whether I'd trust any of them, sir. Especially with it being the King and all. We've got to be careful on this one. No, I can't think of any I'd trust. Except Beth.''

''I see. Well, it isn't to be, then.''

I'd tried.

Jenkins sat still, his eyes fixed on the floor stones, as if pondering some weighty question. He looked up. ''You say the King hasn't been with *anyone* since he was wounded?''

''Not that I know of. He may fear that no woman will have him. Or the threat of failure may deter him. Foolish, perhaps, but that's my brother. He'll just have to get over it one way or another.''

Jenkins stood, and then spoke, a hint of reluctance in his voice. ''I tell you what, sir. I'll ask Beth if we can't make an exception. Just this once. If it's all right by her, it'll be all right by me. I can't promise, now, but I'll ask."

"Well, if you're sure you want to ask her. . . ." I handed him my purse. "I know she doesn't need the money, but give her whatever she feels is fair."

"Aye, sir." He hefted the purse, and made for the door.

"Sergeant Jenkins?"

He stopped.

"I thank her. I thank you, too."

He shrugged. "Yes, sir," and then went out, mumbling in the corridor. "The things I do for my country."

Murdock watched him leave, and then cast me a bemused glance. "You know, Arn, they have a name for men who do what you've done."

"Yes, but they take money. I give it."

"That's a point in your favor. But let's not make this a regular habit, shall we? There are other professions if you're tired of royalty."

We chatted a bit more, made further plans for the journey, and at last he left me to enjoy a moment of solitude. I sat back in my chair, put up my feet, and puffed away at the pipe in languid comfort. I am a man of simple pleasures. A good meal, a warm bed, a woman of charm. These were all I needed to be content. And yet the world kept intruding upon my peace, besetting me with nagging details of administration and unhappy citizens. And now another worrisome mission.

So, it was to be the road again. First it had been the Beastwood, and now Texan, hundreds of miles away from the safety of Kenesee. I might enjoy the comforts of the castle for another month or so, and then I'd be off again on a frolicking adventure, traveling weary miles, being cold and wet, and eating stale bread. Not to mention trying to stay alive when others wanted to kill me, and living in daily fear of discovery. About the only bright spot in the picture was that I would leave behind the burdens of administration. Why, with luck I might even escape the headaches and indigestion. That thought made me feel better. It's always best to find the bright spot—when there is one.

I finished my pipe in leisurely fashion, tapped out the ashes, and headed downstairs. Thinking about stale bread had made me hungry. The last of the kitchen staff were putting away pots and pans under the supervision of the new cook. The previous one had accompanied the royal party during the summer campaign, and been killed in a ridiculous defense of his kitchen wagon during the retreat from Yellow Fields. A brave man. Stupid, but brave.

I missed his pastries.

The new cook was a grumpy woman of solid proportions who frowned when I came in. She knew my habits well. "Prince or no prince, you don't go messing up my clean kitchen." Her cooking made up for any lack of respect. The woman could do wonderful things with a side of beef.

I took a bread roll and cheese, after which she shooed me out into the hallway. I peeked into the dining hall. The tables had already been cleared and the floor swept. Now the servers sat together at one table, two lamps lighting it brightly while they pored over books and scratched pen upon paper. School assignments from Professor Wagner and his colleagues.

Most of the young went to school for a few years to learn the basic skills of reading, writing, and 'rithmetic, and then entered the trades as apprentices or went to work with their fathers. The children of the wealthy received three or four more years of instruction before their education was complete. Only the few who showed unusual intellectual ability—whether born in the humblest farmhouse or the castle of a nobleman—were chosen to attend the university as regular pupils of Professor Wagner.

The servers were a bright enough group, but they weren't among the academic chosen. Yet, in the king's castle they were enjoying the equivalent of a university education—when they weren't clearing tables. Thus, the offspring of nobles and civil leaders received additional education that was impossible to find elsewhere in Kenesee.

The servers were busy at their task, over a half dozen eager young men and women seated beneath the trophy heads of swamp beasts mounted on the wall. My eyes focused on one young woman a year or two older than the rest, an auburn-haired creature of sturdy grace and unpretentious charm.

Angela. Orphaned daughter of the Mayor of Lexington, her father killed in battle. The only woman who had ever been able to ease my melancholy with just a smile. She had finished her year as a server and was now—thanks to my intercession with Professor Wagner—a regular student at the university. She often came and helped the servers with their mathematics, as she was doing now, leaning forward over one boyish-faced youngster and pointing out an error in his calculation.

He was as enchanted by her presence as I, it seemed, for he gave shy glances of appreciation as she leaned over, concentrating more on her features than on the page of figures. Some men might have been made jealous by the admirer, but I wasn't bothered. If done with gentlemanly discretion, such appreciation should never offend. To look is one of the pleasures of life. If I can't do that, then you may roll me into my grave and shovel in the dirt.

I left the students alone, retreated to the second hall and strode in before noticing the backs of two heads just visible on a bench before the fire. I heard a giggle and was about to back out when a head turned and a hand waved me forward. It was Kendall, his one arm resuming its position protectively around Megan as she cuddled against him, her head resting on his shoulder. The two made a contrast that gave pause. Kendall, the king's advisor from Pacifica, might have been mistaken for a bookkeeper. His long, homely face was topped by a balding pate, his form marred by an empty sleeve, the arm lost in a mission against the Alliance. Noblewoman Megan Sims was a classic beauty, her blond curls flowing down over her lover's arm, her features clear and even, her athletic form most firmly and definitely curved.

Yet Megan's beauty was marred by a pensive look that never quite left her anymore, a somber thoughtfulness, a sad remembrance. She and Angela had been together at Lexington, where they had been assaulted in the Castle of Sims by the soldiers of the Alliance. When the brooding deepened, Kendall would comfort Megan with tales and songs of the Old World, just as he had when she was young. It was as a child that Megan, about to enter womanhood, listened to Kendall with wonder and made her choice of love.

I bowed to them. "Didn't mean to disturb you."

Without realizing it, Kendall stroked the blond tresses. "I was just finishing a story. Nothing either of you haven't heard, but I think Megan liked it. Hmmm?"

She took his hand in hers. "Yes, I did." She gave a smile, but it soon faded as she turned back and stared into the fire.

All of her smiles seemed to fade since Lexington.

I knew when it was time to leave. "Well, I'll leave you two in peace."

"No need," Kendall stated. The two untangled themselves. "We were about ready to go up to my—to our rooms. You can have the fire to yourself."

"My Kendall is going away again, Arn," Megan stated.

Nothing unusual about that. Kendall was always disappearing for months at a time on one journey or another, not even the king always knowing his purpose or destination, but sure that his efforts were on behalf of Kenesee and the Codes of the nations. Such an itinerary does not always please the women at home. What startled me was that Megan spoke to me at all. We were often cast into social gatherings together and I had once considered her my friend, but it was rare since Lexington that she said anything to me. I could understand that. She and Angela had me to thank for their suffering.

I suppose I should be thankful that Angela had forgiven me—or at least, that she had learned to accept what I had done. During the pleasant days of early fall, I'd heard Angela and Megan talking one day on one of the terraces, and had hung back, out of sight on the level above, watching the birch trees stir in the breeze while shamelessly listening to their conversation. It took me a moment to realize the topic of their discussion.

"You should be nicer to him," Angela had stated. "He still considers you his friend, in spite of everything."

"Easy for him to be friendly," Megan had intoned.

"Oh, Megan."

"I don't see," she stated firmly, "how you can just forgive him like that. It was his decision. We didn't have to endure what we did. He allowed us to suffer with all the rest. Us."

"It makes no difference."

"No? None? You don't feel any resentment at all?" Megan asked in skeptical tones.

There was a sigh. "I didn't say that. I am human. I will never forget what happened. But I have learned to accept, and to forgive. He was a victim too, you know. And he is all I have left. Everything else that I loved is gone. My father. Lexington. All gone. And now he has all my love. He is my anchor, the only anchor I have left. Without him, I would be set adrift, and I fear the rocks would have me."

"You have me, too, Angela. I will always be your friend."

"Yes. I know that. I cherish our friendship. And it is for our friendship that I ask you to put aside your resentment and accept him as he is."

There was a pause before Megan replied. "I will try. But I cannot promise more. The hurt goes too deep. Perhaps if I loved him as you do, it would allow me to forgive. But I fear I cannot, in spite of what I might want for your sake. Not yet. Perhaps not ever."

"But you will try," Angela said. "And no one can ask more."

I left them at that point, quietly retreating across the terrace and into the castle, where I went to my room and found occupation studying the patterns in the mortar of the crete and stone walls.

So it was that I understood Megan's attitude toward me. She had tried, for Angela's sake. Megan became civil, correct, polite in her dealings with me. But of warmth, there was not the tiniest flicker. And thus her attitude toward me when I entered the second hall.

Given my musing, Megan had to repeat her comment. "Are you listening? My Kendall is going away again, Arn."

I answered simply. "Oh?"

"He won't tell me where."

"I see."

"Is he going with you?" Her eyes were not cold when she asked that question. In fact, they were full of warmth. But it was the fire of anger, not passion, that fed them.

"No, Megan. I can state in all truthfulness . . . that he is not going with me. I didn't know he was going anywhere."

"That's true," he confirmed. "Arn doesn't know." He took her hand and led her toward the door. "Come with me, and we'll talk about it some more. No use disturbing Arn."

"I want to go with you," she said with a grim resolve as hard as metal. "I warn you. I will not be left behind."

"Now Megan, you know I can't let you do that." And then they went out. Strong-willed, was Megan. I gave thanks that Angela was more reasonable than Kendall's proud lady. That's the problem with nobility. They think they should get their way all the time.

I sat down, the bread and cheese making a fine snack to "fill in the corners," as Murdock liked to say. All I lacked was a beverage to wash the small meal down.

"May I interest the Prince of Kenesee in a cup of cider?" A filled cup appeared over my shoulder, held by a familiar hand.

I took the cup, grabbed the hand, and Angela came around to sit beside me. My arm went around her. "Yes, you may interest the Prince of Kenesee in a cup of cider. Ahh, I see other cups of interest too."

She smiled enticingly. It had taken months for Angela to recover from the horrors of Lexington. The physical wounds were taken care of by the recuperative powers of youth, but the wounds to her mind and spirit were not so easily healed. It was only in the last month that her cheerful smile and bright disposition returned. No longer did she have to make an effort at them. Her womanly behavior had been subdued for a while, and I had been exceedingly gentle. But then her passions returned in force, and we resumed as we had before, though not exactly. There was an element of the wanton, a lack of inhibition which had not been there before, that I both enjoyed and worried over.

I had asked Angela to tell me of her experience one time, and reluctantly she had, what she could remember.

I never asked her about it again.

She ran a finger through my hair. "I saw you at the dining hall entry, and thought you might come here. You look so tired. What did you do today?"

"The usual thing," I explained. "Leading armies. Deciding the fate of thousands. Nothing interesting. And your day?"

That opened the floodgates, and she proceeded to tell me of her studies under the guidance of Professor Wagner, and of a chat with Megan Sims, and the gossip of the cooks, and the arrival of the Texans, and my plans to leave on a journey.

I stopped her. "Where did you hear that?"

"I didn't. I just said it to see if you were listening."

Devious woman.

"I listen to what you say." And I did. Usually. Unless I was thinking.

She looked at me suspiciously. "Arn, are you going away?"

Well, I had to tell her sooner or later.

I sighed with just the right tone of regret. "Yes, I am."

"Oh, no! When? Where? For how long?" Her face held a look of anguish that made me look away.

"The Beastwood. Robert asked me to serve as temporary ambassador. It will just be a few months, I'm sure. And I won't be leaving for weeks. First I'll go to the Great Swamp for a bit of hunting, and then straight from there to the Beastwood."

"The Beastwood?" She became thoughtful. "That isn't so far. You'll need a servant or two, I'm sure. Perhaps you could take me along."

I began to tread very carefully. I was not going to end up with a wrathful woman. That was the last thing I needed, especially since Angela can deliver a devastating slap. I had seen her in action. This would take quick wit and soothing words. "Uhhh . . ."

"After all," she reasoned, "the beastmen are friends now, and their forests should be no more dangerous than our own."

So much for my first argument. So much for my only argument. My mind raced for an answer, and then I had it. Give a blind man enough arrows. . . .

"I'm afraid that won't be possible," I said solemnly, with dignity, as befitted a member of the royal family entrusted with a mission of grave import. "Ambassador Sokol mentioned that only the Wizard Murdock, Lorich, and I would be allowed into the Beastwood at this time. That's why I'm going, to finalize a treaty by which open commerce and free travel can be established between our two nations."

"Oh." The resignation in her voice told me I had found the right excuse. If only the three of us were allowed, then there was nothing she could do. She accepted that, not questioning why a mere wizard's apprentice should be included in the party. Poor girl, she trusted me.

"Arn?" she ventured, languidly.

I grew wary. "Yes?"

"Have you considered exchanging promises?"

I gulped. "Exchange promises?"

"I'd be willing, if you want. We could do it before you go. And then, when you return. . . ."

"But Angela, that sounds so—so permanent."

She jabbed me in the ribs and sat up. "Oh, Arn. Be serious. Yes, that's what it is. Permanent." And for the first time, doubt and uncertainty crept into her voice. "Unless—you don't want it to be permanent."

I learned long ago to give my word but rarely, and have often regretted even those few times. Now I was being asked to make another promise, a promise as great as any I had ever given.

The promise was a simple one. The intent to make the other your permanent companion after a year and a day, sanctified by church or legalized by common law in the institution of marriage. Nothing there I wasn't willing to agree to.

Yet I knew I could not respond as she wanted. I had to think the problem through, to deal with a threat that only now began to clarify in my mind as a reality that I had felt but not realized. I needed time. I cast about for a response and found my previous months of administrative decorum served some purpose after all.

I took her arms and stared into her eyes. That was the easy part, staring into her eyes. Or so I thought, for after a moment I was swept away and almost spoke the words she waited to hear. But I caught myself and went on. The next part would be harder. My voice was resolute, the proper pitch of regret and pride and duty commingled. I had practiced variations of the tone on the many supplicants seeking, asking, begging of the royal house for acceptance, approval, aid.

"Angela, I am a servant of our people. Each new task, every new journey, is a trip into danger." I almost stopped to think about that. "I can't ask you to commit yourself to me. Loneliness may be all you gain. When we have treaties with the nations, when the need for journeys is past, then we'll have this discussion again, and I'll give you a different answer."

Wonderful words. I listened in amazement even as I spoke, pleased with their effect, and perhaps for the moment believing them. Angela threw herself into my arms with tears of adoration—or at least, so it seemed to me, though others might say they were the mere expression of disappointment. To each his own truth.

We have a ballad that is sometimes sung, and the words seemed fitting:

> *Where are ye going, oh wandrin' lad,*
> *And when will ye come back to me?*
> *I go now for duty, oh lass most fair,*
> *The road ever on, for me.*

Better those words weren't spoken that night, of course. I'm not a complete fool.

4

Departure

The weeks went by quickly, too quickly, filled with the affairs of state—and of the heart—while preparing for the journey to Texan. First, with elaborate ceremony and formal celebration, the modest but most capable O'Dowd was officially appointed High Wizard of Kenesee, with the reluctant agreement of the one promoted, and the smug relief of Murdock. A few days later, the royal herald hauled down a drunk singing on the Speaker's Stone and then climbed up and made announcement that the honored and beloved Prince Arn, Scourge of the Alliance, would be taking a well-earned rest by going hunting in the Great Swamps. Rumors were carefully put into waiting ears that I would be going to the Beastwood thereafter as ambassador, and the "secret" quickly spread throughout the kingdom. The tailor came and was informed of our needs, looking first surprised at the list of garments required, then pleased, leaving with a wide grin on his face and a promise to return on the morrow for measurements. My adventures were making him a rich man.

The first one to tell was Sergeant Jenkins, who heard it in the security of my room. The news of our coming dinosaur hunt he took with casual and good-natured acceptance, already knowing of it and assuming he would lead my squadron of guards as usual. He took the news of our secret mission to Texan with surprise and interest. He took the news of our clandestine travel plans with less enthusiasm.

His face had turned bright red upon hearing the plan. "What? A theater troupe? Prince Arn, has everyone gone crazy? You want to saddle us with wagons and nags in the middle of Texan? You want to give shows and put us on display for every passing sheriff and deputy? Good Lord in Heaven. Why not just sail in and turn ourselves over to Murphy's guardos when we hit the docks?"

"High Wizard O'Dowd and Wizard Murdock feel it will work."

"They do, do they?" he exclaimed, pacing up and down the confines of my chamber. "And what did Sergeant Major Nakasone have to say about this idiocy, sir?"

"He agreed it might work."

That stopped him in midstride. He shook his head, then began to pace again. It was a long minute before he spoke. "They honestly think we have a chance?"

We had a number of people who made discreet and not-so-discreet inquiries about joining my party, some who knew where we were really going, and some who did not. The unemployed Patron of Mexico, Carlos Esteves, as bored as he was boring, asked if he might go to hunt for the great beasts, and was politely turned down. Esteves was not really a bad sort, as such men go. He had been one of the more reasonable leaders of the Alliance, wishing to get the unpleasantness finished with as little bloodshed and ill feeling as possible. Still, he had gone along with Rodes and Murphy in their plan of conquest. Now he was without position, without power, and without purpose, his country glad to be rid of him.

The beastman Kren was a different matter. Major Kren and Ambassador Sokol were the only two outside the king's council of advisors to be informed of the true mission. It wouldn't do to mislead them at this stage in our relationship with the Beastwood, which would be quite impossible anyway since the planted false rumor had the Beastwood as my destination. While they both were strong supporters of closer relations between our nations, not all of those on the beastman senior council were so inclined. It would take time to change that situation.

I encountered Kren one morning at my laps around the inner castle wall. I used to do the run with Robert, but since his wound I ran alone. The beastman was on the other side of the castle grounds, already speeding around when I came out. I did some stretching exercises with the guards and began to run. Sergeant Major Nakasone stood in the center of the training area and watched me with a critical eye, shaking his head in exasperation. "Faster, sir," he shouted. "You'll never outrun the dogs like that!" I was already moving at a goodly step, so I cast him a scowl and held my pace—and my peace.

Kren caught up and fell into an effortless stride beside me. "Good morning, Arn. Beautiful day, isn't it? Ahh, the feeling of cold air in the lungs. Invigorating."

I gave him a scowl, too, and he laughed. He chatted on about nothing of consequence until the requisite miles were accomplished and I slowed to a walk, the beastman matching my stride. Kren's pelt was sleek with sweat, and he was breathing deeply, but the beastman still looked as if he could run for another hour or two.

"I have a favor to ask of you," he said.

"Favor?" I gasped, my lungs burning with the cold air.

"I'd like to go along with you on your journey. To Texan. I've chatted with King Robert, and he has no objection. Sokol likewise. I discussed it with Murdock, the High Wizard, and the Sergeant Major. They all gave their approval. Given how you'll be traveling, I can go as a sideshow. 'Kren the Beastman! He walks, he talks, he makes bad jokes!' Who knows, I could be useful. What do you say?"

Why not? What could be more natural? Every theater troupe had a hunchback and a beastman and a wizard and a scarred prince, no? It was crazy. But if O'Dowd and the rest saw nothing wrong with it, why should I?

"Agreed," I panted.

"Good," the beastman responded. "Good."

We continued to walk, Kren silent for a good while before he spoke again.

"Do you remember Captain Mendel?"

I rubbed a hand over my cheek and felt the smooth skin of the long scar that marked my jaw. Yes, I remembered Captain Mendel, the beastman who had given me that scar. "What about him?"

Kren made a face. "He's been promoted to colonel."

"A colonel? Mendel?"

There was anger, disbelief, and sadness all mixed in Kren's response. "They transferred him to another battalion, and when its commander retired, he was placed in command and promoted to major. He led his unit at Lexington with great courage, I've been told. For his performance he received another step up and command of a brigade."

Mendel had friends on the high council of the Beastwood. Kren's major supporter was Sokol. The ambassador was no longer the commander of their army, no longer their senior councilman. He was far from the center of power—a probable reason for his appointment as ambassador, no doubt. The Beastwood might open itself to the outside world, but not with the speed that Sokol advocated. Their leaders were more cautious, and wary of the impetuous general who had embroiled them in Kenesee's war, victory or no. As Sokol's friend, Kren shared his unofficial exile.

I stopped and faced the beastman. "I see. While a former subordinate leaps up in rank, Major Kren of the Border Watch is forgotten in Kenesee, his future bleak. That's why you want to come along on my little adventure. A chance for glory."

He grew thoughtful. "There is that, I must admit. If I sit here at the castle stewing over this I'll turn sour. Bitter. I don't want that. But there's more, Arn. I've always been a wanderer at heart. I like walking the roads and trails and seeing new things. It's almost as good as commanding a battalion. And most of all, there was that brief time when you and Murdock and Black and I were out of the Beastwood and heading for the Rift Gates. I enjoyed that. It was a good time. I felt content, as if . . . as if there were a rightness about being together. Sounds silly, doesn't it?"

It did, but I wasn't going to tell him that. Any reason was acceptable, as long as it wasn't just a search for glory. I didn't need any heroes acting stupid and getting us killed.

* * *

Angela had been the first person to ask if she might go with me on my journey. And it turned out she was also the last person to ask. The first time she'd thought it was to accompany me to the Beastwood, and I'd carefully turned her down. The second time, she knew the truth of our travel.

Sergeant Jenkins and I were alone in the castle library, studying maps of the Coast Road. The fireplace was drawing badly, the room was cold, and after hours of map study I was chilled and in low spirits over our departure the next day. Therefore, I was quite happy at the pleasant distraction when Angela bustled into the room. Until she spoke.

"Arn. Where are you *really* going?"

My look turned to one of confusion. Not about the question, but about the answer. I glanced at Jenkins, who was watching with amusement. No help there.

"Why would you ask a question like that?" I stalled.

There was no smile from Angela this time. Only a firm look of resolve.

"I spoke to Major Kren about your journey to the Beastwood. His answers were less than satisfactory."

"He said something wrong?" I would have to talk to Kren about this. First I let him go along with us, and then he does this to me.

"It wasn't what he said," she came back quickly. "It was what he didn't say. Arn, where are you going?"

What had happened to the sweet, agreeable girl I knew? Megan must have been giving her lessons. I looked at Jenkins, who shrugged. What was left but the truth?

"I'm going to Texan to overthrow General Murphy." That stopped her cold, and I took advantage of the temporary opportunity. I explained our plan, who was in the party, and how we were traveling. And then I said one thing too much. "Now you know why I couldn't let you come along. It would be too dangerous."

Her features softened as her eyes lit up with enthusiasm. "Arn, I'm not worried about the danger. If the Beastmen wouldn't let me enter the Beastwood with you, that was one thing that I couldn't prevent. But there's nothing to stop us from going together now. I'm sure I could be helpful to the party. Why, all of the theater groups I've seen have women in them. You have no women in the party. I can remedy that. I see no reason for me to stay here when I can be with you."

I shook my head. "I can see a reason. Think of what could happen. You could be killed."

"You could be killed, too."

Aha. An excellent reason for me not to go. But I had to. I had exhausted every honorable argument, and had to discard several that were dishonorable.

"That's different. I'm a man."

"And I'm a woman."

Well, yes, I had noticed that. "And that's why I won't put you into danger."

Her eyes blazed. "Oh, no? You won't put us into danger? And what did we women face at Lexington?"

I was silent for a long time.

Jenkins cleared his throat. "Uhh, Prince Arn, are you all right?"

I took a deep breath. "Angela, I say this for the last time. You cannot go."

Her anger had not abated. "But I will go, one way or another. I will be with you, I swear. I will not be left waiting again when there is a role I can play. Kenesee is my country, too, Arn Brant. I will not be left behind."

"Is there nothing I can say to dissuade you?" I asked aloud, the words rich with exasperation.

She shook her head. "Nothing. Unless you don't want me any more. Is that why you wouldn't exchange promises? Should I stay here, unbetrothed, awaiting your return? Some of the others already think I'm only your plaything. Is that so?"

I could see what she wanted and expected to hear. She thought I would deny her words, to reassure her of my devotion. And if I did, what then? Would she come after me like a willful child, not knowing what she faced? What would become of her? How could I stop her?

And then it came to me. There was one way. She herself had provided the answer. *Unless you don't want me anymore.*

This was going to be hard.

I leaned back in my chair, crossed my arms, and gave her a casual smirk. "Women seek security, and men freedom. Or so it is said."

"What?" she asked. The anger faded from her features, replaced by puzzlement. I had surprised her.

"Angela, my dear. King Reuel once warned me against trifling. I should have taken his advice. I have misled you, and that was unfair. But I am being truthful now, so I hope you appreciate my honesty."

She did not quail, nor blanch. She gave no outward sign that my words had any impact at all. She just stood there in silent dignity while ages passed. And yet the hurt in her eyes was like the darkness of a deep well. I had never seen its like.

"Do you . . . mean that?"

I could not trust myself to speak. I only nodded, resisting the urge to throw myself at her feet.

She drew herself erect and gave me a cold smile. "I see. Then I will trouble you no longer."

And with that, she strode out.

Jenkins poured me a drink. "I think you made her angry."

"Oh, really?" I said, my thoughts a jumble.

"Aye, sir, but that's the way you have to handle them. Women need a firm hand, an iron hand, otherwise they'll go off and get into trouble. They just don't have the common sense we—"

I stared at him.

"Oh. Yes sir. I'll shut up now."

I didn't see Angela alone during the time before we departed. I observed her at evening meal, where she was respectful and correct, but her manner was cool and aloof. After dinner she did not come to the second hall, nor to the library, nor to my room to look for me. I waited patiently, though by late evening it had become clear that she wasn't going to join me. I had indeed made her angry. But if she thought I was going to come to her room begging, she was mistaken. Besides, I'd tried that earlier in the evening, only to find her door locked and no answer to my persistent knock.

I sat in my room and smoked a pipe, mulling over my celibacy. Here it was, the last night in the castle, the last night in Kingsport, the last night for how long until I could experience some companionship, and I was alone.

I looked up at the sound of the knock, and then stood. My door was open, but Robert waited until I made a gesture before he entered. I gave him my padded chair and took another. The king was the king, after all.

Robert sat back and stretched out his feet to the fire. He took off his crown, laid it on the table, and scratched his head. "The thing does get irksome, at times, though usually I forget it's there. The other night I was in bed before remembering I still had it on."

I raised an eyebrow. "What did the young lady think when you wore your crown to bed?"

He laughed. It was good to hear him laugh again. A real laugh, and not one of politeness. "I was alone that night. . . ." He grew reflective. "In fact, I've been alone most nights. Almost all, to tell the truth. Except that late one evening a few weeks ago, I had a visitor knocking on my door."

"Now who could that have been?" I wanted to say, but remained silent.

"She told me how she had come to be there."

"And you sent her away?" I knew he hadn't.

"I should have. But I was feeling sorry for myself that evening, and it had been a long time, and Beth is a most attractive woman."

"You know she's promised to Sergeant Jenkins."

"She told me. I was surprised that he'd allow it, but then considering her profession. . . . It wouldn't be seemly for the king to go to a guardsman, but if you could, uhh—"

"He's very loyal. I'll thank him for you."

"I'd appreciate that. And I appreciate your attention to my needs. I—I think it helped."

Helped? I should say it did. The effect had been immediate. The morning after Beth's nocturnal visit, we all stood as Robert entered the hall for breakfast, and eyes widened as they saw him cross to his table. Instead of dragging himself about like an old man, he entered with a jauntiness and smile that made us forget he was still limping. Many of the diners looked at each other and whispered, "What's happened to the King?" A few knew. There were answering whispers to the uninformed, and then the newly enlightened gave forth a knowing "Ahhh. . . ."

After leading us in the Prayer Before Meals, Robert had grabbed Nakasone's shoulder firmly as he sat down. "How long has it been since I've trained?"

"Since before your wounding, sir," the sergeant major replied without hesitation, his dissatisfaction at that state of affairs evident in his words.

Robert forked a slice of ham off the platter and gave him a broad grin. "It's time we started again."

Since that time, Robert had almost been his old self, his dignity and presence enhanced by some of the confidence that had been his. His conversations with the ladies of the court grew more animated, and the light of interest was again in his eyes.

Beth had done her job well. I had to remember to give her a bonus.

"Arn, you've been invaluable to me"—Robert said, staring at the logs as they crackled and popped in the fireplace—"in so many ways. And now I've got to send you away again, into great danger and at great risk."

"Well, if you prefer I stay—"

"If only you could. There are several things yet undone, and your presence would be helpful."

"Undone?" I inquired out of politeness, imagining he spoke of petty matters of administrative detail.

"There are things I can discuss with no one else, not even the advisors. Not until we're clear on the value of the issue."

He had my attention now. "What are we talking about here, my esteemed King?"

"For one thing, Arn, I'm thinking of doing away with the nobility."

Robert waited for my reply. I thought about it. I thought about it some more. "Are you sure you want to do this? That's a lot of people to kill."

Robert laughed. "Arn, you've been around Murdock too long. This is a serious matter."

I'd been joking?

"Perhaps 'do away with' is a poor choice of words," he conceded. "Let's say 'abolish.' Or better yet, 'remove from control.' Yes, that would be the phrase. No reason to actually abolish the nobility, as much as take away their duties and responsibilities. Titles might be kept and passed on, but they would be honorary and ceremonial."

"Isn't our plate rather full right now?" I warned. "The kingdom is just getting itself back in order, and—"

"That's exactly why it is a good time." Robert leaned toward me, intent upon his argument. ''Except for Duke Trudeau and Sir Meredith, the old leadership is gone. The new dukes are young and uncertain. They may not like the plan, but they will not oppose it. At least, not with any success.''

''But will Sir Meredith go along with the idea?'' I countered. ''Even good men will not lightly give up what they have, and the tradition of the nobility is two hundred years strong.''

''Sir Meredith can be reasoned with. Given time to consider it, he'll see the purpose.''

''The purpose? What is the purpose?''

I had no great love for the nobility, nor awe of its tradition. But neither did I have a particular distaste for the institution, especially in consideration of my own place within the system, and so I did not see any immediate need to change it. It was the mode of governance, and it worked with reasonable efficiency. Why stir the pot when the soup is already cooked?

Robert picked up his crown and turned it in his hands absentmindedly, playing with it as I might with my pipe. ''Do you remember when father took us down to the locked room—the dungeon?''

I did remember. It was long ago, during my first year in the castle, and yet the memory was as vivid as if it had occurred yesterday. King Reuel had summoned us two—boys not yet ten—and we followed him across the main floor, through a passage while he explained where we were going. We descended to the lowest level of the castle, and in one passageway reached a sealed door. We stopped before it.

''You've been in there?'' I asked Robert.

''No,'' he said. ''Never. The King would not show it to me before.''

''That's right,'' said the king. ''And now I deem it time. I don't like going down there, but it has to be done each year.'' He opened the double padlocks with a single large key, removed the two wooden bars from their slots, shot back the twin bolts, and pulled open the thick door. The lamplight revealed a narrow passage and steps which led down into darkness. The air from the passage was dry but stale. Each of us took a torch and proceeded down carefully, for the steps were steep.

The stairs ended in an open chamber. On one side of the

room three open doors led into bare cells. On the other side was a single door just as stoutly sealed as the one at the top of the stairs. Along the walls were manacles, and in the center stood a long table of solid oak fitted with various chains, pulleys, and ropes. Next to the table was a long-cold brazier, and on another smaller table were laid out whips, pokers, and metal instruments of various sorts. Dust covered everything, except for a narrow path on the floor which had been disturbed between the stairs and the sealed door.

Robert quickly noted the tracks in the dust to the barred entryway. "Where does that door lead?"

The king placed his hand on its rough surface. "Behind it is a tunnel which runs down to the river. It ends ten feet from the surface, so there is no external entrance, but tools are there for digging. Once each year I come down here alone and walk its length to make sure that it is still in good condition. So now you know that those are my footprints in the dust. The tunnel is not on any of the maps or diagrams of the castle. No living person knows of its existence, except we three. It is the last hope for a surprise sortie or escape should the castle ever be in danger of falling. I pray that you will never need to use it.

"The tunnel is one reason I have brought you down here, but not the main reason." The king gazed around and shook his head sadly. "This room is the reason. The House of Brant has produced a benevolent line of kings, although we have had exceptions. Originally, this level was meant for storage, but King Herbert the Mad converted it into what you see. For two years under his reign it was a dungeon of horrors. The cells were full, and the prisoners tortured upon this rack. It is said their screams echoed through the castle. Herbert would come down and watch for pleasure. I'm not proud of it, but you need to know it's here. What you see has remained untouched for almost a hundred years."

"What happened . . . to King Herbert?" I asked.

"His son, Paul the Good, deposed him. Herbert spent the remaining twenty years of his life in the cell on the left, ranting mindlessly for most of that time."

Robert bowed his head. "Father, I pledge that under my reign this dungeon will remain sealed."

"So I pray," the king affirmed. "So I do pray."

Too bad. I'd thought the room had possibilities.

My mind returned to the present as Robert continued his argument. "Kenesee has been fortunate. The line of Brant has been good for this nation. None of the other nations have been as fortunate. Yet how long can the luck hold? When will another tyrant be born to our family? Or when will the nobility tire of following the line of Brant, and decide it is time for a new dynasty? Too much depends on too few. It's time to prepare Kenesee for a new form of government."

I was totally puzzled now. "And just what do you have in mind?"

He contemplated the ceiling. "Oh, possibly a representative democracy."

"Lord help us," was all I could say.

"There is that old tradition in America, remember. The towns are run by elected officials already, so the people are not unfamiliar with the practice of democracy. All we need do is establish a parliament or congress."

If Robert thought it best, then so be it. One form of idiocy is as good as any other. And yet . . . and yet . . . the change still seemed extreme, unnecessary. I told him so.

"There is another reason," he admitted. "I haven't decided for sure. I wanted to see what you thought. You're right, Arn. It is extreme, given the success we've enjoyed through our system of nobility. However, in the absence of a king to monitor the nation, a democratic council might be more effective than the nobility in running the country."

"And why would the king be absent?" I asked, still not seeing his point.

Robert contemplated his crown. "Because the king would be the leader of the six nations, the head of a new alliance."

I sat back and blinked. "A new alliance? We just fought to end the Alliance."

"No, we didn't. We fought to prevent the Alliance from conquering us unjustly. We were never asked to be an equal partner. We were never told the goals of the Alliance. We knew little about it, other than that it sought to conquer Kenesee for the benefit of its other members. The original Alliance had no worthwhile ends, no valid goals other than the selfish purposes of Governor Rodes and General Murphy.

"The idea of an alliance—a New Alliance—has merit, and

deserves consideration. We might summon the nations to send representatives to a new congress, and set up a confederation. We might bring peace to all the six nations. We might eradicate the evils that still exist in Texan and the Isles. We might spread our knowledge to the Southlands, and to the northern tribes and the plains tribes. With all the six nations united, we might more readily consider and approve technological progress. Think of it, Arn! Such an opportunity has never existed before, and may never exist again. Should we not reach out for it?

I pondered his words. "Should we?"

He smiled. "The voice of doubt. That is why I've spoken to you, and no one else. I need to hear those doubts, to make sure that my decisions are firmly grounded in reality, not self-glorification and self-delusion. Perhaps it is too early to even discuss such things. So much can happen. We may not succeed in Texan. Other disasters might befall the kingdom. Yet, I believe we should keep such possibilities in mind, just in case things fall our way. If we succeed in removing General Murphy, and Governor Rodes decides to—well, think about it, Arn."

"I will think about it," I conceded.

"I'm glad I had someone to share this with. It's been burning at me, and I needed to tell it to you. Think about it, and if you gain any insights, tell me."

"I will." Why, I had eight or ten hours before leaving. Plenty of time to develop a totally new form of government.

He studied my face carefully. "You seem a bit ill-humored tonight. Has it to do with your departure? Perhaps you've yet to say good-bye to your Angela. You know, she's quite devoted to you." A wistfulness skipped across his features. "Some men have all the luck."

I shook my head. "She's not quite so devoted anymore."

"I see. Now herein lies a tale. Interested in sharing it with me?"

Normally, I would have said no, and passed it off as a matter of little importance. Robert and I had not shared intimacies since we were boys, and before Graven's poisoned words had come between us. I had never really voiced private concerns with anyone since then. But the events of the day and the worries of the mission lay heavy upon me.

"We had a parting of the ways," I offered, reluctantly. "Just today."

"And the reason?" he inquired gently.

"I told her the true purpose of my journey. I also told her . . . she couldn't go along."

Robert nodded. "Quite sensible to tell her so. But for that Angela scorned you?"

This sharing of intimate matters was difficult. "A few weeks ago she asked if we might exchange promises. I said no. And today I indicated she was no more than a diversion for me."

He stared at me as if I were crazy. "I've never seen you more content than in her company. Most of us were waiting to hear a betrothal. Did you tell her the truth, or is there more to this?"

My throat seemed dry. "I'm . . . afraid."

"Afraid of betrothal?"

We had come to the hard part.

"Of that, no more than any man. No, I'm afraid of something else." I stood up and paced in front of the fire, then stopped and extended my hand to the mantelpiece, touching the pieces of the boat that lay there. I turned to him again. "Robert, when I let people get close to me—" The words were hard to force out. "They . . . die."

The light went on in his eyes. "Ahhh. So you did it to protect her. Arn, what a tangle you are. Murdock is close to you, is he not? He was at your side through all your adventures, yet he's still alive and healthy. Many have fallen, but not all. Just because you're fond of someone doesn't mean that person is doomed."

I let him go on for a while after that, using his powers of persuasion and good sense, though I didn't tell him they were lost on me. His logic I had used already a hundred times that day, reasoning with myself as the hours ticked by. In my head, I agreed with him fully, but that could not change the way I felt. I saw that it was a mistake even to discuss it with him, or anyone. None could offer an answer to my feeling. I would have been happy to slough my cares off on another. What good does it do to talk about things if there's no solution?

I composed myself, carefully placing a thoughtful smile upon my face. "Why, you're right, of course. I just needed to hear someone else say it.'' I was silent a moment. ''Yes, this has helped immensely. We should talk more often. Well, I suppose we should be abed now.''

Robert rose, pretending to believe me. ''Yes, you must be ready for sleep.'' He hesitated at the door. ''Things tend to work out, in the end. Sleep well, Arn. I'll see you off tomorrow.''

A few minutes after he left, I heard the pad of slippered feet in the hall, and turned to the open door in anticipation. It was Megan.

I hid my disappointment. ''Hello, Megan. Looking for Mr. Kendall?''

''No,'' she said curtly. ''I'm looking for you.'' And with that, she hauled off and delivered a ringing slap that felt as if she were wearing an iron gauntlet. ''Unfeeling swine,'' she called me, and stormed out of the room.

Apparently, she and Angela had talked.

I was long awake in my bed, thinking about Robert, thinking about the nobility, thinking about a New Alliance and the fate of men, and listening for a knock upon my door that never came.

Breakfast marked our departure with little ceremony, but with far more food than would normally have been served. The tables offered bread and jams, sweet rolls, boiled eggs, ham slices, and roasted potatoes. The hall was two-thirds full, as many had come to see us off, and the royal guards accompanying the party ate in the hall with us, rather than at the second seating with the rest of the guards.

My companions and I were all seated at the king's table in honor of our departure. Just a few months before I might have expected to see Angela serving the platters. Though she normally took morning meal with the rest of us, today she was nowhere to be seen. Nor was Megan. Though disappointment hindered my appetite somewhat, I still managed to put away a helping of ham and potatoes, topped off by sweet rolls. Murdock pointed at my plate when I filled it a second time. ''You see, Lorich, that's how you prepare to travel. Like Prince Arn. A hearty breakfast in anticipation of the hard times ahead. Why, it might be three or even four hours before we eat again. Time enough to starve.''

"You're a fine one to talk, Wizard," I grumbled through a mouthful.

Murdock spoke to Lorich as if sharing a long forgotten secret. "Did you know, when Prince Arn was young he took 'clean your plate' to a new level of meaning. Bones, eggshells, nothing escaped."

For once, the gullible Lorich looked skeptical. "Master, I know when you're joking."

Poor lad. Wrong again.

Robert had been listening tolerantly, and if he felt uncomfortable at Lorich's presence, he gave no hint. "He may be joking, young Wizard Lorich, but he's using the truth for his jest."

Lorich was confused. "It's true?"

I nodded. "It's true. But I didn't often get eggshells. Murdock ate them first."

Robert shook his head. "Is this what your entire journey is going to be like? Major Kren, I'm depending on you to maintain some semblance of order among them."

"Impossible," the beastman responded.

Ambassador Sokol took in the party and grinned. "They do seem to mesh together nicely, though, don't you think, King Robert?"

"Oh, yes," Robert agreed. "Like inmates in an asylum. Finished, Arn? All right, I know you each have to get your things for departure. We'll meet in the courtyard when the clock strikes the hour."

No one was waiting in my room, so I used my last moments to make ready to depart. All I really had to fetch were my saddlebags, greatcoat, and weapons, for my other supplies were already safely mounted upon one of the pack horses. I was dressed in the traveling clothes of a prince, warm and comfortable garments of subdued designs in dark cloth, but the fabric was excellent. For weapons I had two swords hanging on the wall from which to select. My ornamental sword for ceremonial occasions was, of course, locked up in the tower with the royal treasury. Of the two blades, the first was a regulation officer's sword of the highest quality, ornate in a straightforward way but well designed for its purpose, a fine weapon for a prince, effective whether wielded on foot or on horseback. I had worn it during the summer campaign against the Alliance. The second was a merchant's short sword, plain but functional in an unadorned scabbard. The last was the weapon I had carried throughout my journey to the Beastwood, and during the struggle for the Rift Gates. The officer's sword came down and was strapped about my waist. And the short sword came down too, to be wrapped and placed within my bedroll. Eventually I would leave the longer weapon behind, but the short sword would come with me on the mission. Backing up the swords was the dagger from John Black hidden in its sheath between my shoulder blades. Need and opportunity had never required I use that blade, but its feel was comforting.

Over a year before I had stood in this chamber and my thoughts had been filled with doubts as I looked around for a last time and wondered if I'd ever see the room again. I had been scared of the unknown, not knowing what terrors I might face. Looking around now, I was filled with the same doubts. But this time I was scared not by the unknown, but rather by all the things I knew could go wrong. As I've said, experience makes all the difference.

Saddlebags over my shoulder, I closed the door behind me. The guards on duty at the stairs bid me good-bye. One gave a conspiratorial wink. "Take care, Prince Arn. Have a good hunt."

I tramped forlornly down the stone steps to the main floor, said good-bye to more guards, and found Robert waiting inside the main entryway, alone. He was a handsome figure, the crown standing proudly upon his brow, red hair flowing out beneath, firm chin lending evidence of his strength and determination. And though he still used the cane, his shoulders were square.

He attempted a grin that could not altogether hide his concern. "All ready, I see. Well and good. I envy you this mission. I'd go with you if I could, but that isn't to be. Yet, there is one thing I want you to know. In spite of what I said to the Texan emissaries, I will come for you. If things go ill, or you are taken, I will lead the army of Kenesee to your rescue."

I wished I could have believed him. "No, Robert. You won't come for me. You will do your duty as King, and make the decision that has to be made."

Robert looked at me, and there was a strange look upon his face. A look he had never given me before. It was admiration. "How we underestimated you."

It was exasperating. Robert actually thought I was reminding him of his duty, telling him not to bother with me when the good of Kenesee was at stake. But I was not. I knew Robert too well. When the moment of truth came, he would put Kenesee first. There was no need to remind him of his duty. I was stating a fact, not nobly denying rescue. Actually, I would have felt a lot better if I thought he really might come for me.

I resisted the temptation to laugh at the irony. Noble men—not me certainly, and not those bearing the title from birth, but rather those truly noble in spirit—often harvest suspicion and mistrust, for they speak the truth as they know it, rather than as others wish the truth to be. Yet, while the truly noble go unrewarded, the unworthy such as I garner the laurels. Well, it wasn't for me to remake the world. Robert should have known better.

We stepped out into the courtyard together.

The last time I had departed the castle for a clandestine mission it had been in the dead of night, disguised as a merchant and riding out in stealth and secrecy for a desperate cause. Well, perhaps not so secret. But there had only been three of us, then, and few had seen us off.

This time, beneath the cloudless dawn, the courtyard was crowded with people. On one side, in front of the stables, the men of the Fourth Squadron were lined up on their mounts, Sergeant Jenkins in command, ready to accompany us to the swamps. There should have been fifty of them, but there were no more than half that number. The royal guards had seen hard service during the war, and it would take years to recruit them back up to strength.

On the other side of the courtyard were two more squadrons of guards on foot, the men standing in close order in front of their barracks. Sergeant Major Nakasone spoke a command, and the ranks snapped to attention.

All around the main entry of the king's house were clustered court members and castle staff, enjoying the break in routine. Through the portal of the open gates could be seen the town street, and there, too, a small crowd of citizenry lined the way, waiting for our departure.

It would have been quite touching, had I been in any mood to appreciate it all.

The staff and court members applauded us, and then watched with interest as we made our way to the center of the yard. Wizards Murdock and Lorich, Major Kren, Dr. Amani, and Professor Wagner were already there, dressed in well-made traveling clothes suitable to their rank, waiting beside their horses. The latter two were most appropriate companions for a royal hunt, each for their specialized knowledge in an actual hunt, and for the credibility of our ostensible purpose.

A stable hand held the reins of Runner, a beautiful animal, the first horse I had ever ridden. Runner was getting older now, and didn't have the desire to take the bit in her teeth and run every time I mounted her. But she still knew how to nip me if I wasn't careful. Our truce still existed. I hadn't poisoned her oats, and she hadn't thrown me off for, oh, two or three years, at least.

"Looking for someone, Arn?" Robert inquired.

"Hmmm? No, just taking it all in so I'll remember it."

"I can understand that. We mustn't delay your departure. All the arrangements have been made, and I can think of nothing else. May your hunting trip be a successful one, and may you all come back to us in good health and fine spirits. And now, if Bishop Thomas will give his blessing."

Heads bowed while the bishop droned on about God's protection, but I took the moment for one last glance around. Angela and Megan were notably absent. I scanned the crowd without result until I saw another head not bent in prayer. Jenkins was smiling at an attractive figure standing alone in a far corner of the courtyard. It was Beth, present to see her guardsman off again. And that was when I realized Angela would not be coming. Angela had met Beth, and the two had developed a friendship, unlikely as it might seem. Angela would never leave her friend standing alone at a time like this if she were here.

I supposed I could not blame her, wherever she was. She had asked me to give her my promise, and I had refused. She had asked to come along, and I'd denied that, too. And at the end, I had told her she was nothing but an amusement, the plaything of a prince who refused to make any commitment to her. Of course she was hurt. Of course she was angry. Of course she wouldn't see me. She was right to banish me from her thoughts.

It was over. I understood that now.

Bishop Thomas finished his prayer and the party mounted.

Robert limped up to my horse and laid a hand upon my knee. "Come back, Arn," he said.

Come back? What did he think I meant to do, take up residence in Texan?

The horses wheeled about, and then there was one last person standing next to me, waiting to say some last word. High Wizard O'Dowd gestured and I leaned over. He came close.

"You must be careful, Prince Arn. I haven't told you, but there is something else about this journey you must know."

Another warning. Wonderful timing, these seers.

"Your future, and the future of the mission, are yet unwritten. I have no premonition of what will happen. Your fate depends upon you, and your enemies."

I felt relief.

"But there is another threat you face."

I tensed. "Oh? And what could that be?"

"Heartbreak," he whispered. "Heartbreak."

5

On the Road Again

We left Kingsport by the north gate, passing by the parade grounds where two small infantry companies drilled in cadence. The northern end of the grounds was lined with tarpaulin-covered wagons holding raw lumber, cut beams, rope, tools, metal braces, and other materiel, the disassembled catapults, towers, and engines that made up the siege train of the Alliance. The slow-moving train had dutifully trailed the Army of the Alliance during the spring, only to be captured by advancing Kenesee cavalry after our victory. Now it all sat ready for rust and rot, more equipment than we could use even if our shrunken army had planned on besieging and storming cities and fortresses.

More useful were the mammoths which had survived the campaign. Four of the great hairy animals had been captured, and several trainers had been taken as well. Now, the animals were guided by our men, and formed the First Mammoth Regiment of Kenesee. We had let it be known to the northern tribes that we would pay for trainable young mammoths, if they could be captured. It was strange to see them maneuvering in this familiar field, and hard to avoid a smirk. Drilling infantry companies got out of the way without hesitation when the beasts wheeled across a line of march.

The parade grounds fell behind us as we followed the road northward along the narrowing river for a mile. There, the road sprouted a western branch that led over a wooden bridge spanning the slow water, while the straight way continued north along the bank, skirting the low mounds of green vegetation that hid ruins of the Old World. We took the branch, crossed the bridge, and began to follow the paved surface of the Coast Road proper. It would, had we been willing to brave the uncertainty of the swampy stretch between the Sippi and Ohio Rivers, take us all the way to Texan.

Unlike the other main roads, the Coast Road was not built over the Old World highways. It had been laid afresh, in response to the new coastline given us by the Cataclysm six centuries before, when the oceans and seas had rolled inland to drown the cities of the Old World. The surface was made with flat, irregular slabs of crete salvaged from ruins and lost roadways, each piece laid and fitted to provide a hard surface for hooves and wheels.

Though the way followed the coastline closely on the maps, the traveler upon it would note that the Gulf waters were often lost to sight, the road weaving miles inland and remaining there for many leagues at a time before wending its way back into sight of the Gulf. Cultivated fields, orchards, and pastures were clustered around the farmsteads, villages, and towns scattered along the road's path, though often far separated from each other by meadow and thicket and wood. Much of Kenesee was covered by forest, and the inland communities were like strung beads, widely spaced and connected only by the slender thread of road.

In standard formation, my party marched with a dozen royal guards before us and another dozen behind, while two scouted ahead a few hundred yards. The horses paced off the miles at a brisk walk. We didn't stop at every village, but our appearance certainly stopped all normal activity. Farmers waved from fields, wives came to their doorways, and children ran alongside the column. Occasionally a guard would hoist one of the little ones onto his saddle for a ride, then lower the child again to rejoin the envious peers. The people were happy to see us.

This part of Kenesee had not escaped the war, and there were still too many scars from the enemy. The Islanders and Mexicans had landed east of Kingsport. But the Texans had landed up the coast to the west and marched through this area on their way to Kingsport. At many places the fence posts stood forlorn, their rails gone to feed the campfires of the enemy. Every so often a burnt farmhouse could be seen, its shell blackened and skeletal. And twice we passed the remains of a village similarly put to the torch.

We stopped for lunch outside one village and then pushed on, making twenty-two easy miles and reaching the town of Douglas in late afternoon, to the delight of the innkeepers. There were the mayor and town elders to see, followed by dinner with them, and at last a chance to retire to our rooms for a night's sleep. The next day we made twenty-eight miles and stopped early at Jackson Town for the night, and so it went.

I had precious little chance to meet the fair sex of Kenesee, and those I met were the daughters of the elders, each marched out with the hope that she might catch my eye and my heart, but closely watched and guarded by her family lest the young prince get to enjoy dessert without paying for it. There was always the future, and with Angela no longer having anything to do with me, I could blissfully seek other arms. Or so I told myself.

In many ways I envied the guards, for when the day's journey was over their schedules often allowed them freedom to tour the towns, while their anonymity meant they could go where they would, to tavern or house of joy, alone or with companions, with nary a pompous official or boring functionary to politely entertain. To his credit, Murdock stayed with me during business, lending his cheer to all who would take it and making it easier for me to look pleased and interested, rather than dour and bored. Murdock insisted that Lorich attend, too, as part of his training, though the boy generally sat there in silence, trying to ignore the stares.

Had it not been for the cold, it would have almost been a relief a few days later when we found ourselves between towns just before dusk. We were nearing solstice and darkness fell early, leaving fewer hours to travel than in other seasons. We would have a half moon that night with clear skies, and so could have pushed on to the next village, but perhaps Murdock needed a night off from social duties as badly as I did.

We camped next to the road where a stream crossed beneath a short wooden bridge before continuing on through the remains of a burned-out village. Horses were unsaddled and hobbled, blankets unrolled, firewood collected, and fires started while the first watch took position and made the campsite secure.

Kren spread his bedroll next to mine and sat down. "Finally, a night under the stars. Now this is more like it. For a while there I thought we were doing 'Inns of the World.' Has the adventure started yet?"

Murdock unfastened a sack and started pulling out our dinner: bread, sausage, and cheese. He cut off a hunk of sausage and tossed it to the beastman. "Now, don't be too anxious for excitement. When things start to happen, they'll come faster than you want. You know that. Friends of Prince Arn never have to worry about boredom. Torture and death, perhaps. But boredom, never."

"Unless attending a dinner with town elders," I muttered to myself.

Kren eyed the sausage with dismay. "Is this all we have left?"

"Such is the hardship of adventure," said Dr. Amani.

Sergeant Jenkins finished his survey of the surrounding terrain and was standing over us. "Prince Arn, the campsite is secure. We've explored the village, or what's left of it. Nothing there. Must have been a scouting party of Texans having a little fun. No new graves, so the people here got out in time. There's some mounds over that way amongst the trees, all covered with brush. Looks like old ruins. We didn't go in."

Lorich perked up. "Ruins? Master, may I explore them before it gets dark?"

Murdock looked to the sergeant, who shrugged and responded. "It should be all right. The village was close by, so there couldn't have been anything lurking. Village children probably played in them. But watch your step, Mr. Lorich."

"Yes, Sergeant Jenkins."

"Old World ruins are tricky, and it's getting dark. The grasses and brush hide the rubble, and it's easy to break an ankle. Worse, one step you're on hard ground, and the next you're falling into a six-foot-deep pit. What's left of their old cellars, I imagine. Most of them have filled in, but it only takes one to kill you. You wouldn't be the first to crack your head open or impale yourself on a shard."

"Yes, Sergeant Jenkins."

"And snakes seem to like such places. Want a guard to go with you?"

"No need, Sergeant Jenkins," Lorich responded, and then with a broad grin of anticipation he limped off for the ruins like a child heading for a new toy.

"Be careful!" Jenkins shouted after him, and then noted our turned heads. "He should be all right," the sergeant said in a level voice. "Now that he can ride a horse without falling off, I don't want my training going to waste."

"A frightful thing, wasted training," Kren agreed. "Here, sit down and eat something. Murdock will know if the boy needs help."

"You can do that?" Jenkins asked the wizard.

"Umm . . . sometimes. It's not as easy as Major Kren makes it sound. I'm aware of Lorich, just as I'm aware of you, when I put my mind to it. But sorting out *who* is feeling *what* is an entirely different matter. And if he's unconscious, then I'd have no idea of his distress. Magic defies simple rules, and varies from magician to magician. It takes much practice to use skillfully."

"Well, then," I added, "how is your esteemed apprentice coming with his magic?"

"He has great latent strength, but control is still a problem." Murdock glanced around at the guards, and then lowered his voice. "A demonstration might be in order—later in our journey."

We chatted on, finishing off the bread and cheese and shaking the crumbs from our blankets as dusk closed in around us. A figure emerged from the darkness, misshapen and swaying forward at an awkward gait. Lorich came into the light, holding something in his hands.

"Our explorer returns," said Dr. Amani. "What have you found, Mr. Lorich?"

The young wizard handed the piece of material to Murdock, who held it up to the firelight. It split and crumbled even as his fingers explored the substance. "As I thought. Plastic. They called it plastic. Like metal and crete, it was a common substance. Plates, cups, tools—they used it for everything. Whatever qualities it had were lost hundreds of years ago. The substance dried out. Became brittle. It had a life of about three hundred years, and then turned into what you see. I wonder if the Old World knew that would happen. They'd only had the substance for a hundred years when the Cataclysm struck.''

Murdock handed the pieces back to his apprentice. ''Not much good for anything.''

The apprentice looked puzzled. ''But what about the things in the museum. Some of them were made of plastic—or at least had plastic parts. That's what you said, Professor Wagner.''

The scholar took a piece of the material and rubbed it between thumb and forefinger. ''That is so. But the ones in the museum are among the last in existence, by care or luck protected from damage through the years, and now the plastic parts are carefully lacquered with preservative. Even then, they're handled with extreme care.''

Lorich squeezed the pieces and let the resulting dust sift slowly through his fingers. ''There's nothing left then that works? Nothing at all?''

Professor Wagner shrugged. ''Other than books? Not much. They had their day, and now we have ours.''

Lorich sat bemused. ''But why? Why did God let that happen?''

Jenkins chuckled in spite of himself. ''Why? Why does anything happen? You take what comes, and you make the best of it. Hope for the best, and plan for the worst. That's what I go by.''

''When you find someone with the answer,'' Kren added, smiling tolerantly at the boy, ''let me know.''

After that we listened to some of the guardsmen tell stories about their exploits during the war, and then we sang songs. We went through several traditional ballads about noble princes rescuing fair maidens, sang a new anthem that had been composed during the war, and Corporal Phillips sang ''Lonesome Tonight.'' He had a surprisingly good voice, and all the men fell silent while he sang the words. Then it was time for sleep, and our party bedded down amidst the guardsmen.

It could not have been more than an hour later that I awoke, realizing I had drunk perhaps a bit too much water washing down supper. Barefoot, I tiptoed over the still forms to keep them from waking. Four guardsmen were standing sentry duty around the campsite at the four corners of the compass, and they watched me carefully while I headed beyond the campfires for the latrine area. I found the spot by smell and looked up at the sky while waiting for the water to flow. Footsteps swished through the grass, and then a stout figure was standing beside for the same purpose. Murdock.

"Did I wake you?" I inquired.

"Being stepped on tends to do that."

"Oh. Sorry." I went back to looking at the sky. The moon had not yet risen. The sky was clear and the stars were out in all their splendor against the velvety blackness. Away from the campfires, the Milky Way was clearly visible, and the constellations were easy to pick out. I could remember a hundred nights upon the castle walls with Professor Wagner and his academics calmly pointing out the clusters of stars and giving us their names, and afterwards King Reuel and Sergeant Major Nakasone just as surely telling us how to navigate by them.

"Beautiful, isn't it?" Murdock exulted quietly. "They seem to go on forever. A hundred billion of them in our galaxy alone, or so the old books say. And perhaps some have planets, and perhaps some planets even hold life. Think, Arn. The stars! The wonder of it."

I finished with my purpose and buttoned my pants, but Murdock continued in his without pause, even as he stared upward. At last he shook himself dry, making me wish for my boots.

We started to head back to the camp when he grabbed my arm and pointed at the heavens. "Look there."

Silently, a starlike glow moved slowly across the sky. "A satellite," I commented. "There are still two or three in orbit, according to Professor Wagner. There was even a space station and moon base."

"And now they circle above us, lifeless," Murdock concluded. "Oh, Arn, to go to the stars. They had so much. So much."

I am not one for idle speculation, but the question arose in my mind. "Murdock, will we ever do it again? Will we ever build up a civilization and travel in space again?"

He shrugged. "Wagner thinks we might, but I have my doubts. The Old World was voracious, and consumed more than we can imagine; there is little left that can be easily obtained. They were digging deep for oil and coal to fuel the world, and depended upon their technology to mine the depths.

The Cataclysm uncovered no new deposits. So what is left? How would we fuel this new civilization? No, society will rise to a certain level, and then falter. The Golden Age can be reached but once. Lost, it's gone forever."

Murdock's mood passed, and he clapped me on the back. "Oh, well. Come, let's get back to sleep." In the firelight a smile played upon his lips. "We'll just have to do without toasters."

The next morning we rode on. Douglas and Jackson Town were already behind us. In the next days we came through Gadsden, Bama and Hartsell. The wind shifted, the good weather left us after a week of travel, and the temperature plunged by twenty degrees as winter extended its grasp to the south. We were careful to know where the next inn was located. The towns of Russell, New Corinth, and Westport all provided comfortable quarters, as well as a half dozen smaller habitations scattered between. In all, it was over two weeks since our departure from Kingsport before we rode into Jackson Harbor just in time for Christmas, which pleased guardsman Patrick Lee no end. The reserve guardsman—when he wasn't called to active duty—was one of the town's sheriffs, and so was able to celebrate the holiday in his own home with his family. I promised I would stop by on Christmas day for a holiday drink at his hearth and to greet his family. And I did. Good for morale.

Jackson Harbor was one of the ten walled towns of Kenesee, and in its history had suffered siege only once. The harbor was good-sized, but narrow at its mouth and guarded by a tower on either point. Beneath the walls of the town lay a stone wharf and neatly ordered docks, busy with trading ships from Arkan as well as a prosperous fishing fleet just in with the catch of the day. The roofs of the town were done in green tile and the buildings in white plaster. There was no castle at Jackson Harbor, for only minor nobility of the Trudeau family lived there, and their participation in civic events was primarily honorary. All in all, it was a pleasant town, and with 9,000 souls had become the second largest in Kenesee.

With the holidays come, we were feted in high fashion for two days. The food was good, the company less so, as we endured the inevitable meetings, banquets, and speeches, too many of which were devoted to the glorification of the great Prince Scar. I had problems staying awake during these events, and if they expected me to speak, I would stand, say thank you, and let Murdock deliver a witty monologue that satisfied every audience. During one meal, serving an excellent fresh-broiled swordfish, a town elder was seated at my side, a Councilman Smith, white haired and dignified, watching me with interest. Of course, most of those present watched me with interest. I caught him looking and he smiled.

"We've never had a chance to talk before, Prince Arn, though we've met at one function or another. You see, longevity brings its own rewards. I've grown so old I'm the senior councilman around, and so I get to sit next to royalty now. I was a colleague of your grandfather, you know. And I knew your mother."

Everyone wanted to talk to Prince Scar, but none had mentioned the Brown family before.

The councilman droned on. "Arnold Brown was an honest and dedicated mayor, though we had our differences, I freely admit. We had some real go-arounds in council, but our disagreements were primarily financial. He always wanted the best for our town, though he didn't always think about the cost of things the way he should have. Still, we're a better town because of him. And I think he counted me among his friends, in the end. You look a bit like him, you do. And you look even more like your mother."

He waited for a response, so I nodded noncommittally.

"I can still remember Nancy Brown meeting her father after council. She was quite a sight, a bit of sunshine to warm the hearts of old men and make them wish they were young again. She never looked happier than when she was chosen to go to the King's Castle. You can be proud to come from the family of Brown, commoner or no. Now, it may not be proper to ask, but at my age I don't pay attention to such things anymore. And so I'll ask. Did you ever find out what happened to her? I still wonder about that sometimes. It would have eased Arnold's last days, if only he had known the answer. I'm sure it must trouble you."

Yes, I had occasionally pondered the answers to that mystery, but no, I didn't lose any sleep over it. I was less interested in my past than in my future. It was none of his business, but

I decided to let the old man down gently. "No, sir, I still don't know. It's a mystery to this day." He looked as if he wanted to say more, but refrained. And with that I changed the topic to the condition of the harbor, and the rest of the dinner passed affably enough.

Afterward we retired across the market square to the finest inn the town could offer, and inside the door we were greeted by the innkeeper, who informed us of another man waiting to see us. We recognized his name, and saw him in the hallway outside the common room.

He was an older fellow, uncomfortable in his Sunday clothes, with hands that were callused from tools. Yet he stood with the confident air of a man used to being in charge. "Good evening, Prince Arn. Gentlemen. I won't keep you long. No one can hear us? Good. My name is Stanley Arthur. I'm the wagonmaker the Castle hired to do a job for you. In secret, like. Well, the wagons you've ordered are almost done. I'll be shipping them this week to a livery man in Arkan, and let's hope a winter storm doesn't get them. Lives in Batesville. His name is Jebediah Immerson, a friend, and he'll make sure the wagons are assembled in good order, and that you have decent teams. He knows how to keep his lip buttoned, as do I, so don't worry about that.

"It's a very good job we've done, I must admit, though it isn't very humble of me to say so. I bought the wagons used, put them in first class shape, and added everything you asked, even down to the secret compartments. Why, I haven't seen such a thing since I built a wagon for a healer back, oh, must be twenty years now.

"I've been told you'll be returning soon? My new livery is outside the town walls, just up the road a piece. A sign outside, so you can't miss it. I'm there until dusk. When you come back to town, just stop by and I'll take your horses for you. Yes, sir. As I've said. Nary a word to anyone. I've done things like this for the kingdom before, and never spoke a word of it. I won't start now.

"No, no need to pay me now. See if the wagons meet your needs first. I'd make a gift of them to the kingdom, but my daughter lost her husband at the Yellow Fields, you see, and it's up to me to support her and the grandchildren now, too. Well, that's all I've go to say, and you're busy people, I'm sure. It's been my pleasure meeting you, and we give our thanks that you've saved Kenesee from the Alliance, Prince Arn. The Lord bless you."

And with that he rolled out, not tarrying even to receive word of thanks.

We went to our rooms. In spite of the quality of accommodations, I did not have my own room, though not from any lack of availability. Sergeant Jenkins insisted I not sleep alone when outside the security of the castle. Maybe he thought it forced an assassin to make a choice of which sleeping figure to stab, though with two guards at the door and two more below the window, I did not greatly worry about such things.

Murdock was my roommate, and he had already slipped into his bed as I finished washing. I hesitated for a while, and then, almost hoping he might be asleep, whispered his name.

"Yes, Arn?"

I had finally decided to explore the matter raised at dinner. I told him about the conversation with Councilman Smith, and then forced myself to press on. "Murdock, do you know anything more about the matter? Perhaps Graven mentioned something . . . ?"

The magician turned over and propped himself on one elbow. He scratched his head. "I know a bit. Not all, mind you, but enough. Are you sure you want the story?"

"Yes," I responded, not at all sure.

"Parts of the tale I pieced together over the years. The rest was told to me by Graven just before his end at Lexington. It was almost—a confession, I guess the Catholics would say. Yes, you were right. He was involved. The High Wizard was my old companion in adventure and a dear friend. But he saw a world full of threats and dangers, and he did love to stir the pot. Perhaps I should have looked into such matters years ago and talked to him. I can only be in one place at a time, and I don't like the heat of the kitchen. Those are just excuses, of course.

"Well, regrets are just that. It's over and done, and only the story remains to be told. It's a sad one, I'm afraid to say. You know that. It starts with the daughter of the mayor of Jackson Harbor coming to the King's Castle to spend a year as server. Just as your Angela was a server, so was Nancy Brown more than twenty years ago. When Queen Jessica was pregnant with Robert, King Reuel had a brief tryst with Nancy. The queen didn't really mind Reuel's tumbling a serving wench while she was heavy with child. Such was the prerogative of kings, as it is said.

"Queen Jessica was angered when she found out that Nancy was pregnant. She did not know—perhaps no one knew, although Graven suspected—that Nancy was also the lover of John Black, Corporal in the King's Guards at the time. Graven, and possibly even Nancy, could not be sure who the father was.

"The queen, ignorant of Nancy's other lover, assumed the baby would be King Reuel's, and she was furious. Another child besides her own might be in line to the throne. Her pride in her family and her bloodline was overriding. She could not be angry with the King, for that would not be seemly. So she took her revenge on Nancy Brown. Queen Jessica went to Graven for counsel, and together they evolved a plan to remove Nancy and her offspring from the picture.

"Assuming his suspicions were true, Graven threatened dire consequences upon Nancy's baby and her lover, John Black, should she not agree to his terms. Nancy—little more than a girl really—was ensnared in the plots of queen and counselor. She could see no choice but to do whatever Graven said. Otherwise, she put the baby and John at risk."

Murdock paused. "Do you want me to continue?"

I nodded.

Murdock reached for a mug of water, sipped, and went on. "Graven hired a man—Zavakos, I think his name was—to take Nancy and the child out of Kenesee. Zavakos came for her, waiting in the darkness of the night with a carriage. Nancy Brown slipped out of the convent with the baby and came to the road where Zavakos waited. Graven saw them off on a ship headed to Texan. He sent money to Zavakos for a few years through a ship's captain, and then Zavakos disappeared. Never showed up at the ship carrying that year's payment. And that was all Graven ever found out."

I lay back on my bed. "Do you think she's dead, Murdock?"

Murdock paused. "Nancy? I'm afraid she is. Reuel thought so. John thought so too. You wouldn't know, but John told me that after her disappearance he planned on going to search for her in secret. Before he could put in his request for special leave, the king—whether suspecting Nancy's relationship with John or not—came to him and asked him to do a special service. Reuel wanted John to go and search for Nancy. Reuel financed the search, but after six months held little hope. John would not give up, and the king reluctantly allowed him to continue his search. John sailed to Arkan, Texan, Virginia, and the Isles for word of her. But there was no trace of a lone woman and child. John couldn't know that she was with Zavakos—man, woman, and child traveling as a family. After two years, Reuel ordered John to return. John came back in despair, fearing that Nancy and the baby were dead. And so she must be, agreed those who knew her when you were found, for she would never have abandoned you to the streets if she were alive. It would be nice to think she still awaits rescue, but hope can only stretch so far."

Murdock leaned across the space and patted my arm. "And that's the story, Arn, as much as I know. What happened to Zavakos and Nancy, and how you got back to Kenesee, are still mysteries."

Oh, well, it had been a long time ago. There was nothing more to be done. Nothing at all. "Thank you, Murdock."

"I wish I could provide some comfort. Why God allows such things to happen, I don't know. Perhaps He has some higher purpose. We're in a forest and can't even see through the trees. The mountains are distant and obscure, but if we could stand there, perhaps we could see the whole valley and understand how everything fitted together."

Murdock was silent after that, and by the light of the fireplace I watched the shadows flickering across the ceiling. I tried to think of valleys and mountaintops, but was lost amidst the trees in the forest. There was no clear view to be found.

6

The Hunt

We left Jackson Harbor on the cold dawn of the twenty-sixth, regaining the Coast Road and making our way northward toward the Great Swamp. We were still a good seventy miles from the southern edges of the swamp, where the vegetation grew year-round with the relative warmth generated in the volcanic depths of the earth. Jackson Harbor was subject to all the vagaries of season. The very last of the leaves had fallen, so that trees and bushes were all barren, with only the firs and evergreens to lend foliage amidst the stark timbers. If not for the lack of clouds and the unusual amount of sun we enjoyed, it would have been a dreary December, indeed.

Our progress was slower now, for we had added the Royal Weapons Wagon to our column. Yes, the very wagon used during the Rite of Manhood trundled along with us. It was stored in Jackson Harbor for those infrequent occasions when it might be needed, and the guardsmen had been at work the night before making sure it was properly equipped and ready for use. A strange feeling, seeing it again after four years.

There were no towns in the next fifty miles, although a half dozen villages filled the emptiness between Jackson Harbor and Wickliffe, small beads between greater ones on the slender thread of the road. The lowlands between the hills were rich and fertile, where they weren't marshy. The villages became more formidable as we advanced. One village had wooden gates at the ends of narrow streets, so that it could be sealed off at night. The next had a wooden palisade all around. The last village, and closest to the swamps, was Monterey. This settlement was smaller than the others, and yet lay within a stone wall ten feet high which boasted four wooden towers as well. It was a veritable fortress in miniature. Monterey would not be caught unaware by man or beast.

Its strength reminded me of the architecture to be found along the northern borders, where raids by past generations of the northern tribes had dictated a fortress mentality to defeat the incursions of the barbarians. But the size of the sharpened stakes protruding from the base of the wall and the thickness of the gates in Monterey warned of a different foe, a foe of massive strength and tonnage. I don't think we have evidence of any large beast leaving the swamp and attacking a settlement itself, though on occasion the bigger carnosaurs might wander out and grab an unsuspecting cow or farmer from a field before returning to the safety of the swamp. Perhaps the defensive precautions of the villagers foiled even the threat of such an assault.

However, the smaller predators—dromaeosaurids up to man size—tended to form nomadic packs, and in their wanderings had been known to leave the marsh and try their claws at easy meat. Such packs might besiege a village now and then, roaming the fields with impunity and running down any cow or horse not safely locked in stout barn or stable. Few of these monsters ever returned to the swamp because they would overstay the feast by greedily stuffing themselves and falling into a sleepy torpor. Eventually men would bring out the village ballista-wagon and hunt the creatures down.

Still, such events were only occasional happenings, and we did not trouble ourselves as we approached, though the closed gates of Monterey offered the first clue. The sound of a horn greeted us from afar, and as we neared the gates swung open and several score of villagers—mostly women, children, and gray-haired men—tumbled out to wave hats and aprons. One of the few men of military age held onto the hand of a young woman who led him forward, his mouth hanging open in a wide-eyed stare that peeped from beneath the floppy brim of his hat. The woman did not look as happy as the rest, and had to restrain the man from jumping up and down with excitement. I was afraid he was going to drool, and he did.

I looked away.

"The people do love to see Prince Arn," Lorich exclaimed.

"They do," agreed Murdock. "But their enthusiasm today may have other cause."

We drew to a halt before the crowd, and a man in his thirties came forward to greet us, an army cap upon his head, his right arm in a sling, and a veteran's badge pinned upon his coat. He saluted with his left hand, a grin of relief upon his face. "Good afternoon, Prince Arn. I almost didn't recognize you with the beard. And Wizard Murdock. And—"

He stopped at the sight of Kren, who had already gained the attention of much of the audience, and then remembered himself. "I'm Peter Dennehy, Mayor of Monterey, and lately sergeant in the Tenth Regiment of Infantry. I was with you at Wickliffe and the Crossroads, Prince Arn. Thank God you've come."

I returned the salute and introduced the rest of the party. Mayor Dennehy's earlier fascination with Kren shifted to Professor Wagner when I introduced him.

He stared at Wagner in disbelief. "You are *the* Professor Wagner who wrote *Creatures of the Swamp: Life Patterns of the Dinosaurs*?"

Wagner perked up. "Why, yes. Yes. I am."

The mayor was awestruck. "What an honor to know you, sir. Dinosaurs are my hobby, and I've spent many an hour studying them. My knowledge has helped the village. I have your book, and refer to it constantly. A brilliant work."

I had read it and been bored to distraction. Who wants to know how many eggs a ceratops lays?

Wagner sat up straight, satisfaction radiating from him. "We must talk sometime. And I'll be happy to sign your copy, if you like."

"I would be honored," the mayor gushed.

I interrupted the worship services.

"Mayor Dennehy. To matters at hand. Does my coming really inspire such joy among the villagers, or is there another reason?"

"And why," Murdock ventured, "were your gates shut during daylight?"

He looked from one to the other of us. "You mean you don't know? Then Fischer didn't make it through. We gave him the fastest horse in the village three days ago. He volunteered. He was to reach Westcott to bring help. A pack of swamp beasts—dromaesaurids—have been roaming about. They took a woman from the fields. We thought you were coming to our rescue."

Murdock nodded. "We have, whether intended or not. Well, Arn, we came to hunt dinosaur, and I guess we can do it here as well as anywhere else. It's been a long ride. Mayor, you don't happen to have any refreshments for the brave dragon slayers, do you?"

We set up camp in the street just inside the town gate, or rather the royal guards did. I and my companions took up quarters in the village inn. Unfair, perhaps, but that was the way of it. Next time they'll know to be born princes.

The mayor went with us to the inn. The common room had only a few small tables, but looked familiar. We sat over mugs of beer brought by a hefty woman with streaks of gray in her hair who looked tough enough to lead an infantry company over ramparts. Yet her features belied her nature, for she smiled upon us with warmth and served with courtesy, as pleasant to the private as to the prince.

The mayor waited impatiently as she chatted while handing out the mugs. "It's been a long time since we've had royalty stay at our inn. You were just a boy then, Prince Arn, on one of the royal tours. I had a great time flirting with the guardsmen." She giggled like a school girl. "Drove my husband to fits, it did. Paid him back for eyeing the girls the way he did. How do you like it, I asked him, which stopped that nonsense. It seems like yesterday. Yesterday. . . ."

Throughout, Jenkins stood at the door, mug in hand, eyeing those who clustered about outside until the mayor joined him and shooed the villagers back to their homes.

The server continued. "I recall more recent when King Reuel and Prince Robert and you and the whole royal party came for the Rites, and camped outside the village before going into the swamp for the hunt. That was a day to remember, I can tell you. I thought it crazy to send you boys after those devilish creatures. But you both came out, with trophies and all. Well, enough of that, for you've got serious matters to discuss, I know, and Mr. Dennehy will give me the grief if I keep talking. You just call if you want for anything."

Dennehy took advantage of the opportunity. Sparing frequent glances at Wagner and Kren, he explained the troubling events that had befallen Monterey. "Five days ago, just at dusk, a woman was taken within sight of the village. Two of the beasts pounced on her, and a third joined them as they dragged the body off into the woods. You can see the spot from the wall, for it's just before the wood line. The watch rang the warning bell. Fortunately, most were already back from the fields and the animals put to barn. We don't know if any of the farms were prey, but normally they can hear the bell.

"We saw one or two of them roaming through the fields the next day, so we waited. We saw them a third day, and decided to send someone to notify Westcott so they could send help. One of the prisoners of war, a good man from Virginia named Fischer, volunteered to go. We knew that you were going to the swamps for a hunt, Prince Arn, but we didn't know when you'd be passing. The village could have waited a few days for your arrival, but some of the farmsteads might be in difficulty. We couldn't be sure. Naturally, on your appearance we thought Fischer had met you at Westcott and described our needs."

I considered the situation. "You have a ballista-wagon?"

Dennehy nodded. "Yes, sir. You're wondering why we haven't taken care of the problem ourselves. Prince Arn, the village of Monterey fielded four squads of infantry. Those are still serving on active duty at Wickliffe. The only adult men in the village are myself, two other maimed veterans, six oldsters, and one prisoner of war. We had a dozen prisoners before, but after harvest ended most went to Wickliffe to work on road and bridge repair. I didn't feel it wise to go hunting with the men we had available."

Murdock nodded. "A prudent and proper decision, don't you think, Prince Arn?"

"So it would seem," I agreed. Dennehy was looking at Kren again. "Mayor, didn't you see enough of the beastmen at Lexington?"

"What? My pardon, Prince Arn. My pardon, Major Kren. No, I was wounded at the Crossroads and missed the rest of the campaign. The Major is the first I've ever seen. I meant no discourtesy or offense."

"None taken," Kren reassured him. "I should state, though,

that I am an incredibly handsome member of my race. Not all are so distinguished looking."

There was a great rolling of eyes. Wagner cleared his throat.

"I see," the mayor said. "You are friends. Those of the Beastwood are men after all."

Kren feigned hurt. "What else would we be?"

"To serious matters," I said.

"Yes, sir," said Murdock. "We came to hunt dinosaur. The village is beset by the beasts. I think we may accomplish two ends at the same time."

Reluctantly, I admitted to myself that there was no escape. I had hoped to have Kren and Murdock bring down one or two moderate-sized creatures of the plant-eating variety, obstinately rejecting any pleas they might have for finding more challenging game. I had no desire to challenge a carnivore. But a task had been set in our path, and I could see no viable excuse for refusing it.

Perhaps there was a bright side, though. This would save us from penetrating into the interior of the swamp, and we would miss all the gnats and flies that so enjoyed the visits of royalty. And then I remembered that it was winter, and even though most of the swamp enjoyed a misty warmth during that season, the flies and gnats disappeared between November and March. Thus, there was no bright side. Unless—

"You mentioned the beasts were dromaeosaurids?" I asked.

"Oh, yes sir. I'm sure of that. I saw them roaming myself. They match the drawings in Professor Wagner's book. I can't say what a pleasure it is finally meeting him. No one knows more."

"Yes, he is quite the expert," Murdock affirmed.

"On just about everything," Jenkins mumbled.

"What size were they?" I asked hopefully. Maybe they were some of the small ones, like dromaeosaurus.

Dennehy shook his head. "That's the bad news, I'm afraid. They're deinonychus."

"Dynamite us?" Lorich repeated.

"Deinonychus. And they're man-sized," Wagner stated.

Dennehy nodded at the pronouncement. "And more. Three hundred pounds of death. That's why we waited for help."

Murdock folded his hands and rubbed his thumbs together in thought. "Mister Mayor, do you have any recommendations on how we should go about hunting the creatures?"

Dennehy shrugged. "Such need is infrequent. Professor Wagner in his book suggests there are no more than a half-dozen hunter packs in the entire swamp at any one time, maintaining a balance of nature. The smaller varieties of mammals and reptiles seem to have quite a yen for dinosaur eggs, and so only a few predators ever reach maturity. It's quite amazing how it all works out so well, considering how they once ruled the earth. . . ."

We waited patiently, Wagner smiling benignly.

Dennehy noticed our silence, and the manager won out over the academic within him. "Sorry. For all their ferocity, the beasts tend to avoid large groups of people. They'll likely fade away into the bushes if you go trundling down the roads after them with wagons and horsemen. And they seem to be nocturnal hunters, or at least to limit their activities to early morning and late evening. That's why we have little concern during the day proper. It's only the dawn and dusk that give us concern. So early morning would be the time to start. You've brought a ballista wagon, and with ours, we can set up hunting sites north and south of the village, a dozen men at each. I'd say the north site is a bit more likely to encounter the beasts, since that's where we spotted them grabbing Mrs. Johnson in her field. Of course, Professor Wagner may have suggestions too, and I would defer to any he might have."

Wagner shook his head. "I like your suggestion. It's a very sensible approach to the problem."

I liked it, too. I liked it because it reduced my chances of personally encountering a deinonychus by half. My party would have to take the northern site, of course, but if I was lucky, the other group would take care of the problem for us. If the enthusiasm of my wizard and beastman was unabated afterwards, we could still go hunting for a nice gentle herbivore.

We began our task the next morning under a gray sky and cooling temperature, dividing into two groups as Dennehy had suggested. We were all afoot, leaving only the draft animals pulling the wagons to worry about at the hunting sites. A dozen guardsmen were sent with the village wagon south of town, under the guidance of the mayor, who was named huntmaster of their group. With them went an ex-soldier with a limp and four gray-headed townsmen who had more pride than good sense. They might be too old for the war, but they would not miss the hunt.

My party and a dozen guards under Sergeant Jenkins dutifully marched north along a cow path for less than a mile before turning off into a half-plowed clearing with good lines of fire. A shallow stream formed a small pool nearby and then continued on, a trickle of water in a wide bed that quickly deepened into a gully meandering off behind us to the east.

The two horses were led a dozen paces away to the south, securely tethered to a hitch line, and hobbled as well. Preparations complete, Jenkins had the guardsmen take their positions around us. All veterans, they sank into the tall brown grass, the butts of their lances thrust into the soft ground so that the weapons stood upright, a dozen evenly-spaced points marking a circle around us. The spikes were comforting. Bows in hand, the guards waited expectantly, a firm line of defense should the ballista prove inadequate.

Mounted permanently on the wagon, that weapon now pointed to the sky defiantly, looking like a giant crossbow. The inch-thick bolt that it fired boasted a barbed point that should give pause to any dromaeosaurid. Behind the bolt shooter, the cage waited to give sanctuary to at least one seeker of refuge, and the racks and equipment boxes offered spare weapons and armor. Less than fond memories were invoked by all this, for it reminded me too well how I, a boy of sixteen, had faced the terrors of the swamp, alone and afraid. My portrait had just barely avoided joining the other six unlucky princes adorning the trophy wall at the king's castle.

Dinosaur hunting is much more enjoyable with friends. And guards.

Jenkins familiarized Murdock and Kren with the workings of the giant bolt shooter. "Now remember how it was practicing yesterday. These things shoot high. Lead your target, aim low, and you'll hit right enough."

He jumped down and regarded who was left. There was only Lorich and Professor Wagner. Dr. Amani had been left at the village, a central position in case anyone needed medical attention. It turned out the table server at the inn was also the village healer, and most willing to help the doctor set up shop in a room of the inn.

"Well, now," said Jenkins, as he opened a weapons box. "Here you are, Mr. Lorich. A good bow and a quiver full of arrows. Make sure you've got good tension when you string it. And keep in mind what I taught you back at the castle. One long, smooth motion, and lead your target. And for you, Professor Wagner—"

The scholar shook his head. "Oh, heavens. No. I won't be needing a weapon."

"Let's hope not, sir," replied Jenkins. "But just in case, you buckle on a short sword and take this shield. There are spears on the rack right beside you."

The meadow was quiet, except for the fluttering wings of a few honking geese swooping in to float on the small pool of water. The woods around were brown and bare, branches thrusting upward from bush and tree. We would be able to see or hear anything approaching.

"Are you ready, mighty hunters?" Jenkins asked. The guards chuckled at our expense. "All right, then. Private Tompkins, do the honors."

Tompkins fetched a jar from the wagon and carried it outside the circle of lances. The guardsman unsealed the lid and poured a nice glop of bait upon the ground. I sniffed the air and my nose wrinkled reflexively, punished for my curiosity. The glop stank as badly now as it did when I was sixteen.

I crooked my finger and Sergeant Jenkins came close. "Uh, any special ingredients in the bait?" I whispered.

"Special ingredients? Ohhhh." His voice dropped to match mine. "You know about that, do you? Well, no poison this time. That's only for the Rite of Manhood. Pitting a sixteen year old against one of these things is murder. By the way, don't tell King Robert. He'd use us for bait next time."

"Why don't we just set out poison and go back to town to wait?"

Jenkins chuckled quietly. "And you accuse the others of too much joking."

He winked at me, and then stepped to the wagon, picked a long spear out of the horizontal rack, shook the weapon, and nodded approvingly. He tapped the butt of the spear against a wagon wheel, speaking in his best parade ground voice. "All right, guardsmen and hunters all. We've had our fun, and now it's to serious business. We don't want anyone killed or maimed for carelessness. Guardsmen, keep watch to your front, and signal if you suspect something. The Mayor spotted three of them, and Professor Wagner says a pack has four of the beasties at most, so we should handle them without too much trouble. Just don't be distracted after the first makes an appearance. The others could well be circling in from the sides. That's what they do. Until we spot four, each guardsman should watch his front. Don't be distracted by what's happening elsewhere.

"Hunters, be ready to swing that bolt shooter wherever I tell you. Stay close to the wagon, stay alert, and we'll have a fine day. Any questions? Good. Hunters, let's keep the chatter down to a minimum. That includes you, Wizard Murdock. And you, Major Kren. Guards, silent status until we make contact."

I crawled under the wagon, stretched out on the dry grass, and laid my cap over my eyes. With my vast experience hunting dinosaurs, I knew that we had plenty of time before anything happened. No reason not to catch an hour or two of sleep.

A booted toe nudged me in the thigh, and none too gently. "Prince Arn, what are you doing?"

I peeked out from under my cap at Sergeant Jenkins. "I'm taking a nap."

He shook his head. "We'll have no naps during a hunt. Let's go. Up and at 'em, sir. Now."

Jenkins tone was not that of a request, but of an order.

"Wait a moment," I sputtered. "I'm the prince. You're the sergeant."

"'Aye, sir, I surely am," he said, enjoying the situation immensely. "But you made me huntmaster, and so huntmaster I'll be."

I rolled out from under and saw Murdock and Kren grinning.

"Ah, it's hard to get good help these days," Murdock stated.

Jenkins eyed them critically. "And are you two fine gentlemen scanning your fronts as instructed? Wizard Lorich, these two stalwarts I assign to you. They need watching."

Lorich looked appalled.

Before he could speak, the sergeant raised a hand for silence. One of the guardsman to the north had waved a hand slowly back and forth, signaling he'd heard something. The guardsmen to either side of him waved. And then a guardsman to the west waved too. The beasts were coming at us from two directions. Nasty little creatures with no sense of fair play.

The party was silent now, and we could hear the predators ourselves. There was the far-off rustle of leaves and the distant snapping of dry branches upon the ground. It sounded like they were moving fast. The noise grew louder.

Jenkins clutched his spear. "Still want to take that nap, Prince Arn?"

"Perhaps later," I replied.

A deep breath. This wasn't really so bad. After all, I had a dozen guardsmen, not to mention my loyal and battle-tested companions, between me and the dinosaurs. All were armed and prepared. Certainly they could handle three or four deinonychus without mishap.

The sergeant gestured. "Sir, I want you in the wagon backing up Wizard Murdock and Major Kren. Otherwise you'll go off trying to kill half of them by yourself. I won't have that. No use risking you just for—"

Jenkins pointed. Through the underbrush to the north we could see two forms coming rapidly, their normal stealthiness replaced with an eager rush to the source of the odor. One's head swiveled around, peering about with deadly purpose before fastening its gaze upon us. The creature was perhaps six feet tall from head to foot, but its thick tail gave it a length of at least ten or eleven feet. The lizardy skin was a dirty gray in front, fading to a smeary brown on its flanks and back. Beady eyes peeped out above an ample mouth filled with pointy, inch-long teeth. From its chest, forelimbs could stretch out with three clawed fingers. And to complete this fearsome engine of destruction, each foot had an oversized, curved claw that could rip open chain mail. All in all, the beast was as frightening as it was ugly.

Lorich gasped when he saw it, while Kren and Murdock stared with wonder.

"They are magnificent," Professor Wagner agreed.

"Two more coming up from the west," said Jenkins.

Kren could not tear his eyes from the creatures. "Amazing how they maneuver to the attack."

Murdock gestured to Kren. "Your shot, or mine?"

The beastman bowed. "Wizards first. But wait for it to close. It's too easy to miss at this range."

"I think there's four," warned Jenkins. "Yes. Four." To the north were two beasts. From the west came two more. The creatures cleared the trees and stopped on the edge of the meadow, surveying our position.

As if on cue, the beasts started forward, bounding in powerful, rhythmic strides toward us. I grabbed a wheel and began climbing up into the wagon, intending to follow Jenkins's instructions to the letter. We couldn't risk a prince, now could we?

I found a spear and waited.

The beasts had halved the distance to us when the wizard let loose with the ballista, which made a distinctive *pffft-thunk* as the bolt left the giant bow. The bolt flew true, but the dinosaur took that instant to sidestep a boulder rising out of the ground, and the missile flew past harmlessly. The creature looked back, sniffed, and came on.

Arrows were flying now, pairs of guardsmen concentrating on targets. Kren cranked the giant bow up for another shot, while Murdock slid a bolt into the slot. Just a few seconds, and they would be ready.

Normally, the sight of so many men might have deterred the beasts, but the pungent bait must have set their mouths watering. They put away all thoughts of prudence. With loud hisses, the predators closed.

The two deinonychus from the west went for the horses, and were met by a half dozen guards. The other guards put themselves between us and the northern beasts. Those with lances fended them off while their fellows tried for killing shots with the bow. They were no longer concerned about our rear, since Professor Wagner had assured us four were all there could be.

I glanced at Murdock and Kren to see if they were ready with another bolt, and saw a flicker of movement to the left. East. Our rear. A deinonychus bounding out of the gully. And another. And another.

Seven. The professor's book would need a revised edition.

I yelled as the first closed the distance in a half-dozen bounds and leaped up onto the edge of the wagon, tottering there uncertainly on the side board, arms and one leg flailing as it tried to regain its balance. The beast's great jump had set the wagon to rocking so much that we could barely keep our feet, and instead of attacking the beast, Murdock and Kren cowered back from its flailing limbs, while I fell flat on my back. With a terrible hiss it fell backward to the ground, rolled over and was on its feet just as Jenkins raced around the wagon to put himself between the fierce beast and his precious prince, jabbing at it with his spear as the monster tried to get around the flashing spear point. Foolishly, Lorich and Wagner came around right behind Jenkins. The two stood to one side of the guardsman, the young wizard loosing an arrow while the professor—to my surprise—raised his shield and pulled out his sword.

Fortunately, the next beast went straight for the bait, but the other—the largest of the seven, of course—came bounding right up to the wagon. The beast leered up at me with open jaws, and instinctively one of its feet lifted and then slashed downward, the great claw on it raking the wagon wheel and clattering along the spokes, leaving a deep furrow in the wood. It gathered itself for a leap into the wagon until suddenly distracted by Lorich's arm in front of its eye. The lad was pulling another arrow from his quiver, concentrating upon the creature Jenkins was dueling. It was a common occurrence in battle, even among veterans. Your attention shrinks down to one opponent, oblivious to everything else.

It was a good way to die.

The beast saw how easily it could snatch up Lorich in its jaws. Professor Wagner saw it, too. He stepped in front of the young wizard and jammed his shield in the beast's face. The creature shook his head and slammed the shield aside. It turned slitted eyes upon Wagner and reared back to strike, eager to turn the greatest living authority on dinosaurs into the greatest departed authority.

I must admit, it was hard to believe what happened next, and I watched the moment with wonder. Kren threw himself at the creature, landing on its back and wrapping his arms around its powerful neck. The beast staggered sideways with the impact and weight of the beastman, but in testimony to its strength did not go down. Instead, the dinosaur twisted its neck, made a vain attempt to bite and shake off this unexpected presence, and then went jouncing around the meadow in a slow trot with the beastman still upon its back.

All this, in just seconds.

The ballista went *pffft-thunk*, and suddenly the dromaeosaurid finishing off the bait looked up, hissed, and fell over trembling in its death rattle, skewered by an inch-thick bolt. "One down," stated Murdock. A wise choice of target. Though Jenkins's dromaeosaurid was closer, the angle was bad, and Professor Wagner might not have appreciated a bolt through the back of his head. Besides, the sergeant and Lorich were doing quite a good job on their opponent, who was backing off with two arrows in his side and a half dozen wounds where Jenkins was jabbing him with a spear.

Murdock grunted and began to crank the bow up for another shot.

The ballista went *pffft-thunk* again, followed by a distinctly squishy sound. A beast harried by guardsmen arched its back, hissed, and went down, the bolt buried deep in its chest. Beyond it, another beast lay near the horses, porcupined with a dozen arrows. One of the horses was down, its throat torn open, and the other was pulling wildly against its rope. Of the beasts, a fourth was close to toppling as two guards thrust at it with their lances. It went down at last, still snapping its jaws at the lance points and clawing at the men. But one guard was flat on his back, and covered with blood. Another poor devil was sitting up with a torn shoulder.

I climbed slowly to my feet. Two of the beasts were being harried by the guards that converged upon them from all directions. First one, then the other struggled to get around the spear points while arrows penetrated their vitals. They impaled themselves futilely, and finally toppled. Six down.

Across the meadow, Kren still rode the last reptile, arms and legs wrapped about it, his head pressed to the creature's neck where claws and teeth could not reach. That was all he could do. Loosen the grip of arm or leg, and he would be finished.

The creature came bounding past us, Kren's face turned towards us on this pass.

He called out, forcing a word between two jarring bounds. "HELP!"

The creature turned around and came past again, Kren's face away from us. We could still hear his calls.

"We'll save you!" Murdock called out to the beastman on his third pass.

Jenkins scratched his head. "And just how are we supposed to help him?"

I gave Professor Wagner a look of disgust. Four beasts. At most.

The idiot.

Kren held on.

Wagner didn't seem to notice my anger. "The bolt shooter?"

Murdock said, "We could end up hitting Kren. Same for arrows."

Jenkins clasped his weapon. "Well, then, spears it will be."

The guards grabbed their lances, while the party emptied the wagon of long spears. Murdock stayed, manning the ballista. The wounded guard was brought over and gently laid against a wagon wheel. The rest of us formed around the sergeant, all watching Kren and the reptile making circuits of the meadow. "All right, lads," said Jenkins, "Here's how we'll—Lord, no!"

The beast had been staggering about, his head forward and down, tail extended behind him, clearly tired but still formidable in strength. Suddenly he jerked erect and skidded to a halt, almost throwing Kren. The creature shook itself once, and then again, and at last the beastman came flying from his seat in a low arc. He hit the ground hard, rolled, and was still. The beast cocked its head at Kren and hissed with delight at the victory. It took a step forward, and then another, until it was standing over the beastman, eyeing him wickedly. It sidestepped, sidling its way around the still figure, gloating before leaping upon its victim and rending him open with the giant claw upon either foot.

Kren did not stir.

We were no more than sixty feet away. We knew what would happen next, and yet could not prevent it. All we could do was take our first steps forward, shouting and waving our spears, hoping to frighten the beast away, or at least distract it. Yet the creature paid us not a second's notice. *Pffft-thunk.* Above our heads a bolt flew past, zipped by the creature and continued on, missing it by a foot to one side. Not a bad shot considering how the target weaved about above its victim.

There was no time to fire another bolt.

"KREN!" Jenkins shouted as he ran, his small form leading the rest of us. "Kren, roll away!" But the beastman didn't stir. And the creature stopped circling. Time to pay back its late rider. Its head went down, its tail up, and legs flexed as it prepared to leap atop the prey.

Suddenly, and inexplicably, the head of the deinonychus jerked erect, eyes bulging, every muscle in its body stiffening. And then it collapsed onto its side, lying only inches from Kren.

Guards dragged the beastman away while others watched the creature warily, lances ready to thrust into its twitching form. But the thing was finished, its eyes glazed with death.

Fortunately, the same could not be said of Major Kren. Jenkins felt for a pulse. "He's alive." Then we loosened his clothes and felt his neck, arms, and legs, trying to tally the damage. A low groan escaped the beastman's lips, and he opened his eyes. "If the dinosaur didn't kill me, why must you? Ouch. Everything hurts. Help me up."

He stood shakily and stretched . . . cautiously. "No ribs broken. No bones. No sprains. Then why does everything hurt?"

Professor Wagner helped steady the beastman. "You were clutching the dromaeosaurid in a death grip with every muscle in your body. That's why. I don't think there has ever been a recorded instance of a man—or beastman—riding a dinosaur. You are the first, Major Kren. Congratulations. I will include it in my next book."

Jenkins turned to Wagner, stood toe to toe, and wagged a finger at the face towering above him. "How about correctly stating the number of beasties in a pack, Professor? That little mistake almost got us killed."

It was true. We had wiped them out, but at a high cost. One guard was dead, his innards ripped out, and another might well lose an arm. Not a bad exchange, given the number of creatures we faced. If Kren hadn't leaped on the big one, if Murdock had missed his other shots with the ballista, then half the party or more might be down. We had survived because we were well trained, formidably armed, and, perhaps most important, completely ready. Anything else would have been fatal.

Wagner drew himself up at Jenkins's accusation. "Our knowledge grows," he glared down at the sergeant. "We share knowledge as we gain it. Doubtless others will learn from our experience today. It is not your place to—"

"What do you mean, not my—"

Kren stepped up to the two. "My esteemed colleagues. Sergeant Jenkins, you were very busy with one of the dromaeosaurids. You may not have seen the professor save Lorich from the one I rode."

Jenkins stare shifted to the beastman. "What?"

"Wizard Lorich was busy helping you out with your beast. Mine came at him from the side. Professor Wagner threw himself in front of the creature and turned its strike with his shield."

Jenkins peered up at the professor. "You did that?"

Wagner became reticent. "Well, yes, but you see I really didn't have time to think about it."

Jenkins took a step back. "Well. So you rescued Mr. Lorich. All right, then."

"In any case," Wagner went on, "the deinonychus would have taken me if Major Kren had not leaped when he did. *That* was a willful act of heroism. To the beastman goes the honors."

Kren shook his head, grimacing with the effort. "Farthest thing from my mind. One second I'm safe on the wagon, next I'm on the monster's back. Don't ask me how I got there."

Murdock had abandoned the wagon and arrived in time to hear the last few exchanges. He looked at me with a knowing smirk, and then spoke. "Don't forget Prince Arn. Were it not for his warning, the last three beasts from the gully would have had us."

"For Prince Arn!" Jenkins called out, and as the butts of spears and lances were drummed on the ground, a chorus of cheers rang out. Even the wounded guard resting near the wagon gave forth a feeble hooray. The one person whose actions had been involuntary, the one person who had sought safety, the one person undeserving of praise—was the subject of their adulation.

It made me angry.

I prepared to deliver a few choice words to the imbeciles, and then noticed the tear in Murdock's coat and the dark drops of blood that dripped down his arm and stained the grass. "Murdock! You're wounded."

He looked at his arm and sighed. "So I am. I hadn't noticed. Nothing to fret about, I'm sure."

Lorich grabbed the wizard by his good arm. "Come, Master. We must get you back to the village."

"Not yet," Murdock corrected him, and looked down at the deinonychus. "I want to know. What happened to it?"

"I can't say," said Kren. "Certainly nothing I did."

Jenkins shrugged. "Exhaustion?"

Wizard Murdock looked at the arm holding his, and traveled up its length to young Lorich's face. The young wizard's pale skin was flushed with excitement and exertion, but the features were set into a grimace, as if he were suffering pain.

"Perhaps the answer will become clear in time," ventured Murdock.

Lorich averted his eyes. "Yes, Master. Perhaps."

7

The Casualty

We brought Murdock, the wounded guardsman, and the body of the dead guardsman back to the town by midmorning without too much difficulty, removing the cage and equipment from the weapons wagon so that the lone horse could pull it with the two men seated in back and the covered body lying by them.

"We've wrapped the wounds to stop the bleeding," Jenkins informed Dr. Amani and his new assistant, Healer Diane, who handled both men with calm efficiency after we carried them in, the more seriously wounded guardsman going into the treatment room first while we waited outside in the common room. In a short time the doctor and healer came out.

"I want to take a quick look at Wizard Murdock," Amani stated.

"It's not that bad," Murdock told the doctor while the healer unbuttoned the shirt, the sleeve of which was red with blood. "Help the guardsman. I'll be fine in a minute, though I fear it's needle and thread again. I hate stitches."

Dr. Amani focused on the assortment of old scars covering Murdock's torso. "Good Lord, man. Where did you get those?"

"Here and there," the magician sighed. "But too often there."

The doctor examined the arm wound. "A nice gash you've got, and bleeding freely, though no major vessels seem to be damaged. How'd you get this?"

Murdock was about to shrug, and thought better of it. "A creature jumped on the wagon. Its limbs were flailing for balance, and a claw caught me."

Dr. Amani peered at the wound closely. "You see, Healer Diane. The laceration will be a rather straightforward matter. The important thing is to make sure we've cleansed it adequately. The claws of those beasts are covered with bacteria. Infection is our concern for this man. We'll flush the wound quickly, and then leave him while we take care of the other."

It was late afternoon before a weary Dr. Amani, seated on a stool with his shirt sleeves rolled up past the elbows, completed the last stitch on the magician's arm and pulled the thread tight. The magician winced in his chair. "Torturer. Sadist."

Dr. Amani smiled at him. "So, you're going to treat me like you treat Jason the Healer, eh? All right, then, I can play that game."

"Game? What game? By the way, you need to frown more. Jason would never smile like that."

"I suppose you expect me to say 'serves you right,' " said Dr. Amani. "Hunting dinosaurs at your age."

"I'm still in the prime of my manhood," Murdock protested.

Amani did not bother gracing the statement with a reply.

The wounded guardsman would keep his arm, though it might be of little use to him. Amani had spent long hours working on the torn flesh and muscles of the man, and now the steadfast guardsman was resting in a deep sleep induced by the Healer Diane's powders.

Kren sat in a corner waiting his turn, for though he did not have any external wounds, we'd insisted he be examined too.

Amani cut the thread after the last stitch and straightened. "A fine job you did, Healer Diane," he said to the woman behind him. "The wounds are clean and well-tended. You say you haven't had any formal training?"

She looked around the room, smiled sheepishly and blushed with pleasure. "Thank you, sir. No, just a summer spent with Dr. Hunta from Westport. A good doctor, he was."

In her healing duties, the woman was as sparing with words as she had been generous with them in the common room. Two different personalities. But two different tasks.

"I should say he was," Amani confirmed. "And you have the knack, too. You deserve a reward, and I'm sure Prince Arn will provide it."

She glowed with pleasure. Well, it's not every healer gets to take care of a royal party.

Dr. Amani continued to examine the wizard's torso. "Amazing, all those wounds. What's God keeping you alive for?"

Murdock tried to move his arm, and grunted in pain. "Some great purpose, no doubt."

"Master Murdock will live forever," Lorich pronounced.

"At this rate," Dr. Amani countered, wrapping a bandage around the wizard's wound, "in a few years, all he'll be is a lump of scar tissue." The doctor put the arm in a sling. "There, that should do. I've sterilized the laceration as best I can, but I'll want to take a look at it each day. Then, if all goes well, we'll take the stitches out in a week or so. Do you have any objections, great wizard?"

Murdock laid back down and sighed. "Would it do any good?"

"No, not at all. I'll give you a powder each day to prevent infection, and an opiate for pain, if you wish."

"An opiate? No. Opiates aren't the best for magicians, I'm afraid."

"Why is that, master?" Lorich asked.

"Their effect can be unpredictable, at least initially. Some opiates cause paradoxical effects upon those with magical talents. Many such users gain a temporary, euphoric state of enhanced physical and mental capabilities instead of the normal state of sedation. These capabilities can be dangerous to the user as well as to others around him. And while opiates are addictive to all, magicians are particularly susceptible. There is a saying. 'The first two times, you take it. The third time, it takes you.' "

Amani nodded. "There is truth in what you say. However, I've been studying some medical books. Even the Old World was uncertain about the reason for such addictions. Over and above the physical, it was felt that those of weak character—unhappy people, if you will—were particularly susceptible to becoming addicted to opiates and other powders. Those of strong or healthy character who became addicted to painkillers through treatment for wounds, for example, had little difficulty breaking the addiction once they had convalesced. They were not dependent upon the drug to solve their weaknesses of character and spirit."

"I yield to your knowledge and expertise," Murdock stated. "Still, a wise magician will approach any opiate with great caution."

"As for wizards, perhaps it is as you say," Dr. Amani admitted. "Now, who's next? Major Kren. Please take off your shirt."

Kren pulled off the garment, wincing.

Healer Diane shook her head in awe. "So much hair!"

"We prefer to call it fur, or pelt," Kren stated as Dr. Amani poked and prodded.

"Animals have fur. Animals have pelts," Dr. Amani corrected. "Men have hair. Your condition, or a version of it, was known even in the Old World. Congenital Hypertrichosis Lanuginosa."

"Cogenial hyper-trickle what?" Lorich repeated.

Kren mouthed it out silently.

"The term means abnormal growth of hair over most of the body. I looked it up in the old medical books, and Jason discussed it with me over the campfire last summer. It occurred rarely in the Old World. We don't really know what triggered it among so many newborn after the Cataclysm. Maybe a change in the composition of the atmosphere from volcanic eruption promoted the genetic mutation; or maybe something released from the old laboratories. I doubt if we'll ever really know."

He felt the beastman's ribs, and Kren yelped. "Ow. I don't think I've ever ached like this in my life."

Dr. Amani continued with his exam. "You never rode a dinosaur before, either. You strained all your muscles."

"He saved my life," Lorich told the healer, his tone reverent. "It was the bravest thing I ever saw."

"Brave, indeed," Murdock agreed, still lying prone. "Now, that's the way to fight dinosaurs. Barehanded. Major Kren has shown us the way."

The doctor chuckled at the banter. "Well, nothing broken, nothing torn, nothing sprained. You'll be fine in a few days, which is a miracle, because by all rights you should be dead. You and Murdock will go down in medical history. There. All done. Put your clothes back on, Major Kren." Dr. Amani dumped his instruments into a bowl and handed them to healer. "If you could boil these for me, I would be very appreciative. I'll do the alcohol soak myself. Healer Diane, thank you again for your aid and expertise. Kenesee owes you a debt."

She glowed again. "Oh, Dr. Amani. It's little enough, but I do what I can." Reluctant to leave, she backed to the door. "Well, I guess I'll be going. Your instruments will be ready soon. Just call me if you've need."

When she had gone I smiled brightly at Murdock and Kren. "Well. Are we happy now? Have we had enough hunting for the week? Or maybe you'd like a bit more. I have an idea. Why don't we go into the swamp for a week or so and give you a chance at one of the big ones. A carnosaur, perhaps. Hmmmm?"

Kren looked at Murdock, Murdock looked at Kren, and then both gave me a feeble smile. "Perhaps next trip."

I nodded, satisfied.

Kren made a low rumble in his throat. "Then again, in a

few days we'll be feeling better and possibly we could—Arn, where are you going?"

I shook my head in despair and rose to leave, but Dr. Amani waved me back into my seat, and then remembered whom he was directing. "If you please, Prince Arn."

I was magnanimous. "If you wish." Actually, now I was curious. What topic was he about to take up?

"There is one bit that puzzles me," he stated while closing his bag. "Major Kren was clinging to the back of this creature, and did not deal it any mortal blow. Is that correct, Major?"

The beastman snorted. "A mortal blow was the farthest thing from my mind—or ability. I was hanging on for dear life."

"And you didn't choke off its windpipe?" the doctor asked.

"I certainly didn't cut off its air," Kren affirmed. "I could hear and smell it breathing in great stinking gasps. My grip was too low on its trunk to try choking it to death. But I think it was getting tired."

Dr. Amani nodded. "I see. Sergeant Jenkins, you say no one fired at the creature."

Jenkins stood in one corner with his arms folded across his chest, looking smugly self-possessed. "No, sir, I didn't say that. I said that nothing hit the creature. Wizard Murdock managed to fire. The bolt missed."

"And no one else hit it with an arrow or throwing spear?"

"No, sir."

"Not even around the wagon before Major Kren decided to take a ride?"

Jenkins stopped himself. "I can't say that, sir. I was busy with another of the beasties."

"I can answer that," Kren volunteered. "I watched its approach. Other than brave Professor Wagner sticking a shield in its face, nothing touched it. Everyone was busy with one or another of the creatures."

The healer looked at each of us in turn. "So the beast was perfectly healthy, with no wounds, able to breathe, though perhaps a bit tired when it threw Kren. There was nothing to prevent it from chewing open the throat of our friendly beastman, or tearing his gut open. Instead, it has a spasm and falls dead. May I be so indiscreet as to ask what killed it? Has anyone figured that out yet?"

There was silence as we looked at each other without finding any answers. Murdock stared at the ceiling. And then from the corner of the room, a furtive voice spoke up. "I think—I think I did it."

Heads swiveled. His face rapidly turning a bright shade of red, Lorich sat with legs asprawl on a stool in the corner nearest his master's bed, his long arms close to his sides. His hands were still, his eyes focused upon the floor, his thin hair hanging across his forehead in fine clumps above his wide, jutting nose. One shoulder was thrust up, belying the hump that swelled across his back.

"Ah, Lord, that does it. . . ." With a groan, Murdock grabbed a sideboard and hauled himself erect until he sat up in bed and faced the younger wizard. "I should have talked to him before, but now the tree has fallen. You might as well explain yourself, my boy," he directed in a soft tone.

I had an idea of what was coming. After all, the leaders of Kenesee had to understand magic in order to use it to advantage. Long ago, High Wizard Graven had given my brother and me an orientation, and since then Murdock had expanded my understanding of the mental powers.

Lorich gulped, and then, still sitting on the stool, drew himself erect—or as erect as anyone could who was blessed with such a misshapen form. It reminded me of the day he had been chosen at the School of Magic, when High Wizard Graven had asked him whether he would accept the apprenticeship. Lorich had at first shrunk from the challenge, and then squared his shoulders and faced it in just such a manner. Not devoid of fear, but refusing to surrender to it.

Still, with all watching him, he could not hide the quaver in his voice. "Yes, Master. When Major Kren leaped on the dinosaur, I couldn't help him because I was shooting at another one attacking Sergeant Jenkins. Later, I wanted to shoot at Major Kren's beast, but couldn't because the chance was too great of hitting him. It takes several arrows to kill such creatures. When the Major was thrown off, I knew my arrow would not be enough."

Dr. Amani waved his hand impatiently. "Yes, yes. But what did you do, lad?"

Lorich looked at each of us, hesitant. His glance stopped at Murdock. The young wizard realized his mistake now. He should have kept quiet about the dinosaur's demise.

"Go on," Murdock stated evenly.

"Master, are you sure?"

"The cat's out of the bag. I've figured it out, and they will too, eventually. Tell them."

Reluctant now, Lorich continued. "I knew only magic could save Mr. Kren. So I reached out at the creature and I—I squeezed."

Dr. Amani's eyes opened wide. "Squeezed?"

"Its heart. Or at least, I think it was the heart. I thought of its brain, too, but couldn't decide which would be better. At the last moment, I had to make a choice."

I took out my pipe. I needed it.

Kren had paused with his shirt half-buttoned, and looked at the boy with new respect. "So you killed the dinosaur just—just by willing it to happen?"

"Not by the will of the spirit," Murdock clarified. "But by the power of the mind. That is the source of 'magic,' after all. The power of the mind."

Kren's face lit up. "Ah, I see. You mean telepathy, telekinesis, precognition, and such?"

Wizard Lorich let the surprise show on his face. "Major Kren, what do you know of such things?"

"So much for the closely guarded secrets of wizards," sighed Murdock.

"I inquired before leaving the Beastwood with you last year as emissary," Kren replied. "We have no 'wizards,' of course, probably for the same reason that your magicians can't detect our presence. No telepathic abilities. Yet our scholars are quite knowledgeable about the existence of such powers. Our spies report—uh, we have ways of finding out such things. Still, I was told magic was very limited in its effect, at least telepathically or telekinetically, and so I have observed it to be on the battlefield. Murdock even mentioned once that he had no effect upon reptiles."

The wizard swung his feet off the bed. "In for a ten-penny, in for a dollar. An old saying, perhaps not inappropriate to the situation. Well, then, we shall have a class in magic. Our hairy friend is correct. I cannot influence reptiles, but I can influence mammals upon occasion. It's not complete control, you understand, but merely the ability to—predispose, shall we say—

the feelings or emotions of the subject or subjects. To make them look upon me and my verbal suggestions in a positive light.''

Jenkins shifted his stance. ''And that's why you're such a lovable old coot, heh?''

Murdock drew himself up. ''My personal charm and warmth are merely expressions of my natural personality.''

''Yes,'' agreed Kren. ''Like my incredible attractiveness among beastmen.''

Amani was not deterred from his interest. ''Wizard Murdock, you were telling us of magical powers.''

''Yes. Well, our young wizard's power is quite extraordinary. Quite extraordinary, indeed. I know of no other magician who has ever had that power. It is indeed a potent weapon.''

''And can such a weapon be used against men?'' Amani persisted.

Murdock pursed his lips. ''I don't know. The telekinetic powers don't usually work against sentient creatures. We cannot affect flesh and blood. For an answer to that, you must ask Lorich.''

The young wizard shook his head. ''I don't know, Master. I didn't know I could do what I did. I just—tried.''

''And I'm glad you did,'' said Kren.

Amani considered the matter. ''If it works against men—this is a great power the boy has. It must be used wisely.''

Murdock spread his hands. ''Indeed, it is. But I must ask that for now, this knowledge not go beyond this room. The six of us must keep it a secret. Even Professor Wagner should not be told. Lorich's power must be kept hidden if he is to use it to the benefit of the kingdom. May I expect such discretion?''

''You may,'' affirmed Amani, ''except for the King. Duty requires that I report it to him.''

''Of course. That was assumed. But ask him to guard the knowledge as well.''

Later we had supper in the common room, which had been closed to the villagers and turned to the use of our party and guards. Professor Wagner had returned from his examination of the dromaeosaurid remains. ''It was really quite fascinating. I've measurements on all the beasts, and examined the stomach contents of two. Tomorrow I will dissect one of them. Doctor Amani, perhaps you would like to participate? It should be fascinating."

The doctor declined. "My patients will keep me quite occupied. However, I'm sure the mayor would be most interested in the opportunity."

Conversation continued along these lines into the evening. Most of the guards had finished evening meal, and left for whatever guards do in their off time. We were thinking of bed ourselves when Jenkins called our attention to the two villagers waiting patiently in the hallway with Mayor Dennehy, all under the watchful eyes of the guards on duty at the door. It was the woman and the drooling man from the crowd of villagers. He still wore his floppy hat and wide-eyed stare.

The senior guard gestured at the pair. "Sir, the mayor has brought this woman and her husband." He eyed the husband with a mixture of pity and distrust. "They would like to see you. And the doctor."

I didn't mind the guard's distrust. That was good. But his pity could get me killed. One more thing to talk to Sergeant Jenkins about.

I glanced at Dr. Amani, who nodded. "Have them come in."

The mayor gestured for the woman to go first, and she led her spouse into the room by the arm. She wore a common neck-to-ankle woolen dress under her coat, while her husband had on a clean shirt and pants under his outer coat, the shirt neatly tucked in at the waist and the collar buttoned. The woman might have been pretty had not a tired sadness surrounded her. The man stepped away from his wife and stopped in front of me. He began to bounce from one foot to the other, like an impatient child waiting for dessert. His face grew animated with excitement. "Prince Scar. Prince Scar. Shake hands."

He stuck out his hand.

I took it and smiled at him. He smiled back.

At least he wasn't drooling.

The handshake went on, and on, and on. I kept smiling. My companions stared at the floor. Shaking her head in despair, the woman grabbed her husband's arm and freed me from his grip. "That's enough, George. You wanted to shake his hand, and you did. Now say thank you."

"Thank you. Shake hands. Prince Scar." He started drooling.

She looked at us for understanding.

The mayor broke the embarrassed silence. "He's wanted to shake your hand ever since you came. I'm sorry we bothered you with it, but it meant a lot to George."

"Thank you. Shake hands. Prince Scar."

"Quite all right," I told the woman. "Glad to be able to help. Did you need anything else from me? Money, perhaps?"

"No, nothing. The pension has started. And the village helps out."

Dr. Amani was watching George. "You wanted to see me, too?" he asked the wife.

She gave him a look dreadful in its plea. "Can you do anything? Can you help?"

"Help," repeated George. "Prince Scar. Help. Shake hands."

Dr. Amani shrugged and looked at the woman. "What's the cause?"

The woman took off George's hat. His dark hair was cropped close, so that the damage to his head was easy to see. A slice of the skull had been chopped away, and the scalp had newly healed over the opening, forming a two-inch-wide trough from forehead to top.

"He took a sword cut or two at Yellow Fields from enemy cavalry," the mayor explained. "Alliance doctors found him wandering after the battle. His brain was exposed. All they could do was sew up his scalp. The wound healed, but he's been like this ever since. A pity; he was the brightest man in the village. We know there's not much can be done. . . ."

"Nothing can be done," Dr. Amani stated in frustration, and then caught himself. "I'm sorry. I can't work miracles."

The woman nodded. "I thought so." She stroked the arm of George with a residue of tenderness. "Then I must live with it as I can." Her shoulders sagged a bit more than when she had come in. "Sorry to have bothered you, Doctor. My thanks to you, Prince Arn, and to all of you."

She turned away, and the mayor led her to the door.

"Wait," ordered Amani. He stood by the man, considered

the wound, and then studied the woman for a moment. "Perhaps I can do something. I could operate, just go into the skull and explore. Perhaps there's a fragment of bone floating about that could be removed. It might make a difference. Or not. There is a risk, as always. . . ."

Hope came into the woman's face. "Would he be better?"

Dr. Amani cleared his throat. "Perhaps a bit. A small chance. There's no way of telling for sure."

"And the risk?"

The doctor gazed at her without blinking. "Not much—no, I'm sorry, that's not true. I want to lie to you, but I can't. There is a risk. A very serious risk. His chance of surviving might be only one in two."

The woman grew thoughtful. She looked at George. He was still bouncing from one leg to the other. "If it might help him. . . ." A gob of spittle ran down his chin and splattered to the floor. She watched the cascade, then clenched her teeth and shook her head. "No," she said. "No, I don't think so. You were right not to want to tell me." She stopped herself. "I should be going now. Thank you, sir. Your offer was very kind. Come, George."

She led George away, his boots clumping heavily at each step

Dr. Amani looked after her, his face troubled. "I was the serpent in her garden."

Professor Wagner regarded the doctor. "What do you mean?"

"I offered her a chance to escape. I tempted her. If George had died, she would have been free. And she refused the temptation."

"Yes," Murdock agreed. "The risk made her face the truth of her motives. She didn't really think anything could be done for her husband."

Kren stroked the hair on his chin. "She might have gone along with it if you hadn't mentioned the risk. Why did you tell her? Why not lie, and leave it at that?"

Dr. Amani picked up a mug and drank deeply of the beer. "Why? Because then the moral burden is upon my shoulders. I dare not play with others' lives, for good or ill. My oath is to heal and save—not to court a patient's death for the benefit of relatives. If I am to do a procedure, it is for the benefit of the patient."

"Fine words," Murdock avowed.

"Yes. Fine. But too often, I am tempted too. Such a tragedy. Poor man. Were I in his shoes, I would wish a doctor to help me escape such a state, and set my loved ones free. Would that God gave me direction to follow. For whatever I do, I feel damned by God, or damned by myself."

I knew how he felt.

Jenkins stirred in his corner. "Well, Dr. Amani, you'll pardon me, but I think it was wrong to offer. Now, I know the Church of Kenesee permits such things, but it still seems wrong."

Dr. Amani looked at the guardsman through narrowed eyes. "Oh? You think so?" He shifted his gaze to me. "Prince Arn, how many men have you killed?"

"By my hand, or by my order?"

"Never mind. Sergeant Jenkins, how many men?"

"Nine, by my count," Jenkins responded readily, not without a hint of pride.

"Nine," Dr. Amani repeated. "And you, Major Kren?"

"Five. Four hairless—and one beastman." Kren noticed eyebrows rise at the latter admission. "It was a long time ago."

"Murdock?" the healer persisted.

"I stopped counting long ago. Too many."

Dr. Amani smiled grimly. "You have enough blood on your hands for any gallery of rogues. And you say what I offered was sinful?"

"But mine deserved killing," Jenkins countered.

Dr. Amani stood up. "Did they? No doubt they felt the same about you. Good Lord, man, do you think the Heavens are smiling on our bloodshed? If I offer the poor woman escape, is that so bad?"

Jenkins remained obdurate. "And if you had George under your knife, what would you have done?"

"I'd have performed the exploratory procedure to the best of my ability, with all due regard for the care of the patient. No, Sergeant. There would have been no slip, no accident to blame. If God wants a patient of mine, He's got to pry him out of my hands, and I'll be fighting Him all the way. All I offered the woman was a chance, not a guarantee. Am I still so wrong?"

The sergeant hesitated before responding. "I don't know."

The doctor met the guardsman's eyes. "Nor do I. But I follow my conscience. That is all I can do. Perhaps I am wrong."

Murdock waved a hand. "Perhaps I am tired, and perhaps such matters should be left to God's judgment."

And so we did. Each of us retired to bed. But if any stayed long awake pondering the shifting sands of morality, he was not alone.

We gave Murdock a few days of rest, celebrated New Year's with the villagers, and then rose one early morn to leave Monterey and its grateful villagers behind. Under a gray sky the heavy clouds loosed a cold rain into our faces, muting the cheers which rose as we mounted. The bedraggled mob of admirers meant well, of course, but I suspect the sodden figures were not only cheering us, but our impending departure so that they could hustle into their cozy houses and dry out before the hearth. With them would rest the wounded guardsman we left behind to recuperate. He would eventually make his way back to Kingsport bearing messages of our progress.

There would be no such comfort for the royal party. We could look forward to nothing but a soggy day in the saddle, hoods pulled over caps and coat collars turned up, testing the integrity of our waterproofs. Our departure was delayed while the villagers assembled in the village square and Mayor Dennehy gave a short speech full of praise and glory for Prince Scar and his entire party. And then we were off, turning northward on the road and heading for the Swamp and Wickliffe. And so we proceeded for the better part of an hour, until we were full into the wilderness, and not a habitation was to be seen within miles.

And that was where we parted ways.

Under the shelter of several large pine trees, Professor Wagner cut my hair, the locks that had grown back over the year falling away. In a hand mirror I saw the shorthaired stranger I had come to know on my mission to the Beastwood the year before, though now a three-week growth of beard covered my cheeks and would soon totally obscure the slash running down the line of my jaw. Murdock, too, had several weeks growth of beard, and he had dyed black the fringe of graying hair around his pate. I changed out of my fine clothes, Jenkins changed out of his uniform, and Murdock, Lorich and Kren likewise doffed their well-made traveling clothes for the rougher, inconspicuous garments of the common classes. Except for the beards, Murdock and I looked quite as we had on last year's journey, comfortably dressed with brimmed winter hat, travel boots, warm pants, shirt, sweater, and a heavy knee-length great coat which was hooded, waterproofed, and cloaked to the waist. Kren, Lorich, and Jenkins were dressed likewise.

One of the guards, Tompkins, whose hair had been growing suspiciously long, doffed his uniform and put on common traveling clothes too. He would be playing the role of "Prince-Scar-in-disguise" going in diplomatic secrecy to the Beastwood, as had been rumored in journals throughout Kenesee. Of course, anyone who knew me and actually saw Tompkins face to face would know the truth in a second, but no one was going to be allowed to meet with the hooded figure who would go straight to his room at each inn. And from a distance, there was a passing resemblance. Who else could it be, the commonly dressed traveler escorted by the Royal Physician Amani and the Royal Scholar Wagner and a squadron of royal guards, than Prince Arn of Kenesee?

That, at least, was the plan.

We exchanged horses, the guards taking my companions' mounts, while my understudy Tompkins took Runner and gave me his sturdy mount. Jenkins, riding another guard horse, kept his own.

"We part at last," Dr. Amani stated, the rain dripping from his hat in slow drops.

Professor Wagner clutched his arms to his sides in an effort to stay dry and warm. "I see the wisdom of keeping your true destination secret even from us, but it is maddening not to know where you will be."

"Yes, Professor," said Amani. "It is better so, though I feel the same curiosity. Well, I'm sure it must be necessary, or we would not be taking such measures. Some are made for such adventures, and I believe you five are as likely to succeed as anyone, whatever your purpose. May God keep you all, and bless you with success."

We shook hands all around, even giving each of the guards a shake and taking their blessing and good wishes in turn. Jenkins made one last, short speech to his men.

"You'll continue north to Wickliffe, then on to Louisville and Lexington before returning to Kingsport. A nice, leisurely ride for the lot of you. Corporal Phillips will be in command as acting sergeant. You reserve sergeants remember you aren't active service anymore, and listen to what he says. You know what you have to make it look like, so do it. And if any of you utters a word of all this, I'll see that you're court martialed and hanged. On this you have my solemn oath. Now go on with you, and do the kingdom proud."

The guards mounted, Phillips gave us a salute of honor, and with Tompkins tucked discreetly into the middle of his column between Dr. Amani and Professor Wagner, took his score of guards off northward on the Coast Road.

We watched them go, I with distinctly uncomfortable feelings. I *liked* having royal guards around. And now there was only Jenkins. We mounted and retraced our road southward. Our intent had been to hurry past Monterey to avoid the villagers, but there was no need. Everyone seemed to be inside, avoiding the cold rain and perhaps discussing the events of the week in the inn over a hot mug. Our horses held to their trot, and we went by the open gate to Monterey and kept going, only the village watch in his tower noting the passing of five hooded travelers bent against the wind and hurrying to get to their destination.

We had two days' travel before we would get back to Jackson Harbor.

And from there, we would begin our journey into danger.

8

Under Sail

The next evening we arrived at the livery of Stanley Arthur, the wagonmaker whom we had met on our last visit to Jackson Harbor. He took our horses without question, wished us well, and we left him standing and waving as we walked down the road and through the town gate, one more good citizen upon whom we depended for the secrecy and success of our mission.

The sun began to sink behind the hills. Time was short.

We slipped through Jackson Harbor at a hurried walk, five hooded figures, boots and leggings spattered with mud from the previous day's rain, and carrying well-stuffed saddlebags looped over our shoulders. The darkening streets were almost deserted now as citizens took their evening meal at home or tavern, and those few still out had better things to worry about than five strangers courteously staying to their own half of the street and minding their own business. We stuck to the narrower ways to avoid meeting any sheriffs, yet we were well aware of the need to reach the Harbor Gate before nightlock.

We turned a corner, and there under the gate lamps stood three men, chatting. One wore a sea captain's hat and carried a lantern, while the other two wore gatekeeper uniforms. The one in the captain's hat was a stocky man, compact and composed, with a resolute, weather-beaten face.

"Here they are," he stated calmly, his eyes darting from one to another of us. "My passengers."

The older gatekeeper crossed his arms and eyed us suspiciously. "So you know them all, Cap'n Grayson? No need to check their papers?"

The captain nodded. "I vouch for 'em. Loyal and true, one and all."

"Well, then," agreed the man. "If your word isn't good enough, no one's is." He shook Captain Grayson's hand. "Have a good voyage, Cap'n. And a good voyage to you, gentlemen. We'll be closing up now for nightlock."

The gates swung shut behind us as we followed Grayson along the deserted stone pier. He beckoned us onward with the lantern. "There's my ship, gentlemen. The *Windsprite*. We'll talk when we're aboard."

The *Windsprite* was drawn up beside the stone quay and lit now by a dozen lanterns. She was a typical cargo vessel, a two-masted fore-and-aft schooner, almost seventy feet long, with a beam of fourteen feet. The main deck ran the length of the hull, broken by masts, two hatches for the holds, and two low entryways leading below, as well as the capstan, the long-boat, and the rudder wheel. With spars and rigging to watch out for, it seemed crowded. Crewmen bustled with last minute preparations, stowing final items of cargo and clearing the deck for sailing. We followed the captain aboard, sailors giving informal but respectful nods to the man as he passed. He led us to an entryway, down steep steps to a short and narrow central passage, through a door at its end, and into a neatly arranged cabin of modest dimensions but moderate comfort: the captain's cabin.

Captain Grayson closed the door behind us and hung the lantern. "I passed you through the gate, but now I want proof. Show me your papers, gentlemen." We uncovered our heads, reached into coat pockets and drew out documents. He inspected each set of papers in turn, giving the owner a close look before passing on to the next. He shook his head in amazement as he studied Kren, who was still greatly concealed beneath his winter cap, but made no other comment about the beastman. The captain kept our documents, put them in a box, and locked it. Carrying identification from this point on would only endanger us.

"Well, the paperwork is correct. But I have to make sure." He reached out to my face but paused as he noted Jenkins's hand move to the hilt of his sword. "Just an inspection, Prince Arn, if you don't mind," he reassured us, and then parted my beard at the line of the jaw and peered at the skin below. "I see the scar right enough, and a nasty one it is, too. But there's one last check, I'm afraid.''

He stood waiting.

It took me a moment, and then I remembered. The birthmark. I hadn't used that as identification since I was found. True, over the years there had been a lady or two who had, in private conversation, expressed some interest in my birthmark. Not willing to let their curiosity go unsatisfied, I would find opportunity to—

''Prince Arn?'' the captain inquired patiently.

''Oh. Certainly.'' I dropped my britches.

''Pumice or sandpaper will confirm its authenticity,'' Murdock suggested, straightfaced.

The captain peered with clinical detachment. ''No need. There's no doubt.'' I pulled up my pants. He smiled for the first time. ''Prince Arn, I'm Timothy Grayson, captain of the *Windsprite*.'' He shook my hand while I held up my pants with the other. ''Sorry about the indignity. I saw you at a naval review when you were a boy, but not up-close since. I had to make sure.'' He shook hands with the others as I introduced them. ''Wizard Murdock. Major Kren. Sergeant Jenkins. Wizard Lorich. Welcome to you all. We'll be leaving just as soon as I can get topside. It's a deep water port, so no need to wait for the tide. Baggage for 'Mr. Thomas' has already been checked and loaded. Is everything else in order? Anything I should know about before we leave?''

''Uh, I do have a tendency to become seasick. If you have a bucket. . . .''

''Each cabin has one. I won't crowd on all the sail, but the Gulf is the Gulf, and I do want to make this a quick passage. Just yesterday a merchant, the *Steadfast*, spotted a fast ship closing with her until she came into sight of Jackson Harbor. She couldn't tell who they were.''

Kren raised an eyebrow. ''The Alliance?''

''Maybe,'' Captain Grayson responded. ''Or maybe pirates.''

Kren gaped. ''You're joking.''

The captain shook his head. ''No joke. The Pirate War destroyed their fleet, aye. Still, a few survived, scattered here or there amongst the smaller islands that wouldn't join the Isles.''

"Yes," Murdock agreed, "but they prey in waters off the Southlands now."

"So they have," the captain explained. "But we lost a good two-thirds of our warships last year. That would be tempting to the southern pirates. Don't worry, the *Windsprite* can outrun most even in rough seas, like today. We'll be fine."

Pirates to take my mind off seasickness. How thoughtful.

"You'll be wanting me to use your travel names, I presume?"

"Yes," Murdock confirmed. "From this moment on, I am Papa Thomas. These are my two sons, Andrew and James," he said, pointing to me and Sergeant Jenkins. He put an arm on Wizard Lorich. "And this is Luke, an orphan taken into the family." He grinned wickedly at Major Kren. "And this is Klod, a man we've hired to play 'beastman.' "

"Klod?" the beastman repeated. "*Klod*? You didn't tell me my name would be Klod."

"I decided that you four should keep the same first letter as we normally call you. Arn becomes Andrew. Jenkins, James. Lorich, Luke. Easy to remember."

Lorich ventured a question. "Won't this be confusing when Ar—when Andrew writes the chronicle of our journey?"

Kren answered. "He can just use our regular names as he writes to avoid confusion, and tell his readers we actually used our aliases as we traveled and spoke to each other. And that way he won't keep recording *Klod* for history."

Captain Grayson shook his head. He wasn't used to us yet. "If that's all, good sirs, we'll get you to your quarters and shove off."

We were given the two passenger cabins, each tiny cubicle barely large enough for two short bunks, with drawers below each bunk and cabinets above. At one end was a washstand with bowl and, on the floor below it, the inevitable bucket. The captain apologized for the lack of space. "I can string a hammock in the mates' cabin, if you like. I'd give you my cabin, but that would just alert the crew that you weren't ordinary passengers."

"Quite all right," Murdock assured him. "Andrew and I will take this cabin, while James and Klod can have the other. Luke will sleep on the floor between their beds."

"Well, then, you're loaded, and we can shove off." The

captain left us and we settled in, emptying our saddlebags into the drawers as the ship started to rock gently. I took off my clothes and slid under the covers of my bunk. "We must be getting under way," Murdock commented, and then noted my position. "Arn, are you tired? Aren't you going above to watch the departure?"

"I just want to be prepared."

"Oh, come now. Certainly it can't be that bad. Even old Speros was able to rouse himself unto deck now and then."

The ship started to roll as we cleared the mouth of the harbor. I swallowed hard, and managed a last few words. "What did the captain say? Rough seas today?" Suddenly my head began to spin and my mouth was filled with drool. Murdock's eyebrows lifted in surprise. "Good Lord, I've never seen anyone turn that shade of green before."

He handed me the bucket just in time.

At some interminable point later, I lifted my head and stared into a face. Sergeant Jenkins. "Arn, are you still alive?"

I groaned. "There is movement, but no life. Go away."

"Sorry, Arn. We need you."

I rolled over and lay on my back, eyes closed and mouth open. "Why?"

He splashed a pitcher of water in my face. "Pirates."

I stumbled up the ladder after him.

Actually, getting up and moving about were an improvement in my condition. My stomach was settling, and the deadly disorientation and dizziness was almost gone. It didn't feel like we were in port. More like we were sailing a river. I could sail rivers. I felt almost . . . hungry. Always a good sign.

On deck, I could see the reason for the improvement in my condition. We weren't in port, as I had first thought, but still on the open sea beneath sunny skies. The ship was almost at an even keel, the wind from the east a mere breeze, warm and gentle, and the sea covered with wavelets that did not break at the top.

My companions were already on deck with the captain, who was using his spyglass while the others stared off in the same direction. Their faces were sober, thoughtful. I joined them. "I'm still alive."

Kren turned first, still wrapped in his cap and hood. "Andrew, you're up! We'll need you."

Murdock smiled, but his eyes went back to the horizon. "Well, you almost look human. And just in time, too."

Captain Grayson, gestured to the port side. "A ship, coming up from the port side and upwind."

"Pirates?"

Grayson checked his sails. "She's showing no flag, and that means pirates. Probably the same as tried to catch the *Steadfast* last week."

The ship came on, closing slowly. "Can we outrun them?"

The captain handed me the spyglass. "She's waiting for us, anticipating how we'll come up on her so she can intercept. This weather is a curse. It's not often like this, mind you, but it happens. Bad luck. The winds are too weak to offer us any chance of running by her, and if we turn back and try to close haul, I think she'd have the best of us too. So, it looks like we'll have a fight on our hands."

"I knew this would be an interesting trip," said Kren.

"We may be able to help a bit," offered Jenkins.

"Aye, I believe you will," Grayson nodded in agreement with an appreciative look at each of us until his glance fell upon Lorich.

"And your crew?" Murdock asked.

"We've a crew of twenty seamen, besides myself. The *Windsprite* served as a merchant raider during the war, and haunted the Alliance ships after they unloaded troops. Took one trader, and fought off a Virginian raider. The men have tasted battle, and they're true."

"How many will we face, Captain?" I asked.

Grayson frowned. "Pirates like to have the odds, so they sail with large crews. I'd say they'd have fifty or sixty."

Lorich stared at the ships forlornly. "Fifty or sixty. And we number less than thirty."

Kren sighed. "For once it'd be nice to have even odds."

Murdock responded to the captain's remark. "That estimate sounds about right, Captain. I was at the Battle of the Isles, you know."

"You were? So was I. The Pirate War was a long time ago, and I was just a boy, a midshipman. I can remember those ships burning on the sea. A terrible sight, seeing a ship burn.

But it was a great battle, and a great victory. We'll have to talk of it later. For now, gentlemen, I think we'd best prepare for action. May I expect your obedience if it comes to that?''

The others looked at me, and I nodded. ''We are under your orders, sir,'' Murdock responded formally. ''And among our number are several formidable warriors. There is hope yet.''

Combat. Mortal danger. Terror.

Again.

There was one small consolation. I wasn't in command.

Captain Grayson knew his business, of course. That's why he'd been chosen. He'd served in the Kenesee Royal Navy for twenty years, including five years as captain of a man-of-war before retiring to commercial ships to have more time with his family—though how any seaman has time for a family at all is beyond me. Now he barked out orders to the ship's mates, and it was as if a stick had been taken to a bees' nest. Sailors popped out of entryways while others disappeared into them.

We went below, the wizard talking as we jostled past each other in the tiny space of the cabin, getting our weapons. ''Well, Arn, we haven't had any excitement in awhile, so I suppose we were due. Still, the odds are a bit steep again, aren't they?''

I buckled on my sheath belt gloomily, making sure everything was in place, and touched the throwing knife at the small of my back. Perhaps it was like a good luck charm. I had survived every encounter, and never had to use it. At my belt the other knife and the sword were sheathed, ready to be drawn. Nothing else to do. ''In the old days,'' I grumbled to Murdock, ''I would have searched for an excuse to remain below here. Keep myself in reserve, so to speak.''

''What do you mean, the 'old days'?'' Murdock stopped a moment, suddenly serious. ''Maybe that isn't a bad idea. You're the key to this whole venture, you know. If we lose you, there's no one to rally the Texans against General Murphy.''

Well, if he really thought it was best. . . .

''Yet if the pirates take us, that will be the end of it right there. No, we need every man this time. Sorry, my boy.''

On the washbasin was a basket with bread, a small cheese,

and apples. My uneaten supper for the last two days. I popped a chunk of cheese into my mouth. Good. Very good. The bread was chewy but tasty. The apples wrinkled but sweet. I stuffed two apples in my pocket, stuck the loaf of bread under my arm, and held onto the cheese. My hunger was sharp, a surprise since appetite seemed to vanish for me whenever danger threatened. Perhaps I was maturing? Perhaps not. My two day fast must have subdued that habitual response. With each mouthful renewed strength flowed into my limbs. I kept chewing as I followed Murdock up the ladder.

On deck, Murdock and the others tried to determine the most advantageous positions during combat. The side rails were low, and offered little barrier to boarders. Near the bow the *Windsprite* mounted her only armament, a small catapult with a narrow arc of traverse to either side, a weapon hastily added for the war and not yet removed.

The crew was still busy with preparations. A number of sailors were dashing buckets of seawater against the sails, soaking them thoroughly, while other men splashed masts, rigging, and deck with more buckets. Captain Grayson watched their work carefully. "I won't have my ship burnt," he explained with a clenched jaw.

Off the port side, the pirates were much closer now. They had closed the distance quickly. "Uh, shouldn't the crew be getting their weapons now?" I whispered to Murdock.

He shook his head. "There's time. Trust the captain."

Grayson looked on the crew's handiwork with approval, and shouted out to the first mate. "Mr. Clancey, have personal weapons issued to the crew."

Murdock grinned sheepishly. "Well, maybe there isn't time after all."

Other crewmen sprinkled sand upon the deck, and then left full buckets ready at hand. One task completed, they went to the forward entryway and descended, emerging moments later, each with a heavy basket. They began to empty the baskets near the catapult, building two neat piles of hefty rocks. One crewman started placing rocks into thick burlap sacks, one rock per sack. Another set jugs of oil nearby and lit a torch. Saturate the rock-sack with oil, apply a torch, launch it, and one had the naval version of the fireball. A moment later, one of the fireballs was indeed flung at the pirate vessel, but the range was too great, for the flaming missile fell short.

I finished the bread and cheese, chomped down the last apple, and washed it down with loud swallows from a water-skin I'd brought up. My own kind of foresight.

The pirate ship had changed course slightly, and was bearing in more quickly than before. If we kept going on our present course, they would soon be upon us. Grayson looked up at the sails, studied the courses of the two ships, frowned, and gave further orders to the man at the wheel, who tacked away from the other ship. For a moment we had to watch for the spars that slowly came around until the wind took hold of the sails.

Grayson was not going to make it easy for them. However, the change of course had swung the bow away from the other ship, and our catapult would not be able to shoot at this angle.

"They'll grapple with us," said Murdock.

"Murdock the Mariner," intoned Jenkins. "Sees all, knows all."

The wizard frowned. "So many deeds. So little respect."

In spite of the captain's efforts, the pirates were much closer now. We could see individual weapons being waved in anticipation, and shouts drifted to us from across the water. Yes, there were a goodly number of them crowding their decks. My stomach began to churn in its traditional style, and I regretted eating the apples. And the bread. And the cheese.

Crewmen who had been filing below now began to emerge. Most bore cutlasses and shields, though a half dozen wearing green armbands carried bows and quivers in addition to their swords. First Mate Clancey approached, followed by two crewmen bearing extra shields and cutlasses. "Excuse me, gentlemen, but can I offer you any weapons for the coming festivities?"

Jenkins brightened. "Aye, sir. Shields." The round shields were about two feet in diameter, made out of wood and painted red. Rough-hewn, but they would do. We each took one and then waited awkwardly amidst the spars and rigging, trying to figure out a position of advantage. There seemed to be none. The captain spared us a glance. "They've a fast ship. I'll try to outmaneuver her but it doesn't look good. I think she's going to catch us. Our crew can't hold the whole deck, we'd be spread too thin. I'll station a section of men in the bow to defend the catapult, in case we get a shot. We'll give the pirates the midship, and put the rest of the men defending the stern. That's where I'd like you, if you please. It's going to be a tough fight. Good luck to you all.'' And then he was off, shouting orders to the mates and the men redeployed according to his instructions.

There was a snap, and from the bow of the pirate a round stone went arcing up between the ships, and then came down through one of our sails, ripping a long, decisive tear in the fabric. Either a lucky shot, or a very well-trained crew. What little hope we had of outmaneuvering the pirate vanished with that one shot.

The pirate vessel was very close now.

''Prepare to repel boarders!'' Grayson ordered. The pirate ship was coming on as fast as the wind would allow, the distance between us narrowing rapidly.

The bowmen on each ship opened fire, so that arrows passed each other in flight. One or two came our way. ''Stay down, Arn,'' Murdock instructed, watching the flight of the shafts even as he spoke. I was already crouched behind the rail next to my companions, peering carefully around my shield.

Grapples came flying across the space between the hulls, catching on rigging and rail. Some were hacked free by our crewmen, but others were not so easily removed. The pirate vessel's own momentum brought her quickly to our side.

The pirates were individuals now, a horde of eager figures in all colors of skin and dress clustered along the side of their vessel. Most had cutlass and knife, others mace and small shield, a few ax or morning star. All shouted defiance or howled in anticipation.

Standing on the rail so that he stood above his men, a dark-skinned figure with a mass of frizzled hair eyed our ship greedily. The pirate captain, perchance? He wore tan leggings and a deep blue coat resplendent with generous applications of gold lace on sleeves and chest. No honest merchant or naval captain would have been caught dead in such a gaudy display, but such fashion restraints did not seem to apply to the likes of our opponent. I had to admit, he did look quite splendid in the outfit, his gold lace and white teeth gleaming in the sun, a bold leader both handsome and imposing.

I opened my mouth to ask Murdock if Lorich couldn't do

something about putting a "squeeze" on our dashing opponent when the two vessels bumped together at last, and I had to reach out to keep my balance. And then there was no time.

A number of the pirate crew went down with arrows in them, one falling into the water, and there came the crunch of bone as the two hulls ground the man between them. But the rest came on with brash fierceness, confident that their numbers would prevail. The pirate's starboard bow had met our port side amidships. Since the pirate's deck rode a foot or two higher than ours, its crew had little difficulty swarming over the rails and onto our deck at that point. None of our sailors were left there, and the pirates hurried fore and aft to get at us.

We had already formed a line of battle across the stern with Grayson's crew, Jenkins against the rail on my left, and Kren on my right. Behind us, Murdock and Lorich waited. Murdock had his sword in hand and his shield up near the rail, Lorich stood similarly armed behind him. And that was how it had to be. There was no safe spot on the deck, and every man's sword, even Lorich's, was needed.

Jenkins and Kren—their eyes alight with anticipation, warriors about to go into battle—watched the enemy come. "Wait for us," Jenkins admonished me. "Don't you go leaping to the attack thinking you can do it all by yourself."

Leaping into the attack . . . ? There was no help for it; it was my duty, and I was needed as a man-at-arms, just as Jenkins and Kren were. Almost three score of pirates were on our deck now. This battle would be won by sheer hard fighting, and it would have to be won quickly, or not at all.

I looked behind me one last time to ensure Murdock was all right, and saw three pirates—greedy fools with more courage than sense—leap across the gap that separated the hulls at the stern of the boat. The wizard was already rushing to meet this threat to our rear, while Lorich limped after him. They would be killed, no doubt of that. I would have turned to go after them, but it was too late. The pirates were upon us. Jenkins and Kren gave a yell and waded in. Grunting in disgust, I went with them.

Hard, mean-faced men met us with scorn, and were cut down swiftly, unpleasant surprise upon their faces. For all their fierce demeanor and ruthless bullies' courage, they were not trained warriors. They expected to encounter sailors like themselves, not hardened fighters. The three of us had spent years practicing daily with sword and shield, and in contrast their feints and thrusts and blows were slow and obvious. We stepped over their bodies and engaged the pirates behind, who were puzzled to see their comrades go down so swiftly, but did not yet realize who they faced.

My opponent parried the first blow with his shield and tried to slip his cutlass under my guard. I met the thrust with my shield, feinted low to draw his down, and then stuck the point of my sword in his throat. He spouted blood like a fountain. Kren and Jenkins were dispatching their opponents just as quickly. From the left edge of my vision I saw a pirate leap upon the rigging and raise his mace above Jenkins's head. An arrow went into his chest and he spun around, showing the arrow point and a good three inches of shaft protruding from his back. Our archers were firing from no more than a dozen feet away, and at that range their missiles would skewer any human target. Unfortunately, the same could be said of the pirate arrows, one of which whizzed by no more than an inch from my nose.

We three stepped forward again, and another trio of pirates went down. We had cut down nine of them already, and the odds were improving. If all the boarders were as clumsy, we would clear the deck without difficulty. I actually began to feel less terrified.

Another mistake.

For that's when the pirate with the gold-braided jacket jumped in front of me. The pirate captain himself, worse luck. The man was no fool. He'd seen what was happening, and leaped forward with his mates to stop us. I quickly found that pirate leaders were handy with weapons. The captain had no shield, but held a cutlass in one hand and a long dagger in the other. Up close he was the same dashing fellow of brown skin and blazing eyes I'd seen before, but on his face the greedy look had been replaced by a cool grin of certainty. "Now you die," he stated, thinking he could intimidate me.

The pirate captain certainly knew his man.

He swung with his sword, and thrust with his dagger, and suddenly it was I on the defensive, parrying his blows. He was quick, very quick. The dagger flashed, the sword darted in and out, and the realization came that I faced a master of the art. It was like the practice sessions with my brother in the old days. I could hold him off for awhile, but eventually a thrust would slip through. Only now, I would die if I missed even a single parry. Any hope for succor from my companions was dashed, for Jenkins and Kren were likewise engaged with the mates of the pirate ship, who were also formidable opponents. The air was filled with the thunk of metal on wood, the rasp and clang of metal on metal, as we fought amidst the yelling pandemonium of the deck.

The captain parried my blows with his sword and jabbed with his dagger—up at my eyes and down at my groin—my shield moving to cover his thrusts. I had to do something, but what? Our eyes were locked upon each other even as we moved, and I gave ground, a few inches only, back-stepping carefully, anticipating the bodies and the blood of those we had killed. But anticipating was not enough. A thick red pool under one boot betrayed me, and I fell backward onto one of the bodies, my shield aside and my sword down.

A gleam came into the pirate's eye. It was all he could have hoped for. I wouldn't even have time to scream. He darted forward, drawing back his sword for the final cut, and instead impaled himself upon the ship's pike which suddenly jabbed out over me. Captain Grayson pushed forward, still driving the point into the chest of the pirate captain, whose eyes had widened in the puzzlement of death.

Stunned, I saw Kren and Jenkins still locked in combat almost above me, and without thinking thrust my sword into the heart of Kren's man. The pirate dropped like a stone. The beastman shook his head in regret. "Ahh, Arn. I was just about to finish him." Deprived of his fun, he chopped the edge of his shield into the head of Jenkins's pirate, and the man slumped.

They helped me rise and Jenkins assured himself I was all right. "Stay back a moment and get your wind, sir," he said before they advanced behind Captain Grayson, who had pinned the gold-braided corpse to the deck with the pike. I stood in a daze, shaking, trying to rouse myself for another effort. But none was needed.

Though the pirates still more than equaled us in numbers, their morale had been broken with the fall of their captain and his mates. They were scurrying back now, trying to regain the false security of their ship. Those who panicked and tried to flee were cut down from behind, but most had sense enough to make a fighting withdrawal. One of the pirates was shouting "*Cast off!*" but this was not so easily done.

Our men followed them up to the railing, and then over it, onto the pirate ship. Captain Grayson and Jenkins and Kren led the way and broke any effective resistance. "Surrender now," Grayson bellowed, "or we'll slaughter every one of you!"

"The Rights of Prisoners!" one of the pirates had the sense to counter, but Grayson shook his head.

"No! Surrender now, or die!"

By that time half the pirates had already thrown down their weapons, and the rest had no choice. Swords and shields clattered to the deck, and a score of healthy prisoners lay face down, threatened with instant death by a dozen watchful sailors should they move. Two other crewmen hurried to open the hatch of the forward hold.

It was then that I remembered the wizards.

Murdock and Lorich were both still on their feet, three dead pirates sprawled around them. Murdock leaned upon the rail tiredly, his sword red and the bloodied pirates lying nearby in mute testimony to his feat. He held his arm, the sleeve of which was again red. He did ruin more shirts that way. . . .

"Murdock. You're wounded again."

"No, I just reopened the wound from the dinosaur. I'll need a few stitches. Lord, I hate stitches."

I swept my hand at the carnage. "You did all this?"

He chuckled. "No, even I'm not that good. I held the three off for a few moments, but I only accounted for one. Captain Grayson got another when he saw we were in trouble, but then had to rush off to help you—and just in time, it seems. Wizard Lorich took care of the last one, and with his sword, no less. The man had only one arm, but Lorich had his limp, so I think it was an even fight."

Lorich was looking at the man he had slain, a grimace on his face.

"Your first kill, Lorich," I said to him. "How do you feel?"

His face was pained. "I'm not sure."

"You won't be, for a while. Later you'll feel quite the giant slayer. Later still, the bad dreams will start. Those will pass, too. He might have—"

"Arn," Murdock interrupted me gently. "He already knows. I told him."

"Oh. Well."

Lorich wiped a bloodied hand across his forehead. "This man wasn't the only one, sir."

"What? You killed others with swordplay?"

Murdock answered for him. "He used his talent."

"So." My voice was a whisper. "It works on humans."

"It works on humans," Murdock repeated.

"How many did he get?"

"He took out an archer who had you as a target. Another pirate slipped behind Jenkins and he stopped him, too. I think that was all."

"That was all, Master. Just the two. And this one."

"Splendid job, Lorich." I congratulated him. "But always go for the leaders."

"Yes, Prince Arn. But even when you're about to be killed by someone else?"

"Ummm—that's the exception."

"That was the problem. There was always someone in danger, and I didn't have time." He squeezed his eyes shut. "Master, it hurts."

So the pained look on his face wasn't emotional, but physical.

"Worse than at Yellow Fields?"

"Yes, Master. Much worse."

Murdock winced. "Sorry, my boy. That's the price of magic, and you've accomplished a feat never done before. You have to pay the price now. Great feats, great pain. But I have a powder that might help."

Kren and Jenkins made their way back to us.

Murdock won a frown of disapproval from Kren. "Murdock, are you wounded again?"

"No, not this time," the wizard denied, and explained what had happened. He shook his head. "You know, I've come full circle. In my youth as an apprentice I guarded my master the aged Speros at the Battle of the Isles, and he destroyed the enemy fleet. Now I guard my young apprentice Lorich, and he saves Arn and the ship. I am but a spear carrier among the great actors on stage, alas.''

Captain Grayson came back and was told how Murdock and Lorich—by dint of shield and sword, according to the version he heard—had kept our rear clear of the pirates.

''As I know from personal observation,'' he agreed, and gave them a bow.

Second Mate Dawes stepped up to his captain. ''Sir, we have the casualties.''

''Aye?''

''Five gone, including Clancey. And another six wounded and down. It was a close thing, Captain.''

''Aye, a close thing,'' Grayson repeated. ''And costly. We have prevailed when we had no right to win. Most of the crew fought with me last year, and had experience at this sort of thing. We owe it to that. And we owe it to our passengers.''

Congratulations are all very well, but I had other matters to attend to. The sea wasn't that rough yet, but the cause was too much bread and cheese. Too much deadly excitement. I leaned over the rail and emptied my stomach.

The second mate's voice registered his surprise. ''Even in calm seas, would you believe it! Worst case of seasickness I ever saw.''

ARKAN

1

Landfall

Grayson did not waste time.

The prisoners were crammed into the forward hold, the hatch battened down and guarded by two crewmen. Our wounded had earned more luxurious accommodations than their hammocks in crew quarters. The captain and mates' cabins each took two, while Jenkins, Kren, and Lorich lost their cabin to the last two wounded. The captain and Second Mate Dawes would sleep in crew quarters. My party would stagger its sleep schedule, our three companions taking the bunks when Murdock and I were not using them.

Wizard Murdock joined Second Mate Dawes below in order to treat the men for their wounds, and for a time that activity had priority as we all helped to carry the wounded down the ladder. Captain Grayson did not rest. "Vinny! Your section help Mr. Dawes, and make sure he has everything he needs. Get hot water boiled; get bandage cloth from stores, alcohol and spirits from the dispensary. Here's the keys, and mind you don't have a nip. Stein! Your section get the deck squared away. I'm going aboard the pirate."

That ship still drifted before the wind with us, hulls rubbing together at times, but the mild weather—which had contributed to our encounter with the pirates—now kept the ships from doing great damage to each other while riding the waves together.

Grayson went to inspect the pirate vessel, and I went with him, my party (minus Murdock) coming along. The wind and waves had picked up a bit, but were amazingly calm for the open gulf. Danger over and stomach empty, only a hint of queasiness remained, and I was actually able to function in a relatively normal manner.

The surviving pirates taken prisoner on the ship's deck had already been put away safely in a hold aboard the *Windsprite*. The pirate ship held no other living soul. When a pirate crew attacks, *everyone* in the crew attacks. The ship was built for speed, and not cargo. The small cargo holds held few things besides the extra food and water a large fighting crew would need. The ship was as neat and clean as the *Windsprite*, squared away above and below; the pirate captain had kept a tight ship. In his cabin we found charts, ship's log and captain's journal (the man could read, to our surprise), and the strongbox.

Captain Grayson was quite interested in the books and charts. "Ahh, now these'll be handy for tracking where these swine have come from. For where there's one pirate, there's more, and maybe one day we can go in again and burn them out for good."

Those few items were our only find. After an hour of searching, the captain was convinced there was nothing else worth saving. There were numerous small personal items of the crew in their quarters, but as Grayson commented, "They'll be having little use for them, shortly. As to this ship, I'd take her into port as a prize, but that won't do under the circumstances. With our casualties, even a scratch crew would reduce the *Windsprite*'s complement too far. No, we could sail her, right enough. But it would look strange when we put into port. We don't want word of this spreading too soon. I'll drop you off in Batesville and head straight back to Kingsport, where we'll announce the attack. We'll imply it happened on the return, and that will separate the incident from you."

"What will you do with the pirate ship?" Kren asked.

"She's a beauty, but we'll have to sink her."

On deck, we saw that the crew had put the dead pirates aboard the empty ship, the bodies piled like cordwood. A tall sailor—Stein—approached as we boarded the *Windsprite*. "Everything's squared away, captain. Mr. Dawes and the passenger, Mr. Thomas, are still working on the wounded. Extra weapons are collected and locked away. We put our dead over there, and covered them with a tarp. The pirate bodies have been put on the pirate ship. I didn't want to throw them overboard till you gave the order. The decks have been swabbed down. Shall I assemble a prize crew to take the pirate into port?''

"No. We're not taking it into port. There are foul things aboard that ship, and they can only be cleansed in the sea.''

"Aye, sir. It's sad. Men going wrong, that way. What makes them so? Is it their natural bent, or has someone twisted them to it?''

"Even the ancients couldn't answer that question. You're a good sailor and a good seaman, Stein, and have served loyally and bravely for—what—five years? I'm promoting Mr. Dawes to first mate, and I need a second. Would you like to be an officer?''

The man's face betrayed mixed emotions. "Sir? Aye, sir. Second Mate Stein? I'd like that. But I'm sorry it comes about this way. I liked Mr. Clancey.''

"So did we all, Mr. Stein. Get me the sledgehammer and wedge from storage. Then see to the crew, and make sure the prisoners are under control.'' The new mate hurried away while Captain Grayson stared at the pirate vessel for a long minute, we passengers just standing and waiting. Mr. Stein came up the entryway with the hammer and wedge. The captain took them and sized up each member of the party. "I think finishing the pirate should be done by me and one other. You, Mr. Klod.''

Kren winced at the name. "Me?''

"You look like you can swing a sledge fair and true. Come with me. Mr. Stein, make ready to cast off the pirate.''

They crossed to the other ship, disappeared down a hatchway. There came a muffled thud that vibrated through the pirate. And another. And a whole series of rhythmic thuds, repeated twice more. Silence returned. The captain and Kren reappeared with the sledgehammer and crossed back aboard the Windsprite.

"Mr. Stein, prepare to cast off.''

"Aye, sir.''

"Cast off.''

The last two grappling lines were released, and sailors with ship pikes pushed off. The pirate gradually slid by us until it was clear and the seas slowly opened between the two ships. Five feet. Ten. Twenty.

"And now,'' stated Captain Grayson quite evenly, "let us see to our prisoners.''

Murdock and Dawes had finished their work, and joined us on deck. My party and I settled along a railing out of the way. For once, I had nothing to do but sit and watch. There was nothing we could do to alter the course of matters, of course, nor were we inclined to do so. Even Lorich kept silent and still. Almost being killed will do that.

A drumhead court was held at sea, Captain Grayson, Mr. Dawes, and Mr. Stein presiding. Their hands tied behind them, the pirates were brought up one by one and given their moment. The first was in his thirties, a good-looking man tanned a magnificent bronze, but dull-eyed and slow. He was questioned, and answered what he knew in a desperate attempt to win our favor.

In the end, he was asked if he had anything to say for himself before the court rendered judgment. He was stupid enough to ask for mercy, though he had given none in his years. A noose was put around his neck and he was hauled up the yardarm.

He was still kicking and squirming when the second pirate was brought up. And so it went. The *Windsprite*'s crewmen actually became tired from hauling the victims aloft, but didn't complain. Except in the rare case when there might be ransom, pirates took no prisoners. In a few hours it was done. The prisoners were gone, the pirate ship sunk, our voyage resumed.

A man of many admirable qualities, the captain.

The mood aboard ship was sober that day, with no laughter and little talk; but by the next morning the thrill of being alive had taken over, washing away the stain of the previous day from our thoughts as the sea water had scoured away the pirate blood from the deck. A crewman rang out "land ho," in the late morning, and by midafternoon we were close to land.

To the left and right the land was rocks and grass and the green of pines, a rugged but not unattractive coastline. And that's all there was. There might have been individual cabins scattered here or there, but from miles out they were invisible, though almost directly in front of us there was a haze above the coast, as if from the smoke of a thousand fireplaces. Yet, we saw nothing.

Wizard Lorich voiced our thoughts. "But Captain Grayson. There's nothing there."

Murdock exchanged a knowing smile with the captain, who

tucked his hands into his pocket and rocked gently back and forth with the motion of the ship. The weather had held calm, and I was still up and about. Miracles do happen.

"Nothing there?" the captain repeated. "Why, certainly there is. Can't you see it?"

"No sir. I cannot."

"Well, perhaps things will become clearer ahead."

As we neared land, it became evident that there was a gap in the coastline, an opening or inlet a good quarter mile wide. We sailed through the gap and into a long, calm bay that took an immediate dogleg to the south until it abruptly narrowed to meet the mouth of the White River. And there, at the end of the leg and nestled next to both bay and river, was a walled town, the faint haze high above it marking where it was laid at the base of the hills, protected from blasts of weather from the sea and from the land.

"You see," grinned Grayson. "Batesville. The town was here all the time."

I stood next to him on deck and nodded mutely, thankful that we had at last reached landfall. I had watched wind and wave anxiously throughout the two days I'd been up, expecting that the wind would pick up and the waves grow high, as was the norm in the winter waters of the Gulf. But the weather had fooled even the captain, the wind remaining but a steady breeze, the seas maintaining their calm. And now, the placid waters of the bay made the world seem a place of peace and quiet, with neither storm nor worry.

Batesville, one of the larger towns of Arkan, boasted eight or nine thousand inhabitants within its high walls, the normal trades and crafts supplemented by shipbuilding and fishing, which were served by extensive wharves stretching along the waterfront outside the walls. Except for the size of the bay and the banners and flags that flew over the town, it reminded me of Kingsport. The construction of the walls was standard fortification style, the gates square at top, the ships at the wharves close in design to our own. Arkan and Kenesee shared much, and it had been all the more surprising and painful when King Herrick had thrown in his lot with the Alliance against Kenesee. The fact that he'd been coerced and intimidated did not excuse his decision. A leader who does not stand up for right amidst adversity is not a leader.

Captain Grayson docked the *Windsprite* without incident,

yelling out and shaking his fist only once as a returning fishing boat cut across our bows and forced us to give way.

The ship secured, Grayson shook hands with us, speaking softly and watching that none overheard. "Gentlemen, my thanks to each of you, and my best wishes for your safety and success. We'll be sailing as soon as you're disembarked. If we stay, someone will talk about the pirates, and you don't want that kind of attention."

There were few signs of our life and death struggle in the Gulf. A few gouges and cuts in the wood of the ship, and a decidedly smaller crew, were the only clues that anything was amiss. The wounded were belowdeck, and would have to wait until their return to Kenesee for treatment. Some would not make it. Yet, the risk of taking them ashore was too great. More casualties of war.

We had come to Arkan, each of us using his new traveling name and facing the first test. Murdock gestured at the town. "Captain Grayson is right to be cautious. Remember, we're in Arkan now. A different country with a different ruler, even if a benevolent one. To be discovered here should not mean we lose our lives. In all likelihood, we'd be detained, and after a month or two sent back to Kenesee. It would be merely a diplomatic incident in the history of the nations, possibly an embarrassment to King Robert. But it would doom our mission to failure, and that is reason enough to go carefully."

Grayson listened without comment, for he was one of the few men who knew the true plan and purpose of our journey. "I'll take word back to King Robert of your safe arrival. If there are any messages from him, I will try to get them to you, one way or another." He had been watching the pier. "On your guard," he warned us, and waved to an unpretentious figure with an embossed metal plate hanging from a chain about his neck who strode towards the ship. "That's Hardy, a port inspector," said Grayson. "He's honest and does his job well. We've gotten to know each other over the years. I'll try to get you past him without too much problem. Once he issues your entry papers, you'll be all right. Hello, Inspector Hardy. How are you?"

"Very well, Captain Grayson," the port inspector called out in a friendly manner, stopping at the gangplank and noting our shipping trunks, which had been brought up onto the deck. "And welcome to you, too. What cargo?"

"Kenesee tobacco and brandy. And passengers."

"Yes, I see," Hardy said with interest, eyeing us with the calculating appraisal of officialdom.

"As soon as they're offloaded, I'm sailing to Trentwood, then back to Kingsport."

Hardy raised an eyebrow. "Not going to spend a night in port?"

Looking uncomfortable, Grayson's voice fell to conspiratorial level. "Well, my wife and I had a bit of an argument before I left, and—"

Hardy bestowed him a knowing look. "Ahh. The wife is left stewing and alone. Not a good problem for a sailor. Aye, you'd best be getting back, captain. Well, let's get your cargo and passengers off."

"Come with me," Grayson said to us, and led the way across the deck and down the gangplank to the dock. By the laws of the sea—technically, at least—we were safe as long as we stayed aboard the *Windsprite*. Once off the ship, we would be subject to Arkan law and Arkan justice. I tried not to show reluctance, but almost stumbled with my last step unto the wooden pier. Behind us, the crew began to offload trunks and cargo.

Grayson shook Hardy's hand with a warm smile. "Let me introduce my passengers to you. They were quite a merry bunch on our trip over, and won my favor."

"Well now, the approval of Captain Grayson is something to be prized," Hardy stated sincerely, taking another appraisal at close range. "How did you good men manage to impress the captain?"

With a flourish, Murdock bowed from the waist, oozing charm and goodwill. "Allow us to introduce ourselves. I am Alex Thomas, of Thomas's Traveling Theater. These are my two sons," he continued, stepping between Jenkins and me and putting his arms around our shoulders. "The scrawny little one is James—"

"The scrawny little one?" Jenkins bristled, his face turning a nice reddish hue.

"—And the dullard with the beard is Andrew."

Me, the dullard? I opened my mouth to speak.

Murdock chattered on, ignoring us. "Now, you may see differences between us, and wonder. Why is the father darker than the sons? My wife was fair skinned and that could account for it. But no, that is not the reason. The other differences are too great. I am intelligent. I am personable. I am tall and handsome. While they—the truth is, my friend, that when I was away on business one week, a tinker came by and knocked upon our door. My wife took pity on him because he was so slight and small. And thus my first born, James.''

Port Inspector Hardy was grinning broadly.

''And here, my dullard second son, Andrew. Look at him.'' Murdock tweaked my nose as he spoke. ''How could there be such a difference between us? Mr. Hardy, that tinker came by years later, and knocked as he had before. My wife took pity upon him again because he lacked wits. A woman of great heart, my wife. When someone knocked, she let him enter.''

Murdock left us and went over to Lorich. ''And here is a young waif my wife and I took on as a servant. We call him Luke. No, don't be put off by his infirmities, for he is one of the most gifted actors of our century, blessed with a form and manner which allows him to play characters twisted in both body and mind.''

Lorich blinked while he thought about that one.

''Enough,'' said Mr. Hardy, laughing. ''I can see you're in the theater, no doubt. But what about this last one in your troupe? Who's he? Can't see much of him with that cap and hood covering his head.''

''Ahh, him.'' Murdock leaned close to Hardy. ''This is Klod. He'll be our beastman during the tour.''

''A beastman?'' Hardy asked in astonishment, as if hoping Kren really were from the Beastwood.

Murdock gestured, and Kren reluctantly undid the flap of his cap. ''Take a look. I met him in Kingsport, and hired him on the spot. Hairiest man I'd ever seen. He'll make a fine beastman, don't you think?''

Hardy nodded. ''He's a hairy brute, I grant you. No one'll be fooled, but he'll provide some fun.''

Kren stopped short. ''Fooled?''

The port inspector burst out laughing again. ''Captain Grayson, I can see why you like them. Just one or two more questions, then. Where are you from?''

Murdock gestured back out to sea. ''We come from Kenesee, good sir. Indeed, most of us were born there. Our tours have been in the north of the kingdom—Louisville, Lexington, Knox, and all the smaller towns of that region. We even visited Loren once."

"I see," the inspector stated thoughtfully, as if he were trying to remember what a map might show of the geography. "And why have you come to Arkan?"

The smile faded from Murdock's face. "Ahh. Now that is a sad story. The war was hard on Kenesee. Hard. The north suffered mightily, and Lexington was burnt to the ground. The people have not much to offer a wandering troupe of performers. We thought Arkan might provide new opportunities for fame and wealth. And if not, at least we will have the appreciation of new audiences unburdened with memories of destruction."

The wizard's persuasiveness was a marvel. Even I almost believed him. The port inspector was completely taken with Murdock—or, perhaps more precisely, taken in.

Hardy sighed in commiseration. "It is sad. All right, gentlemen. But are these trunks all you have for baggage?"

"Our wagons were shipped before us to Mr. Immerson's livery here in Batesville. He should have teams for us."

"Two box wagons? I remember Immerson got them, right enough. Inspected them myself. Good wagons. Nothing suspicious, except for the secret compartment I found. Under a drawer. It was empty."

Inspector Hardy watched how Murdock would react. The wizard chuckled in admiration. "So, you found it. Well, I didn't think it would pass the eye of a trained professional. If all goes well, it'll hold a good purse of coins before the summer. Do you think it will deter a common thief, or do we have cause for worry?"

Murdock's reaction had apparently met the inspector's approval, for Hardy nodded and was unable to hide a flush of satisfaction at the implied compliment to his skills. "Oh, it'll do, unless some rascals take your wagon apart. I might have missed it myself, easily enough. Well, bring your goods to the inspection office so we can take a look and write up your entry paper."

We shook hands with Captain Grayson one last time, waved good-bye to the crew, and then went with Hardy, a dock hand following with our trunks piled on his cart. The inspection went quickly, Hardy examining each trunk and noting the brightly-colored garments and props we had included. No opiates nor tariff items to be found. Paperwork not his forte, the inspector slowly and painstakingly filled out an entry paper listing each of our names, affixed the official stamp, and handed the sheet over.

"There you are, good men. Arkan's laws are not far different from those in Kenesee, though we're harsh on thieves, if you get my meaning? Good. As long as you don't get into trouble, you should have no difficulty traveling through the kingdom. Oh, I do have to mention, the roads are patrolled, but we've had word of a nasty band of cutthroats further south, so be careful if you go in that direction. I'm sure they'll be taken shortly, for we have someone on their trail who doesn't fail. That's about it. You're staying in town tonight, certainly? Then I recommend the East Gate Inn. Good food, clean sheets, and no troublemakers. Right through the gates and straight up Clarke Street a block. Do let me know if you're going to give a performance before you leave town. I'll bring the family."

Batesville was similar to most large towns in Kenesee. New World English was the language here, as it was at home, the signs showing the same familiar words for bakery and butchery and bath, though the style of printing seemed to tend to greater flourishes. We were to find small differences in language. We referred to "evening meal," while the Arkans spoke of "dinner." We had a "pipeful," while they had a "smoke." Nothing we couldn't readily get used to, since you heard both versions in either country. It was merely a matter of frequency.

Architecture bore a close resemblance to the Kenesee mix of crete and timber, though perhaps only half as much wood was used, and some of that pine rather than oak or maple or other good wood. The great trees of the north weren't quite so plentiful here. Otherwise, shops and homes looked the same inside and out.

Dress and manner were likewise close to Kenesee. We might have thought ourselves strolling down a street in Kingsport except for the slight accent that marked the speech of the Arkans. We would have to practice that accent and lose our own.

Port Inspector Hardy had steered us rightly. The East Gate Inn was one of several taverns and inns along the street, though it enjoyed being the oldest and largest. We procured rooms and settled in, while Murdock and Jenkins sought out Immerson's livery to have him prepare for the morrow.

When they returned with reports that all was well, we went down to evening meal, which was a pleasant change for my companions from the tasteless fare they had suffered in the wardroom of the *Windsprite*. Culinary appreciation was not one of Captain Grayson's concerns aboard ship. The East Gate Inn was known for its table, and was popular with sailors and townspeople both. The large common room enjoyed a respectable crowd, one or two tables even seating families of parents and children. There was a good-natured boisterousness evident among the sailors, but the usual curses and topics one might hear in their conversation were tempered as they watched their language and behavior.

We found a vacant table in a corner, and took our seats. Murdock flirted with the serving girl, commenting about the well-behaved diners. She laughed. "They'd better be. See Mr. Mohammed?" She pointed at a powerfully built giant of a man, with dark mottled skin and a thick black beard that extended over his apron top. "That's the innkeeper. Break his rules and see what happens."

Dinner was as good as we'd been led to expect. Each of us enjoyed a large sea trout broiled and topped with sauce. With it came a platter of baked potatoes and an urn of melted butter, escorted by a long loaf of dark bread. We washed it all down with beer, and found that even dessert was included in the meal, a thick tart made with apples and a sugary crust.

As we finished, the innkeeper sauntered by our table, peering at the empty plates with a critical eye. He stopped, looming over us like a mountain, and gave us each a telling glance before directing his question to me. Perhaps it was because I was wolfing down a second large piece of tart, still hungry after my fast aboard the *Windsprite*.

"How's the food?"

I gulped the last of the crust. "An excellent meal in all respects, and the apple tart was superb. Just the right amount of cinnamon, the apples cooked but still firm. My compliments to the chef."

''And to you for keeping such a fine inn,'' expanded Murdock. ''Our rooms are quite nice, and the service all we could hope for.''

With Mohammed standing there, we would have said the same if the meal had tasted of sawdust and the rooms been full of fleas.

Mohammed nodded. ''Good, good. I'm pleased. Enjoy your stay.''

Kren watched him as he went away. ''I'm certainly glad he was pleased.''

We sat nursing another beer, discussing the weather and similar topics safe for other ears until Lorich yawned. Murdock noted the fatigue on the young wizard's face, the dark circles under his eyes. ''Perhaps you should turn in. You can do my boots tomorrow morning.''

''Yes, master. Thank you.''

As the boy departed, Jenkins leaned toward us, speaking softly to Murdock. ''He looks terrible. Is he all right?''

The wizard shrugged, and responded just as softly. ''He'll be all right in a day or two. The greater the magic, the greater the price.''

Jenkins watched as the young wizard clumsily mounted the steps to our rooms. ''I didn't believe anyone could do what he did.''

''No one else *could* do what he did,'' Murdock agreed, pensively. ''None has ever had such power.''

''He saved me in Kenesee. He saved us at sea,'' said Kren. ''And he's barely eighteen. What will he do when he's grown to manhood?''

The families and half the diners left after eating, and the noise died down from a loud rumble to a lower chatter. Murdock noted the change. ''Well, perhaps it's time for us to be abed, too. Go ahead. Arn and I will join you two in a moment.'' Jenkins hesitated. ''Don't worry, James. I'll keep alert.'' Kren finished his mug, adjusted his cap and hood, and departed, followed by a reluctant Jenkins.

Murdock scanned the room diligently while talking. ''You're thinking about Lorich.''

''No,'' I corrected him. ''I know he'll recover.''

The wizard gave me an impatient frown. ''That's not how you're thinking about him.''

Aha. I was caught. ''Well, we have quite a potent weapon in the boy.''

''Yes, we do,'' Murdock admitted. He leaned close in his chair, and we both watched the room. I tried not to be distracted by the tavern maids.

''What concerns me,'' Murdock continued, ''is the extent of his power.''

I nodded in agreement, finished my beer, and looked to see if Jenkins had left any in his mug.

''Don't ever make him mad.''

He looked at me seriously. ''Yes, that's the crux of it, you know. There is something new under the sun. I've never heard of a magician who could manipulate and control living tissue. It just doesn't happen. I've tried, and my mental grip just slides off. Yet he's able to reach out and crush key organs. Constrict the heart—or the brain—and the victim is dead. There is no external evidence, no way of telling how the victim died, nor who did the deed.''

''A powerful weapon,'' I concurred, thinking of quick and easy ways to end our quest without the danger of a military campaign. ''He could walk through a castle, and the guards would drop before they knew what happened. He could stand in a crowded throne room and execute half the court. He could—''

''I don't think so,'' Murdock countered. ''I've talked to him. The dinosaur was not easy to target, and it wasn't easy to kill. It took him several seconds to—uh, get a grasp, shall we say—and a great expenditure of force to actually compress the organ. He almost blacked out doing it. And you see the price he pays for the two he finished aboard ship. He was exhausted afterward. The power is limited.''

Oh, well. So much for sending Lorich in singlehanded to take care of Murphy and his minions. ''No use for me to worry, then. But why do you worry?''

He stroked the lip of his mug with one finger, preoccupied with his thoughts, and unaware of its glazed smoothness beneath his skin. ''Power twists the soul. For the first time in his life, Lorich has power.''

''Bosh,'' I answered. ''Lorich is not an evil sort. In fact, he's an innocent. Not a mean bone in his body. There's no reason to fear him.''

"Oh, I don't fear *him*," Murdock answered quietly. "I fear *for* him."

We slept in the next morning and had a breakfast of oatmeal and honey before we headed for Immerson's livery well after sunrise. We brought our saddlebags and trunks, which were piled neatly behind the driver of a two-wheel goods cart. The streets of the town all seemed to lead uphill, but at last Murdock signaled our arrival. Kren and Lorich waited with the cart driver while Jenkins and I went with the wizard.

It was rather a large establishment, a house and barn combined in one structure taking up a wide front on the crete-cobbled street it occupied near the West Gate. Above the barn door were painted two lines of white letters, JEBEDIAH IMMERSON & SON, WAGON MAKERS & LIVERY, while a sign above the smaller door swung gently in the breeze, the picture of a team and wagon etched black into the wood.

The barn door was open, and the clang of metal on metal could be heard from within. The hammering came from the efforts of a sullen young metal worker who wore a dirty leather apron and labored steadily at a red hot strip of metal, pounding and turning it on an anvil. He worked in a space that was half workshop and half barn, with a workbench, forge, tools, metal strips, water barrel, and stacks of wood along one wall, while along the other wall were empty horse stalls and wagons under repair.

To Murdock's inquiry for Mr. Immerson, the metal worker silently pointed to the rear of the barn, where another door opened into the street beyond. We headed that way, and were met by a slender man of middle age just coming in who broke into a smile when he saw us. "Ah, Mr. Thomas! And these must be the other members of your theater. Welcome, good sirs. I'm Jebediah Immerson, and that is my nephew, Mark. Please, come with me. The wagons are out back." He led us toward the rear door, and spoke confidentially as we left the sullen young man. "My nephew's a bit curt. He doesn't do well with people, but he's an excellent waggoneer."

Murdock nodded. "Mark was helpful, never fear. And is your son about?"

Immerson's smile faded a bit. "He died of the fever at age five. I'd already had the sign painted, and didn't have the heart to change it. Well, here we are. My nephew and I inspected your wagons after they arrived, and found them in good order, no damage taken during shipment. I've kept them in my barn since then, as instructed. The teams I bought two weeks ago when the trader said he had some good ones for me. I'd told him to watch out for a good buy. We do business together often. He brought the teams this morning, and I was just about to harness them."

Almost filling the street were the wagons, beyond which stood two matched teams of draft horses, one of blacks and one of grays, waiting at stone hitching posts on either side of a wooden watering trough. The wagons were not new, but had been reworked in Kenesee to our purposes. The exteriors had been painted a bright red while the roofs were covered with green shingles. A wide border of yellow swirls and waves decorated each side, framing the ornate letters that announced our trade.

THOMAS'S TRAVELING THEATER
Drama! Comedy! Magic!
Feats of Skill and Wonder!
Entertainment for Young and Old!

Jenkins looked at it, looked again, and then grunted. "A bit gaudy, isn't it?"

"Now, James," Murdock corrected, "perhaps that's why we've never done very well as a troupe so far. We were too restrained. That's why I ordered the wagons to be rebuilt in Kenesee. This time we'll do it right. Color. Action. Appeal. That shall bring us success in Arkan."

Immerson waited while we inspected the wagons. "Stanley Arthur did a good job, didn't he? Surely, take your time and look at the undercarriage all you like. You'll find no flaws there. Now, if you'll come this way. Two steps for easy mounting. Watch your footing. A well-fitted door with window. Stanley used good aged pine on the box to keep the weight down, tarred and shingled the roof and sealed all the cracks in the walls. Each has two bunks, a built-in washstand, and stove, all the rest of the space going for storage. These wagons are some of the neatest work I've seen in a while.

Stanley has a genius for this sort of thing. He also completed the, uh, special work you wanted."

"The secret compartments?" Murdock clarified. "Show us."

There was one under the floorboard, and another in a false-bottomed drawer of one wagon, and another in the wall of the other wagon. Not large spaces, but enough to put a sack of coins, papers, or other items better kept hidden. It had all been done as we'd instructed by letter to Mr. Arthur in Jackson Harbor.

It is nice to have competent people on one's side.

We stepped out of the wagons and Jenkins joined us. "I've inspected the horses. They look well enough. Healthy, well-treated and fed, though we'll have to see how they take to the traces."

"Oh, no worry there," Immerson reassured us. "The grays have pulled together for two years, the blacks for three—or so the horse trader told me."

We led the teams around, and they backed into the traces with easy familiarity, ears cocked forward and then turning independently of each other as they listened to our voices. Alert but calm. Good animals.

Jenkins patted the flank of a gray. "These are good, Papa Thomas. You can pay him."

Good animals. Good wagons. But not the way to outrun pursuers. Well, it was too late to change plans. A theater troupe we would be.

2

An Unexpected Audience

We concluded financial matters with the wagonmaker, transferred our clothes and supplies into the wagons, and left the travel trunks with Mr. Immerson to dispose of as he would. As we'd anticipated, there was just no room for us to take them. Mr. Immerson shook our hands before we left.

"I wish you good fortune on your tour. You have good wagons and good teams. May they help bring you great success."

Murdock glanced back at Immerson and gave him a wave as we started off.

"Does he suspect anything?" I asked.

Murdock drew the reins between his fingers until he was comfortable with the feel. "If so, he didn't let on. Let us take that as proof of our acting, and hope other performances will be as easy."

Murdock drove the front wagon and I sat beside him in regal idleness. Jenkins drove the other, Kren and Lorich squeezed onto the bench beside him. We passed the market and stopped to pick up food before continuing on to the western gate. The gatekeeper checked our entry paper, reading it as laboriously as Inspector Hardy had written it. He took a glance inside the wagon boxes to make sure we weren't making off with the town maidens, and then passed us on. Outside the gate there was a dense cluster of shops and stables and houses, soon giving way to tilled fields and farm houses.

The well-greased wagons rolled along smoothly, or as smoothly as any wagon can ever roll, springs or not. The teams, well-trained and strong, pulled without a balk, enjoying being in harness again after the monotony of the horse trader's stable. All in all, it was an auspicious start. Even the weather started off clear, though within an hour of our departure clouds formed into a gray blanket overhead, lending a bleak and chill attitude to the hillsides that we passed. When far from village and farm we pulled into a field edged by a small stream.

I was surprised. "Setting up camp already?"

"Yes. We have to get organized. We can pass by the villages without raising comment. They're too small to make it worthwhile for us. But we'd better be ready to perform when we get to the next town. Unless you feel we're ready right now, my dear son Andrew?"

"Uhh, no." We unhitched the teams and tethered the horses, started a fire, had lunch, and sorted through the clothes before storing them away in the storage drawers of the wagon. Jenkins grimaced at a costume of red and silver, and tried on a tightly cut, bright green outfit with gold lace at neck and wrist, topped off with a jaunty hat of green. It fit perfectly.

He looked at himself, appalled. "I'm supposed to wear this?"

"A very versatile costume," Murdock answered cheerily. "And you said the same thing when you tried it on at the castle. You can wear it during your display of swordplay with your brother, and during some of the dramas. And of course, during the knife throwing."

"Knife throwing? What knife throwing?"

"I thought of it at the last moment. It should be a wonderful act, an exciting part of the performance."

I pulled out a felt-lined box, opened it and showed Jenkins the half-dozen matched knives inside. I hefted one. "Quite nice. They're a good bit heavier than mine, but a little practice will take care of that."

Kren picked up a knife and gave it an admiring glance. "Nice and sharp."

"Uhh—why do you need me for the act?" Jenkins ventured.

"Someone has to be the target."

"Target?" He looked around, uncertainly. "That stump, brother Andrew. Try it."

I took careful aim with the knife and let fly. It went sailing past the stump and sank into a tree trunk just beyond. Jenkins turned pale. Even a brave man has his limits.

"Well," said Murdock, "then again, maybe knife-throwing isn't such a good idea. Don't worry. I'll think of something else."

I put the knives away. Maybe we could get a good price for them.

Under gray and cold skies we spent the rest of the afternoon working out final touches on the various acts of the performance that we'd planned, trying on costumes, organizing the props, and finding places on the wagons so that everything was carefully stored but still readily accessible during a performance. Murdock's experience was invaluable, and by late afternoon all was in place.

We gathered around the fire, enjoying its warmth. The wizard seemed quite satisfied. "Done at last. It's been a good day's work. We are safely and legally within Arkan. We have good wagons and healthy teams. Our costumes and props are all accounted for, and with a few days of practice we'll be ready to give our first performance. Yes, things have progressed quite nicely. All that's left is for us to gather enough firewood for the night. Andrew and I will work this side of the camp, Klod and James the other side. Luke will begin our evening meal—that is, our dinner."

Murdock was having fun with our new names, using them as often as he could. There was a purpose behind it, of course, though none of us pronounced the names with the same pleasure he seemed to derive from their use.

We each collected an armful of suitable fuel from the deadwood littering the ground beneath the trees, stacked it in the campsite, and went out for a second load. While searching I could hear Jenkins bragging to Kren about a trip with Lorich to the Street of Pleasure.

I started to laugh.

Murdock eyed me. "Are you laughing at my jokes before I tell them, or is something else amusing?"

"Yes. I just overheard Jenkins talking."

"Oh? I didn't hear anything."

"He's right over there with Kren. They're talking about—well, you can guess. I'm surprised you haven't been listening."

Murdock looked at the men, then stared at the ground thoughtfully. "Arn, our companions are a good thirty yards away and talking quietly. Besides that, they're downwind of us. I haven't heard a word." He scratched his chin through his new beard. "Let's try something. You stand here and I'll go over there by that tree. You listen and tell me what I say."

He strode over to the tree and stood with his back to me.

"Willing women," he said clearly.

"Warm beds and dry boots," he added, softly now.

"Good food and cool beer," he concluded, quite faintly. I could barely hear him.

He walked back. "Well? What did I say? Tell me exactly."

I told him the exact words. "You must have been whispering at the end," I added. "I could barely make out what you said."

The sorcerer put his hands on his hips and eyed me critically. "By my mother's bones, who would have thought it!"

"Thought what?" I asked with concern.

"I really must tell O'Dowd. On second thought, perhaps not. No, this should be our little secret."

I started to worry. "Murdock, what are you talking about?"

He laughed. "You have a talent. A magical power!"

I took his arm. "Come along. These past few days have been too much for you. Did you take any knocks to the head from the pirates?"

"No, no, it's true. I should have seen it before."

"In that case, Papa Thomas, have you been abusing yourself?" I asked cynically.

"What? Hardly at all. Why."

"Because you're going insane."

"Listen to me. The first time I spoke softly. The second time, my whisper was barely audible to me. The third time I moved my lips, but couldn't hear the words myself. Do you understand? All I did was mouth the words. That's all."

That stopped me. I always had wondered why people were so indiscreet as to hold conversations where others could eavesdrop. Perhaps the reason was because no one could have heard—unless they had a talent.

"You mean I can hear people think?"

"In a manner of speaking. Sometimes."

"Then why can't I hear what everyone around me is thinking now? I don't hear anything."

He grinned. "It's not easy hearing another's thoughts. A magician has to focus in and listen carefully. Even then one may just hear certain individuals attuned to them. I suspect you're only able to hear when the subject frames his thoughts with words, and physically mouths them as well. You'd have to practice intensively to do more."

I was skeptical.

He gestured wide. "Magic is an art, not a science. Each talent has many variations on a common theme. Those with even great talent rarely hear pure thoughts without training and practice, and even then only with difficulty. It is a very imprecise ability. At any distance, only a presence is felt, or an emotion is recognized rather than a reading of conscious thought. The air is ripe with the emotions of men, beasts, even the birds. Most commonly, that is what the talent would detect. But even that is subject to distraction."

"So. I'm a wizard."

"Andrew. Let's not get carried away."

A thought struck me. "You have several talents. Do I?"

He shrugged. "Possibly. Or, more likely, you have just the one. In any case, I doubt that you could do much with them. Your training would be starting too late. We usually bring boys to the school no older than thirteen."

I tried to think of some way to use my new knowledge of this power. I couldn't, but perhaps Murdock would know. "So. What difference does this make?"

"Difference? Why, none. You are still Arn, Prince of Kenesee. You can still listen in on some private conversations, just as you do already. Hardly an ability to win kingdoms. All that we have cleared up is why you have such extraordinarily good hearing."

No difference. Well, that was good to know, at least.

"Except for one thing," said Murdock with a smile. "Don't ever listen to my conversations."

"No? Why not?"

"I'll break your arms."

We had a simple dinner of fried sausage and bread, and then retired. Kren had lit a fire in each of the tiny stoves and they worked quite well, taking the chill out of the wagons. One of us was always on watch, so the lack of a fifth bed was of little concern. The bunks were small, but the wagon interior was much more comfortable than sleeping outside on the cold ground.

For the next few days we traveled in the mornings, slowly following the coast road southwest past the occasional farmhouse and halting briefly at village or inn to have lunch and replenish our supplies. We'd move on for another hour or two in the afternoon before finding an empty field or meadow with a good water source and ready firewood where we could set up camp. A large fire would be lit, and the afternoon and evening would be spent practicing and rehearsing.

Murdock had brought a battered old volume of Shakespeare in the New English translation, and this he consigned to Lorich, who was put to memorizing various scenes. All in all, we were making good progress. "Another week," said Murdock, "and we'll be ready for our first performance."

As it turned out, we didn't have another week.

The next day we arose to the cold dawn. It was certainly winter, gray and bleak and windy in the morning. Yet, it was not as harsh as it might have been, and our southward progress since leaving Kenesee must have had something to do with it. We had morning meal, and were quickly on our way.

Other than the lack of female companionship, I was actually enjoying our journey through Arkan. My companions provided pleasant company, we slept warm and dry, and meals were tasty. At times I even forgot that we were in a foreign land under threat of capture and imprisonment. So quickly are we lulled into complacency, and so quickly shaken out of it.

By midafternoon we had set up camp and had a nice kettle of cider warming on the edge of the fire ring and waiting for a nice bed of coals to heat it properly. Jenkins and I had taken out our shiny dueling swords and were about to begin another rehearsal when Murdock stood up with a frown and gestured with his hand. We fell silent, waiting. "We shall have visitors," he explained at last. "Men on horseback, I should guess, coming from the south. A dozen or two."

"Too many for common travelers," Jenkins stated. "Then it's either a military patrol or bandits."

It was too late to hide the wagons, and running into the

woods ourselves would leave them suspiciously abandoned. Murdock reminded us of that. "We have to play our roles. Everyone make sure you have your sword belted on, but otherwise act as if these are normal travelers who mean us no harm. After all, that's probably what they are. Lorich, you stay in the wagons as much as possible. Come out to prepare evening meal for us, but pay attention to what's happening. If it comes to fighting, use your talent. Take down the leaders first, then as many of them as fast as you can. We'll handle the rest. Is that satisfactory, my son James?"

Jenkins nodded. "In a fight, everyone stay near the wagons. For the rest, I was about to recommend the exact same thing, of course."

"Of course. Any suggestions, Klod? By the way, you may want to put your cap back on, and your hood up."

The beastman followed Murdock's direction and closed the chin flap. "Sounds reasonable to me. Not bad for a withered old magician."

"Careful, or I shall turn you into a frog," Murdock warned.

"You've already turned me into a Klod. What could be worse?"

"Well, I considered naming you Krud. Now, everyone sit down and relax."

"There they are," Jenkins stated calmly. Coming up the road they were just visible in the distance through the bare trees and underbrush that lined their way, two files of horsemen proceeding at the walk. They came on, reached the clearing in which we rested and the horsemen looked our way curiously. A hand went up from a figure in front, halting the column. They were aligned with neat, military precision, their lances and shields at rest position, outer tunics in the gray tones of the Arkan Army covering their winter coats and leather armor, shiny helms of metal and leather on their heads.

Jenkins counted. "Hmmm. More than a score of trained Arkan horsemen against us." He grinned. "We could form square. That would be one for the books. A five-man square. And without long spears."

"At least they're not thieves," I said, trying to find the best side of a bad situation.

"Smile," commanded Murdock, and we all showed our teeth in joyous welcome. Leaving their followers waiting on the road, the two lead riders turned their horses and trotted across the meadow, reining in before our fire. We stood up in greeting, teeth still gleaming upon the visitors as they reined up.

Both men were in their early thirties, held themselves with quiet confidence, and projected an air of incorruptible efficiency. They carried their rank upon shoulder and sleeve, an officer and a sergeant.

"Good afternoon, gentlemen," Murdock welcomed them warmly.

The officer was soft-featured except for a rather large nose, and he tended slightly towards portliness. But his eyes were sharp, sweeping across our faces, our clothes, our wagons, our campsite with the look of a man who noticed things. The sergeant was well-formed and square-featured, probably a favorite with the women.

The officer nodded. "Good afternoon. I'm Major Miller. This is Sergeant Nordstrom. May we ask your name and business."

"Certainly," Murdock replied. He introduced us as the famous Thomas's, and explained our livelihood.

The two gave no reaction this information, other than another question. "You have an accent. You're not Arkan?"

"Oh, no," Murdock admitted, and then explained how we found ourselves in their fair kingdom.

"So," said the major, "you're a theater troupe, fleeing the ravages of war in Kenesee to seek new lands of opportunity."

"Yes, sir, that's exactly it. If you had seen the destruction of war, you would know why we've come."

"I have seen it. Briefly, and too much."

"Ahhh. Your unit participated in the invasion?"

"We did. This performance of yours—what is it?"

The wizard was ready for that question. "We offer a variety of acts and entertainments suitable for all ages, Major Miller. Scenes of drama and humor, a swordfight, a magic show and other entertainments."

"Other entertainments?"

Murdock was caught. "Oh, a bit of music and a songfest. And . . . a beastman."

"A real beastman?" rasped the sergeant, his voice like sandpaper.

"Uh—really and truly."

"Excellent," said the major, a disbelieving frown on his face. "Your troupe can give our men a performance this afternoon."

For once, Murdock was surprised. "Sir?"

"The Major wants you to perform," the sergeant clarified.

"This afternoon? We wouldn't want to delay you, sir. We'll be giving other performances in the towns. I'm sure you could see us then, and save yourself a delay."

"We're in no rush," stated the major. "Sergeant, have the men set up camp here. We'll join Mr. Thomas and his theater. And let the men know we'll be having some real entertainment—one way or another."

The Arkans' camp was quickly established next to ours, a dozen two-man tents set up in a precise row, horses grain fed, watered, unsaddled, and tethered, fires going and firewood piled, a thick layer of pine boughs cut from trees and laid under their tents for ground cover, a latrine set up. And it was still not dusk. The soldiers were experienced, and went about their business with good-natured joking about the entertainment to come.

"No women?" asked one. "There ain't no women? These shows always have women."

"How many shows have you seen?" a comrade asked the first.

"One."

"No women," confirmed Jenkins. "Sorry."

We had just about completed our nervous preparations by the time the Arkans sat down on two tree trunks dragged up from the woods. Murdock checked us over behind the wagons, making sure our costumes were on correctly, and telling Lorich to tuck in the his shirt-tail.

"There. You all look fine. Is everyone ready?"

We were a unanimous chorus. "No!"

"Neither am I, but we have no choice. Now, if you forget a line, or miss a cue, or something doesn't quite go right, ignore it and keep going. Make things up if you have to. They won't know what's supposed to come next, and if you keep your heads about you, anything you do will look fine. Now go and do your best," he smiled beatifically as we went our ways, and then looked heavenward and mumbled under his breath so low that none of the others could hear. "And Lord grant us a miracle."

A moment later, dressed in a shiny blue robe and tall conical hat that were covered with silver stars and crescent moons, Murdock bounded out from between the wagons that served as the backdrop for our "stage" and tossed a handful of dust into the fire. The flames roared up in a whoosh, and the Arkans jerked back, startled. The flames subsided, and they looked at each other and laughed sheepishly.

Murdock smiled. "Welcome, good men and gentlemen, welcome to Thomas's Traveling Theater. Today we will present for your enjoyment a number of acts. We will show you feats of magic." With dramatic flair, he pulled brightly colored scarves out of his open hand. "We will sing for you, and with you. We will present great scenes from Shakespeare—"

"Shake-spear?" one soldier asked another.

"It's a contest with spears," the other replied knowingly.

"—We will show feats of skill and daring," the wizard continued, ignoring the muted voices from his audience. "And, as an added treat, you will see a creature never before seen in Arkan, brought to you from the lands of the north where they live secure in their forest. A beastman!"

There were more exclamations from the audience. He had them. He really had them—most of them. The major and his sergeant sat in quiet judgment, their faces unreadable.

"And now, for our first act, the marvelous magic of your humble host, Thomas the Talented, Sorcerer Supreme!" Murdock stepped behind his magician's table and, with a constant stream of jokes and stories, started to run through the basic tricks and illusions of a magic show. He was still a bit rusty. Fanning a handful of playing cards, they suddenly spewed from his grasp, fluttering to the grass in an embarrassing snowfall. The Arkans burst out laughing. Murdock grinned and winked at them while Lorich gasped and ran forward to pick up the cards. Murdock took his wand and beat the apprentice over the head with blows that might have felled a sick kitten. "Why did you make me do that?" Murdock asked. "It's all your fault!"

The soldiers guffawed. "Sounds like what my wife tells

me,'' said one, and they broke up again, even Sergeant Nordstrom chuckling.

Once Lorich had scuttled away with the cards, Murdock took up a box and commenced the disappearing coin trick, which ended when the side flap fell away and revealed the secret compartment. ''I never did trust that box,'' the wizard admitted, and the Arkans roared again.

The rest went pretty well, the laughter coming from Murdock's jokes and expressions rather than mistakes. At last he took a deep bow to hearty applause, beckoned for silence, and introduced the next act.

''Enough comedy, my friends. We must give you a chance to rest. Our next act will be a dramatic scene from a famous historical play, *King Richard the Third.* A great battle is to be fought for the throne of England, a land that existed across the seas before the Cataclysm, and the twisted and evil usurper of the crown, Richard the Third, will see his army defeated. Let us join Richard as he wakes from a dream and contemplates his murderous deeds.''

Murdock faded back and Lorich limped forward in kingly battle dress, sword in one hand and crown upon his head. He looked around dazedly, though whether it was fine acting or his true state, I was not sure. He took a deep breath and began speaking the lines he had been memorizing since Kingsport, his voice hesitant and low:

What do I fear? Myself? There's none else by.
Richard loves Richard, that is, I am I.
Is there a murderer here? No. Yes, I am.
Then fly. What, from myself? Great reason why—
Lest I revenge. What, myself upon myself?

Lorich became thoughtful, as if he were Richard himself pondering the duplicity of man's consciousness, and his voice grew in strength and depth.

Alack, I love myself. Wherefore? For any good
That I myself have done unto myself?
O, no! Alas, I rather hate myself
For hateful deeds committed by myself.
I am a villain; yet I lie, I am not.

He delivered the rest of the lines of that speech, and then moved directly into the battle of Scene IV, and Murdock rushed out to play the role of Sir William Catesby exclaiming the wondrous battle deeds of Richard as the tyrant fights on unhorsed. Murdock's Catesby urged him to flee.

Withdraw, my lord, I'll help you to a horse.

Lorich's Richard gave Murdock's Catesby a look of scorn.

Slave, I have set my life upon a cast,
And I will stand the hazard of the die:
I think there be six Richmonds in the field;
Five have I slain to-day instead of him.
A horse! A horse! my kingdom for a horse.

Everyone was silent, listening with rapt attention. All in all, Lorich was doing an impressive job. But as luck would have it, just as he concluded his last line there came a sharp snort from one animal and a long whinny from another on the Arkan's tether line. The attentive audience dissolved into laughter. Lorich froze in confusion. Murdock whispered something. The boy bowed and exited, the laughter dying out and honest applause following him as he left.

The major lifted an eyebrow, but that was all.

"They laughed. They didn't like it," Lorich stated as he joined us behind the wagons.

"They laughed at the horses," Kren reassured him. "The applause is for you."

"For me?"

Murdock introduced the next act. Jenkins and I took a deep breath and stepped forward, each of us with a dueling sword in hand. The soldiers took a look at our fancy costumes and snickered. We faced each other, bowed, and went into our act. The camp site rang with the clang of sword on sword as we thrust and chopped and feinted and parried, each move carefully rehearsed time and again. The snickers stopped as they followed our whirling swords. The blades were carefully dulled, but could still inflict a mean bruise, at the least, should there be a miscue. I let Jenkins force me back . . . back . . . until I was jammed against a wagon wheel. Then I took the offensive, driving him back. He leaped upon a rock and fought me from there. Then he drove me again. Back and forth the combat moved for one minute, two, then three, and at last Jenkins thrust his sword between my arm and side. I squeezed his sword to keep it in place, screamed convincingly, and died.

There was applause, and some appreciative comments. "They know how to use those swords," Sergeant Nordstrom whispered to Major Miller.

The major nodded slowly. "I wonder where they learned."

Murdock came out again. "And now, as the next act of our show, I have the privilege of presenting a sight never before seen in Arkan. Good men and gentlemen, I present to you Klod, King of the Beastmen!"

Kren emerged from behind a wagon, dressed in a set of blazing white robes lined in silver lace, with a deep hood over his bowed head. Standing before the Arkans he slowly reached up, drew back the hood, and lifted his head. He grinned at his audience. There were gasps from the susceptible and grunts from the cynical.

"Look at him, a beastman!" said one.

"Beastman, my eye," scoffed another. "Beastmen have long fangs and pig noses and eyes like a cat."

The first one grew thoughtful. "Well, I suppose you're right. His hair is rather scruffy looking."

Kren blinked and frowned. For a moment I thought he was going to wade into the audience with his bare hands, and that would have been a fight worth seeing. His good sense got the better of him, and he merely glared. He gathered his dignity around him, sniffed, and strode off our makeshift stage, joining us behind the wagons. "Did you hear what they called me? Did you hear?"

Murdock tried to hide a smirk. "I seem to remember someone calling me scruffy on a snowy mountainside in Kenesee last year—and that while I was assisting new life into the world. Don't worry, we'll make you a false nose and some fangs, and you'll look like a real beastman. Now get back out there and finish your act."

Grumbling, Kren stomped back out, recited his little speech about growing up under the trees of the Beastwood, safe and secure deep within their forest, wanting only to live and let live with their neighbors, the hairless ones. And then he recited a poem about the dear trees of the Beastwood, and finally retired to polite applause.

"Time for the last act," said Murdock, and we followed him onto our stage, the sky darkening with night as he introduced the first song. Unfortunately, none of us played an instrument. Kren, with the best voice among us, led off with a solo rendition of "Lonesome Tonight." We followed with a group version of "Home on the Range," and then invited the Arkans to join us. Several among them had good voices, and soon we were belting out "Red River Valley," "Green Leaves of Summer," and finally, "Falling in Love with You."

At last Murdock held up his hands. "Thank you, thank you. You've been a wonderful audience, and we thank you for your participation. This concludes our performance of Thomas's Traveling Theater, and we wish you all a good night." We bowed in unison and exited the stage to quite respectable cheers.

Easily pleased, these Arkans.

Behind the wagons, Murdock gave a gasp of relief. "Not bad. Not bad at all, considering. What the major thought, we shall have to see."

We put away our props and changed, but were not bothered by the soldiers, who huddled around their fires, warming sausage and bread for their evening meal. They had mess kits, but no cooking pots or kettles. Traveling light, and hard if need be.

We prepared our own meal, keeping it as simple as theirs, and the soldiers began to come over to chat as we ate. Murdock greeted them warmly, though as Jenkins and Kren and Lorich each became involved in conversation with one bunch or another and shared information about the fabricated history of our theater and ourselves, the wizard looked upward and mouthed a silent prayer for mercy.

God must have been in a good mood that night.

Our companions delivered their stories skillfully, and steered the conversations into less dangerous paths, as they'd been taught by Murdock. The weeks of practice and planning were paying off. The Arkans shared their own stories.

"We're chasing bandits," said one soldier importantly. "They've been too much for the local sheriffs, so the king put Major Miller on it. He's executive officer in our regiment. He asked for a half squadron to take on the road, and so here we are. Duty in winter isn't as much fun, I'll tell you. We've been up and down the coast twice, and haven't found them yet."

"Aye, but the bandits are cutthroats, they are," another chimed in. "Maybe as many as a dozen of 'em. We heard what they did. A band of pilgrims was going to the cathedral in Prescott. Three men, two women, and a little girl. From what could be figured out, the men had been taken and bound, and forced to watch while the bandits did the women and girl. They killed the women. And then they killed the girl. And then they killed the men. Sick bastards. Well, the major'll find them, if anyone can. He's not a king's constable for nothing."

The major decided his men had had enough time with us. Sergeant Nordstrom gave an order for turn in, and the Arkans finally sought their tents, three guards left on watch to pace the perimeter of our camp. We sought the wagons for a night's rest, exhausted from the long performance—onstage and off—that we had given throughout the afternoon and evening. At least for once we would not have to worry about robbers, though we still locked the wagon door and took turns on watch through the night. One never knew.

The next morning dawned gray and cold as usual, with the sky threatening rain once more. We heated water in our kettle and pot, dipped crunched coffee beans in a strainer bag, and as the aroma wafted through the campsite, asked the major if his men might like a cup. He nodded once, and the soldiers gathered round readily enough, enjoying the warmth as much as the taste of the brew. I noted that Major Miller and his sergeant were each casually making rounds of the men, questioning them, no doubt, about what we might have said to them the night before. The major also walked entirely around the campsite yet again, eyeing the wagons from all sides, near and far, as if studying them for purchase. Apparently, he could discover nothing amiss, for he went back to the fires and finished his own cup of coffee. His men toasted the last of their bread over the fires, ate, and were ready within minutes.

Murdock ambled over to Miller to bid him good journey. "Well, major, we part company. I presume you are headed to Batesville?"

"Yes. And then we shall return this way." The last words implied warning. Not for us, but to us.

"Ahh. Are you on patrol?"

"Bandits have been plaguing the coast road," the major explained with a nod. "They're clever, and have eluded us so far. We've been assigned to track them down. I recommend you take care."

"We shall."

The Arkans formed up, the sergeant and his men mounting. The major lingered a moment longer, looking at us and our wagons. "I thank you for the coffee. The men appreciated that. They liked your performance last night, though I thought it a bit . . . unpracticed, shall we say? I don't know what it is, but something smells about all this. I've a nose for such things."

And indeed, with his great beak he could sniff us out if anyone could. Murdock stared a warning at me as if he thought I might make a comment about the major's dominant feature, but he needn't have worried. We didn't need the ire of this Arkan, nor any other.

Major Miller surveyed the camp one last time. "I have always held that actors were empty people, and they played roles to fill themselves up, to give them shape, if you will. Yet, I think you are not empty. No, not empty at all." He put foot into stirrup and mounted ponderously. "I can't figure out quite what is wrong here," the major continued, "but I'll think upon it.

"Mind what you do," he warned, and at last his face broke into a smile. But it was one of irony rather than warmth. "Who knows, perhaps we shall meet again."

3

Lorich's Mistake

We broke camp less than a half hour after the Arkans, heading south to their north, resuming our trek along the coast road under a cold drizzle that lasted perhaps an hour before the sun broke through with a distant warmth. The gray clouds gave way to scattered puffs of white. The sky was a brilliant blue across which wedges of geese flew, as well as one immense flock of smaller birds weaving northward over the trees.

The land was hilly, even mountainous in places, with all that meant for overland travel. The horses strained as they pulled the wagons uphill, and then on the downhill side our drivers rode the brake hard. Progress was slow, if steady.

The road was not maintained as it was in Kenesee, or perhaps it was never built with care, or perhaps both causes were at fault. Portions were decently paved with odd-shaped chunks of flat crete carefully patched together into a smooth surface, while other stretches were rutted and muddy paths over which the horses pulled with difficulty. It was a vivid reminder of the value of the old roads in travel—and in war.

At one point the road crept up a hillside to avoid a small bay, and from it we could see both the Gulf and our way laid out before us in brilliant relief. The breeze was brisk off the water, the surface spotted with whitecaps that sent one small fishing boat bouncing with the waves. We could look southwest and see the coast of Arkan stretching out into the distance. The land flattened out ahead, the villages and towns and fields and rivers forming a continuous patchwork of blue and green and brown. Had it been later in the flush of spring, the scene might have been quite spectacular.

Our tiny caravan halted to enjoy the view. Lorich sighed. "It's beautiful."

Kren breathed deeply. "I thought there could never be anything to match the hills and forests of the Beastwood. But now, I don't know. A man could love this, here above the sea."

"It's not bad," Jenkins admitted. "Except we've got to climb the damn hill."

We went on, and that evening set up camp outside the village of Drury. Having performed for the soldiers, Murdock felt we might as well continue practicing before live audiences. Held on the village square and playing to three score adults and children—literally everyone in the community—the performance went better than expected. Murdock got the magic box trick to work, and Lorich was able to finish his kingdom-for-a-horse speech without a single whinny. But Jenkins lost his footing and fell during the duel with me.

Still, if the show wasn't yet perfect, the villagers were pleased. They gave us an enthusiastic ovation at the end, and the troupe was invited to the village tavern for free drinks. Leaving Lorich to watch the wagons—young wizards do seem to get that type of unfortunate duty with appalling frequency—the rest of us went. No fool, the tavernkeeper. Most of the men of the village followed us in, jamming the tiny room from wall to door and bringing him more business than he normally had in a week.

Each of us was surrounded by listeners, but Murdock and Kren had the most, the magic user attracting admirers to his warm friendliness like bees to clover, while others clustered around the beastman and asked him who he really was and what it was like to have so much hair and, after enough beers, what the fair sex thought about it all. About who he really was, Kren remained jokingly noncommittal. About the fair sex, he was more forthcoming.

We stayed within our practiced stories, and steered the conversation to news picked up at other towns and villages. After several beers the stress of the performance told on us, so that I was yawning and feeling a pleasant heaviness upon my eyelids. When we had done our duty by the villagers, Murdock collected the members of his troupe and led us out the door to the farewells of those remaining.

And that's when our problems with women began.

The fire we had built in the square had burned down to glowing embers which cast little light, but two lanterns still hung from our wagons, showing us the way. Lorich waited near the fire. A short, stout figure waited with him. She came forward when we approached. The light revealed a plain, pimply-faced young woman who gave off an unwashed smell. "Mr. Thomas?"

She touched Murdock's sleeve shyly to get his attention, but peered at him with shining eyes. "I—I've been waitin' for you. I liked your magic show. I never saw nothin' like that before."

Murdock smiled upon her. "I see. Well, thank you. I'm glad you liked it. Have you been waiting long?"

Her glance never wavered. "Oh . . . not long. Not long. Just since the show."

We had been in the tavern for—a half-hour? More likely an hour.

The wizard nodded. "I see. And where is your family?"

"Papa's home sleepin'. He don't know I'm here."

"He didn't come to the show?" the wizard inquired.

She glanced furtively behind, as if someone might be sneaking up on her. "Papa would never take me. Said such things was devil's work. I ain't never seen a show before."

"And where do you live?"

She pointed. "Farm is outside the village a ways."

He smiled gently. "Well, a young woman should not be about this late by herself. I could use a walk before retiring. May I escort you home?"

"Ess-coort?"

"May I walk you home."

"Walk me home? Oh, Mr. Thomas, that'd be won'rful."

"So, a walk it shall be," Murdock said, taking a lantern. Jenkins was grinning at him. "James, a little less grinning and a bit more duty, if you please. Andrew, see that everyone is settled in by the time I return." He ambled off slowly, following the road in the direction the girl had indicated. She fell in beside him. "Now, my girl, tell me your name. . . ."

When they were well on their way, Kren and Jenkins exchanged knowing looks.

"He has a kind heart," said the beastman.

"Oh, is that what it is?"

"But he's kindling hope where he shouldn't," Kren concluded.

I interrupted. "Our beastman has first watch. We should get some rest."

The wagon box was cold. Lorich had forgotten to light the stoves. I brought in some coals from the fire to start the wood burning, slipped off my boots and got into bed with clothes still on, pulling the blankets up over me. The wagon swayed gently as Kren sat down on the outside stoop. All was quiet, but after a while could be heard the sound of the other wagon's door opening and closing.

Someone coming out, still awake?

Lorich's voice addressed Kren. "May I join you, Mr. Klod? I couldn't sleep."

"You may," permitted the beastman.

I could imagine the hunchbacked young wizard sitting down on the other wagon stoop, wrapping his coat about his misshapen form and extending his feet toward the fire before he spoke. "That woman. Master is being . . . charitable . . . isn't he?"

"Yes," Kren stated. He was probably sitting with his arms folded across his chest, eyeing the embers of the fire.

"He doesn't intend to make love to her?"

"No," Kren admitted. "I don't think so. Our wizard has quite a way with women. If he wanted, he could pretty much have his pick, I should think. Yet, he's a very careful man."

"Careful?"

"Your master has a kind heart. He would do nothing to hurt a lass, nor anyone who might love her."

There was silence for a moment, and then Lorich spoke again. "He pities her."

"I don't know. Maybe. I guess you could say that."

"Isn't—isn't that being a bit unfair? To her?"

Kren hesitated before replying. "Unfair? Well now, that's a tough one to answer. Our wizard is not exactly lusting after this young woman, you know. There's nothing for him to gain. If he gives her a little of his time, a few minutes of conversation, a bit of flattery, is that so bad? He doesn't have to make love to her, after all. The poor girl is probably lonely. Perhaps no one has taken an interest in her before. A bit of attention can go a long way, for some."

"It's still unfair."

"Possibly. But that would be for the young woman to decide, don't you think?"

Lorich thought about it. "I mean no disrespect to my master, but it isn't right to be nice to someone because of pity."

Kren's voice was soothing. "You may have a point there. It would take a better man than I to know what is right and wrong in such a case. I guess we have to look into our hearts and do what we think is best."

Lorich's voice was pensive. "I don't want to be pitied. I don't want to be lied to. I want. . . ."

"You want to be loved, as you deserve. And so do we all, my boy. As we all deserve. But some of us won't find love. And those of us who don't must make do with what we can to fill the void."

"Sir, do you think a woman could love me? In spite of my appearance?"

"In spite of how you look? Well, now. Women enjoy a handsome man. No doubt about that. But notice that when women search for someone to listen to them, and father their children, and be there when they need them—well, it seems that's when the rest of us get our chance."

"So you think a woman could love me? You think there's a chance?"

"Everyone has a chance. You just have to know when they're interested. Wait! I know what you're about to ask. How to know when a woman's interested, right? Beastmen or hairless, from all I can see it seems to work exactly the same. And yet I'll be darned if I can figure out exactly how one knows. I mean, you can see it when it happens between others. But when it's just you and the woman, then it's a different matter. Of course, women don't have this problem. Just men. A woman can tell when a man's interested because we look like eager puppies. But it's harder to tell what a woman's thinking. She's sly about such things."

"Like dogs and cats."

"Hmmm?"

"Nothing, sir. Sorry to interrupt."

"Still, if you look carefully, you can catch them glancing. Or giving you a particular smile. Or a quick hand to their head pelt to brush the strands into place when they notice you're watching. All good signs, lad."

"And after a man sees a sign?"

"Why, then you have to take the offensive. Sure as hell, they're not going to do it. Even the most forward of women will just make it easy for you to express your interest openly. They figure they've left you the signs, now you'll act on them—if you're interested. As stupid as we men are, more often than not we miss the signs and walk away frustrated, not even knowing the woman is just as disappointed. It's a strange game. Just watch for the signs. And then express your interest. The worst they can do is say no."

"They can laugh at me!" Lorich objected.

"Aye, that too. But all the more challenge to turn their laughter into interest."

The Relation of the Sexes, as discovered by the great philosopher, Kren the Beastman. Although he did have the right idea. Why couldn't women be clearer? Why is it men are the clowns in such matters? Quite unfair.

"Mr. Klod? I have another question. Why?"

"*Why*? Why, you ask. Can't we narrow that down just a bit?"

"Why am I like this?"

"Like what? Getting into trouble? Talking too much?"

"No. Not that. My appearance. Why am I malformed? Why am I ugly? Why can't I be whole like the rest of you?"

Kren took a long time before he answered. There was a soft, rhythmic sound, as if he were tapping his stick against a piece of firewood. "You've come up against one of the great mysteries. Why is there suffering in the world? Why is there pain? Unhappiness? Loneliness? Why do men kill each other? Why do horrible diseases plague us? Why do the innocent suffer while the guilty grow rich and prosper? Why, why, why?"

"Exactly!"

"Don't you think every man worth his salt hasn't asked himself those questions as he saw an innocent child suffer, or a loved one die? Yet though we ask, there is no answer. I used to think there was, but then—then I found out differently. But you should talk to your master."

"What would he say?"

"Your master? We've talked. I know what he'd say. He's said it. To me. He got that what-is-this-all-about look, and started in on me. 'What?' he asked. 'How can you say that? Can you see all ends? God is silent, but that doesn't mean He is evil. The natural world is violent, with one thing eating another. Only man has the opportunity to do more. That is the world God has given us, to see what we do.' "

"That was his answer?" Lorich pondered the words.

"That was his answer. He almost had me believing him. You know how he can get. You want to trust him like he's your mother and father and spouse all rolled into one. You want to believe. Ah, well. Don't you think you should be getting abed now? Dawn comes early."

"Yes, sir. I'll think about what you said. And thank you for talking with me. May we speak again?"

"When you have the need, I'll be here. Answering a few questions is the least I can do, my young friend. There is hope. For you. For everyone."

"Master is coming back. I'll go to bed now. Good night, sir."

"Good night, lad. Don't trouble yourself over all this. Sleep well."

The sound of a creaking wagon spring. A door opening and closing.

Footsteps approached. Murdock's voice. "Lillian. I know you're out there. Go home."

"A problem?" Kren asked.

There was a note of exasperation in Murdock's voice. "I saw the girl almost to her cabin. Said good night. And then she followed me back."

"What did you say to her?"

"Nothing, except a few kind words," the wizard explained.

"Apparently that was too much. You can't set the whole world right, my friend."

"And yet, when the needy find their way to our door, should we slam it in their faces?"

"You tell me."

"Tomorrow I'll warn her father and the village mayor. We don't want her following us."

"Is that her?"

"Lillian, go home!"

* * *

Murdock did as he'd stated, and Lillian was watched as we left the village. She did not follow, thank goodness, and we continued our travels, polishing our acts both onstage and off. Murdock carved out a pair of fangs for Kren, and molded a false snout that he could secure over his nose with paste. After that, he looked like a real beastman.

There was one village we stopped at where we didn't perform. The Coast Road formed the main street of a large crossroads village by the name of Duttonhill, another way branching off to the northwest from the middle of the habitation. We drew up in front of the village inn to inquire where we might set up for a performance that evening.

The innkeeper was embarrassed. "Well, you're certainly welcome to make camp on the green north of town. There's a stream feeding the river there. But as to a show, I'm afraid that might be a problem."

Murdock looked surprised. "A problem?"

"Umm, some of the people don't feel too kindly about such doings. There's Deacon Carroll coming," the innkeeper stated guardedly. "Maybe he'd better tell you."

The deacon was a short, slender man in working clothes, over which he had put a formal church coat. He strode down to us with a pinched look on his face. The innkeeper made preliminary introductions, related the conversation so far, and then stood silent.

The deacon's voice was surprisingly rich and deep, coming from that skinny chest, but the words were strident as he stared at us as if we had crawled out from under a rock. "Entertainment is the work of the devil, and will not be allowed here. You must leave."

A friendly sort. Well, we had believers with similar ideas in Kenesee, too. A village or town would get swept up in a heated fervor stoked by some inspiring representative of God. Funny how most of them seemed to have that same pinched look about them, as if they were in pain all the time. Maybe they were.

The innkeeper cleared his throat reluctantly. "Deacon, I've already told them they could use the green for the night."

The deacon glared at him. "This matter should have been referred to me. I am the mayor now. Do not forget yourself."

The chastisement completed, he turned back to us. ''Since hospitality has been extended, we will abide by the custom, but those engaged in sinfulness do not deserve such courtesy. You may use the green for tonight. Tomorrow morning you will leave.''

Murdock studied the two men carefully, and bowed. ''With all respect for your customs and beliefs we will give no performance, and thank you for your generous hospitality.''

''Do you have any women with you? You don't? Good. Then at least our men will not be tempted by your harlots. And you will treat our women with courtesy and respect, otherwise we will have a reckoning.''

He stalked off. The innkeeper kept his face neutral. ''And with that, gentlemen, I have my own work to do. I wish you well, but advise you respect the Deacon's wishes—for your own good.''

Our bread was gone, so we stopped at the village baker's, where Lorich and I hoped to purchase a half dozen loaves. An attractive but stern-faced woman of perhaps twenty-five ran the place. I knew Lorich was taken by her, for he turned shy as he ordered.

''Uh—bread. We want bread.''

''We have bread,'' she replied impatiently. She pointed at a basket and stared at his hump while he emptied the few loaves remaining.

''Three loaves,'' said Lorich. ''We need three more.''

''My husband will get more. Louis!'' she called out in a harsh tone, and the baker's head pushed out from the curtained doorway leading to the oven. ''Louis, the bread basket is empty. I need three more loaves.''

Louis nodded to us politely, and disappeared. The woman crossed her arms. ''You're visiting?'' she asked with a bored air.

''We are in the theater,'' Lorich responded quickly. ''Thomas's Traveling Theater. Our wagons are outside. We'll be staying on the green overnight, but we won't be giving a performance.''

Her face changed as he spoke, her eyes darting to each of us in turn with new interest. ''A theater? I wish I could see that. Where are you going next?''

''Oh, just working our way down the coast,'' I blurted out

before Lorich could say something indiscreet. ''A show here, a show there. Wherever we can bring in a good audience.''

The baker stuck his head out. ''The bread's not ready to come out yet. Another quarter hour. Sorry, gentlemen.'' The head disappeared behind the curtain.

The wife turned back to Lorich. ''You're camping on the green? If you would like to pay me now, I will bring the loaves after we close.''

''How kind of you,'' Lorich gushed, and plopped down an Arkan ten-penny. The woman made change, and smiled for the first time. ''I'll look forward to seeing you later.''

''Yes, later.'' Lorich limped out, his eyes bright. ''A very nice woman, sir, don't you think?''

''Very nice,'' I agreed. After weeks away from feminine comfort, it was getting very hard to resist the physical imperatives. Murdock had warned us we would have various temptations on the road, but other than money-for-services transactions, we must have nothing to do with the women we met. Too much could go wrong.

The green was a pleasant enough site, with the village on one side and a wooded stream on the other providing water and firewood. There was even an outhouse in a far corner we could use. Camp was established without difficulty, but except for a few children who stared from a distance, no curious idlers came to chat. Our only visitor was the baker's wife, for whom Lorich had been carefully watching. He limped across the green to meet her before she could even reach the wagons, and the two stood talking for a goodly time.

Kren watched them curiously. ''Our good young wizard seems to have made a friend.''

''Yes,'' I commented. ''So it seems. She's the baker's wife.''

Murdock glanced my way. ''Do I detect some concern about that?''

I had to think about it. ''I don't know. Certainly, he was taken by her.''

''That's understandable,'' Jenkins contributed. ''She looks pretty enough.''

''Yes,'' I admitted. Why Lorich would be interested in her

was obvious. But why would she be interested in Lorich? That question hung in the air, unspoken.

After a quiet night we broke camp in the morning, several village folk watching us with curiosity, and not a few looks of regret at opportunity missed. Sinful or not, entertainment was rare enough for any village. We left Duttonhill behind without regret.

Several hours later, Murdock lifted his head, as if listening. "Someone coming up behind us," he warned. "Could be another patrol. Why don't we pull off, eat, and let them go by."

We found a clearing and halted the wagons on dry ground next to the road. Kren jumped down and stretched. "Ah, that feels good. Now, for something to eat. Too bad we couldn't find a turkey. Or a wild boar. I'm hungry enough to eat one myself."

"Careful," Murdock advised. "If you eat like me, you'll look like me."

"Anything but that," Kren retorted heading for the back of the wagon where we kept the supplies.

"Oh, let me get it for you," Lorich said, still climbing down.

"Quite all, right," said the beastman, opening the door of the wagon. Lorich stopped, suspended on the spoke of one wheel. Kren backed up a step. "Oh oh. My friends, we have a problem."

We hurried back to join him and peered into the wagon box. Seated on one of the bunks was the baker's wife, her face unreadable. Lorich hung his head. Murdock extended a hand and, reluctantly, the woman took it and was helped down. She was dressed in a shift pulled in tight at the waist, accentuating her figure. Somehow I didn't think she had much opportunity to wear it with Deacon Carroll around.

"And you are . . . ?"

"My name is Regina."

"Well, Regina, may I ask what you are doing in our wagon?"

She straightened her back proudly, which accentuated her figure even more. "I wanted to come with you." She gestured at Lorich. "He said I could."

We frowned at the young wizard, who smiled weakly. "I'm

sorry, Master. I hope I haven't done anything wrong."

"Wrong?" Jenkins fumed at Lorich and the woman. "You've stolen away a man's wife, and you hope you haven't done anything wrong? Don't you know what's going to happen?"

Regina stepped back before Jenkins' anger. "Well—"

"They'll think we've taken her. And they'll come for us. And what will happen then? Did you think of that?"

"I did. But I wanted to help."

Regina held out her hands to us. "You are my only escape. Please help me. Let me come with you."

"Why do you flee?" Kren asked.

Her gaze shifted to each of us as she spoke, meeting our eyes in supplication. "My husband is brutal. A violent man. No one will protect me."

"I will protect you," Lorich said softly.

Murdock sighed. "Our visitors should be arriving. Just . . . about . . . now."

Regina tried to get back into the wagon, but Murdock blocked her way.

There were more than a score of men in Arkan Army uniforms, the same we had met before, for leading the troop were our old friends Major Miller and Sergeant Nordstrom. They were bound to come across us somewhere.

Riding with them were the village baker and Deacon Carroll.

"Well, well, well," said the ubiquitous Major Miller. "We meet again."

We were in a nice dilemma now. If they thought we were guilty of taking her, they'd try to arrest us and we'd have to fight them. If by some chance we won, we'd be criminals hunted down and killed for defending ourselves against them. If we lost—well, we wouldn't have anything to worry about. Ever.

I wanted to wring Lorich's scrawny neck.

The baker leaped down from his horse and approached his wife, an angry scowl upon his face. Regina took a half step back and bumped against Lorich, who put a hand on her arm protectively.

The major looked on with interest. "We seem to have a situation here."

The deacon glared at us from horseback. ''You have stolen this woman. Taken her against her will.''

Our wizard bowed to the deacon, who was ablaze with righteousness. Murdock's words carried wisdom and logic, and were imbued with the warmth and good will that I had felt at crucial times before. ''Deacon Caroll, we have just discovered her inside our wagon. We did not take her against her will. Note that she bears no signs of binding. Nor did we travel far in a rush to escape.''

The deacon continued to mull his suspicions, but the major spoke. ''Is this true, woman? Did you go with them?''

Her face was blank. ''I—I. . . .''

''So,'' said the baker, sadly. ''It was as I thought.''

''She asked to come with us,'' Lorich said to the Arkan officer. ''The others didn't know. It was my fault. I let her.'' He turned to the baker. ''You're cruel. You beat her. You don't deserve to have her back.''

The baker's shoulders slumped. ''So, she's using that line again, is she? She said that the last time she ran away. Regina, why do you do this?''

Lorich was indignant. ''You deny it?''

Several of the soldiers passed looks of bewilderment to each other.

The baker laughed bitterly. ''Hah. Take a look at her. You say there are no marks of binding? Well, do you see any other bruises or scars? Regina, show us where I've beaten you. Don't be modest. You've never been modest. Show us.''

Regina did not respond. The woman's skin was unblemished. I thought of other women who had endured a beating, and what the results were.

''Does he speak the truth?'' Murdock asked the deacon.

The churchman snorted. He was having to answer accusations, rather than make them. ''It's true. Brother Stevens does not believe in such punishment, though it is his right. And perhaps if he had done so, we would not be engaged in this farce.''

Murdock nodded. ''And we speak the truth also. The woman appealed to my young wizard, and played upon his kindness. He allowed her to come along, but she hid in the wagon, and we did not know of her until we stopped for noon meal. She has not been touched, and we would have returned her so."

The major addressed the deacon. "Do you accept this explanation?"

Deacon Carroll gritted his teeth. "I can see the truth in their answer. We will take the woman and they may go on." I think he was disappointed they wouldn't be able to smite us high and low.

The major nodded. "I agree with you. Come, baker, take your wife and return to your home."

The baker held up his hand in denial, his eyes brimming. "No, Deacon. I'm tired of this. If she wants to go, I'll let her. Do you hear, Regina? Are you sure you want this? You can go, but you can never come back. Never."

The woman sheltered against Lorich's side and stared back at her husband. Something played across her face. Doubt? Regret? Indecision? Hate? Whatever went on inside her heart, she made no move, nor spoke any word.

At last her husband shrugged. "Well lad, she's your problem now," he said, his face pained, and turned away.

"If my woman did that," Jenkins whispered to me, "I'd give her what for."

The baker mounted. "I'm sorry we've troubled you. I'm sorry . . . about everything."

"You see, I told you no good would come of such people," said the deacon. He turned to Major Miller. "God's Will brought you to our village this morning, and we thank you for coming with us. We will return to our home now." Without another word the two villagers rode off.

The Arkan officer considered us for a while. "You seem to be admirably well behaved for a theater troupe. No items missing or stolen at the villages you stay. No fights. No cheating at cards or dice. I was becoming worried about you. But this was more like it. Until next time." He gave a quick order, and the column went off at a trot.

Regina took a step away from Lorich, his hand falling loose from her arm. "Thank you, Lorich, for defending me." She bowed. He bowed in return, and despite his ungainly form attained a bit of dignity in the ritual.

"The fair maiden has been rescued by the young hero, it

seems,'' Kren observed. ''So just what do we do with her now?''

''That is the question, isn't it?'' Murdock stated with an air of doubt. ''What should we do with you—Regina?''

She looked from one to another of us. ''Take me with you. I can be useful. I can cook. I can sew.''

''Can you do anything else?'' Jenkins asked with a leer.

Lorich gasped.

The woman drew herself up. ''I am not a plaything, sir,'' she answered, meeting his stare.

Jenkins nodded and turned to the young wizard. ''Sorry about that, lad. Just had to make sure what we were dealing with, here.''

Murdock scratched his chin. ''Do you know anyone in the surrounding villages?''

''No. But I have relatives in Prescott.''

''Then you may accompany us to Prescott, but no further. You will take care of housekeeping duties to pay your keep. Is that clear? Good.'' He turned his attention to Lorich, smiling ominously.

Lorich wilted under the gaze. ''Have I done wrong, master?''

''Come with me,'' was all the wizard had to say. He strode down the road, the boy following dejectedly.

''Does he always get this angry?'' Regina asked.

''He never gets this angry,'' Kren replied sharply.

Jenkins watched the two move off. ''I wonder if Lorich's ever had his arms broken before?''

We could still see them, but only as tiny figures far down the road when Murdock turned, put his hands on his hips, and began to share a few astute observations with Lorich. The wizard was quite out of earshot for normal conversation, but I could still hear him.

Then again, everyone could hear him.

4

Toil and Trouble

We continued on with a chastened young wizard, an angry Murdock, a sullen woman, and three men—or two men and a beastman, if you will—who could only shrug their shoulders and shake their heads. Regina rode in Lorich's wagon. Kren sat with the reins between her and Lorich, singing patriotic songs of the greatness of the Beastwood, such as "Trees of Green" and "Death to All Hairless." Kren stated they were going to retitle the latter song. Eventually.

Jenkins joined Murdock and me on the seat of the second wagon. After a mile or two Murdock's temper mellowed, and they had the opportunity of regaling each other with their adventures in bed and out. They also took a few moments to wonder what had led the baker's wife to abandon her husband, what she had said—or done—to Lorich to gain such devotion, and how to warn the gullible youngster not to look upon her with too much hope.

The days and miles passed. We ignored the rutted paths and dirt roads that led off westward from the coast road and wended their way inland, and other trails that led down eastward a few miles to small fishing villages on the coast. Our party made its way past a dozen sizable villages located on the road, and noted five towns on or near the old highway. We had to stop at the towns and give a performance, for to pass them by would have aroused suspicion. But of the villages, we stopped and performed only at those conveniently close to the end of our day's progress. In this way we made eight or ten miles a day, and kept to the tentative schedule of travel we had laid out in Kingsport.

Regina did her duties well and without complaint. She was polite and correct with all, though there was seldom a smile for anyone. She did not ask untoward questions, and listened to our innocent banter without interrupting. Though aware that she was an attractive woman alone among appreciative men, and enjoying the courtesy she received as a result, she might have been surprised that none of us made any moves upon her. What conversation she had came from Lorich, who was attentive to the woman with a simpleminded optimism that was both touching and disturbing to those of us who watched. Yet we kept our tongues, though Kren expressed it well, if sadly: "His reach exceeds his grasp."

On a gray and rainy afternoon after three days of storm, we reached the walled town of Trentwood. The town was a friendly place situated on the north bank of the Arkan River where it flowed into the Gulf, and surrounded by neat squares of plowed fields which in summer would be thick with everything from cotton to oats. The gatekeeper questioned us and took a cursory look inside the wagons to make sure nothing was amiss, then directed us to the market square, where we set up camp and hoped the rains would stop before dusk.

In the pouring rain the town sheriff visited us that same afternoon, accompanied by two deputies. Murdock gave the usual greeting, and the sheriff asked the usual questions while his men searched the wagons. At last he asked, "Any opiates?"

"No, sheriff," Murdock answered politely.

"Did you run into any trouble on the roads? Any sign of bandits?"

"No, sir. Major Miller warned us there was a gang preying on travelers, but we encountered no one but innocent travelers."

The sheriff perked up. "You know Major Miller?"

"Yes, sheriff. We met him twice. Once on the road south of Batesville, and again at the village of Duttonhill. We even gave a performance for his men."

"Well, if Miller enjoyed your performance, then I guess our town can, too." He called to the deputies, who hurriedly finished their search and exited the wagons. We hoped we were not too obvious about watching them to make sure *they* did not steal anything.

The rain let up that evening, and we were able to give two performances—though the audiences had to stand, given the puddles in the paved market square.

The next day, a familiar face strode out of the crowds and greeted us. "There you are," beamed Captain Grayson, a wide grin beneath his captain's hat. "Thank the Lord. I thought I might have missed you. I was late getting away from Kingsport because of passengers, and then a winter storm hit. Blew up out of the south fast, Lord help us. Devilish seas. For a time I feared we might—but the *Windsprite* is a good ship. We rode it out, though it cost us two days' sailing."

Murdock, Kren, and I joined him in the wagon while Jenkins and Lorich casually made sure no one came too close. We had arranged with the captain to meet us at various points in our travel, estimating when we might be at the various ports along the Coast Road. If we were delayed, Grayson was to record the news in an innocent appearing letter and leave it for one of his many friends in each port to pass on when Thomas's Traveling Theater came to town. We had not anticipated that it might be Grayson who would be delayed.

"How has it gone for you?" he asked, and we told him of our progress. Robert would want to know the details.

His news was not quite so positive. "King Robert is well. But Governor Rodes of Virginia has ordered new regiments to assemble at their home towns and begin active training. Rodes is building a formidable new army, at least in numbers. It will outnumber the Army of Kenesee when finally assembled. Robert does not seem overly worried. He's ordered the field regiments to begin active training, though he isn't organizing any new units. But he did call up two cavalry regiments to guard the Coast Road."

There were other bits of information Grayson related, and then he hesitated. "Well, that's about all. . . . Anything else will be made clear in its own good time. Good luck to you, and continued success. I'll see you in Prescott, New Harbor, or Tyler, storms or no." And then he was gone.

We stayed in Trentwood three nights, giving two shows each afternoon, one before dusk and quite suitable for children, and one at dusk, where some of the songs' bawdier verses were not omitted. All went well, our acts gaining greater approval with each performance, so that the audience grew each time we took the stage.

On both nights, at least one woman without escort stayed after the last performance to talk of the theater and acting and Shakespeare, or strolled conveniently past our campfire so we could engage them in conversation. Yet though we might talk to the women within the security of the camp, Murdock would allow no one, including himself, to go with any of them, nor to allow them within our wagons. He wanted no further problems.

"A little celibacy will be good for us," the wizard explained. "Look how much you'll appreciate it if you do without for a while."

Jenkins snorted. "I don't have to do without it to appreciate it."

"We'll be at Prescott in a fortnight. They have a Street of Pleasure, if I remember correctly. You can wait till then, I trust?"

Our virtue intact, thanks to Murdock's strictures, we left Trentwood on the third morning after our arrival by the west gate, gained the Coast Road just outside of town, and crossed the timber bridge spanning the Arkan River above the town. All seemed well, but it was only a few miles further south that the next incident occurred.

It was a sunny afternoon, though cold enough that we saw our breath misting. We were slowed by a gentle upward slope of the road. Murdock noted two or three people were somewhere ahead, possibly women. They were probably just farmers or such, and since we outnumbered them, there wasn't much to worry about. The wagons had just topped a rise, Murdock and Jenkins each on the reins while the rest of us walked alongside to ease the load on the teams. I trudged along with my eyes on the road to avoid tripping over exposed corners of crete paving, when Kren nudged me

"Good Lord, look at that!" he said.

I looked, and for a moment could not believe the sight. In a clearing beside the road burned a campfire. From a tripod over the fire was suspended a cauldron that steamed vigorously. Around the fire, each with a long wooden spoon thrust into the cauldron, were three bent figures dressed in ragged garments of black and brown, a wide-brimmed conical hat atop the head of each. Under the hat, straight black hair dangled in dirty clumps to their shoulders. They had long crooked noses and faces lined with ugliness. They were old, veritable hags. And they laughed. No, not laughed. Cackled. Yes, cackled with delight at the sight of us.

I was glad it was daytime.

"Visssitorrrs," said one with a hiss. "We have visssitorrrs."

"Yyeesss," shrieked another. "For dinnnn'rrrr."

"Meeeaaattt," gloated the last. "Forrrr the pottt."

Jenkins set the brake, leaped down, and put himself before me, his hand on his sword.

Kren's eyes were wide. "Does anyone believe in witches and ghosts?"

There were no such things as ghosts. When you're dead, you're dead, a one-way trip to God-knows-where. I was sure of that.

Witches were another matter.

"Klod!" Jenkins called out. "Cover our rear!"

The hags cackled together and began to sway in unison around the cauldron as they chanted.

Double, double, toil and trouble,
Fire burn and cauldron bubble.
Such nice young men, amidst the rubble,
Leave their women alone with worry
While off to hated war they hurry.

The three burst into cackles again.

Murdock stepped down from the wagon. "Lorich, take Regina and continue down the road for a mile. No, not a word. Take her and go. We'll catch up shortly."

Swallowing his objections, the apprentice grabbed the woman's arm and dragged her along. "But I want to see!" Regina exclaimed as they went off. They were soon far down the road.

Murdock joined us, bemused. "I've known witches, but none looked like these. And none quoted lines from *Macbeth.* They belong on a stage, wouldn't you say?" He grinned. "Well, who better to deal with such dangerous creatures than Murdock the Magnificent? Here, here, good women. A first-rate performance. Your point is made. You may stop now.''

Silent now, the three bent forms straightened.

''And who will uncover first?'' Murdock asked.

One stepped forward. She peeled off her beaked nose and pulled off her hat and black wig together, golden hair tumbling out around her head. She rubbed the powder and paste from her face with a wet cloth.

''Megan!'' I gasped.

Megan Sims shook out her hair. ''Who were you expecting? Shakespeare?''

A second witch stepped forward. Nose, hat, and wig came off, thick black curls of hair taking their rightful place about her face. Makeup was wiped away.

Her eyes were on Jenkins.

''Beth?'' he asked in disbelief, his mouth opening and closing like a fish. ''Is—is that you?''

''Yes, it's me,'' she said, standing proud and yet timorous. He walked up to her, put a hand to her cheek, and then she melted into his arms.

''A firm hand,'' Murdock whispered to him. ''A firm hand.''

''And who,'' Kren stated with a smirk, ''could the last be?''

I looked at the third witch, and needed to say only one word.

''Angela?''

The hag did not bother to remove her costume, but bounded into my arms and buried her face in my shoulder. The large nose came off, revealing a smaller, perkier one. I gently pulled the hat and wig free, and auburn hair poured out upon her shoulders. I was once again amazed by how a woman could be both soft and firm at the same time. Her scent, her sigh, her touch was enough to put all else from my mind for a long moment, and I might reasonably have feared her ribs would crack as I clasped her to me.

''Oh, Arn,'' she whispered. ''Robert told me how you felt. You did it for me.''

And then a part of me felt quite differently. How *dare* she disobey me and put herself in danger. How dare she put *me* through this. She would be the cause of endless worry. I had wanted to wring Lorich's neck a few days before. Now it was Angela's I wanted to wring.

I put my hands on her shoulders and gave her an angry shake. "What are you *doing* here?"

Her eyes misted, and tears began to trickle down through the makeup on her cheeks. Megan marched up, pulled her from my grasp and wiped her face clean with the cloth. Then she turned on me and shook her finger beneath my nose. "How dare you do that? This woman comes across the sea for you, endures hard travel for you, waits anxiously and without complaint for you, and all you can do is berate her?"

I jerked my head back from the wagging finger, a most dangerous weapon when commanded by a righteous female. But her words tempered my anger.

The women were clustered together now, and despite their raggedy costumes and my own distress at seeing them here, I could not help noting that three more attractive creatures would be hard to find. I was not the most objective observer in the world, yet I trust that most men would have found them highly acceptable at the least, whether for the noble beauty of Megan, the enchanting smile of Angela, or the sensuous allure of Beth.

Murdock took the opportunity to step forward, his hands clasped behind his back. He began to pace back and forth before the three, and under his scrutiny they fell silent, Angela ceasing her sniffles, Beth's words of comfort to her friend fading away, and even defiant Megan's objections dying on her lips. Murdock was all seriousness.

He glanced at me. "If I may?"

I nodded. "You may, indeed."

"Prince Arn will have to make a few decisions, and to do so he needs information. Now tell us, Angela. What are you doing here?"

The wizard had chosen the woman he thought would be most ready to answer truthfully. Megan realized this and opened her mouth, but a single look from Murdock made her think better of it.

I'd have to ask him how he did that.

Angela took a breath. "We have come to join you on your adventure."

Murdock's eyebrows went up. "Ahhh. To join us. And do you know where we're going?"

"You are pretending to be a theater troupe, but you're actually going to Texan to overthrow General Murphy.''

''And what traitor told you this?'' Jenkins asked.

''Prince Arn,'' Angela responded readily. ''And you were there.''

Jenkins grimaced. ''You're right. I forgot.''

She continued, guileless. ''We tried to hide our plans, but they found us out.''

''They?''

''The king and the high wizard.''

Murdock lifted an eyebrow. ''They knew what you were planning, and you still got away?''

Angela nodded. ''They sent us.''

Megan decided she could risk speaking. ''Robert was going to put us under guard, but High Wizard O'Dowd convinced him we should be allowed to go. He said it would be for the best.''

Murdock mused upon her words for a moment. ''I see. . . .''

''So what do we do with them?'' Kren asked.

''That is the question, isn't it? The decision, of course, is up to Arn.''

Up to me. Well, I wanted to get a few things straight, first. I looked at them sternly. ''Harumpf. Just whose idea was this?''

Unable to stop themselves, Angela and Beth cast the briefest glance at Megan, and then stared at the ground in a futile effort to undo their betrayal.

I wagged my finger in Megan's face, a fitting comeuppance. ''Aha! I thought so. You're the troublemaker. You instigated this.''

Angela shook her head in loyal defense of her friend. ''I wanted to be with you. It was for me that Megan made our plan.''

''And for myself,'' Megan added. ''I wished to see Mr. Kendall.'' She still called him Mr. Kendall. ''He's there, somewhere. In Texan. Or he will be. And he'll join you, won't he?''

That was true.

''And so, Beth, it's the same with you?'' Jenkins asked. ''You came to be with me.''

Beth shook her head. ''Why, no.'' Her answer left Jenkins perturbed. She indicated her companions. ''I came to keep these two out of trouble.'' Now the other two women were perturbed. She noted their reactions. ''Jenkins, my dear, you know how to take care of yourself. But these two helpless babes don't. They have absolutely no idea how to handle men.''

Megan's eyes narrowed. ''I don't know how to handle men, you say?''

Murdock and I looked at each other, and shrugged.

Angela put a hand on the arm of each companion and moved the discussion to less dangerous ground. ''Megan and Beth were very clever, and we had almost no problem. We traveled in old clothes and put up our hair and wore hats and dirtied our faces, so we weren't really bothered . . . that much.

''The king arranged for a ship with a very nice captain by the name of Grayson, and we arrived yesterday, late by several days. We had a terrible storm. One of the crew said we'd have foundered if Captain Grayson hadn't been the best sailor on the Gulf. The captain dropped us off at Trentwood. He checked for us and found you had just arrived the day before. Everyone knew your plan to leave today, so we had a cart bring us out here this morning before dawn.''

Jenkins looked on in disbelief. ''Don't you think it might look a little odd for three women to wait in the middle of nowhere?''

''Oh, no,'' continued Angela. ''We told the cart driver we were joining our theater troupe and wanted to surprise them.''

''Uh-huh. That you did. And what is all this?'' I responded, gesturing around us at the cauldron and their costumes.

Angela smiled shyly, hoping to lure me out of my anger. ''Another act for your show. We have the entire witch scene from *Macbeth* down, and we're practicing—''

I gestured for her to stop, and looked beseechingly at Murdock. ''Is there any alternative?''

He shrugged. ''Normally, I'd say send them back to Kingsport. But if High Wizard O'Dowd thinks they can help. . . .''

''A firm hand, sir,'' said Jenkins. ''A firm hand.''

We picked up Lorich and Regina, and went on.

The arrival of the women meant more changes in our routine. We ended up giving them the bunks in the wagons, while the men slept on the ground beneath, with a thick layer of pine boughs spread to keep us off the ground, and a good fire going to keep off the chill. Their first evening with us, I took Angela to gather some firewood. Grinning, Kren mentioned that Jenkins and Beth had already wandered out into the forest for the same purpose. "They went south," he said. "You may want to go north." Excellent advice. With Angela in tow, I ventured out before it grew too dark, and we spent a goodly while searching before heading back to the wagons.

You can never have enough firewood.

Accommodations—and other such matters—were the most easily arranged. Adding the women to our performance was a bit more trying.

"Well, we can use your 'three witches' scene," Murdock admitted. "And it will do nicely to have some female attendants in our other acts. I can even use two of you in my magic show."

"What would we do in your show?" they asked, eager to help.

"Oh, stand nearby and look pretty."

They looked bleakly at each other. "Stand and look pretty? That's all?"

"Well, you could hand me things on occasion."

Somehow, Murdock survived.

That evening we rearranged the wagons as the women unpacked their travel bags.

"I assume you've brought costumes with you?" Murdock asked them.

When the women tried out their outfits for us, conversation stopped abruptly. "My goodness!" Murdock exclaimed in awe.

The women's hair was combed and ribboned, clean faces shone brightly upon us. They wore form-fitting jerkins belted over short skirts that swirled about their thighs. Above the jerkins white blouses covered their charms, cut discreetly but still giving an enticing hint of what lay below. Their legs were encased by dark stockings that seemed to go all the way up to their waists.

Jenkins elbowed me with a self-satisfied smirk, "We do know how to pick 'em, sir, don't we?"

* * *

The "three witches" scene we stuck in after Lorich's act. Beth wanted to do Lady Macbeth's "bloody hands" herself, and the three scenes would form "a trio of Shakespeare's best," as Murdock would present it to our audiences. Megan knew how to play the flute, so she had her own act with "Greensleeves" and "Are You Lonesome Tonight." Her flute also gave us instrumental accompaniment for our songfest at the end of the performance. She wanted to have an archery act as well, since she'd continued the sport until just a year before, and was really quite an excellent archer. But Murdock felt we had enough acts already.

My Angela volunteered to keep the ledger, take over fee collection, and generally manage the business of the troupe. We hadn't been concerned with financial matters since we had as much money with us as we imagined needing and none of us wanted to meddle with accounting sheets and such, but Murdock confided that it couldn't hurt, and would give her something to do. She set to her duties with a vengeance, counting our coins, asking how many people we'd had in each audience, which villages and towns we'd stopped at, and generally talking us to distraction until she'd filled in all the previous days and created a complete ledger.

The first show with our women was for the large village of Sherrill, where we set up outside the village proper on a small green to the north. It went handily enough, though I could see why Murdock thought their assistance would be helpful to his act. The men ignored the wizard's tricks and watched his assistants with drooling admiration, while their own women glared venomously. Still, the three witches scene became the most popular act in the show, Megan did a beautiful job with the flute, and Beth gave a surprisingly good performance as Lady Macbeth. Jenkins complimented her on her acting.

"Are you surprised?" she asked with a sly look. "I've had plenty of practice."

Jenkins considered that.

After the performance ended, the women went inside the wagons to change out of their costumes, with Regina helping them as part of her duties. The rest of us kept busy putting away the props and getting the campsite ready for the night. Men started drifting towards us in ones and twos, and forming a line near one of the wagons. Even as we watched, the number waiting stretched to a score, with more coming.

"How did you get out of the house?" one of the men asked another.

"Told my wife I was going over to help you."

Another looked in surprise at the older man behind him. "Papa! What are you doing here?

Jenkins ambled over. "Evening, good men. Can we help you?"

"We're ready," the first in line stated eagerly. "How much will it be?"

Jenkins cocked his head. "How much will what be?"

"I want the blond," said the first in line. "How much?"

"It's the black-haired one for me," stated the second in line.

"Good," said the third, relieved. "That leaves the brown-headed girl. That's the one I wanted."

In Arkan, apparently, theater troupes provided more entertainment that we had realized. Jenkins chuckled. "Ahh. I get you, now. It's the women you're after. And I can understand why."

They nodded in agreement, eyes gleaming with anticipation in the firelight.

"Unfortunately," Jenkins said, "they are not available for business of any sort. We're just a traveling theater, not a brothel. Sorry, men. Have a good night."

They did not like what they heard. "That's not fair. You gonna keep them all for yourselves?" one challenged.

Jenkins smiled. He did love a challenge. "As a matter of fact, we are. Anyone have an objection?" he said pleasantly, placing his hand on the pommel of his sword.

The man looked at the weapon, remembered our demonstration of swordplay during the performance, and shut up. They dispersed, a few grumbling in anger, most just disappointed, like the first. "Damn. I was really looking forward to the blond."

After that we had the women resume precautions. Long shapeless dresses, bonnets, bound hair, and dirt-smudged cheeks made them plain enough for traveling. They kept their hair up during performances, and we substituted much more demure costumes when they assisted on stage. We also moved their witches scene toward the end of the performance, and they stayed in costume for the songfest at the end. That cut down drastically on the lines of eager males, though there were always one or two hopefuls drifting into the camp after each show, who were politely informed that entertainment was over for the night.

Once again we settled into a routine, and I thought things were going quite well. I was pleased with how well everyone in the party was getting along, and told Angela exactly that. She shook her head. "It's not quite that easy, my love. Not everyone gets along, you see."

"Oh?"

"Megan and Beth argued about who was in charge during the journey. Megan didn't want to hide her hair and wear that shapeless dress all the time. So Beth called her a cow and said she didn't have enough sense to—"

"Wait a moment," I interrupted. "*Beth* called *Megan* a cow?"

"Yes, she did. But that's not the point. Beth and Megan don't really care for each other. Megan's a lady, you see, and can't quite forget what Beth was. Beth, on the other hand, regards Megan as a spoiled child with an ill temper. Sometimes it's hard to be friends with both when they're quarreling."

"But they each get along with you."

"Oh, yes. I'm in the middle, neither nobility nor—well, you know."

"And is Regina proving any problem?" Regina had accepted our explanation of the women as troupe members with an uplifted eyebrow, but no other comment. She did her chores.

Angela pondered my question. "Regina says little, but she does her work well, and she has been respectful to us. She knows her place. But I fear Lorich is going to be disappointed once we reach Prescott. She is nice to him, and Lorich feeds off her attention. They are not lovers, I think, though Lorich would like to be. But she is a woman, and he is still a boy."

It was as I'd thought. "Except her reluctance may not only lie in their ages."

"I know," she said with sadness. "He will have to look far for love. And yet it's not impossible. There's always hope. But not with Regina."

It was as Angela had guessed. When we reached the walled town of Prescott, Regina thanked us and made ready to depart, Lorich hovering near her as she collected her tiny bag.

Murdock and Kren were gone, departing camp in great haste after our arrival since Prescott was known to house a brothel or two, and under Jenkins's escort our three women had gone to market. So only I was around to listen to the little drama being played out. I watched from a distance, and I admit to shamelessly eavesdropping on their parting. I have never claimed to be honorable.

The young wizard argued gently, already knowing, I think, that it was impossible. "You could stay with us, Regina. I could ask Pr—uh, my master. I'm sure he'd let you come with us. Please stay."

"I can't," she said, brusquely, sorting through her things.

"Why not?" Lorich asked. "'Why can't you stay with us?"

She turned on him, perhaps with a sharp retort on her lips, but that died as she saw his face. She sighed. "You're making this difficult, Lorich. Listen. I've lived in a village for five years, and I'm sick of it. I'm tired of scrubbing pots and cooking meals. I'm tired of being bored. I'll stay here with my sister for a while, and enjoy everything this town has to offer. Then, I'll go elsewhere. To Trentwood, or Batesville, or maybe even Tulsa. And I'll meet someone with money, and I'll be a woman of position. Yes, a woman of position. I never knew what they meant by that until I married my husband and lived in that miserable little village. I want more."

"We can give you more," Lorich pleaded. "I can give you position. I can."

"Are you rich? Are you a great merchant? Are you traveling with princes? Posh. You're actors. You have nothing but the wagons and the clothes on your back and—" She stopped herself. "I don't want to be cruel. You and your friends have been kind to me, and I appreciate that. You are a nice boy. Almost like a brother to me. I will remember you."

"A brother?" he asked in dismay.

"Good-bye. I am going now. Good-bye."

And with that she took her bag and left behind a crestfallen young man, a misshapen figure who looked after her with realization dawning upon him of the reality of his place in the world. And there was nothing I could do. Neither king nor prince nor commoner can solve the problems of the heart.

I could buy women for Lorich, but I could not buy him love.

5

Crossing Over

"Awaken, oh mighty warriors! You too, great noble one," Kren called out, prodding me with the toe of his boot. "Today, we face another trial. Another challenge on the road of life. Another mountain to climb. Another—"

"Please," I moaned. "No more. You're beginning to sound like Murdock."

"Good Lord, anything but that!" the beastman said.

I pushed Jenkins's foot out of my face and turned over, peering out through the spokes of the wagon wheel at the brightening day. Yes, it was well past dawn. And then I remembered what we had to do today, and my stomach turned queasy.

We had slept in this day, our last in Arkan, for we needn't be at the ferry until midmorning. We wanted to be well-rested and well-prepared when we set out, for we had reached a critical moment—a dangerous moment—in our adventure. All our planning and practice would be put to the test. Today, we would cross the Red River, and pass into Texan. And our lives would be forfeit should we take a misstep.

Murdock and Lorich were already stirring. I jabbed Jenkins. He jerked. "I'm awake. I'm awake." He carefully looked around to make sure none but our party were near. "A royal guard never sleeps."

"For one who never sleeps, you do a lot of snoring," said Kren.

The women had heard our commotion and were already issuing from the wagons, looking—with their brisk efficiency and attentive glances—for all the world as if they had been up for hours. They set to preparing breakfast while the men headed down to the stream. Barely a hundred yards from the wagons it widened into a gentle pool a dozen yards across, ringed with willows and a footpath, before tumbling down to join another stream that flowed into the river.

Apparently, spring came early in southern Arkan, for the inhabitants thought the weather totally normal for the beginning of March. Arriving at the small Arkan border town of Foreman early the day before, we had taken advantage of the warm weather and done our laundry in the pool that afternoon. The women had bathed afterwards while we kept guard from a discreet distance. This morning it was our turn in the pool. Perhaps it was simply the beautiful spring weather, or the realization of what we faced, or simply Murdock trying to relieve our anxiety with a dose of his charm, but for a half hour we frolicked naked in the cold water like a bunch of schoolboys on a holiday. My companions shouted joyfully, swimming, dunking each other, or leaping off the bank into the deepest water with joyful results.

Kren, a grin of delight on his face and his brown pelt dripping with water, crawled out onto the bank and leaped with a boastful yell, a tremendous splash sending waves racing across the pool. We had learned that besides the soles of their feet and the palms of their hands, there were one or two other places on beastmen that the hair does not grow.

Assured by Murdock that no threat was near, Jenkins floated placidly through the waves and then dived beneath the surface to cross to the end of the pool where Lorich tested his breaststroke in the shallows, the hump upon one shoulder rising above the water like an island in the sea. Jenkins corrected the boy's stroke, scanned the surroundings out of habit, and then relaxed and went back to floating. Murdock sent a handful of water splashing over the guardsman and laughed until Kren pulled the wizard's feet out from under and dunked him.

I stood waist deep in the pool and watched them with a deep realization of the moment, not so much unable to share their exuberance as sobered by the fleeting nature of their enjoyment. Had I the power, I might have recorded that instant in time and preserved our swim for eternity, endlessly replaying it with a half dozen other carefully chosen scenes from my life that had struck me similarly. But that was not to be. I could only enjoy the minutes we had, giving thanks that I could take the memory, at least, into whatever dungeons I might enter.

Still, memories only get you so far.

Murdock swam up while Kren and Jenkins engaged in a race across the pool. He stood, revealing his portly torso, old whip scars covering his back, newer burn scars on his sides, the marks of various healed wounds dotting his chest and arms. He looked at my own collection. "Hmm. Well, you've got some ways to go yet. Your back is untouched, and there's barely a mark on your chest. Still, you've made a good start for one so young. Have you noticed how women like such things? Some are impressed, others feel motherly. Either way, it is some small recompense." He looked at the others frolicking, silent for a moment before speaking. "We get few such moments, don't we?"

My companions and I emerged, toweled, dressed, and returned to the smell of coffee brewing over the fire. The women eyed us with smiles as we sat ourselves on a fallen tree trunk that had served this purpose often before. "You were gone so long. But you all seem to have enjoyed yourselves. We could hear you from here."

Murdock folded his hands and assumed a posture of simple innocence. "Ahh, such is the contentment of men when they know loving women are near. Yet it was wise that you did not try to spy upon us while we bathed. The sight of so many handsome men would surely have been more than you could bear."

The women looked at each other and burst out laughing.

He lifted an eyebrow. "Are you laughing with me, or at me?"

Beth put her arm in his. "We are laughing with you . . . and at you."

"It's good that God gave us men," Megan continued, "or there would be no humor in the world."

"You mean you would have nothing to laugh at," Murdock

corrected as he was handed a piece of buttered bread and a mug of steaming coffee. "Laugh if you will. Once more I have fulfilled my purpose by bringing happiness to women."

Jenkins sat himself next to the wizard. "And how many women have you brought happiness to?"

"How many? How many, the good man asks. Does a gardener count the leaves on a tree? Does a farmer count stalks of wheat in his fields?"

Jenkins snorted. "Do we count the words of a wizard?"

The banter ceased as we all worked on mouthfuls of bread. Murdock finished his piece, took a long draught of coffee, and then rubbed the crumbs from his hands. "And now, time to be serious. Finish your breakfast while I talk."

He looked at me, and I nodded approval. Officially, I was the leader of the party, and as such was responsible for making decisions, good or bad. But Murdock handled the day-to-day matters of running the party so well that I rarely exerted my authority. It was a relief to let him take care of such matters, and conform to our false identities as well.

The wizard looked around but there was no one within a hundred yards. Murdock was satisfied. "Tonight, if all goes well, we'll be in Texan. Danger will be with us every day, but perhaps no more than today. We have made mistakes on our journey through Arkan, ranging from simple lapses of memory and slips of the tongue to involving ourselves in local matters."

Lorich hung his head under Murdock's glance.

"But there can be no more mistakes, no more lapses, no more slips. We must play our roles at all times, avoid compromising situations, and allay suspicions. We'll be acting both on and offstage, and our roles offstage will be infinitely more difficult. I would not advise we proceed unless we were ready. I believe we are. You know your roles, and have practiced them well. Unless we are beset by ill luck, our mission will succeed. Anything you want to add, Andrew?" He looked at me and I shook my head. "Then let's break camp, and may the Lord's Blessing be on us all."

Our camp had been perhaps a quarter mile west of Foreman, set into a clearing between a road and a low rise which both followed the curve of the river. We'd given two successful and well-attended performances here the evening before, and it was with some reluctance that we at last got rolling.

The town of Foreman was set upon the edge of an embankment overlooking the north bank of the Red River. Situated opposite it upon the southern bank was the town of New Harbor, one of the eleven walled towns of Texan, its battlements topped by flags and pendants. Below the embankment, on a narrow lip of earth that had been paved with chunks of crete, was the ferry landing.

Murdock and I got off the seat and made sure Megan was out of the wagon box before Jenkins put his foot solidly to the brake as the wagon went down the ramp to the ferry. No room remained on the landing until the ferry was loaded, so the other wagon had to wait at the top of the embankment. Little other traffic was to be seen this late in the morning—which was why we had waited. On foot we followed the first wagon down and Murdock dickered only briefly with the ferryman before agreeing to the standard and fair rate.

It was then that Megan gestured up the embankment at a column of Arkan horsemen which had appeared. "Soldiers are coming," she whispered. "Shouldn't you have warned us?"

Murdock snorted. "No, I shouldn't have warned you. They came through the town, and there are over a thousand people in Foreman. No one could pick them out from the townspeople."

The column halted at the top of the embankment and the two file leaders spurred their horses down the ramp to the landing but remained mounted. Murdock greeted them with a broad smile. "Major Miller! Sergeant Nordstrom! How good to see you again."

Miller nodded. "Mr. Thomas, we meet again. I understand from the townspeople that you're crossing into Texan."

"Yes, that's right. We mentioned to the audience that we would only give two performances before crossing over."

"You won't mind, then, if we conduct a search of your wagons." It was a statement, not a question. Sergeant Nordstrom put up two fingers then pointed to the wagon on the embankment and the one on the landing. Without a word, four horsemen dismounted, two heading for each wagon.

"A search?" Murdock repeated. "Of course we won't mind. We have nothing to hide. Andrew, Klod, open the wagons and assist them in any way you can."

A woman's voice came from behind the wagon. "Careful with that. Don't get it dirty. When you're done, put it back exactly as you found it."

"Yes, ma'am."

"By the way, are your hands clean?"

I think it was Angela.

Miller listened, and then turned his attention to Megan, who stood unobtrusively beside a wheel. The major dismounted. "I'd heard there were women with your theater now. I would like to talk to them."

Murdock gestured, and soon Beth and Angela stood next to Megan, the three falling under the scrutiny of the Arkan major. They were in their demure mode, covered neck to ankle by shapeless dresses, hair hidden under bonnets, faces smudged.

"Three women. You had a fourth with you. The woman who ran away from her husband."

"She left us in Prescott to join her sister—and seek her fortune."

"So I had heard. Good women, take off your bonnets," Miller ordered.

After a brief hesitation, and a glance at Murdock, they uncovered. Jenkins opened his mouth, thought again, and shut it. The three—in uncharacteristic modesty—avoided the Arkan officer's stare. Are all women born actresses? Miller looked at each in turn, then stepped up to Beth, and lifted her chin with a surprisingly gentle hand. He put a finger to her cheek and rubbed. The smudge came off readily.

His eyebrow lifted. "Tell me, good woman, you are with the troupe?"

"Oh, yes sir. We came to join them of our own decision." Beth smiled at him, and for a long moment he was still—beguiled, perhaps—before shaking his head and taking step back.

For a moment I felt empathy for the Arkan. Do women realize the power they have over men?

Major Miller forged onward. "Then you are here of your own free will? The men do not threaten or coerce? You can speak the truth. My soldiers are near, and we'll protect you if need be."

Beth shook her head. "Your concern is most appreciated, sir, but unnecessary." She gestured towards Jenkins. "That one chains me to him, but the chains are around my heart.''

Jenkins puffed up, a pleased grin spreading from ear to ear, and Miller gave him a long look. ''He is a lucky man, then. Very well, the others. Yes, you two. You are here of your free will?''

''Yes, sir,'' Megan and Angela replied in unison.

He asked them more questions about their travels, to which they replied with answers that were generally true. A successful cover story must always use as much of the truth as possible. And the untruths, when necessary, were certainly handled well. The major seemed to accept their stories without hesitation.

Eventually, Sergeant Nordstrom reported to his leader. ''Both wagons checked, sir. The boys couldn't find anything. Just costumes and props and clothes. Most of them we saw before. If they're smuggling something, it's nothing big. Only thing left worth considering is opiates, but no need to smuggle *them* into Texan.''

''Thank you, Sergeant. Get the men mounted.'' Nordstrom bellowed out his order while Miller sauntered up to where Murdock and I stood with Jenkins. He stood close to us, arms folded across his chest, his voice low. ''What a strange traveling theater you have, Mr. Thomas. It appears perfectly normal. Normal, except that you indulge in no smuggling, no crooked games of chance, no stealing, no trade in opium or alcohol, no fights, no seductions, and no ten-penny girls. There is nothing at all to hold you on, nothing that other troupes engage in. Now, why is that?''

Murdock pressed his fingertips together and looked at the sky. ''Is honesty not valued? Is morality now a vice?''

Miller considered him. ''You know, Mr. Thomas, you still remind me of someone. And I've thought of who it is. I'd have to say that you resemble someone I saw in Kenesee when my regiment surrendered. A wizard, I think he was. But that couldn't be, now could it? For what would a famous wizard be doing here in Arkan? And why would he go into Texan? Why?''

My companions and I refrained from looking at each other. Beside me, I could feel Jenkins tensing.

''Well, you're leaving Arkan now, and it's good riddance, for that's one less worry. But it would grieve me to see these good women come to harm. So perhaps a word is in order. They're a suspicious lot over there, if you understand me. They'll be looking for your little "angle," so you might want to have one they can find. A game of chance after your show, for instance. No need to cheat, for they'll think you're doing that anyway when they lose. A few coins to the authorities will restore peace, shall we say? Well, enough said."

The Arkan mounted smoothly, and Murdock stepped up to the horse.

"Major Miller?"

He stared down at the wizard. "Yes?"

"Thank you."

The soldier nodded and was away, his horse scrambling up the ramp, and then the Arkan patrol clattered off, leaving us staring after them. Jenkins shrugged. "I guess he wasn't such a bad sort after all."

The ferryman had come forward as soon as the soldiers departed, and heard Jenkins remark. "Who, Major Miller? He's made a bit of a name for himself in Arkan solving a murder or two up in Trentwood. He's a stern man, God bless him, and no one gets away with anything when he's around. We had some robbers start preying along the coast road when the cavalry was sent north against the horse tribes. But haven't heard any problems since he started patrolling. Lead your team onto the ferry. Slow now. It'll be easier that way."

The wagon was put aboard, the ferryman and his assistant securing the wheels with ropes and hooks while Jenkins and Murdock calmed the horses. Angela would join us on the first trip over. Kren and Lorich would make the second with Megan and Beth. The ferry itself consisted of a low, flat-bottomed boat large enough to take a wagon and team. Two thick ropes were attached to old crete pylons still standing upon either bank, and the ropes fed through large metal staples on each side of the ferry. A ratchet and pulley on either side pulled the rope through the staples, and could thus be used to move the ferry back and forth. When landed at either side, the ropes were made slack, so that they sank even further into the water at center passage and allowed ships to navigate upriver.

The ferryman and his younger assistant each took a side and began to work the device with a steady rhythm that slowly and surely pulled us away from the landing and out into the river. The ferryman chatted away while he worked the handle in smooth circles. "I'm sorry to see you folks leaving Arkan. Saw your show last night. Pretty good one, I gotta say. 'Course it's been a while since any shows came down this way, so we aren't too partic'lar. Still, I'm old enough to have seen a few, and I know a good one when I see it."

The ferryman eyed the ropes and the riverbank. "Keep her steady, boy," he cautioned the younger ferryman, then glanced back at us. "This only gets tricky when it floods. We just draw in the ropes and wait for low water. Other boats go back and forth any time, and that takes care of most traffic that has to get across. Your wagons are a diff'rent matter, you see."

"You have an important job," Murdock stated sincerely.

"I 'preciate that. Don't many think about what we do, nor care. But they should. We're all little cogs in the clock. But if the cog doesn't do its part, the clock ain't gonna work. Trick is, you got to admit you're just a little cog, not a big one."

Murdock gave a slight bow to the ferryman. "The greatest wisdom is often found far from the halls of kings."

The ferryman chuckled. "You seem like nice folks, so I'll tell you somethin' since we're gettin' close t'other bank now. Texan ain't like Arkan. You got to watch yourselves. The border guards know most of the folks we haul over each day, so they don't hassle them too much. But they ain't gonna know you. Unless it's Inspector Smith, slip them one or two five dollar pieces and it'll help."

"Five-dollar pieces?" Angela sputtered in surprise. "Why, that's—that's outrageous."

"I agree with you, ma'am, but that's the way things are over there. I'm not sayin' a coin will get you out of trouble, but it might keep you from gettin' into it. Well, here we are. I'll get your other wagon across quick and safe, never you worry."

The landing was just upstream of the dock area. There was no steep embankment on this side of the river, just a gradual rise of ground toward the walls of the town that were built a hundred feet from the river bank. The space between was filled with one-story wooden structures housing the trade that bustled around the docks. Between the structures a crete-paved road ran along the river bank, while another went from the docks to the gates of the town. Striding down the latter road in silent cadence were four gray-uniformed officials with helmets and swords, followed in step by two shabbily dressed men. The local welcoming committee, no doubt.

We greeted them with our best let's-all-be-friends smiles.

The uniformed officials stopped, a gray-haired one with a badge of position on his collar eyeing us suspiciously. He looked like a brawler. His nose was flattened and pushed to one side, so that he had to breathe through his mouth, which remained open. The man was missing most of his front teeth, and his others looked as if they wouldn't be around much longer either. His rough appearance was tempered only by the fact that he carried a ledger in one hand, and a pen and ink bottle bulged from a pocket. He didn't bother with pleasantries. "Who are you?" he snorted wetly.

"Good morning, good men," Murdock greeted cheerily, clinking two Arkan five dollar pieces in his hand and launching into his story with enthusiasm. "As you can see from the wagon, we are—

"Thomas's Traveling Theater," said the official, squinting a bit but reading clearly and smoothly.

"Our second wagon will be across soon with the other members of our troupe. We've just concluded a successful tour of Arkan, and hope to bring our entertainment to the good people of Texan where ever they may—"

The Inspector cut him off with a wave of the hand, and then poked a finger into Murdock's chest. "No, not that. I want to know who—are—you?"

The wizard's smile never wavered at the evident failure of his charm. He continued to rub the two coins together. "Ahh, I see. How stupid of me. My name is Papa Thomas, the owner of Thomas's Traveling Theater."

"What do you bring from Arkan?"

"Bring? Nothing, sir, except our wagons. They contain only our clothes and items for the shows we give. Nothing more, I can assure you."

"We'll see." He gestured, and the two shabbily dressed men went at the wagon, knocking on the sides, peering underneath and tapping, inspecting the cracks between boards. Satisfied with the outside, they opened the back door, went in, and were soon carrying out every container and drawer in the wagon, laying them in the street, and opening everything for inspection. The uniformed officials began to stir through our possessions with a surprising efficiency, which gave way to silent smirks when they found the women's costumes. The two shabbily-dressed helpers went back inside the empty wagon. Soon more thumps were heard as they searched for secret compartments.

The Inspector waited impatiently throughout, breathing through his open mouth with slurping draughts of air. Murdock continued to rub the coins, now numbering three. He was worried. "Inspector, is this really necessary? I'm sure we can reach some accommodation without spilling all our clothing into the street like this. Here, allow me to make a charitable donation to your favorite cause."

The Inspector stuck out his hand, which was immediately gifted with three five-dollar pieces. He stuck the coins into his pocket without a glance. "Did you see that, men? The outlanders tried to bribe me."

"I saw it," one official nodded. "Doesn't do any good to bribe you, Inspector Smith," he added with a wistful sigh.

An entirely corrupt organization, and we get the only honest official left in town. We were certainly a lucky bunch.

There was a commotion behind the wagon. One of the officials emerged with a small sack. It was the one we kept in the false bottom of the floor. "Isaac found a secret compartment, Inspector. This was in it."

Inspector Smith took the sack and opened it. "Arkan dollars," he said with satisfaction. "Must be hundreds there. What kind of thievery have you done for this, eh?"

Murdock shrugged in exasperation. "Please, sir, be reasonable. That's our money."

"A small fortune, is what it is. I've never seen any travelers with so much money. I think we'd better hold you for questioning. The deputies will find out what you're up to."

I eyed Murdock, who was discreetly judging distances. How could things have gone so disastrously wrong so quickly? To be held for the sheriff could be disastrous. A cursory questioning on the street was one thing. A formal interrogation at the local jail quite another. Even without physical persuasion, an hour or two of questioning would reveal our stories to be riddled with holes.

The ferry, laden with our other wagon and companions, was

halfway across the river and drawing nearer with every second. We would have to dive into the water from the landing and swim for it, then force the ferryman to take us back to Arkan. Murdock and I might have done it, using the advantage of surprise to make our escape good. But what of Angela? Would she react quickly enough? Could she swim in her heavy dress and shoes? For that matter, did she know how to swim? We'd never discussed it.

As if on cue from some invisible stagemaster, Angela glided forward until she stood before Smith, her bonnet off and her hair undone. When had she accomplished that? "The sack holds five hundred and forty-three Arkan dollars to be exact, Inspector Smith," she said, looking down at the short man and giving him a smile that would have lit a darkened room. "I keep the books for our theater. That's our life savings, sir, the profit from years of performing. Where else would we keep it?"

He stared at her. She had his attention, for sure. "I've got my duty," he said reluctantly.

She eyed his ledger. "You are a man of learning. Do you keep account of those who enter?"

He nodded, bemused.

"I keep account of our theater. Here, let me show you." She went to a drawer and returned to stand close beside him. I could see him eye her and swallow as she opened the ledger and explained it to him. "Here, Inspector Smith. You see the dates, and the amounts? Good. Those are all the performances and our moneys from each. In the other column are entries for our expenses, labeled and listed. Please. Take a few minutes to look. I am very proud of my ledger."

The deputies, disbelief on their faces, looked at the book, at Angela, and then at Murdock and me. We shrugged.

Smith took the book from her and began to paw slowly through the pages, studying each, Angela occasionally pointing out interesting entries in the various columns. Were our lives and freedom not at stake, the excitement of examining ledgers might have put us all to sleep. But Smith's skeptical sneer gradually faded to appreciation.

"You keep a very good ledger. I like the way you arranged your expenses and moneys on daily and weekly lines. I tally people and items. Here, look.'' He opened his own ledger and began showing her his entries.

We looked at the deputies. They shrugged.

Finally he closed the book, appreciative comments warming him. Her smile faded into a sad plea. ''Please sir, we've done no harm, and we mean no wrong. Your men have found nothing except that money. There is nothing else. What do you fear from us? Look at our wagons. We can go nowhere unnoticed. We can't run anywhere, nor have we cause. Come to our show tonight, and you'll see we're simple actors trying to make our way in the world, bringing a bit of joy into dull lives.'' Her pleading tone changed, until it was a voice soft with promise. ''After the performance I can answer any questions you might have. Perhaps we might discuss accounts and bookkeeping.''

I refrained from speaking. I knew that come-hither voice, but before it had always been for me alone. Now, showing her wits, she was using it on this mangle-faced Texan. And possibly saving our lives in the process. I was quite proud of her.

The Texan should have known better, really. And yet, when the hunger and loneliness grow too great, any man can watch his good sense disappear like mist in the sun. Inspector Smith's eyebrows uncurled and the frown faded, revealing a troubled expression. He swallowed and nodded. ''All right. You made your point. You can go after we search the other wagon. If we don't find anything, I'll give you a document of entry. But I'll be at that show tonight. I'll be watching. Remember that.''

Angela smiled. ''Of course, you will. And I'll be looking for you. Thank you, Inspector.''

''Indeed,'' Murdock added. ''Our thanks to you, Inspector. We trust you'll enjoy our entertainment. Ah, here is the ferry with our other wagon.'' He stood placidly beside me and whispered from the side of his mouth. ''Lord, that was close. I thought we'd have to swim for it.''

''We're fine for now,'' I responded in a like voice. ''But what about tonight?''

Yes, what would we do—what would I do—when the Texan came for Angela?

I would have to think about that.

TEXAN

1

Solving Problems

Inspector Smith was kind enough to recommend that we set up camp on the green just outside the northwest gate, although the recommendation had the tone of an order and the spot was conveniently under the sharp eyes of the gate watch. We did as we were told.

Our site was immediately beset by several score of children, most wearing clothes appropriate for commoners of the merchant, artisan, and laborer classes. However, too many wore the filthy rags of gutter rats, and so we left our props safely locked inside the wagons while Murdock and Jenkins shooed them away, establishing with a ball of string and a few sticks the boundary of our camp, after which Jenkins informed the children one and all that to cross the string was to invite death, or at least a good beating.

They believed him.

While our companions set up camp, I grabbed Angela's hand and led her around the wagon to a quiet spot just within the boundary string. I took her other hand and held both in mine. That way, she couldn't hit me.

I looked at her sternly. "Angela, that was a stupid thing to do."

She lifted an eyebrow. "Oh, was it? The troupe was in danger. I thought it was quite the right thing to do."

"The right thing? And just what do you think will happen when Inspector Smith comes here this evening?"

"I shall go with him."

That stopped me. "You—you will?"

She sighed. "What choice do I have?"

She was right. If it was reasonable for us to risk our lives on this quest, then it was reasonable for her to risk her honor. She could give the mangle-face company, yet refuse companionship—though that would be risking his displeasure still again. No, it made sense for her to do whatever was necessary. And yet. And yet . . .

"I won't let you go with him," I objected, totally without logic.

And then the corners of her mouth turned upward, and a smile burst forth upon me with all its dazzling power. "You would sacrifice all for me," she murmured with satisfaction, and shaking loose of my grip took my face into her hands. "No woman could ask for more."

"Well, it's just—uh. . . ."

She traced the line of my brow with her fingers. "I know you don't like it, nor do I. But if it comes to it, I will do what I must to save us, and especially to save you. I would gladly die to keep you safe, my love. Never forget that." She gave me a long, light kiss which earned a roar of giggles and snickers from the children clustered watchfully beyond the string, and then dropped her hands and hurried back around the wagon.

I stood staring after her, and silently cursed Robert for getting me into this mess. The children hooted and I glared at them. They stopped laughing.

There were eleven Great Landholders in Texan, each situated near a walled town, each dominating the smaller landholders and running the affairs of the region, their power balanced only by local officials—regimental commanders, mayors, sheriffs, and border guards—who reported directly to the state of Texan. The state, of course, was the President of Texan, General Jack Murphy.

The Great Landholder for New Harbor and its surroundings was a Mr. Lyle Parsons, whose home—or hacienda, as the Texans called a home of such size—was located a mile outside of town. This was apparently the norm among the largest landholders, who were the equivalent of our own nobles in power and prestige. Rather than have a castle in or adjacent to the town, the landholders apparently felt better building their holds separate from such habitations. Perhaps this arrangement was dictated by an old distrust of the landholders for their own people. Whether this separation of strong points strengthened or weakened them against an invader, I leave to the armchair strategists.

Murdock and I would have gone to Landholder Parsons's estate once camp was established, but the constant gaze of the gate guard precluded us from such a venture. We were still not done with Inspector Smith, and wished to give him no excuse for further suspicion. We stayed at the camp, and for a coin sent a message to the landholder with an arranged word to reveal our identities in an innocent offer to perform at his hacienda. A leisurely meal around the campfire followed. And soon after that, it was time to entertain the folk of New Harbor, who were rapidly collecting upon the green for a mid-afternoon performance.

Angela, Megan and Beth made their way through the crowd, seating those in front rows for two pennies, and others behind for a penny. Most people brought blankets or sacks to sit upon, though the green was dry and grassed. There was quite a crowd, for we had over two hundred paying members in the audience, as well as a few dozen gutter rats we allowed to sit on the sides. The rats had a partially obstructed view that was not at all bad, considering they were watching for free.

Our first performance went well, as did our second in the late afternoon, though between the acts of the latter I noted Inspector Smith standing silently at the back of the crowd, watching intently. The audience perhaps most enjoyed our sing-along, bellowing out "Red River Valley" and "Deep In the Heart of Texan" with great enthusiasm before giving us a final, thunderous round of applause. Afterwards, many surged up to congratulate us and bask in the attention of these larger-than-life players who had held there rapt attention for the last hour or more. They had to wait, for we were busy stuffing away the props before the gutter rats got them.

Amidst all this I saw Inspector Smith approach Angela, who had just changed into her normal street clothes. I watched them together, watched some more, and tried to make up my mind about what to do.

Murdock approached in the company of a dark-skinned, middle-aged man. "Andrew, my son. I'd like you to meet Mr. James Montrose, the steward for the Great Landholder of this area. The Landholder would like us to come out and visit him now in order to discuss a private performance at his estate.

I've told Steward Montrose we can leave immediately, and he has a carriage waiting. Do you see any problems with that?''

I looked over the wizard's shoulder, met Angela's glance, and we stared at each other across the space. Inspector Smith looked up, followed her eyes, and saw me staring back. I looked at him and smiled bleakly. His expression, unreadable, did not change. Angela extended her hand to take his arm and, chattering gaily all the while, began to lead him gently toward the town gates. I saw his battered face one more time as he looked back at me, and then he disappeared with her into the town.

''Andrew? Andrew?'' It was Murdock. Talking to me.

''Oh, yes. Sorry.''

His voice was not unsympathetic. ''I know you have some things on your mind right now, but I think this is an opportunity we cannot afford to miss, wouldn't you say?''

I ground my teeth. ''To see the Landholder? Yes. Quite the opportunity. Quite.''

The carriage turned out to be merely an open wagon with benches pulled by a single team. Steward Montrose gestured to the second seat. ''Your pardon. I could not use the carriage for it is reserved by the Landholder. For distinguished guests only.'' The last he stated with a laugh and a shake of his head. Murdock and I clambered up, after which he mounted the front seat and took the reins. ''It's less than two miles. We'll be there within a few minutes.'' With a snap of the whip we were off through the twilight.

It was not yet dusk. The way was generally flat, with only the occasional gentle roll of ground; we passed by both fenced pastures and woods. Beyond the town, the land flattened out into large, cultivated fields divided by lines of trees and brush that followed the meandering courses of small streams.

We traveled without a word passing between us, and soon a stone wall could be seen looming in the midst of the fields to our left: the estate. The steward turned onto a lane paved with chunks of crete, and then we were passing through the gates of the wall and into a courtyard. The outer stone wall was only ten feet high, except at the four corners where round towers rose twenty feet into the air. The wall formed almost a perfect square enclosing the buildings, which were a cluster of stables and cottages and storage around a larger two-story house. Almost all the buildings were made of timber, though such material must have been expensive here—we had seen ample pine, but other types of trees were less plentiful. Against one side of the landholder's house was a square tower perhaps twenty feet on a side and thirty feet in height, made of crete rather than stone, the final redoubt in case attackers carried the outer walls. The manor did not seem the most formidable of bastions.

A slave scurried up out of the shadows to see to the horses, while other slaves closed the gates behind us. Steward Montrose led us inside the house to a small but comfortable waiting room. "Please, make yourselves comfortable and I'll be right back."

Murdock touched his ear, pointed at a wall, and gestured for silence before seating himself in a comfortable chair. He folded his hands across his lap and closed his eyes as if he were taking a nap in the safety of Kenesee. My nerves were wrought enough for both of us. I lit my pipe and slowly paced up and down the room, puffing in the tobacco and thinking of soldiers bursting in and making us prisoners. Nothing like a little danger to take the mind off women.

Steward Montrose returned shortly and sat down, quite unperturbed. "Landholder Parsons has been informed that you've arrived. He will be here after he has kept you waiting a sufficient time. It would not be seemly for him to come too quickly. Illustrious visitors you may be, but to others you're just performers. Oh yes, we can talk safely here. No one can overhear."

Murdock raised an eyebrow. "Illustrious visitors? You think we're more than just poor actors?"

"Oh come now, gentlemen. Your secret is safe with me, Wizard Murdock. It *is* Wizard Murdock, I trust?"

Murdock made a decision, and nodded. "You have me."

"Excellent. I was told you would probably accompany the Prince. But first, gentlemen, I know that there are two signs I must see to confirm your identities." He looked at me. "If you would, sir."

I parted my beard so that he could see the scar.

The steward nodded. "And the other?"

I made ready to drop my pants.

"Ahem. Quite all right. I've seen enough. So this is Prince Arn, the Hero of Kenesee."

"Some call him that. We call him Chimney."

The steward was puzzled for a moment, and then understanding dawned as the smoke swirled about me. "I see, it's a joke. Well, we have our smokers too, only they puff fouler stuff than tobacco."

Murdock grimaced. "The opiate."

Steward Montrose nodded. "Aye. It took my younger brother years ago. He went to town, bored with life as the second son of a steward. And soon a full pipe in the opiate house was all he cared about."

"There is a saying," Murdock ruminated. "The first two times, you take it. The third time, it takes you."

"Aye, Wizard Murdock, there is great truth in that old saying. It killed my brother, eventually. It kills all of them. And our President Murphy allows it to go on. He even has a hand in it, you know. Opiates form a very lucrative trade."

"Ahh," Murdock noted the revelation. "And that is the reason you have little love for General Murphy."

"That is one reason, but not the greatest."

"Slavery?"

"No. I have had doubts about men owning men. Still, it would take long to change, and many hold it their right to own slaves."

"So. Does Landholder Parsons share your feelings?"

"We are of like mind on the matter of General Murphy," the steward replied grimly. "He lost his eldest son at the battle of Lexington. And . . . I lost mine."

"I'm sorry," Murdock stated sincerely.

"So am I," the steward replied. "But it was our fault. We tolerated Murphy because he fed our greed. We were caught up in running the estate and gaining land and making money. And then you hear your child is dead, and nothing else matters, after all. But too late we learn."

The door opened and Steward Montrose rose from his seat, as did Murdock and I. A short man entered, even darker-skinned than the steward, with a crinkly gray fringe of hair marking him a few years older than his steward. The man carefully closed the door behind him. There was a resemblance between landholder and steward. A shared ancestor, perhaps.

"I am Parsons," stated the landholder as he shook hands with a dignity that bordered on pomposity.

The steward introduced Murdock first, since the landholder

already held his hand. "This is Wizard Desjardins Murdock, advisor to King Robert Brant. And this," he added with a verbal flourish, "is Arn of Kenesee."

Arn of Kenesee. That was all. Arn of Kenesee, as if no other title were necessary. If this kept up, it would soon be The Great Arn, or perhaps *The* Arn, or just ARN.

Idiocy. It made me angry.

"You saw the mark?" Landholder Parsons asked doubtfully, seeking reassurance.

"I know it's there, sir. And the scar. Would you like to see?"

"No need, no need." The landholder waved away the thought, and seated himself in a chair that the steward brought up. "Do sit down, gentlemen," he invited once he was himself settled.

Even were I not a prince, courtesy might have seen the guests seated first. But what else could you expect in Texan?

Parsons conducted himself with imperious calm. "So. This is Prince Arn. So young. So young. And yet, the one who defeated the Army of the Alliance. The one who killed our sons."

Well. There wasn't much to say to that.

He sighed and shook his head. "No use lamenting. No use. On to matters before us. I know of your purpose. Landholder Mason visited us."

Mason? Oh, yes, Peter Mason, who'd started this all by seeking us out in Kingsport with the general's senior aide, Chalmers.

Parsons continued. "Mason stated that you would come to us, and bring help when needed. And now you are here, and that says much for your courage and resolve. We will need such qualities, I fear. I do not mind admitting that I've wavered about what to do. No, not about General Murphy. He should be removed from power. That need is clear. I wonder about our chance of success. Should we fail, not only would our own lives be forfeit, but our loved ones would be killed or thrown into the slave pens. If it comes to revolt, we risk all. All. . . ."

He fell silent for a long moment before continuing. "Well, you are here. What do you have to say? What do you have to offer?"

Murdock had rehearsed me enough on those questions. I spoke with little difficulty. "Landholder Parsons, I represent my brother, King Robert, and the kingdom of Kenesee. We are committed to the removal of General Murphy because of the ill he has brought upon Texan. We are committed to the freeing of Texan from his tyranny, and the resumption of friendship with your people."

Actually, I didn't care a penny for the Texans or their friendship. But the right words are important at such times, empty or not. Who knows, he might even have believed me.

"All well and good," he replied. "But what support will Kenesee offer when the regiments march? How many besides Prince Scar will join us on the battlefield?"

"As many men as ships can bear," Murdock stated before I could speak. "King Robert will not deny his brother the means of victory—"

"That is well," the landholder interrupted with satisfaction.

Murdock nodded. "But such strength as we extend is to aid you in your victory, not our own. Texans must provide the army of revolt. Kenesee will provide the margin for success. We cannot do what Texans will not do for themselves."

"Yes, I think you are right," Parsons agreed. "I think it will happen. You will meet the eleven Great Landholders at the Gathering in May?"

"That's why we've come," I stated truthfully. "Landholder Mason told us of those he thought safe to approach. I will visit each of those, so that you will go to the Gathering confident of our resolve and committed to the cause. Your name is one of three he gave us, and the first we have come to."

"And the other names are Landholder Fields of Tyler and Landholder Martinez of Cheraco, are they not? Strange. Cheraco, Fields, and I have never gotten along very well, and yet on this matter, we agree. Mason and we see what must be done," Parsons said. "But the other landholders waver, afraid to choose sides lest they choose wrong."

"And that," Murdock affirmed, "is why we are here. To rally the landholders."

"And the military commanders," I added as a thought came into my mind. "Which raises a question. There is an infantry regiment headquartered in New Harbor, I believe? Is the commander sympathetic to your cause?"

The steward grinned. "Oh, yes. Most sympathetic."

"Then shouldn't he be here too?"

"He is here," the landholder stated. "My steward is colonel of the Fourteenth Regiment, appointed by General Murphy himself, as are all the regimental commanders. For Murphy, to criticize is to be disloyal. He could not imagine that my steward Montrose could give voice to criticism and still be a loyal subordinate. Murphy assumed he would have another set of eyes spying for him within my house."

Montrose nodded. "He has seen us quarrel, and assumed I thought ill of the Landholder. He did not realize we quarrel about most things. His mistake. I will lead the regiment against him, and welcome the day. My only regret is that Texan blood will be spilled on both sides of the battlefield, when we have already lost so many. There are only eleven infantry regiments left to us, as you probably know."

We knew, indeed. The other eleven had been destroyed in Kenesee.

We discussed plans for the Gathering and the rebellion, and then after more handshakes we slipped out into the courtyard. Steward Montrose took us back to town, halting the wagon in the darkness on the far edge of the green, where neither comrade nor gatekeeper nor guard could overhear our whispers. We got down, and he shook our hands from his seat. "You can trust Mr. Parsons. Whatever his faults, his word is his bond."

"That's good to know," Murdock stated.

"I'm sorry you'll have to waste a day here just to give a performance at the manor tomorrow night, but not doing so would be too hard to explain. We may not have an opportunity to talk again. May God watch over you."

"And over you," Murdock responded. "Tell me. Are all the stewards so capable?"

The man paused in the lamplight. "You are very kind. I have had no higher praise. But to answer truthfully, no, not all are capable. Nor can all be trusted. My Landholder and I are related by blood. Our great-grandfather is the same man. His grandfather was a son by marriage. Mine was a son by lust. Our family has held the title of steward ever since, father to son. And we have served faithfully, regardless of the man we served, be he wise man or fool. In some generations, our role has been—how shall I put this—more important, let us say, than at others.''

''And is the role more important now?''

He smiled, and climbed back onto the wagon seat. ''Our prayers go with you. Until we meet again.''

After the steward had driven off, we crossed the green in silence. The crowds were gone, and even the games of chance that we'd planned were over. Blanket-wrapped figures lay beneath the wagons, and only Jenkins was awake, pacing around the wagons in a slow amble, watching everything. He faced us as we approached, and we reassured him that all had gone well. Then I raised my own concern.

''Has Angela returned?''

''Yes, sir, she did. She's in the second wagon, all alone.''

I did not like that answer. Normally she and Megan shared a wagon. ''Is she all right? Did she get hurt?''

''No, sir, nothing like that. She came back safe and sound perhaps an hour ago. But we thought maybe she'd—maybe you both—would like a little privacy, after all.''

I climbed into the wagon box and shut the door quietly, trying not to wake her. But the voice, drowsy, came out of the darkness as soon as I'd lain in the empty bunk. ''Is it you?''

I extended my hand and it found hers despite the gloom. ''It's me.''

The bedding rustled as she stretched and turned. ''Are you all right? Did things go well at the Landholder's?''

''Aye. I'm well, and things went as we'd hoped. And for you?''

She squeezed my hand. ''I'm well.''

''Will Inspector Smith leave us in peace now?''

''Inspector Smith won't give us any more problems. He said we could go wherever we wanted tomorrow.''

''That's very good,'' I stated softly.

''Yes, it is, isn't it?'' I gave no response, and after a time she spoke again. ''Do you—do you have any questions you want to ask?''

''You did what you had to do,'' I said slowly, trying to keep the thickness out of my voice. ''Now you're here. You're safe. That's all that matters.''

"All right."

The silence stretched on. I released her hand. But there was one thing more to say. "Angela?"

"Yes, my love?"

"No one else can say it, but—thank you. For doing that. For all of us."

I heard her lift her head. "Would you like to come into my bunk for a little while?" she asked.

She could not see me shake my head. "I'm a bit tired tonight. Perhaps it would be better if we just slept."

"Yes. Perhaps."

I lay staring into the darkness.

"Arn?"

"You shouldn't use my name," I corrected her. "It's Andrew for now."

There was another rustle, and then I could feel her breath on my cheek. "Arn," she whispered, "Nothing happened. I didn't do anything. Inspector Smith didn't do anything."

"Hmmm?"

She went on in anxious little breaths. "He asked me if I had a lover, and I told him. He asked me how I felt about you, and I told him that, too. He said he would not take what belonged to another. After that, all he wanted to do was talk, Arn. Just talk. And I listened. He was very nice, actually, but very lonely, and very sad, like Lorich. Do you hear me, my love? Do you believe me?"

For reply, I dragged her down beside me, amazed again how two people can squeeze into a narrow bunk. Hopefully, the creaking of the wagon springs did not wake the others. And a long time later she got back into her own bunk and we slept.

But I never did answer her last question. Did I believe her? I thought about it some more, and realized it didn't matter. Whatever happened or didn't happen, she had done it for me. And that was what mattered.

And with that, the petty jealousies within quieted enough that I was able to sleep, and I dreamed of Inspector Smith with a noose around his neck and hanging from the branch of a large tree.

He swung quite nicely.

2

Two Men and a Girl

The performances at Landholder Parsons's estate went well, though Angela insisted he pay us a good fee before we went onstage, which he did with a laugh of approval. We did the first performance inside the hacienda for the household, and the second for the field hands and slaves in one of the barns. The second was won during Angela's negotiations. Parson could not understand why he should have to pay for the slaves' entertainment, but was buried in an analysis of the cost-effectiveness of having two performances for a single fee.

It was quite a study in contrasts. The household was comfortably arrayed in rich clothes, family and servants alike used to the comfort of the hacienda. The field hands and slaves wore rough working clothes, and the latter poor devils each wore a leather-wound ankle iron in addition, men, women, and children, all. We had seen slaves in the streets these last two days. But to see dozens all assembled with the proof of their position displayed below ragged pants and skirts gave us pause.

"Get used to it," Murdock warned. "You'll see some unfortunate things in Texan, and we can't do anything about them."

"Not yet," Kren promised.

The morning after our performances we left the Parsons hacienda and headed south along the Coast Road, making six or eight miles and more a day and giving our usual performances without much incident.

Oh, we were watched, wherever we went. And we were questioned. And there was danger, real danger, each and every time we were approached by a suspicious Texan. And almost always there was the coin pressed into a waiting hand. Yet, after a time the inquiries became a part of the routine of each day, a repetition of questions and answers that we knew well, though complacency could easily lull us into a mistake.

We noticed that our improbable, slow-moving theater garnered less suspicion than other strangers encountered. For example, in one town we saw a newly-arrived peddler hauled off to a cell. He couldn't remember the name of the village he'd slept in the night before. The idea of traveling as a road show had been a good one. Merchant disguises would not have gotten us far in Texan.

Three weeks after leaving New Harbor we arrived at Tyler, a walled town situated on the edge of a small, natural bay. The bay was really quite stunning, particularly at dawn. More important to us than natural beauty was its use. Tyler was home port for the Texan Navy, and a half dozen ships floated at anchor or in their docks. Those ships would have to be dealt with before any troops could land from Kenesee.

We were allowed to set up camp at the end of a street that backed onto the wall of the town, and enjoyed two successful performances that evening. The next morning Murdock and I went out the north gate on our way to visit the Great Landholder of the area. There was a scattering of buildings along the road outside the gate, with one wide building surrounded by open fields with cut grasses. As we came closer I saw that what I had taken for the side of a building was actually a solid-faced, eight-foot-tall wooden fence surrounding an area about the size of a farmyard. It certainly smelled like a farmyard—or perhaps more accurately, like a latrine.

"What is that?" I asked.

"Can't you guess?" he asked, frowning at the structure as we approached.

And then I saw the sign over the gate.

SHAW'S SLAVES

The Finest Human Property

Field Hands. House Servants. Breeding Stock.

Healthy. Skilled. Obedient.

Boarding and Training at Reasonable Rates

"A slave pen?"

Murdock nodded pensively. "A slave pen. Traders keep their stock there until it's sold at market."

"Uh, is this where you—that is, were you held. . . ."

"In this one? No, not here. Not here."

Murdock suddenly cocked his head and looked up, as if he were sniffing the air.

"Yes," I agreed. "It does smell bad."

He shook his head. "No, not that. I thought I felt a—well, nothing." But he strode forward with new purpose, and turned in at the gateway of the enclosure. The gate of the pen was closed, and a guard stood on duty outside with short sword at his waist, while a bow and quiver leaned handily against the wood enclosure. Murdock nodded to the guard and gestured at the gate. "May I take a look?"

The guard nodded in return. "Sure. Look all ya' want."

We stepped up together and peered through the slots. Several wooden shacks surrounded a central yard. From the yard came squeals of delight, a noise that must have been heard rarely from such a place. A half dozen children from perhaps six to sixteen stood together in the middle of the compound, naked except for the inevitable ankle iron and ring, screaming with pleasure while a spray of water was pumped over them and they scrubbed themselves with bare hands. The chance to wash, even under such circumstances, was apparently a rare treat. I tore my eyes away from one promising sixteen-year-old female, and took in the rest of the yard. A dozen men, dusty in their ragged clothes, stood on one side, shackled together by a chain and waiting their turn under the water. On the other side a like number of women, still wet, were putting on clean white cotton dresses. One man handled the hose and another pumped from a trough, both of them wearing ankle irons. Four guards with short spears, free men, stood watching the females with interest.

The gate guard jabbered away while we peered through the slats. "There's a couple a' real good 'uns in the lot, if you're interested in buyin'. We're cleanin' them up for the market today. Auction'll be startin' noon in the market plaza."

Murdock stepped back from the gate. "You've been very helpful. Perhaps I'll go to it."

"You won't be sorry," said the guard. "Mr. Shaw ain't got the most, but he's got the best."

It was always good to see such loyalty to an employer.

"Well, judging by the quality of his guards," Murdock stated carefully, "I certainly know what to expect."

The man beamed. "Thankee, sir. Glad I could help ya'."

Our reason for visiting the estate of Mr. Fields, Great Landholder of Tyler, was, ostensibly, to offer him, for the right price, a performance at his estate. Mr. Fields didn't know we had arrived yet, and the pilgrimage to his estate by entertainers would have been the norm. His manor was a few miles outside the town and had a similar layout to the manor of Mr. Parsons, except it was sited to take advantage of a creek running around the outer wall, gaining the benefit of a natural, moatlike obstacle to any attacker.

Landholder Fields was a white-haired old man who walked stooped over his cane and snapped at slaves, servants, and family with equal enthusiasm. The meeting went well, and it quickly became clear, as we discussed the late war, that the refined Landholder Fields had a deep loathing for crude General Murphy. Mr. Fields was interested in discussing the tactics and strategy of the struggle, and bemoaned the fate of the Texan army in Kenesee. After an hour of discussion we got down to particulars, and he readily agreed to our plan. He would openly state his support of the rebellion when the Great Landholders met with us at the Gathering in Dallas. But he had a warning.

"Yes, you have my support, and I will so state it at the Gathering. But only if you're sure about support from Kenesee. Your forces will be landing immediately after?"

I shrugged. "Your meeting is scheduled to begin May fifteenth and end May eighteenth. The troops will be landing here at that time. More, I will not tell you, nor anyone."

He tapped the tip of his cane on the floor stones. "You are cautious. That's good. There will be turmoil and quavering. The knowledge that your troops are about to arrive will fortify the timid. And where will you go after the meeting?"

"To the coast, to meet the forces after they land."

He nodded again. "And see you do. It's going to be a very dangerous and confused fortnight after we declare our loyalties. You won't be meeting with all eleven Great Landholders, you know. Only the two or three others that Mason, Parsons, and I think might join us. But once they all know what's happening, the chance of betrayal will go up with every day that goes by. Remember that, Prince Arn, and keep yourself safe. If we lose you, we lose the rebellion."

Murdock and I thought about that. He thought about losing the rebellion, and I thought about losing me.

"I recommend you take the eastern road to Tyler after the Gathering. I can get you to the coast safely. I'll have some of my personal guards waiting with horses outside Dallas. In case you're pursued, they'll provide the chance of escape."

And so our planning was conducted.

Mr. Fields provided a wagon to drive us back to town, which was fortuitous since the morning had turned distinctly warm, and another sweaty walk back through the dust of the road was not something I looked forward to. The driver dropped us at the town gates, we threaded our way through the streets without incident, and at last found ourselves back at our wagons parked beneath the wall of the town. The women—watched over by Jenkins—were at the market plaza buying supplies. Only Kren and Lorich were there to greet us.

Murdock told them our plans. "We'll break camp in early afternoon in order to go out to Landholder Field's estate. We'll be giving a performance for him at his manor this evening."

"So, I take it all went well?" Kren asked, sweating inside his cap. Yes, he could have taken it off, for many of the townspeople had already seen him in all his glory, though whether they considered him a real beastman or not was debatable. But as Angela had pointed out to him, there was no reason to give them a free show, and we had enough gutter rats and town children hanging around as it was.

"All went well," Murdock assured him. "And I'm for taking a walk down to the market place too. A bit of business might be done."

"May I come too, Master?" Lorich asked eagerly

"Yes, that might be a good idea," Murdock agreed, rubbing his chin thoughtfully. "Do you mind, oh furry one?"

Kren smiled tolerantly at the younger wizard before replying to Murdock. "I can watch the wagons alone, if need be. But perhaps Andrew will keep me company."

"Sorry," I responded. "I need to go, too. Tobacco's running low."

"All right," said Kren. "I'll stay the watch, abandoned and alone. Just tell everyone to get back soon. I'm getting hungry."

"It's almost noon. We won't be long, Klod."

The beastman winced.

The market plaza was still full with the Saturday rush: farmers, traders, and craftsmen from countryside and town hawking their wares over the steady mutter of business and pleasure. I was hoping to spot Jenkins and the women, but could not find them in the swirling crowds of marketgoers. Men, women, and children, in families and alone, all mumbled and chattered and shouted as they made their way up and down the rows formed by the carts and displays of the vendors.

Many of the wives had completed their shopping for bread and cheese and vegetables, but lingered with their little ones to examine metal pots and pans, bolts of cloth, wood and leather goods, and a hundred other items. Their menfolk accompanied them, or puddled into little groups to chat about the local news, or share the latest gossip, or even discuss the wonderful performances of the night before by Thomas's Traveling Theater.

A glorious spring day at Saturday market.

In one corner of the plaza a farrier had set up in front of a blacksmith's shop, and was busily hammering shoes onto a horse. In another corner, a horse trader displayed a line of saddle horses to a buyer. In a third corner was a puppet show. And in the last corner, a small platform had been taken over as an auction block. Upon it stood two men, and a crowd composed mostly of men was gathering around. One of the two on the platform was well-dressed, and telling a joke to the audience to put them in the mood. The other was light haired and stocky, a rough-featured man in his thirties dressed in dark pants and loose white shirt. On his feet he wore only sandals, while from his ankle iron a chain ran to the hand of a guard.

I recognized him from earlier that morning. He was one of

those we'd seen waiting to wash inside the pen.

The slave auction had begun.

Murdock tapped Lorich on the shoulder and spoke softly so that others couldn't hear. "Do you feel it?"

"Feel it?" Lorich replied, puzzled.

Murdock frowned. "It's one thing to block things out. It's another to close yourself off entirely. That could be dangerous. The trick is to find the middle ground."

"Yes, Master."

"Extend yourself," the wizard retorted impatiently. "Reach out. Feel."

Lorich did not move. "I don't—oh, my. Yes. I feel it."

"You should," Murdock chastised him. "It's like a beacon. But what is it?"

"I think . . . I think it's fear."

"Very good. You're learning. Now, where is it coming from?"

Lorich paused, rotating his head slowly left, and then right. "Over there. Over there, Master."

"Exactly right," stated Murdock, satisfied at last. "Let's go over there."

Lorich was not the only one to be puzzled. But I kept my peace and followed as Murdock threaded his way through the citizenry toward the corner of the square where the auction was underway. Murdock's face became grimmer as we approached the corner.

The auctioneer was in the middle of his sale now, standing next to the slave and taking bids from the crowd. He was quite good at his business.

"I have twenty dollars on this fine male specimen. Twenty dollars. Who will make it twenty-one? Twenty-one? My good people! Are you going to let this bargain go by? Look at those shoulders. Look at that neck. This man was born for labor. He has all his teeth and no diseases. A perfect field hand, he'll give you a full day without complaint, seven days a week. Who'll give me twenty-five?"

The slave looked out over the heads of the crowd, listening to the auctioneer without reaction, only an unchanging, sullen look upon his face.

He went for twenty to a merchant who smiled in satisfaction.

"You'll have trouble with that one," an onlooker predicted to the buyer.

The merchant shook his head, the smile broadening. "I'll beat that out of him, soon enough," he stated with certainty, and went up to pay for his new property.

The two magicians stopped and conferred on the fringes of the throng that surrounded the auction block. Lorich pointed toward it. Murdock nodded, and they pushed forward, not in the direction Lorich had pointed, but at a right angle through the crowd. If I didn't know better, I would have sworn they were taking sightings in order to triangulate, as one might do in the woods when marking a landmark to determine a location.

Maybe they were.

The two stopped again, took another sighting, and conferred. "It's from them," Murdock stated, pointing through the crowd at the slaves clustered together in their chains behind the platform.

"Yes, you're right," Lorich agreed. "But which one?"

"Which one what?" I asked.

Murdock grabbed Lorich's arm and spoke into his ear. "Go back to the wagons. You know where the money is kept? Good. Bring me a full purse. Quickly now."

"A full purse, quickly. Yes, Master." His head bobbing awkwardly among the other people, Lorich limped off through the crowd.

I stared at Murdock. "Just what is going on?"

Murdock looked smug. "I'm going to buy a slave."

My mouth fell open. "You?"

"Yes."

"Buy a slave?"

"Yes."

"But why in the world would you of all people—"

"My dear . . . SON. Don't be so difficult. Think. Think a moment."

I thought. Inspiration burst upon me. "Ohhhh. You want a woman for your plaything."

"No, I do not want a woman for my plaything. Be quiet now and watch."

The next slave up on the block was a young woman, olive-skinned, dark haired, and well-formed. She wasn't particularly pretty, nor busty, but she enjoyed a narrow waist above good hips and legs, as her dress showed to advantage.

"Is that the one?" I asked.

"No," he replied carefully. "Not her."

Someone slipped up between us. It was Jenkins. "The women are headed back to the wagons. Guess who we saw."

"Not now," I mumbled to him.

"Not now?" He looked around and frowned. "What are you two doing here?"

I shrugged. "We're going to buy a slave."

His mouth fell open. "Us?"

"Yes."

"Buy a slave?"

"Be quiet," Murdock ordered.

The auctioneer was finishing his warm-up. "And there you have her background, good men and women. A fine, healthy woman taken from Kenesee, and less than a year wearing the iron." He rattled her chain for emphasis. "You can take her home to kitchen or field, and find her skilled at the homely tasks yet strong enough to pitch hay at the harvest. A fine cook and a fine bedwarmer she'll be. And now, who'll start the bidding at twenty dollars. Twenty dollars for this woman."

Several in the crowd made bids, each raising the other by a dollar or two. But at last the auctioneer ended up with two men still in the contest, one of middle-age and in common cloth, the other in his twenties and well dressed. I didn't like the look of the young one. There was something cold and ominous in his smile as he stared at the woman. He reminded me of me.

Jenkins nudged my arm. "The auctioneer said she's a Kenesee woman," he muttered out of the side of his mouth.

"That's right," I admitted sourly.

"Are we going to buy her?"

Murdock shook his head. "Sorry, we can't help her."

"But—"

The magician gave Jenkins a single hard look, and Jenkins shut up in surprise.

"I have a bid of thirty," the auctioneer announced. "Do I have thirty-five?" The older bidder looked pained, and did not respond. The auctioneer looked at him expectantly. "Do I have thirty-two? Thirty-two?" Reluctantly, the middle-aged bidder put up a hand. "I have thirty-two," the auctioneer sang out immediately. "Do I have thirty-five?" Smirking, the young one put up a hand. "I have thirty-five. Thirty-five. Do I have forty? Forty?"

The older man shook his head no and turned away.

"I have thirty-five. Going for thirty-five. Going for thirty-five. Gone for thirty-five dollars to Mr. Hardiman," concluded the auctioneer. With cool arrogance the young buyer went up to pay for and gather his purchase.

Some people, you just want to hit.

"I'll remember his name," Jenkins whispered ominously.

Within a minute or two the third piece of merchandise mounted the block. It was a skinny girl of perhaps eight, with tanned skin and stringy blond hair, unexceptional to all outward appearances.

As she stepped onto the platform, Murdock gave a groan. "On the block already. Just our luck."

"What's wrong?" I asked.

"It's her. She's the one."

"You're sure?"

"Now that she's up there, I am."

"So what's the problem?" I asked again.

"No money yet. If you purchase without cash in hand, they arrest you." That was a problem. "How much do you have on you?"

The three of us pooled our coins. Four dollars and seventy-four cents. Not quite enough to buy a human being.

The auctioneer had started bidding at fifteen dollars for the man, and twenty dollars for the woman, which had surprised me. I was even more startled when he announced the girl's opening bid.

"Twenty-five dollars for this healthy young female. Do I have twenty-five?"

A handsome but kindly-looking gentleman next to Murdock smiled gently at the girl. "She'd be a fine one to teach," he whispered to the magician, and raised his hand.

The price of perversion was high.

Murdock gave him a knowing smile. "Indeed, friend. I agree with you. Would you mind if I bid on her, too?"

"Of course you may," the gentleman assured him with utmost courtesy.

Polite, these perverts.

Murdock's hand went up.

"Thirty. I have thirty. Do I hear thirty-five?"

The gentleman bid.

The auctioneer was most pleased. "I have thirty-five. Do I have forty?"

Murdock bid.

"Forty. I have forty. Do I have forty-five?"

Murdock's opponent smiled again. "This is getting rather expensive. But you don't like to lose either, do you?" He raised his hand.

"I have forty-five. Do I have fifty?"

Murdock sighed. "Sir, you are a most formidable bidder. But I can't give up now. She resembles a child I once loved. My only love. Alas, the child grew up, and I lost her. To have this one would give me the chance to love again." The magician raised his hand.

"Fifty." The auctioneer positively beamed with satisfaction. "I have fifty for this girl. Ah, it's good to have bidders who recognize the value of a good slave. Do I have fifty-five?"

The gentleman bowed to Murdock. "Why did you not say so before, good sir? I would have declined to bid. Please. The girl is yours."

Murdock bowed in return. "You are most gracious. A true gentleman."

"I try to be, sir. I try to be."

"Fifty. I have fifty. Fifty going once. Fifty going twice. Sold to the good man in the back for fifty dollars."

"Now we're in trouble," Jenkins intoned.

There was a voice behind us. "Master! Master, I'm here. Am I back in time?" Lorich arrived, the sweat pouring off him from his hurried errand through town, one hand buried in a pocket of his jacket as if clutching something precious. He took out the purse.

"Just in time," Murdock stated calmly, taking it from Lorich.

The gentleman watched and extended his hand. "Well, it's been a pleasure, sir. Enjoy your new purchase."

Murdock smiled and shook hands with the man. The man

turned away. Murdock's smile did not fade from public view, but he did wipe his hand clean.

The auctioneer accepted the money with pleasure, handing Murdock the end of a rope which was securely knotted to the girl's ankle iron. Murdock took the rope and returned to us, the child reluctantly following.

"It's time to go back to the wagons," he declared, and we left the auction behind, another poor soul up for sale. When we were out of the plaza and the crowd had thinned, Murdock stopped and turned to the child. She stared up at him with large eyes, the eyes of a frightened animal.

Maybe there were worse things than being a gutter rat.

Murdock looked at her critically, nodded approvingly. "It's going to be all right now. No one will touch you. No one will hurt you."

And, to my surprise, I felt that everything would be all right, though the words, and the power of the wizard's charm, had not been meant for me. For Murdock, the girl smiled back.

His voice was gentle. "What's your name, little one?"

She hesitated only a moment. "Sabrena. I'm Sabrena."

"Sabrena." Murdock savored the name. "I like that. It's a good name."

The child nodded in agreement.

We found out more as we walked. Sabrena had been sold to a dry goods trader a year before—by her parents. When the trader had tired of her, he'd sold her to the slave dealer. And that was how she ended up on the auction block.

We listened to her tale, and exchanged glances.

Well, what did my companions expect? Could they deny the existence of depravity, perversion, greed, wanton cruelty, or a dozen other failings of man? As a child I had seen such degradation in the alleys and backways of humanity. If I had missed being the victim, I had been the observer. A powerless observer. Soon, perhaps, I would not be so powerless.

And there would be a few changes made in Texan.

We arrived at the camp and the troupe surged forward in a wave of questions and concern.

Kren shook his head. "What's this all about?"

"You bought a slave?" Angela exclaimed.

"Wasn't that dangerous?" asked Megan.

Murdock freed the rope by which he had been leading the girl and threw it into the fire.

"The poor child," Beth clucked, spotting the ankle iron. "Can't we do something about that *thing*?"

"Not yet," Murdock stated regretfully. "It will be safer for her if she wears it in Texan. I am now her legal owner, and if she's separated it will identify her. If the Texans are good at anything, it's getting slaves back to their owners."

Angela took the girl's hand. "What's your name?"

"My name?" she answered, her eyes distracted by something else. She was staring at the cloth sacks of food the women had bought. Loaves of bread stuck out the top. Finally she remembered to answer. "Sabrena."

We gave her a hunk of bread, which disappeared with amazing rapidity.

Sabrena looked up and swallowed a mouthful of bread, a look of rapture upon her.

We had only water to give her after, but even then, I think she was beginning to realize she had a good thing going.

When our story was shared with the others, Kren stroked his chin. "So you left the Kenesee woman and took the child. Why?"

Murdock looked around to confirm that none but troupe members were anywhere near. "She has talents. Power."

"A magician?" Jenkins asked, surprised.

"A sorceress, to be more precise. I first sensed her at the slave pen outside of town, but I wasn't sure how strong she was. Then, I felt her across an entire square full of people. She's strong for her age. Quite strong."

Megan looked up from the circle around the girl and strode over. "Are you going to keep Captain Grayson waiting all day?"

"Captain Grayson?" Murdock asked.

She looked accusingly at Jenkins. "You mean you haven't told him?"

"How could I?" he retorted. "First I got shushed, and then we're busy buying every slave in the city."

"What is this about Captain Grayson?" Murdock persisted.

"He's in the wagon," Megan explained. "He was coming to find us when we ran into him at the plaza and brought him back here. We didn't think it would be good if he stood around in the open, so we had him wait out of sight."

"Quite right," Murdock intoned solemnly.

He climbed into the wagon with me on his heels. Megan was about to follow us in when I shut the door in her face. She did not look happy about that.

Sprawled in a bunk upon his back was a familiar figure, his captain's cap resting upon his face. From beneath it came a loud buzzing. The captain snored.

I had to shake him awake. He peeked out from beneath the brim of his cap. "Humph? What? Oh, it's you." He sat up and swung his legs to the floor. "Sorry, thought I'd take a nap. I sleep very lightly aboard ship, but when I get ashore . . . anyway, it's good to see you, uh, Mr. Thomas and Andrew."

His wits weren't addled, sleepy or not. He'd remembered to use our traveling names.

"And it's good to see you," Murdock assured him. "Is there news?"

"There is." He leaned forward, speaking softly. "Robert sends his greetings. And wants you to know that the Virginians are assembling for an invasion of Kenesee."

"*What*?" Murdock and I chorused, taken aback. "Has the Alliance formed again?"

Grayson shook his head. "No. No other nation will have anything to do with Rodes. He plans to do it alone."

"Virginia alone?" Murdock asked, incredulous. "And with only green troops?"

Grayson nodded. "I know, it sounds crazy. But from all we can tell, Governor Rodes plans to attack along the Coast Road. The Beastwood has declared its neutrality in all future affairs of the nations. With the beastmen removed from the equation, Rodes figures he can still outnumber our army. The defeat of the Alliance gnaws at him. He wants to play the game again."

Murdock was silent. I voiced my thoughts. "So, that ends our efforts to help the Texan rebellion."

To have come so far, just to turn back. Strangely, I almost felt regret at our failure.

"On the contrary," said the captain. "If your safety is not compromised, you are to continue as planned. Those were Robert's instructions."

Murdock sat pondering. "Success will be difficult. Robert

won't be able to help us. And without Kenesee troops. . . ."

Suddenly, in a flash of inspiration, I knew. "Robert is going to send us the regiments anyway."

Grayson smiled. "I see you know your brother. Yes, he's staying with the original plan. He'll support you even if it weakens him in the face of the Virginian Army. The King's Call went out the day I left port, and I must admit the Easterners provide a perfect excuse for mobilizing our troops. But if Governor Rodes is just bluffing, trying to rally his citizens against an external enemy, then word that Robert has split his force might actually prompt Rodes to attack."

"How is Robert?" I asked.

"He looks well. But he's worried about you and your companions. He's a fine man, but quite young to carry such a burden."

"Not so young," I said. "Not so young."

"There's one other thing," Grayson added reluctantly. "The High Wizard sends his regards to you all. But—"

"Yes?"

"He fears for Arn."

"How so?" Murdock inquired.

"He didn't know, exactly. But when he thinks about Arn, he's troubled."

Wonderful. Just wonderful. I could have beaten Grayson over the head with a stick.

"Is there anything else?" Murdock asked.

"No. That's about it. Unless you have any messages for me to carry back."

We shook our heads. "All goes as planned. We have been fortunate."

"So be it. Well, I'll be on my way. May God keep you safe."

And then he was gone.

3

Zavakos

Jenkins was the first to notice the crazy man.

Up to this point, our mission was making fine progress. We had visited Landholder Martinez of Cheraco without incident, and confirmed his support in the cause, as well as the support of two more regimental commanders whom he called to meet me. We were in the town of Canton, a bit better than halfway inland on the road from Cheraco to Dallas, when Jenkins pointed the man out to me. It was the first performance, and the sky was still light. We were looking out from behind a wagon after just completing our swordplay act. "Look there," Jenkins said, wiping the sweat from his brow. "That scrawny old man in the third row."

The man was seated on the lawn, thin as a rail, eyes darting back and forth between the girls. His rotted teeth showed in an eager grin as he watched, his gray beard stained yellow below his mouth from tobacco juice.

"What about him?"

"I saw him for the first time in Tyler. He came to a performance. Then I noticed him again two days ago in Bryan village. And now again tonight. He's following us."

"Umm, maybe. If he's a peddler on foot, it wouldn't be unusual to come along behind us."

"And pay good money to watch the same show three times?" Jenkins countered. "We may be good, but we're not that good. Besides, there's something else."

He waited for me to ask. I gave in. "All right. What's the something else?"

Jenkins beamed with satisfaction. "He forgets all about the

girls when you get on stage. He stares at you as if you were—well, I don't know what. But he doesn't take his eyes away while you're up there."

"Maybe he's just taken by my good looks." It wouldn't be the first time we'd encountered—admirers, shall we say—of the same sex. Murdock had warned us such might happen. "The glamor of the stage will be upon you, at least for the moment, and that can be very appealing. But there's no reason to berate the poor devils. Lord knows, they have a hard enough lot in life."

The women seemed to have fewer problems with such things. We knew how to handle the men's expectations of our women, putting out word early to interested ears that our three were actors, and nothing else. If any doubted us, Jenkins and Kren moved them on with a few choice words. Those simply smitten with the women were allowed to chat, and then sent on their way by the women as it grew late. All in all, we had things well in hand in that regard, although Kren stated that "hairless" females were looking better and better to him as time went on.

But that had little to do with the man in the audience.

"No," Jenkins replied. "He's not taken by your good looks. Would anyone be? It's something else, but I don't know what. Just be careful."

I took particular note of Jenkins's words when, during the second performance, I saw the same man sitting in the audience again. As Jenkins had said, we weren't *that* good. Afterwards, when members of the audience came up to shake hands and congratulate us on our performance, there was the old man again, waiting on the fringes until most had left. He came up to me then, a dirty fur cap in his hands that his fingers stroked nervously.

His face was pasty-looking, and there were scabs on his neck and the backs of his hands, as if some disease were slowly eating away at him. His eyes were yellowed and streaked with blue veins, almost feverish as he looked at me unwaveringly.

I tested my footing in anticipation of danger even as I gave him a nod. "Hello."

He grinned that rotted grin. "Evening, good sir. I watched you in the show." In spite of his appearance, the voice, rich toned and clear, still held an echo of culture and sophistication.

"Well, I hope you enjoyed it," I said. Jenkins, unnoticed by the man, casually took position behind him.

"If it would be convenient, I'd like to talk to you."

"Oh?"

He leaned toward me, whispering. "I have some information for you."

I smelled his breath and took a step backward. "That's interesting. What information do you have?"

"Oh, not here, my good man. Not yet. We have to—to negotiate. Yes, negotiate. We will negotiate."

"Negotiate?"

"If you would consent to come with me, we will go to a tavern I know."

"I don't think. . . ."

"It will be very beneficial to you. And I promise you will come to no harm. None at all."

"Why can't we take care of the matter here?"

He grew petulant. "Because I'm thirsty and I want to sit down and rest." He caught himself. "The tavern is not far, and it's well lit. Or pick the tavern you want. Now, if you will be so kind."

I was not about to go off alone with a stranger for such an uncertain reason. The man was left waiting by the wagon while I went inside and changed into my normal clothes, making sure my throwing knife was set in its sheath between my shoulder blades. But I didn't put on my sword belt. In Texan they didn't take kindly to people wearing swords in town, whether it was inside or outside the gates. Jenkins came in and changed quickly. "I'll follow a dozen paces back. Watch yourself."

I joined the man and he led us along a road that followed the curve of the town walls. Soon, we reached an inn tucked next to a stable. The faded sign above the door was hardly readable in the lanternlight, but showed a rough metal key. The inn was ill-kept and dirty, befitting its clientele. The man fit in well, though I earned stares. "Watch your purse," he stated. "There are thieves about."

Oh, really?

The man and I took a small table in a corner, his seat against one wall, mine against the other. I was closer than I wanted to be to him, but I was not going to leave my back exposed.

He immediately got up and went close to the fireplace, toasting himself before it front and back for a good five minutes in spite of the heat of the day. During that time, Jenkins sauntered in, hiding under an ordinary worker's cap. Although others gave him the same suspicious stare I or any stranger seemed to receive, the simple disguise worked in that the man at the fireplace gave him only a cursory glance before returning his gaze in my direction, as if afraid I might disappear while he basked in the warmth. All the corner tables were taken, so Jenkins seated himself at a lonely bench against the far wall.

The man ordered two beers, and I inspected the rim of my mug carefully for cleanliness before drinking. I had drunk from worse.

A small sip. The beer was quite good, surprisingly.

The man gulped half the mug down in a single chug. "Ahhh . . . that's why I stay here when I travel this way. Good. Very good." He sat contentedly, grinning and staring at me while his eyes glazed in some unknown reverie.

"You have some information?"

"Information?" he focused with a new gleam of interest. "Oh, yes. Yes, I have, my good man. You might be interested."

"What kind of information?"

His eyes darted around suspiciously, and then he leaned forward. "I saw you before. I've been watching your show, in Tyler, and in Bryan, too. I watched you come out the first time, and I said to myself, 'Now that lad looks familiar. Why is that?' " And then I think back years and years, and I look at your forehead, and your nose, and I say to myself, 'Aye. Maybe it's him. Maybe it is him.' "

I felt a gnawing at the pit of my stomach. Did he suspect who I was? Did he *know* who I was? If so, then he could betray us, to our ruin. "And just who," I asked, speaking softly and trying to remain calm, "am I supposed to be?"

"Supposed to be? Well now, that's the question, isn't it? Who are you supposed to be? A man sits down in a tavern and enjoys a good beer, and who knows who he might be talking to? He could be a rich merchant, or a landholder, or a noble, or even . . . a prince."

The man had just signed his own death warrant.

I swallowed. "Yes, he could be . . . anything. Take you, for instance. Who are you, and what do you want?''

''Want? I want money, of course. What else would I want?''

I tried to play the role of confused and impatient innocent. ''Money? Why should I give you money? Go on. Go to the sheriff. I have nothing to hide. He'll settle this soon enough.'' I wanted him to leave the tavern. A gesture to Jenkins, and the man would be dead within two minutes.

''I'll go,'' he said, standing up casually. ''If that's what you want. But then, you won't find out what I have to tell you.''

More patrons came into the tavern, three tired apprentices coming off a job for their master and a couple of night watch deputies taking their late supper, filling in the empty tables at the center of the common room. Nothing to worry about, from all appearances.

''What can *you* tell *me*?'' I asked.

He smiled again. At one time, it might have been quite a charming smile. Now, it was a parody. ''Well, my good man, it's been a long time. You were only a—a little one. That's what she used to call you. 'My little one. My little one.' But I suppose I might have made a mistake, and approached the wrong man. So you wouldn't be interested in anything I have to say, now would you?''

I sat for a long moment while he waited with intolerable self-assurance. ''Sit down,'' I said at last.

He sat down. ''Well now,'' he smirked, ''have I got your attention?''

''You have my attention,'' I admitted, resisting the impulse to pull my knife from its sheath and slit his throat open. ''Your name is Zavakos.''

''Zavakos? Zavakos. I haven't heard that name in a long time. So. You know some of the story.''

''Some. Tell me more.''

''Where should I begin?''

''When you arrived in Texan. Start there.''

Zavakos scratched at a scab on his neck. ''When we arrived in Texan? Yes, that's easy enough. It was just her, and the baby, and me, getting off the boat in Tyler, a pretty little family come to make our fortune in Texan. 'Smile for everyone,' I told her. 'Look happy.' A few coins in the right hands, and we settled into town as neat as you please.''

"What was the woman's name?" I asked.

"Well, now, I think you know her name. No need to mention it. But I called her Nancy-me-dear. Nancy-me-dear, at first because she was my fortune, and later because she was dear to me, you see. I took care of her, and someone back in Kenesee took care of me—with a heavy purse each year. A heavy purse. It was quite nice. There were no more orders from those less worthy, and no more petty rules. No more watching the rich never work a day. No more watching my inferiors have more money than I did. I could sit back and enjoy life.

"And for once I had a woman who wouldn't go running out on me, like they do. Nancy was a fine-looking piece back then, and I showed her a good time between the sheets, I can assure you."

The man was bragging about this—to *me*?

"So she . . . was . . . your mate."

"Of course she was," Zavakos answered. "No woman ever turned me down—at least, not when I was younger, and in better health. She may have objected the first few times, being unused to me, but a little persuasion always helps." He made a fist and winked.

"I see." And I did, all too clearly. No, not in memory. I remembered nothing. But the fist and the boot delivered to those who could not fight back—that I was well acquainted with. "And she never . . . tried to go back to Kenesee?"

"Oh, she tried to leave two or three times," he sniffed. "But I always caught her before she got far. I kept my hand on the purse strings, you could say. And where would she go, a woman all alone? I always tracked her down. Even if she'd gotten back to Kenesee, she knew I'd tell, and then they'd find her, and the queen would keep her promise. It'd go bad for Nancy—and for the child."

"What happened next?"

"Well, everything would have been fine, if they'd just played square with me."

I was listening carefully. "Someone cheated you?"

He nodded. "They were planning to. The high wizard. The queen. I was sure of it. After two or three years in Texan, I began to think of our situation. It was, after all, rather precarious. What if one day those in Kenesee began to worry we might come back? What if they decided it would be better if we could not talk? They might do away with Nancy, and the child, and even me, after all I'd done for them. I was too quick for them, you see. I took Nancy and the child—she wouldn't go without the child—and left Tyler. We went to Dallas, and lived there."

"Quite clever of you. You can't trust anyone."

He took my praise quite willingly. "I knew I was right. I knew it! And they never found us."

"So. Then you lived in Dallas."

"We did. Quite well, too, until the money ran out."

I anticipated where the story was going. "What did you do then?"

"Well, one must do what has to be done. Nancy—oh, found employment, shall we say—and made a good purse. Not as much as we'd become used to, I'm afraid, but enough. She was still a pretty piece, back then, and didn't have problems finding admirers. I found that it took a little persuasion to get her to agree, unfortunately."

"Persuasion?"

He made the fist again. "A few demonstrations with the child, and the difficulties were resolved."

It was at this point that I decided the pox had afflicted the mind as well as the body of Zavakos. For him to know who I was and calmly tell me this story, he had to be crazy. Any sane man would realize he was inviting death. "What happened to . . . the child?"

"Ah, now that was a bit of luck, though I didn't think so at the time. Nancy met another ten-penny girl, and they became good friends. The girl lacked commitment to her man, and planned to run out on him by taking ship. Nancy asked her to go to Kenesee, and take the child. Nancy also stole some of our cash and gave it to the girl, too, which quite annoyed me, I must admit. I never did find out who the girl was, fortunate for her. It seems she reached Kenesee."

"I guess she did," I agreed with a painted smile. So that's how I had returned to Kenesee. What might have happened to Nancy Brown's ten-penny friend, who could say. Perhaps she wasn't as good a friend as Nancy thought. Perhaps she and the child had become separated at some point. Or perhaps she had gone out one night to work, and met her end floating in the river, done to death by those who preyed upon such women. And the child, alone, found refuge in the streets.

"I think it worked out for the best," Zavakos continued philosophically. "I never did like having children around. And Nancy no longer attempted to run away. Instead, she took up the opium pipe. She did like her pipe, I must admit. I think those were the best days of all. No screaming child around, no arguments, a woman to enjoy as I might, and, of course, steady money. A man couldn't ask for more."

"You had everything you wanted," I agreed, regretting that we would have to kill him so . . . quickly.

"You're right. But it didn't last, unfortunately. It never lasts. She caught the pox, and her looks went. She didn't get many customers after that, and I was forced to go out to put bread on the table. But being a clever sort, I found ways of filling a purse."

"I'm sure you did."

"I always liked Nancy. Had a real soft spot for her. She was quite a woman. But when your time is over, your time is over."

"And her time was over."

"Yes. Just so. And that, I fear, is the end of my story."

"I thought it would be something like that." Ah well, at least if the pox killed her, she didn't have to suffer through the years with this sorry excuse for a human being.

"Now, perchance we might discuss a bit of money?"

I nodded. "We can."

His eyes glistened in the lamplight. "The Texan dollar won't buy as much as it did. People just don't trust the state. So I want Arkan dollars. One hundred Arkan dollars."

"A hundred dollars," I echoed, with raised eyebrows.

"Surely, for one such as you, that is no great price."

"I don't have that much on me. It's at the camp. We'll have to go back to the wagons."

"So we shall, then. Together, and you'll give me the money. I trust I need not worry about trickery?"

"No tricks." I had to keep him off his guard. "But no tricks by you, either. That's a lot of money. But we'll pay it for your silence."

He looked puzzled. "Silence? Pay me for my silence? What are you talking about, my good man? The money is to see your mother—"

"My—mother?"

"Naturally."

"She's alive? I thought you said—"

"She's alive. Or at least, she was a month ago. But the pox is eating at her innards now, I'm sorry to say. I don't guarantee she'll be living when you get to Dallas, but if she is, I'll take you to her. That is what your money gets. No more, no less."

I pondered his words for long moments. Nancy Brown was alive. I had never seriously considered that she might still be living, even in Texan. She was nothing to me, of course. There were no pangs of feeling for a mother I did not know. Even the faint and blurry image I held of a tired woman with a sad smile might be the ten-penny friend rather than her. Still, the thought of Nancy Brown still alive, living all these years for her opium pipe and enduring Zavakos, was disturbing. My discovery as a child had been reported across the six nations. The death of Queen Jessica had likewise been spread far and wide. Why had she not heard of these things? Why had she not left Zavakos and come back to Kenesee long ago?

I asked him why she had remained in Texan when it was safe to return to Kenesee and take up her life again.

Zavakos regarded his fingers modestly. "Well I think she would say that she had grown accustomed to me, and thought that I was well suited for her. She often said as much, once the child was gone."

I did not deny his assertion. I didn't believe it, but I wasn't about to deny it. I needed him now. "I can understand that. Such things happen. Well, you were a lucky man."

He eyed the scabs on his arm. "Not always so lucky," he said. "Not always. . . ."

And now was the moment of decision. Give Jenkins the sign to kill Zavakos, or let him live? He was a threat to our mission, a constant danger of betrayal hanging over us as long as he lived. I shouldn't feel anything for this woman, this Nancy Brown who happened to give me birth. And yet, after what I'd heard, there was a curiosity aroused in me, and perhaps a vague, formless, illogical sense of debt. Who was this woman of whom I'd heard? What was she like? And could I help her in any way, this victim of circumstance who had gone into the streets to save me from beatings, and had sent me away to save me?

Without Zavakos, could I find one sick woman in Dallas who used a name unknown to me? Not likely, and not without arousing too much attention. It would be foolish to let him live. Foolish. And yet that was my decision. There would be another time and place to settle accounts with Zavakos—and then, why, I might even do the job myself. Perhaps slowly. Yes, that could be quite pleasant indeed.

"Shall we go?" I asked.

"Go?"

"To my camp. To get the money. A tenth now, Zavakos, and the rest in Dallas when you take me to Nancy. I'll even give you a bonus."

His eyes refocused. "The money. Yes, the money. Certainly. You can trust me, you know. When you get to Dallas, I will find you, and take you to her. I am a man of honor."

I refrained from strangling him. "Never doubted it for a second."

The next morning we packed up and made ready to travel. I'd discussed the new state of affairs with my companions, freely admitting the foolishness of my decision. And yet not one—not even Jenkins—objected. Silly of them. I might have relented.

Just before moving on, I noticed a half dozen boys playing nearby with wooden swords and shields, going at it fiercely for a few minutes. They were shouting and yelling as they beat upon each other. Four boys were getting the better of two.

"Take that, King Robert!"

"Death to you, Prince Scar."

"The Alliance will triumph in the end!"

"Ow! You hit my finger."

They finished their bout, two left lying on the grass and the others wandering over to watch us hitch up the horses.

"Playing war?" I asked the boys who came over.

"Yes, sir," their leader stated respectfully. "We're the good side, the Alliance." He pointed to the two boys recovering on their backs. "They are the enemy from Kenesee."

"My father says they aren't so bad," said a small lad. "He says the Alliance started the war. He—"

"Shut up, Michael!" said a larger boy who had the same

freckled features. He looked around fearfully, to see who might have heard. "Father will beat you for saying that."

The younger boy subsided.

I walked over to the two boys on the grass, sitting up now and nursing their bruises.

"Which one of you is Scar?" I asked.

One groaned, touching a lump that was rising on his forehead, the back of his sword hand covered with scratches. He looked at me warily.

The battered hero sprawling in the dirt.

"You're Prince Scar?" I asked again.

He nodded and grimaced with pain. "Ouch. It hurts."

"It does?"

"Yes," the boy moaned. "I don't like being Prince Scar."

A shrug. "I know the feeling."

4

The Old Crone

We arrived at Dallas on May 15th, the day that the meeting of the Great Landholders started, a sunny day which seemed excessively hot to me, but was taken as quite the norm by the inhabitants. Dallas, capital of Texan, was larger than any other town in Texan, or in Kenesee for that matter. Set upon the north bank of the Trinity River amid the flat plains of the interior, the walls of the town loomed high and thick, perhaps even more formidable than the walls of Kingsport.

Yet within, towering higher still at the western end of the town, was Castle Corral, the home of Texan's ruler, General Jack Murphy. The castle was as gaily festooned with banners and flags and pennants as our castle in Kingsport, and yet to me the walls and towers of Corral lacked the symmetry, the sense of benevolence that the king's castle held for the citizens of Kenesee. It seemed as though Corral was dominated by its battlements, being only a place of fortification and war that frowned down with tyrannical suspicion upon the lives of its people, though perhaps its citizens felt differently. Still it was forbidding enough to give pause to a tiny band of adventurers dedicated to its downfall. I looked at the structure and felt my stomach stir in protest.

"Uhh—rather formidable."

Even Murdock could only manage a weak grin and a shrug as we drove up to the town walls. "It is said Castle Corral has the largest dungeon in the world."

"Thank you for sharing that with us," grumbled Kren. "Just what we need to cheer us up."

We wanted to set up camp near the eastern gate, but uniformed sentries directed us—in no uncertain terms—to the parade ground near the northern gate. There, just outside the town's brooding walls, we dutifully parked our wagons, set up a tether line and fed the horses, bought firewood, roped off a stage area, and arranged lamps, props, and costumes. Our activities alone attracted an audience of children and adults. Murdock did impromptu juggling and a magic trick or two, announcing that Thomas's Traveling Theater would perform its feats of wonder outside the north gate during two performances that evening and the evening after. The word would spread quickly. It always did, and we had rarely found other advertising to be necessary.

With the camp established and the stage set, we had an hour or two before we needed to begin the first performance. Time to explore the town. I thought it would be just Murdock and Jenkins and me as usual, but Megan fell into step with us as we set off. I suggested to her that she might want to shop with Angela and Beth, but she quickly corrected me. "Whenever we arrive at a town, you three go off and come back with all kinds of tales and information. From now on, I go along." I looked to Murdock for support, but he only grimaced. "It should do no harm—I hope."

We took a quick tour. The town was a confusing maze of streets, large and small, branching and merging with surprising frequency, but the people of Dallas seemed to have no problem navigating the ways. There was the usual mix of merchants, artisans, workers, and slaves going about their business, though I noticed a large number of beggars plying their trade. There were simply too many to be charitable to all, though the women with children earned a penny each. Megan noted that the way a few of the children lay motionless in their mothers' arms was disturbing. How could they sleep so soundly through the tumult of the streets?

"Oh, a child could sleep through it all, if tired," Murdock intoned. "However, these aren't tired, but drugged with opiates."

Megan came to a halt in midstep and faced Murdock, her face blazing. She caught herself, and kept her voice down. "You mean their own *mothers* give them opiates?"

Murdock looked at one woman and child on a corner who seemed to fit the subject under discussion. "They are paying a high price for survival. Perhaps they should ask themselves whether the cost is worth it. Sad, no?"

"I had not imagined such things could happen," Megan said in horror.

"Oh, there are worse things. I pray you will never have to see them as well. Come, it's time to move on."

We came to the town hall, before which stood a small but finely-crafted carriage pulled by a matching pair of white horses. Two slaves dressed in livery were polishing the carriage's gleaming exterior, while another tended to the matched pair of horses. It struck me how complacently I accepted the sight of well-dressed slaves, the leather-bound ankle iron the only sign of their status. Around the carriage, two dozen red-jacketed soldiers stood at ease next to their mounts and chatted. We joined a small crowd of townsfolk watching the spectacle, staying safely to the rear.

"What's going on? Why are we stopping here?" Megan asked, exasperated with us.

Murdock nodded to the building. "The Great Landholders started their annual Gathering today. It will go on for three days."

Megan did not know about the gathering, nor did Angela or Beth. Unfair, perhaps, but every additional person who knew the details of our business meant one more chance for discovery should they be taken into custody. Not that they would willingly betray us, but they wouldn't be the first to be tricked into revealing crucial information during questioning.

Her ignorance accounted for the next question. "But why are we standing here watching the Landholder Guards?"

"Not Landholder Guards. Those men are the Presidential Horse Guardos of General Jack Murphy," Murdock corrected her. "An equal number of Presidential Foot Guardos are probably inside. Murphy always joins the Landholders for the first day of their meeting. There, the meeting is ending for the day, as I'd hoped. Watch."

The horse guardos mounted and took position, a dozen before and a dozen behind the carriage. From the town hall, red-jacketed foot guardos rushed out and sprang into the street, sweeping us with the crowd of watchers back from the entrance. A man emerged, stooping to clear the door frame. When he stood to his full height he towered over the others, at least six and a half feet tall and powerfully built in proportion. He wore the red jacket of the guardos, but his was decorated at sleeve and shoulder and collar with gold braid. In size he reminded me of Montego, our guide in the valley during the struggle to reach the Rift Gates. But his stern face lacked any of the honest good will of Montego. The man's gaze swept the surroundings to make sure all was safe.

"Look at *him*," Megan whispered, impressed. Well, I was impressed, too.

"Who is he?" Jenkins asked

"That is Bartholomew," Murdock replied as softly. "Sheriff Matthew Bartholomew. The most loyal and devoted follower of General Murphy. He's the head of Murphy's security, and despite his size, as clever a lieutenant as any leader could ever want. Besides which, he is an enthusiastic sadist. He stayed in Texan to run the country during the War of the Alliance, the only man Murphy trusted for the job. To all accounts, he is one of our most formidable opponents. Think you could handle him?"

Jenkins sized him up. "Do I have to?"

So, even the fiery Jenkins had his limit.

Bartholomew gave a signal, and another figure emerged from the building surrounded by a half-dozen guardos. The man strode through the door and hurried across the porch, glancing about suspiciously. Murdock and I made ourselves six inches shorter to avoid the eyes of the mean-featured, swarthy face before it ducked into the carriage. Jenkins did not have our difficulty with height, and peeped from between the shoulders of two men, only his eyes and cap showing.

The carriage moved off in the direction of the castle, the street hurriedly clearing before it. The citizens knew to get out of the way of that procession. It wasn't going to stop for man or beast.

Murdock took Megan's arm and spoke into her ear. "That was General Jack Murphy, President of Texan."

"So he's the one," Megan stated. "Pity we didn't bring Lorich with us."

Murdock and I looked at each other, shocked expressions on our faces. Shocked because Megan knew Lorich's secret power. And shocked because she was absolutely correct. How easy it would have been. We were no more than forty feet from Murphy's carriage, well within Lorich's effective range. For all our plans and calculations and plotting, the idea had never occurred to us.

The wizard's shoulders sagged. "Stupidity. Sheer stupidity. I never thought of it."

Megan stamped her foot. "Oh, you men! If you had told me where you were going, I would have suggested it." So, Clever Megan had figured out what role Lorich had played in our adventures.

The opportunity was gone and it would not come again. Discouraging. Quite discouraging.

Stupidity aside, our first day in Dallas went smoothly enough, paying a bribe or two to local officials who wandered by and commented to us upon the wear and tear their poor town was taking from our presence. We kept as low a profile as a traveling theater troupe could reasonably do, and presented the usual two acts the first afternoon to large audiences. We let it be known that we'd be leaving on the third day.

Such entertainments were not unusual to the capital of Texan, and on the whole ours was little different from the dozens of theaters, circuses, and shows that wandered through the nations, at least in the quality of on-stage entertainment. Yet any attraction was a welcome relief to the hard monotony of everyday life, and so our arrival was a cause of interest. Word spread through town, and soon there were few commoners who did not know there was a new theater troupe in town.

And so it was that during late morning of the second day, Zavakos stepped forward and gave a cheerful grin of rotting teeth, his eyes glittering. "Ahh, my good man. We meet again."

Jenkins, casually strolling from the rear of the wagon with his show sword, saw the man and quickly stepped up beside me. I nodded politely to the man, noting that the gatekeeper was preoccupied, flirting with a heavyset woman who obviously enjoyed the attention. At least we didn't have to worry about *his* attentions for the next few moments.

"Señor Zavakos. You've shown up, as promised."

"Of course," he agreed. "Did you doubt me? I am a man of my word. We can conduct a bit of business, if you're so inclined. I can take you to her now."

Murdock came up to join us. He, Jenkins, and I were the only ones at the wagons. The rest were exploring the town, or buying supplies in the plazas.

The wizard considered Zavakos, and then looked about, as if considering the situation. "We can't all go. One of us has to stay at with the wagons."

Jenkins nodded his agreement. "I'll take care of him, sir. Don't worry."

Murdock glanced at the gatekeeper, and then back at me. "Are you sure about this, my son?"

"No, but I said I would go, so I'll go."

Jenkins went into the wagon to get a money purse, and then, reluctantly, the two of us followed Zavakos into town.

I pondered why I did such foolish things.

Zavakos led us from the north gate to the southernmost of the three town plazas, and then west in the direction of the river gate. Before arriving at the gate he turned up a smaller lane which grew steadily more filthy as we proceeded up its length. A trickle of liquid waste ran down the stone gutter in the lane's center, and the walls of the buildings lining either side of the narrow way were dark and grimy, punctuated only by unkempt doors and small windows that were, often as not, broken.

The smell of waste and decay permeated the length of the way, moderated by another acrid odor that hung heavy in the air at spots. The occasional gutter rat (four-legged or two-legged), stray dog, beggar, ten-penny girl and odd unfortunate watched us with questioning looks as we passed, but none dared bother us. We stepped carefully, even Zavakos.

I was not unfamiliar with such streets. There were fewer now in Kenesee, given all that King Reuel had done during his reign. But such places can never be eradicated. There will always be one or two in any large town, dead-ends where those who have slid down the slope of failure and misery find a last refuge for living—if such an existence can be called that.

Zavakos stopped before a door that was in a bit better shape than the rest. The heavy odor that we'd noted before lingered in the air. Zavakos knocked, and then unlatched the door, bowed, and with a sweep of his hat gestured for us to enter. Jenkins put a hand on my chest, stepped forward, and preceded me through the door. My companion looked around, and beckoned us forward.

We were in a narrow, ill-lit corridor, with low doors along either side of the passage. The heavy odor was present here too. Zavakos squeezed past us and repeated his performance with bow and flourish at a door halfway down the hall. Jenkins led us in again.

This time we were in a small room with a narrow table, two chairs, and a cold hearth, a few cooking utensils arranged upon hooks set in the brick. A tiny window let in a bit of light, but the room was still dim, and it smelled bad. The room was divided by a thin and faded draw curtain on a string, though it appeared a lamp or candle burned behind it. A stout woman looked up as we entered, stood, and bowed her head respectfully at us. When Zavakos followed us in, her features hardened.

I studied the woman carefully. Like her form, her face was broad and heavy, dark hair giving way to streaks of gray. The color of her eyes? I could not tell in the dimness.

Zavakos saw me staring at her, and laughed. "Oh, no, my good man. This isn't her. This is Maria."

Maria nodded and spoke, her English heavily accented with Spanish. "Sí. Nancy helped me when I needed help. Now it is my turn. I take care of Nancy." She eyed Zavakos. "Someone has to."

He gave her a look. "You may leave now, Maria."

"I no have to leave. This is my inn. I own it—"

"And I rent this room," Zavakos cut her off. "And as long as I pay you, it is mine. Go now. You can come back and check on her later."

She seemed about to argue, thought better of it, and padded heavily past Zavakos with a resentful jerk of her head. I pointed from Jenkins's purse to the woman, and he got my meaning. He took from it an Arkan five-dollar piece and handed it to the woman. Maria's eyes focused on the purse and the coin with the intensity of those for whom money is the prime weakness. She shut her hand around the coin and looked at us with new eyes. "Thank you, Señor. It is good that Nancy has rich friends who can help her."

Zavakos had looked at the purse with great interest too, but now he closed the door behind Maria. "She's a greedy sort, you know. Likes her money. Not for what it can buy, you understand. Just to hoard. She's got a sackful hidden somewhere in her room, I'm sure. I can hear coins clinking at night, when she gets them out to count. But she's taken care of Nancy, I'll give her that."

I pointed at the curtain. "She's there?"

He nodded. "Nancy always did like her privacy."

"I see." Behind the curtain.

"And now, perhaps we should discuss our arrangement? I've done my part in the bargain. Don't you agree?"

I had to admit it. "So you have. James, pay Mr. Zavakos the amount agreed upon."

We were alone now, and I would have liked to give Zavakos payment of a different sort, but now was not the time. Too many people had seen us come in with him.

Jenkins dutifully opened his purse again and counted out the coins.

Zavakos recounted their number. "That's it, as agreed upon, and a twenty dollar bonus. Quite generous of you. Of course, you're in a position to be generous, aren't you? Well, my good man, it certainly has been a pleasure doing business with you. And now I'll leave you to your moments in private. Stay as long as you like. There is no rush, certainly. I'm sure you'll be able to find your way back across town." He bowed, and left.

I gave Jenkins the signal. "Follow him."

I had not yet completely lost my wits.

Alone, I reached out to the curtain, drew back my hand in hesitation, reached out again and swept it open. Behind the curtain was a bed, illuminated dimly by an oil lamp hung on the wall. Upon the bed lay a gaunt, pox-ridden women wearing a stained bedgown. She rested on her side, the skeletal fingers of her left hand up close to her mouth, and her lips moved, meeting and parting in a slow rhythm. She grimaced at times, and her teeth, the few left her, were rotted as badly as Zavakos's. Her skin, stretched thin and white upon the cheekbones, seemed to be like parchment. Yet the parchment was marred by flaking scabs and open sores that decorated her flesh like a scattering of red hot cinders burning through paper

She was a discarded page, and those who had written so cruelly upon her had left their mark.

The woman was sleeping. I reached out a hesitant hand, and touched her shoulder. She turned over onto her back, and began to snore loudly. I listened to her snort and rasp.

I touched her shoulder again. I shook it. The snort and rasp cut off, and her eyes opened. It was several moments before they focused and turned to gaze at me.

The old crone frowned. "Who are you? Maria! There's a thief in my room. Maria. Come kill him." Fortunately, her voice was low and weak.

"I'm not a thief," I said.

"What?"

"I'm not a thief."

"Of course you are."

"No, I'm not."

"Oh. Then you're looking for a girl. Sorry, I'm too old. Sick. Don't do that anymore. I think Natalia down the street is still working. You go see her. Tell her to give me a coin for sending you."

"My name is Arn."

"Your name? I don't want to know your name."

This rude old crone was my mother? This was Nancy Brown? I wondered if somehow Zavakos had cheated me after all.

"Where's my pipe?" she droned on. "Did Maria take it

again? She won't let me have it too often. Says it'll kill me. Maria, come take this crazy man away."

"My name is Arnold Brant."

"Arnold Brant? Who's Arnold Brant?"

"I come from Kingsport. In Kenesee."

She paused. "Kenesee. I came from Kenesee."

"And what was your name in Kenesee?" Perhaps now I could pin her down.

She had to think about it. "My name? My name was Nancy Brown. Nancy Brown. That was it."

"Yes. And your father was Arnold Brown, a councilman of Jackson Harbor, and a friend of his was Mr. Smith, a fellow councilman."

The woman looked at me with fresh interest. "That's right. I remember. How do you know?"

Around the mulberry bush yet again. "I told you. I'm Arnold Brant. I'm your son."

She laughed. "Hah. My son is a famous prince. He's up north, not down here in this pigsty. Where's Zee? Did *he* put you up to this? How much is he paying you?

I shook her by the shoulders. "I am your son. I am Arnold Brant. I am Prince Arn of Kenesee."

The shaking was an act of anger, and perhaps cruel to do to one so old and so sick. But it gained her attention, and she seemed focused and rational for the first time.

"You're my son?"

"Yes."

"And you've come to rescue me?"

"Umm, no, not really. I didn't know you were here. Not until Zavakos told us."

"My son would rescue me. You're not my son."

"I am."

"Is that so? All right, my son," she stated with sarcastic scorn. "You leave me here for fifteen years, and you still haven't come to rescue me? Worthless men."

"Mother, I have a question for you."

"A question. The crazy man has a question."

"Who was my father?"

"Your father?"

"Was it Reuel Brant? Or John Black?"

Her features changed, the sneer of the mouth softening, the

tight lines around her eyes fading. A distant look came upon her face, not unfocused, but as if seeing a place far away and a time long ago. "Yes. I remember them. Poor Reuel. Poor John. They're dead, aren't they?"

"Yes, they're dead. But which—"

"I knew they were dead. I heard about the battles. But it didn't matter. For me, they were dead a long time. A long, long time."

"Mother—"

"I used to hope someone would come and rescue me. I prayed they would rescue me. But they never came."

"They tried. They searched."

"There is no rescue. Only in the ballads. Only in the fairy tales."

"But I've come back. I'm here."

"But not to rescue me. Damn you."

"Not yet. I have to go soon. But I'll come back."

Her eyes widened. "You'll come back, but I'll be dead. I've been wanting to die, you know. I keep waiting. The pain is very bad, sometimes. Very bad. But my pipe helps. Where is my pipe?"

It was hopeless. I stood up. "I'll get Maria."

She watched me, hesitating. "Aren't you going to stay?"

"I can't stay. I told you. I have to go."

"But you'll come back?"

"You want the crazy man to come back?"

"No. Don't come back."

What could I say to this repulsive old woman with the addled mind who had given me life? She was a stranger. There was a regret, I admit that. Deep down, perhaps I had been hoping to discover a beautiful and intelligent and charming matron, grateful for the blessing of finally seeing her son once more. But Nancy Brown's beauty and intelligence and charm had been beaten out of her. Beaten out by circumstance. Beaten out by Zavakos. Beaten out by an uncaring world. Beaten out by her own sense of hopelessness. And now, there was nothing left but the addle-brained shards of a hardhearted cynic, a calculating old crone who had shut out the world.

"Don't come back."

And so I left her, her last words denying me still. I called Maria into the room, thanked her, and left. The streets were busy with noon marketgoers, and the mixed smell of the town was like a breath of forest air in comparison to the odor of the place I had been. I was careful on my way, watching for any followers. There were none, and I made it back to the wagons without incident. To my companions' inquiries, I stated only that she was old and near death, and didn't recognize me. And that was true.

An hour later, Jenkins showed up. "I followed Zavakos. I think he expected to be followed. He tried to lose me. When I realized that, I looked for a place to take care of him once and for all. But he stayed on the busiest streets in his wanderings, and finally turned a corner, and simply disappeared. He must have gone into one of the buildings, but which one, I couldn't tell. I don't know where he is, and there is nothing we can do, except leave now."

Murdock listened to the narration with me, and thought long before commenting. "No, we can't leave yet. We'll just have to trust to luck, or whatever shards of honor this Zavakos has left. A poor bet, perhaps, but I don't know what else we can do. We're too close to the finish to flee now."

And so we stayed, preparing for our two performances that second afternoon, and acted as if not a soul knew our true identities.

I had a devil of a time with my stomach.

5

The Conspirators

Anyone watching our troupe would expect us to get an early start on the third day so that we could be in the next town before evening. Yet, it was important that we remain through the afternoon. We had to figure out a good excuse for delay. After returning from my visit to Nancy Brown, we discussed the need for a delay the next day. Beth thought of the answer. She handed one of Jenkins's costumes to him shortly after he returned from tailing Zavakos. "Here you are, my hero. Look. You've torn your costume. Beyond repair."

The unsuspecting Jenkins stared at the clothing. "I never tore that costume."

"Clumsy oaf!" Kren admonished him, catching on quickly. "Now we'll have to have a new one made, and it will delay our departure tomorrow."

"But I didn't—Oh, I see." Jenkins got the point at last.

We went to a tailor shop and put in an order for a new costume for Jenkins. The tailor was apologetic. "You say you're leaving tomorrow? Sorry, good sirs, but I have another order to finish tonight. A dress for a Landholder's wife. I couldn't possibly get the costume to you before midafternoon tomorrow."

After a great gnashing of teeth over the delay, we reluctantly admitted that midafternoon would have to do, and Jenkins would just use another costume for the swordfight act that evening. The tailor took Jenkins's measurements.

Such is the stuff of secret missions.

So it was that on the morning of the third day we slept in, had a leisurely breakfast, and slowly packed up our gear. After such a strenuous morning we rewarded ourselves with lunch, and several of us napped in the shade of the wagon. I lay down too, but could not count myself among those napping; my mind was troubled with worry for the afternoon. But Angela lay curled up beside me, her head snuggled against my shoulder, and Murdock gave me a confident wink, so that my worries, if not stilled, were at least quieted.

Sabrena, still quiet as a mouse and still painfully thin despite the decent food, sat and watched. She studied us as if two people simply enjoying each other's company was something she had never seen before. The girl was still reserved, feeling comfortable with Murdock, but much less so with the others in our party. However, she was also developing a real affinity for Beth, who delighted in washing the girl's hair and making clothes for her. About the rest of us she was still making up her mind, though she was fascinated by our beastman.

At midafternoon we roused. Kren and Lorich saw to the horses, while the women saw to our care. Angela busied herself straightening my shirt and brushing off the pieces of grass that clung to my jacket, while Jenkins was the victim of Beth's careful ministrations and worried looks.

Angela finished at last. "There. You're ready." She leaned forward and whispered into my ear. "I shall be very angry at you if you get yourself killed."

I kissed her before she could say more. "I'll be angry at me, too."

Murdock, Jenkins and I nodded to each other, ready at last. Kren watched with folded arms. "I do more *waiting* on this trip. Not my idea of a worthy adventure at all."

Lorich opened his mouth to speak to his master, and Murdock put up a hand. "Don't say it. Everything will be fine. We'll be back in a few hours."

And then we were off, the three of us sauntering back into town and to the tailor's shop, where Jenkins tried on the costume, pronounced it a perfect fit (in spite of uneven sleeves), and the tailor neatly rolled it into a small bundle and tied it with string. We paid and were on our way, passing in front of the town hall. All was calm, for many of the landholders had left the meeting at the formal conclusion of business a good hour ago. Unconcerned that some of their number held back for a meeting of a different kind, they hurried back to their inn, anxious for the drinking and wenching with ten-penny girls that normally followed the official end of the landholders' Gathering.

This time, those lingering behind would not be catching up.

We ambled onto the veranda and to the door, before which stood two men with the bearing of soldiers. They were quite polite. "May we help you?"

Murdock bowed. "I am Mr. Thomas, here to see Landholder Mason. He should be expecting me."

"Certainly. I'll let him know, good sirs. Please wait here."

A moment later he returned and led us into a hallway, and thence to a chamber with a large table and many chairs. More than a score of men were seated there, many of them strangers to us except for Landholders Mason, Parsons, and Fields. Mason was as cool as he had been in Kingsport months before. "Ahh, our honored and long-awaited guests have arrived." He stood and introduced them to us one by one, giving the name and title of each man seated.

A third were the selected landholders great and almost-great who, knowing of this meeting of conspirators, had stayed behind rather than rush off with the other landholders to fun and frolic. Another third, many arrived just that day, were mayors of the larger towns. The last third, dressed in civilian clothes like the others, were colonels of regiments in the Army of Texan. Among them was Steward Montrose of the Parsons Landhold, who nodded at us. Like the landholders, the mayors and colonels had found their way—by strange coincidence—to Dallas at just this time. These twenty were the troubled men of Texan: troubled by the losses and humiliation their nation had endured; troubled by General Murphy's leadership; troubled by the future of their people; troubled by what needed to be done. Not all of them might be fully committed to action, not all might have decided what to do. But they were leaning that way, or they would not have been invited. Our job this day was inspire them, and get them to commit their all to the cause. For that is what it would be, for them. All or nothing.

One was either loyal to General Murphy, or one was dead.

There were others involved, of course, as Mason noted. "There are more of us, certainly, but some could not come, and others must remain hidden until the moment we strike."

Mason introduced the three of us to the assembly, least to

greatest—as the world reckoned us in its ignorance. "First is Sergeant Jenkins of the Kenesee Royal Guards, if my memory does not serve me wrong. Next, Wizard Desjardins Murdock, advisor to the royal family of Kenesee. And last, the guarantee of Kenesee's assistance to our cause, Prince Arn of Kenesee, brother of King Robert. Prince Scar has come, as he promised."

The assembly broke into whispers and murmurs, hope and suspicion mixed together. "*He's* the Scourge of the Alliance?" muttered one landholder. "Barely more than a boy," whispered a colonel. One mayor even shook his head in disbelief and voiced his concern. "The proof?"

Mason gestured the mayor up to our side. "I myself affirm that this man is the same who I met at the King's Castle in Kingsport, recognized by King Robert and all as Prince Arn of Kenesee. But you need not—you should not—take my word alone for it. Too much is at stake. Any who doubt may inspect his face and see for himself."

The mayor who had asked about proof came forward, along with two other doubters. I spread apart my beard so that he could see the skin beneath. "It's there," proclaimed the mayor, "and a wicked-looking slash it is, too."

"Thank you, Mayor Bragg," Mason said. "Now, is everyone satisfied that this man is Arn Brant of Kenesee?"

"What about the birthmark?" asked a colonel of the army, one of the three men who had come up to inspect the scar.

I frowned. Displaying myself as an eight-year-old to King Reuel and his advisors to prove the matter had been tolerable enough. Proving it to Captain Grayson had been discomfiting. Dropping my pants now before a roomful of grown men was downright embarrassing. Perhaps if Texan had been a matriarchy. . . .

Mason grew thoughtful. "I do not think it quite appropriate for such proof to be offered to all in such a manner. Perhaps if you would like to accompany Prince Arn to a private room, you could verify the existence of the birthmark."

The colonel suddenly appeared uncomfortable. "Uh, no. The fact that he would be willing to do so is enough."

Mason refrained from smirking. "Anyone else? No? So, it is accepted that this man is Prince Arn of Kenesee. Now, if we may proceed. We have each considered the disaster that

General Jack Murphy led us to during the War of the Alliance. And we have long endured his tyrannical rule, in which each feared to speak his thoughts to another. It is only since the war that we ventured to share our feelings with each other, and realized the dissatisfaction is broad and deep. So now we come to the time of decision. Do we endure Murphy's tyranny, or do we act?"

"We act!" said Landholder Parsons.

Mason nodded, but waited for other opinions. There were none. "So be it. Does anyone disagree with this course of action? If so, you may leave now, with no ill feelings."

No ill feelings? Not likely. Anyone who tried to leave, I am sure, would have been dead within the hour. By now, these men knew that they were committing treason just by being in the room with me. Their lives were forfeit from this moment on. Those with cold feet would not have come. Any plotter not firmly committed would keep his peace now—and betray us later.

Mason scanned each face for hesitation, and then continued. "It is time to hear from Prince Arn."

He sat, and left me standing before the assembly. I wasn't at a total loss for words. Murdock had guided me in the matter. "I greet the true heroes of Texan." They liked that well enough. "I am here . . . at risk with you. Together, our victory cannot be denied. And now, my advisor, Wizard Desjardins Murdock, will present our plans."

I'd made some progress in speechgiving over the months, but could still easily make embarrassing mistakes, and hanging the audience was not an option. I was happy to turn over such tasks to more talented subordinates. Especially where subtlety and diplomacy were required, I depended upon Murdock, his wizardly "charm" often making as favorable an impact as the logic of his words.

I sat and he stood. "Thank you, Prince Arn. Good men of Texan, let me make our purpose clear. We come not to intrude ourselves upon the affairs of your country. We never desired that, and fought the nations of the Alliance only when they invaded the land of Kenesee. After our victory we marched on no other land, nor made demand on any."

Of course we hadn't made demands. Kenesee was militarily exhausted.

"We are here at the invitation—and the plea—of your own membership. Landholder Mason and another Texan patriot came to Kenesee and requested that we aid you in your rebellion. They asked for a leader of Kenesee to rally your members, and military force to aid your victory."

Murdock gestured to me. "After a long and dangerous journey, Prince Arn has come to Texan in answer to that request. He has come, and put himself at risk for you. He is here to inspire you and your followers. He is here to lead forces of Kenesee into battle beside you. But he cannot win your victory for you. That can only be done by the courage of Texans committed to ridding themselves of the tyranny of General Murphy. Yet, if all here are true, victory will be yours."

The mayor of Denison tapped one forefinger nervously on the table. "They say Murphy is making weapons of the Old World. Is that true?"

Murdock eyed Mason. The landholder motioned, and a man brought a long object wrapped in cloth. I didn't have to wait for it to be unwrapped to know what it was. The man unfurled the cloth and held up the musket. It was little different from the one they had brought to Kingsport.

Mason waited until the shocked exclamations had diminished. The Texans were no less appalled to see the forbidden weapon than we had been in Kingsport.

"The rumors are true. This musket is an early sample of his efforts. We have shown a like piece to King Robert and Prince Arn, which convinced them to aid us. There can be no doubt. Murphy is building powder weapons."

The mayor of Denison stopped his finger tapping. "So. It is true, after all. He has broken the Codes, God help us. If there was any doubt before of what we must do, there can be none now."

"Yet, if he has such weapons," lamented another mayor, "how can we stand against him?"

Mason shook his head. "He cannot have many, or the army regiments would have been given them. His foot guardos have been training in secret, though, out in the countryside, and there can be little doubt that they, at least, will be equipped with these forbidden devices."

A colonel looked dismayed. "A regiment of guardos

equipped with powder weapons? That alone would be enough to defeat us.''

''How can we prevail against such weapons?'' asked another.

Murdock cleared his throat. ''I think it should be made clear that the powder weapons developed so far are primitive versions of those the Old World had at the time of the Cataclysm. The musket we saw could be fired but a few times per minute, and accuracy was doubtful.''

The colonel perked up. ''Then—then we have a chance, after all.''

''Most certainly,'' Murdock assured him. ''More than a chance. It is General Murphy who will be facing the long odds. From this meeting we will be going directly to Tyler. Within a few days, if not already, regiments from Kenesee will be landing. They will fight beside your units, and ensure the victory you seek.''

Mason took over. ''Exactly. It is to Tyler that colonels should bring their regiments as soon as possible. From there, we will march on Dallas. If Murphy hides within its walls, we will besiege him, and rally the countryside to our cause. If he comes out to fight, we will finish him once and for all.''

There were nods.

''So. Are all agreed? Then, we will take an oath. By God in Heaven, we swear to commit our honor and our lives to rid Texan of Jack Murphy. And if any here does not feel this way, we will kill him ourselves, and may his soul rot in hell. So help me, God.''

''So help me, God,'' echoed the assembly.

There was some discussion of details. Towns and bridges that had to be secured for the assembly of our forces, the safest roads for the regiments, march times and distances, supply points, and organization of forces. Finally, all was complete, and Mason stood again. ''It is done, then. Leave Dallas without delay and return swiftly to your counties. Rally your men, and bring them to Tyler. And God be with us all.''

I was anxious to leave, too, but waited for Landholder Fields to catch up with us before we departed. ''Prince Arn, as promised I have horses for you and your companions at the village of Red Tavern, only two hours by wagon from here on the Tyler road. I will meet your group at the east gate outside of town and escort you to Red Tavern. Even this close to Dallas, local officials will not dare detain me."

We could abandon the wagons at Red Tavern and go by horseback, and on fast mounts there would be no danger of cavalry riding us down. My opinion of Landholder Fields went up a notch. We agreed to his plan and left the town hall, making our way through the streets of the town as quickly as we might without arousing the suspicions of any official. So far, so good.

The wagons and friends were waiting as we'd left them, the horses in their traces, harnessed and ready to go, our companions seated nearby on the soft grass of the green. They were watching for us, and stood as we came through the gate. The look of relief was evident on their faces, and Angela's eyes brimmed with tears.

She rushed into my arms and buried her head in my shoulder. "Oh, Arn. Waiting was torture." A gatekeeper watched us from above with an envious look. Angela's show of emotion had been unwise, perhaps, but I have to admit I felt relieved.

"What, you worried? You know I'm Arn the Invincible, don't you?"

"Stop teasing or I'll be angry."

I stopped.

Murdock counted heads and nodded, satisfied. Then he spoke loud enough for all to hear, playing to the listening ears of the gatekeeper. "Well, it took a bit longer than anticipated, but we have the new costume for the swordfight, so we may leave at last. No more time to waste. Everyone up and aboard. We're off now to the next town."

The others climbed up to their seats, and I was about to join them when a voice I'd heard once before spoke out. "Señor. Señor."

It was Maria. She waddled up rapidly, breathing hard, her voice low. "Señor Arn. It is Nancy. She is asking for you."

Señor *Arn*? So. Nancy or Zavakos had told Maria who I was. Our little secrets were becoming less and less secret.

Jenkins joined me on the ground. "Where is Zavakos?" he asked the woman.

She shrugged her big shoulders. "I don't know. He didn't

come back. The day you come, he went out before you left, and he never come back.''

So, Zavakos had figured it was time to pull up stakes. Well, he hadn't survived all these years by stupidity. A hundred-and-twenty Arkan dollars was a hefty sum. He'd be able to establish himself quite well in one town or another on that.

Jenkins shook his head. ''Too risky. We have to be going. He can visit her next time we come back to Dallas. Soon, I hope.''

Her voice became desperate. ''Next time? Oh, no. No next time. Señor, I think she is dying today. I saw my mother die. It is the same. But she asked for Señor Arn.''

Murdock climbed down and stood beside me, his face written with concern. ''You can't go now, Arn. It's too dangerous. We have to be away. You know that.''

Certainly I knew that. The gatekeeper was occupied examining a cart coming into the town. I stood in silence for a long moment. It was not that I felt anything. Not that, of course. But the woman wanted to see me. For the last time. And maybe this time she could be lucid, and give me some answers. The answers she could provide were tempting. And they made a good excuse.

I turned to Murdock. ''Take the wagons and go ahead. I'll follow when I may.''

Murdock looked at the walls of Dallas. He shook his head. ''No, it's too dangerous.''

''I'll be back quickly,'' I assured him. ''I'll meet you at the east gate.''

Jenkins threw up his hands in exasperation and slapped them against his trousers. ''All right, if we have to go, let's go. I'll take care of him again, sir. Don't worry.''

Angela climbed down. ''I'm going with you.''

''Angela, I'll be all right. You can't—''

''I'm going, I say. If you'll be all right, then I will be, too.''

Beth stepped out of the wagon box. ''If Angela is to go with you, then I will go with my Jenkins. Perhaps I can help.''

Murdock sighed. Discipline amongst the troops was falling apart. He looked up. ''And where do you two think you're going?'' he said to Lorich and Megan. ''No you don't. You get back on that wagon seat. These four are going, and that's enough. The rest of us will go ahead, and meet them at the east gate."

Megan was about to say something, but Murdock glared at her, and she sank back into her seat. Lorich hesitated a moment, and sat, too. "Yes, master."

Murdock glanced at Kren, but the beastman raised his palms. "Don't look at me. I do what I'm told."

Muttering, the wizard got back onto the wagon seat and looked at us sternly. "Take an hour, but no more. Don't disappoint me."

Jenkins scowled. "If we're going, we should go. Beth, I'm not happy about you doing this."

"Yes, James," Beth said without concern.

Maria gestured and set off, with us easily keeping up with her slow walk. From the green, Murdock and the others watched until we passed through the gate of the town.

Maria led us through town, down the street of filth, and through the door of her inn. Everything was the same as before, except that the heavy odor we'd detected before was stronger here, the air wispy with smoke. We followed Maria into Nancy's room.

Angela regarded the room with repugnance, though Beth seemed to accept it with a single glance around. They both focused upon the woman at the same moment, their faces betraying nothing. Were they thinking that Nancy Brown could not have been more than forty years old, though she looked not a day less than sixty? She looked much worse than she had two days ago. Her skin had turned gray, and she was even more frail. She rested on her side, a small, clay tobacco pipe in her mouth supported by those skeletal fingers. One might think Nancy too weak to manage it, yet incredibly, from the pipe rose wisps of smoke as she worked it in short, wheezy puffs. The smoke was thicker here, the acrid odor strong in my nostrils. And now the heavy odor was identified. Even on her deathbed, the woman was smoking opiate.

Angela and Beth each clutched one of my arms. "Oh, Arn—" Angela gasped. "The poor thing."

I stepped forward, drew up a chair, and sat down before the old crone. Her eyes were open, but they stared vacantly at the wall behind me, unseeing.

Maria stood in a corner, watching. "Only a little time left for poor Nancy. I will leave you with her." She closed the door as she went out.

"So, is this Nancy Brown?" Beth asked. "Is this your mother?"

I nodded. "From all I could tell. It's her."

Angela stood behind me. "Talk to her, Arn. See if she can hear you."

"Nancy?"

She did not hear. My throat was dry and my head fuzzy from the acrid fumes of the opiate. I swallowed and tried again, louder and more forcefully. "Nancy Brown. Do you hear me, Nancy?"

The eyes seemed to move, each following its own track before coming together and focusing upon me. So I had her eyes on me. Whether there was anything left of her mind behind them remained to be seen.

"What do I do now?" I muttered, more to myself than to the others.

The woman's thin lips curled into a smile around her pipe. "You came back."

"Yes, mother. I came back."

Mother. The term did not come easily to my lips.

The dreamy look on her face sloughed off, her eyes opened wide, and she saw me for the first time.

"So you're Arn," she stated softly but clearly. She placed her pipe carefully beside her on the sheet, bowl upwards, and the smoke continued to curl up into my face. She reached for my hand with trembling fingers.

I stared at the scabs and sores on the back of her hands and resisted the impulse to pull away.

A rotted smile formed again, though without the scorn that had been so prominent on my last visit. "Thank you for coming back. I'm sorry I was so harsh last time you visited. I wasn't myself. I wasn't thinking clearly. The pain does that."

To my amazement, the voice was gentle, the words precise, the tone dignified. Could the opiate make that much difference? Could this possibly be the same person I'd met last time?

I heard a sob behind me, and glanced that way. Angela was wiping her eyes of the tears that trickled down. Beth grabbed a bowl of water and with her kerchief wiped Nancy's forehead and cheeks.

Jenkins looked distinctly uncomfortable, perhaps as much from the old woman as from the danger of the situation. "I think I'll go outside and check to see that everything's all right. Keep the door closed."

Nancy's eyes followed Jenkins out the door, and then considered Angela and Beth. "Are these your friends?" She spoke cheerfully, as if in an afternoon chat with people she enjoyed.

"This is Angela, and Beth. The other was Jenkins. They are my companions, and my friends."

"That's nice to see. I'm glad they came with you. And I'm glad you came. I didn't know if you would. I was so rude."

"As you say, you weren't yourself."

"There is no excuse for rudeness. But that's how I am, if I don't have my pipe. Maria wouldn't let me have it all the time, but now I can have it as much as I want. She thinks I'm going to die soon. There's little pain today, so I think she's right."

That cheery tone still, unfazed by reality.

What to say? "Can we do anything for you?"

"Well, perhaps one thing. My, it's so strange to have you here. I can see your grandfather in you. His forehead and eyes. And his nose. Yes, you remind me of him."

"What can we do for you, Nancy?"

"Do? Oh, yes. One thing. Will you stay with me, Arn? Until I die? It would be nice having you here at the end. We don't really know each other. I can't be anything to you. But for a sick old woman, will you do that?"

"Mother, why—"

"*Mother*. That will take getting used to. Mother. But there isn't any time to get used to it, is there?"

"Mother, you knew where I was. Why didn't you come join me?"

"Join you?" she asked. "No, I'm afraid that wouldn't have been wise. Zee had already sent me out to work in the streets, my dear boy. No one would have wanted me."

So that was why she had not returned. She'd asked herself who would want Nancy Brown after that?

Yet I could think of one man, at least.

She went on. "So I stayed. It was the only thing to do, Arn. But I knew you were safe. That was enough. I did that. I sent you away."

"You did. Thank you for saving me from Zavakos."

"It was very hard to do. But after a few years, I was used to being alone."

Angela broke out into more sobs, and I gave her an exasperated look. Beth tried to quiet her. I turned to them. "Could you both wait outside, please? I would like a moment—a moment of privacy."

They went, Angela most reluctantly. The door to the room closed.

"Mother, I have a question for you."

"Yes, Arn?"

"Who was my father?"

"Your father?"

"Was it Reuel Brant? Or John Black?"

She looked at my hand in hers. "Is that important to you?"

"Just curious."

She closed her eyes, and her breathing slowed, and then grew unsteady, in little gasps. "My pipe. Where is my pipe?" I held it to her mouth, and she puffed, rekindling the tobacco so that the smoke swirled up again.

"Arn?"

"Yes, mother?"

"I don't know."

"What's that?"

"John and Reuel. I don't know which is your father."

Oh. Well, so much for that question. I don't think I would have been disappointed to find out which one had fathered me, and which one hadn't. They were equal in my mind, more alike than different, and to know would not have made any difference in my memory of them. But curiosity can be a powerful motive.

"Sorry to disappoint you," she consoled me.

"That's all right." My arm was getting tired. I moved her free hand up to her mouth, where she could hold the pipe herself. She puffed on it again. We were strangely silent, trying to figure out what to say to each other, her smoke swirling up and around us.

Then she spoke again. "Beth is Jenkins's woman?"

"Yes, mother."

"I could tell. She seems like a good, practical girl. And Angela is . . . ?"

"Yes, mother."

"A bit weepy, isn't she?"

I had no time to respond, for Jenkins burst through the door. "We have to go! Maria's betrayed us. She wasn't in her room, so I went out to look for her. She went straight to a deputy in the street before I could do anything. They went for more help, but they'll be coming soon."

Such news should have sent a bolt of fear up my spine, but I took it quite calmly, feeling not at all worried. Strange. Very strange. I thought through the situation for only a moment before my course was clear to me. "Jenkins, take Angela and Beth. Guard them well."

"You can't stay here, Arn," he countered. "You've got to come with us. There's still time to get away."

"Oh, I'll come. I'll come," I said placidly. "I'll just stay a little while. I don't think it'll be long."

"I'm not going," Angela declared.

Beth took my arm. "This is a mistake, Arn. You're risking everything."

"Perhaps," I answered in perfect tranquillity. "But I have to do it. Jenkins, take Angela along. She won't go willingly."

He shrugged, pushed Angela into Beth's arms, and firmly scooted them out into the passageway despite Angela's protests.

Jenkins hesitated, and stopped. "I'm not going."

"You have to go."

"I have to stay here to protect you. That's my duty."

"There's still time. I'll get away. And if not—"

"Sir, I won't leave you."

"Have you thought what will happen to Beth and Angela? They won't go of their own accord."

Jenkins was torn by indecision. "I should stay."

"But if they take you, who will be left to rescue me?"

He opened his mouth, and then shut it. I'd found an argument he couldn't deny. At times I surprise myself with my own cleverness. With an angry scowl he stomped out of the room, and I was alone. There was the sound of a door down the hall opening, and the protests of a pretty young woman with brown hair were cut off with the door's closing.

I turned back to the bed and sat down. I took Nancy's hand and gave her a smile. "Well, mother. Tell me about yourself."

"Arn, just what in the world is going on?"

"Oh, nothing. Don't worry. I'll stay with you."

"Are you in trouble?"

I was telling her about our General Jack Murphy when I heard the sound of a door opening down the hall, and then closing again. A bolt was shot home. I expected deputies, but it was not them. Yet.

"Angela."

She stood in the doorway of the room, triumphant. "I got away from Jenkins. I think Beth helped, or I couldn't have done it."

"He's never failed me before."

"He'll be limping for a little while, I'm afraid. I wasn't gentle, and caused an awful scene. You men make me mad, thinking you can order us about."

"You shouldn't have come back. You haven't thought of the consequences."

I spoke with amazing surety. The fumes of the pipe drifted up slowly into my face, and I breathed them in. They were not as bad as I'd thought them, before. In fact, the aroma was quite satisfying, once used to it. I felt very good. Very confident.

"Your consequences will be my consequences." Angela stated firmly, and then the defiance left her, and she came up to put a hand on my shoulder. "How is she?"

Nancy's feeble hand pulled the pipe from her lips. "*She* is dying, but that's not the concern."

Loud voices were heard. There was a pounding at the front door of the building.

"Young woman, you take Arn and go. And don't get all weepy. Go now."

I stood. "You're sure you don't mind?"

"Is this what it's like raising children? Go."

"Good-bye, mother."

"Go!"

We were out of the room and into the hall, but even through the noise from the breaking front door, I thought I heard her faint voice rising from the pillow. "None too bright, that boy."

I towed Angela down the hallway, and to a door at the back of the building. I opened it and stepped through. A deputy swung his club at me. I was amazed at how slowly he moved. I wrenched it from his grasp and broke it across his shoulder. Another deputy came from the side. I picked him up and threw him against the wall. I hadn't known I was that strong.

Angela shrieked behind me. I turned and saw deputies grabbing her and coming out the doorway. I stepped forward to help her, but four more grabbed my arms from behind and struggled to hold me. Another took his club and swung it at my head. It seemed to take a long time to get there, but when it arrived, the result was just as sure.

The world went black, and I knew no more.

6

The Dungeon

A bucket of cold water splashed hard in my face.

"He's coming around now, General."

I opened my eyes, saw nothing but a blur and shook my head. The last was a mistake. A wave of pain rolled in, broke against the interior of my skull in a blinding flash, and receded. I tried again, opening my eyes slowly. Light. There was light, hundreds of spots of light. The lights combined and joined and resolved themselves into a half dozen lamps hanging from the walls. And there were people. Their blurred forms came into focus, and suddenly I wanted to be unconscious again.

"Prince Arn!" General Murphy greeted me with a raspy voice that barely contained his glee. He was flanked by a dozen other men, most of whom were unfamiliar to me. But

I recognized two of them. One was Senior Aide Scott Chalmers, the bookish-looking functionary whom I had last seen in Kingsport with Landholder Mason, beseeching us to come and save his people from Murphy's tyranny. The other was Matthew Bartholomew, Murphy's chief of security, whom I had seen for the first time just two days before on the porch of the town hall, towering over everyone in his red jacket with the gold braid. He still had on a red jacket with gold braid. Apparently that was his permanent uniform. Both Chalmers and Bartholomew had evil smirks upon their faces, and I felt my stomach twist.

We had been betrayed. And I was in their power.

"Welcome," the general continued jovially. "Welcome to my dungeon."

Senior Aide Chalmers laughed. "Yes, Prince Arn, that's where you are. Take a look around. You see, it's just as General Murphy has said. This is the dungeon of Castle Corral. You're hidden deep below the earth, far away from sun and sky, and surrounded by crete and stone and mortar and very thick and strong doors with large, heavy locks."

I looked around, and it was as he had said. The only detail he had left out were the cuffs around my wrists, and the chains at my ankles shackled to a large iron ring in the wall. I felt the links. They were very cold—and very strong.

"Well, Prince Arn," Murphy gloated. "Are you going to curse at me? Are you going to say that while chains might hold you, nothing can bind your spirit? Hmmmm?"

"No," I stated reluctantly. My spirit was quite subdued for the moment, thank you.

"A realist!" Murphy exclaimed, "As well as an idealist. How interesting."

There were chuckles from the others. But Matthew Bartholomew did not laugh. His massive jaw was set firmly beneath thick, beetling brows while he considered me with the same interest a hungry cat might have for a wounded bird. His voice was deceptively soft, almost gentle. "Where are your friends?"

General Murphy shook his head, as if saddened. "Ahh, Prince Arn, you see how it is. My loyal follower, Bartholomew, is so anxious to begin business that he would cut short our bit of fun. Then again, Bartholomew's business is his fun. Have you heard of my sheriff, Prince Arn?"

I swallowed, trusting myself to do no more than nod.

"You have? Good. We have you where we want you. Our little plan worked. You came to free our poor people from my wicked rule—and put yourself within my grasp. I knew you would. You're that kind of man, aren't you? Honorable and caring and just full of self-sacrifice."

Honorable? Caring? He must be confusing me with Robert.

"I must admit," he went on, "you had us completely fooled with that inspired acting of yours at Lexington. You disarmed us completely. We actually thought you were a frightened, incompetent fool."

"You . . . had . . . reason," I managed to gasp through lips trembling with fear.

"Come now, Prince Arn, that act won't work again. Fool us once, shame on you. Fool us twice. . . . Now we know just how devious you can be. Take that ridiculous 'traveling theater' idea. One of our deputies saw your show, and he recognized you when you were brought in. You intended to wander through the length of Arkan and Texan without ever being found out? Completely insane."

"That's what . . . I told them . . . too."

Bartholomew nodded in agreement, and then spoke himself, a tone of wonder in his soft words. "And yet, it worked! We were looking for a few men—merchants, perhaps, who would come sneaking into Texan this spring. We never dreamed that we should watch out for a slow-moving circus like yours. Such an idea would be too incredible. But that was the way you chose, and that was the way that worked."

General Murphy studied my face. "Oh, yes. It worked. We didn't know you were here. Not at all. We expected you, and warned our border officials and sheriffs to be looking for a man with a scar, traveling alone or with two or three other men as merchants or such. But we missed you completely. It quite embarrassed Bartholomew to hear the news of your capture."

"Someone has to pay," Bartholomew said to me. "Do you know who's going to pay?"

Somehow, I had a vague feeling of who that someone was.

My stomach flopped, but I held back the sickness. For the moment.

Murphy grinned at his man. "I'm afraid Bartholomew is quite upset with you, Prince Arn. Your plan might have worked, if it were not for that wonderful fat woman who came to our deputies with a wild tale that Prince Scar was in town. When you resisted, they brought you to the castle, and I personally identified you."

"They had quite a time taking you, I understand," Bartholomew continued. "One with a broken shoulder, and one with cracked ribs—"

My mouth fell open. "I did that?"

"Indeed. Quite a feat for an unarmed man. But then, you're noted for improbable feats, aren't you? The deputies weren't too happy with you, I'm afraid. No, not happy at all. But they restrained themselves and brought you to the castle. And here you are. You and the pretty young woman."

I gagged. Angela!

Perhaps it was the effect of the opium I'd inhaled at Nancy's bedside. Or perhaps it was the fear which held me so tightly that I had to clench my teeth to keep them from chattering. Or perhaps it was my own selfish nature. Whatever the reason, I had entirely forgotten that she was with me at Nancy's end. Yet as soon as Bartholomew mentioned her, I remembered. The few rays of hope vanished, and I fought back the cloud of despair that threatened to envelop me.

Angela.

The look on my face must have revealed all. Murphy enjoyed it no end. "Ahh, I see she means something to you. Well, let's see. Bartholomew, have her brought in. That's right, Prince Arn. She's here, as deeply entombed as you are. She offers all kinds of possibilities, don't you think? Ah, here she is."

Angela was led in, her hands tied behind her back, her hair wildly askew in a fashion that merely heightened her attractiveness rather than diminished it. She looked about defiantly until she saw me, and then with a gasp tried to rush forward, only to be painfully restrained by the guard holding her arms.

No, I didn't struggle and cry out and attempt to rush to her. My mind was too clear for that, now. No use inviting further damage until it could be of some benefit. And for all my calculated restraint, for all the fear which prompted it, I still felt a wave of unreasonable anger aimed not at my scurrilous captors, but rather at poor, innocent Angela. Anger that she had insisted on joining our troupe. Anger that she had stayed with me at Nancy's bed. Anger that she stood before me now.

And then the anger was replaced by another emotion. I thought my cup of fear had been full. Now it was overflowing, for I feared not just for myself, but for her.

Murphy stood and put an arm around Angela's waist, pulling her resisting form to him. "And quite charming she is, too. I hadn't seen her before. What is your name, girl?"

She looked at me, and I nodded.

"Angela," she replied proudly, never taking her eyes from me.

His fingers stroked her waist, and then he released her and sat down again. "Angela what?"

"Angela Kauffman, daughter of Andrew Kauffman, late mayor of Lexington."

"Lexington . . ." breathed Murphy. "Lexington is no more."

"Neither is the Army of the Alliance. Were you there with that rabble? Pity you had to leave."

Murphy's swarthy skin turned red. Bartholomew's lips thinned into a tight line. The smiles were gone from their followers. That was my sweet, dear Angela. Infuriating the enemy to no purpose. Let a woman have a little education. . . .

She laughed at them. A laugh of desperation and fear, perhaps, but still a laugh. I could not manage as much. She spoke. "You've held us no more than two hours, and already you congratulate yourselves. Yet, have we told you anything? Not a question have you asked of me, and none would I answer, if you had. And I know Arn would not give you a scrap of information. Let us go now, and perhaps he will spare you."

Was her defiance calculated for my benefit? Certainly, the information she had given me was critical. It had only been two hours. And they had not yet questioned her. Then Murdock and Jenkins and the conspirators might be safely away, or on their way, at least. There was still hope, then. But it was most important not to give away anything.

Bartholomew lifted an eyebrow. "She is clever, this young woman. Did you hear, General, how she passed information to the prince? Two hours. No information. Key facts to give her brave hero as they attempt to delay us and give their friends time to flee. Such qualities are rare.'' He gave her a searching look. ''But we know everything we need to know. Your companions have taken the east road to Tyler. Doubtless, they expect to meet a ship there, or perhaps even a few regiments of the Army of Kenesee? Well, they won't, because soon a company of horse guardos will be hard on its way behind them. I think our guards will have little problem running them down in their slow wagons. But if not, there is no loss. We have the one we sought. The rest are of no consequence without their Prince Scar.''

Good guesses. I made no outward show at the words, but worry for my companions was mixed with hope. Murphy and his minions did not know of Landholder Fields's arrangements. Murdock and the rest had probably reached the village of Red Tavern by now, and so found the speedy mounts provided by Fields. They would be away, and the guards pursuing would remain far behind. Or so I hoped.

But Angela knew nothing of these arrangements. The dismay on her face could not be hidden. ''They have done nothing. You have us. Let them go.''

Murphy enjoyed her futile pleas. '' 'Let them go,' she says,'' and he burst into laughter. The others dutifully followed his example. ''You shouldn't be worrying about them, my dear. You should be worrying about yourself. Yes, and your Prince Scar, too.''

I spoke up again at last. ''This woman . . . is nothing to me.''

''Nothing to you?'' Bartholomew asked. ''Are you sure? Then you won't care if we put her into the regimental brothel.''

I shrugged, and my chains rattled. ''She was a servant to us, no more.''

Murphy waved a hand. ''Enough of this. If she's a servant, then she's nothing to Prince Scar, and he doesn't care about her. If he doesn't care about her, then she is of no use to us. Bartholomew, you may kill her.''

He hesitated. ''Now, sir?''

''Yes, now.''

Bartholomew nodded and drew his knife. Angela's eyes

grew wide and a tremble went through her, but then she drew herself erect and braced for the blow, her lips moving silently in a final prayer before the end.

I had never seen her more beautiful.

Bartholomew's hand came back to strike her heart, the knife gleaming in the lamplight.

"Stop!" I gasped.

The knife point held steady, waiting.

"Please. General Murphy. Stop."

Murphy put up his hand, and Bartholomew lowered the knife. The general looked pleased. "Ahh. Now we're getting somewhere. I take it this young woman is not a servant."

I shook my head. "Not a servant."

"And I take it she means a great deal to you."

I nodded. "A great deal."

Angela tried to move toward me.

"She is your true love, perhaps?"

"I will never . . . have another."

Angela smiled through the tears that welled up. "Oh, Arn."

"Perhaps we should ask him a few questions before it gets too late," Bartholomew reminded the general.

"Yes. Questions. Go ahead. And you must answer them, Prince Scar. Or she will die."

I thought Angela was going to blurt something out, then. Perhaps a defiant "Don't tell them anything, Arn," or a stern "You'll get nothing from us. Kill us, if you will." But her courage had, I think, been stretched as far as it would go. Or possibly she feared for me. Or a combination of the two. In any case, she said nothing further, and I thanked the heavens for her silence.

"Well, Prince Arn, are you ready?" Murphy asked impatiently.

"On one condition," I gasped.

"No conditions," the general responded.

"Promise that she will come to no harm."

"This becomes tedious."

"Promise. That is all I ask."

He chuckled. "You would believe *my* promise? Well, then, so be it. I promise. There, are you satisfied now? In my own dungeon, we can't even have a simple interrogation without prisoners making demands. Whatever are we coming to?"

Bartholomew was precise and efficient, his questions short

and sharp. I answered promptly, but cautiously. This would have to be carefully done, providing truth and lie in a believable package, and keeping a frustrated Murphy from giving the order once again.

He asked about our companions, and I truthfully told him where they were going. He apparently already knew that, anyway, and it was too late to get military units there before the Kenesee regiments landed. He asked what would happen at Tyler, and I told him of our regiments landing. He asked when the landings would take place, and I lied. Three weeks hence, I told him. He asked who was involved in the conspiracy, and I mentioned the names of those I knew except for Chalmers. They obviously knew his double-dealing role. If the rest were not already away to safety, then they were fools, and of little use to the cause. He asked what our plans were, and I told him. After all, any decent strategist could have figured it out as the logical course of action.

Whatever they wanted, I told them, truth and lies mixed in a great deceit that teetered, almost literally, on a knife edge. It would become clear I'd lied. Eventually. But for a day, or two, or three, my answers had to serve as the semblance of truth, for Angela's life was the price if my tale were disbelieved.

My treachery was not as dark as it appeared. The great struggle had already begun. The landholders and mayors and colonels were at that moment spurring back to their lands and towns and regiments, and it would be a slow and foolish one indeed who would let himself be caught by Murphy's horsemen. My own companions should have reached Red Tavern and mounted fast steeds for Tyler. And within the next day or two the regiments of Kenesee would be disembarking, if they had not done so already. There was no time to interfere with that. Even if he ordered his guardos to march at once, they could not be at Tyler within forty-eight hours. And the guardos could do nothing but face the closed gates and high walls of Tyler, while the regiments of Kenesee landed at the port and prepared to march out to give battle to the outnumbered guardos.

All Murphy could prudently do with my information was order the callup of his own forces and decide upon a course of action. It would take a fortnight to mobilize his regiments and assemble them at Dallas. A week ago, such information in Murphy's hands would have been disastrous to the cause, and he would have been one step ahead of us as we attempted to mobilize, assemble, and land forces at Tyler. Now, he could only respond to the course of events. Thus, whatever I said would make little difference at this late date.

However, my capture would have an adverse, perhaps fatal, effect upon our efforts. With me in his hands, a quick march with loyal troops upon Tyler would be Murphy's likeliest course. Without Prince Scar to inspire the Kenesee regiments and reassure the Texan conspirators, the combined forces would be an uncertain army, at best. An energetic General Murphy would have a good chance of crushing the rebellion in a single open-field battle. If—instead of offering battle—the rebels and Kenesee troops refused his challenge and holed up inside Tyler's walls, Murphy could dig in for a siege and rally the country behind him against the cowardly conspirators and invaders. An army that would not come out and fight would gain little respect, and the people would follow Murphy simply because he would seem to have the upper hand.

My actions—and Angela's, it must be admitted—had severely compromised our chances for victory. Well, I had warned Robert not to depend on me.

I answered the last question they had for me, and Senior Aide Chalmers dutifully recorded the essentials in writing. "That should be all we need from him, General. Nothing, of course, that we didn't suspect already. Do you have any other questions for the prisoner?"

Murphy looked at the stone ceiling. "More? No, I don't think so. Anyone else? All right, we are done with him, for now. Prince Arn, we'll spare you for the moment. Senior Aide Chalmers has already pointed out to me that you have notable value as a bargaining chip, and we want you reasonably whole until this little matter is resolved." He bestowed a beatific smile upon me. "After that, well, we'll make a few changes to you so that the darkness down here won't make a difference. That will be fitting vengeance for that trick at Lexington."

I grasped at schemes. "Perhaps—perhaps I could be useful in other ways. You haven't offered me any possibilities, General Murphy."

"Nor will I," he scoffed. "I know you're not a fool. Don't think me one, either. And now, I think our little meeting is at an end. Oh, one last thing. Since we can't yet pay you back as I might like, perhaps we can make you suffer in other ways. Bartholomew, you may kill the girl now."

My throat constricted so that I could barely speak. "General Murphy . . . you gave me . . . your word."

"Yes, I did." He broke into laughter. "Ahh, Prince Arn, you are a humorous fellow. To pretend that you expected me to honor my word. Well, let's get on with it, Bartholomew. I'm curious to see his face when the blade goes in."

Bartholomew spoke. "I will do as you request, General. However, may I make a request?"

The general paused. "A request?"

Bartholomew continued. "She takes my fancy. I would like to—use her." Murphy frowned, and Bartholomew continued quickly. "It would only be for a short time. I will have my—my pleasure—I assure you. Prince Arn will squirm here in the dark, knowing what is happening to his woman, and what will ultimately happen."

Murphy considered it. "Yes, there is a certain satisfaction for us with that. So be it. Bartholomew, you have been a good and faithful servant, and I award you this boon. May it be noted by all my staff that General Murphy rewards those who serve him well."

"Thank you, General," Bartholomew bowed as Murphy headed for the door.

The general paused. "But see what you can do to our prince without leaving permanent marks."

Murphy liked his vengeance, but he wasn't a sadist who had to hear every scream to enjoy the satisfaction of malice fulfilled.

"As you wish, General."

Murphy left, followed by all but two of the followers. "Take her to my quarters," Bartholomew told the men. "Chain her to the bed, and make sure she's still healthy when I get there."

They took her, then, and dragged her out without ceremony, her only words trailing off as they took her down the corridor. "Arn! Don't worry, Arn . . ."

Bartholomew waited until the voice had faded away, and

then ambled over to a table covered with various instruments which I didn't even want to look at closely. He considered the selection carefully, and then picked up a short truncheon, weighing it in his hand before finally deciding that it would do.

"And now, Prince Arn, why don't we get better acquainted?"

It was a very painful acquaintance.

7

The Pacifican

"Prince Arn! Can you hear me, Prince Arn?"

The voice was a loud whisper.

Consciousness had returned, albeit reluctantly. I was seated—sprawled might be a better word—on a cold stone floor, my head and shoulders leaning against what must be a stone wall that was just as cold. I opened my eyes, and went through the same unpleasant focusing as I had before, only this time my eyes adjusted not to myriad lights, but to total darkness. No, not total. A single source of illumination remained. From a small grilled opening a foot or two above me, a dim light filtered through in a small square. I moved, and heard groaning. The groaning was my own.

Bartholomew had been both thorough and skillful in his ministrations. He certainly did enjoy meeting new people.

"Prince Arn?" The voice again. An accent of mixed English and Spanish, overlaid with something else that was vaguely familiar, but that, in my disorientation, I could not for the moment place.

The shackles were still upon my arms and legs, but I could not detect any chain connecting me to a wall. My ribcage protested every movement, and my limbs were stiff and ached unmercifully at the joints. I raised myself onto my hands and knees, and grimaced with the pain. Bartholomew had paid particular attention to elbows and knees. I could have cried out, but that would have hurt too much. I crawled three short steps to just below the square of light, if such the feeble glow could be called.

My head bumped against a flat wooden surface. A door. I had, apparently, been moved to a tiny cell somewhere in this godforsaken dungeon. Leaning against the door, I brought myself up to my knees, and then got both feet under me, an effort which left me panting like a dog. And that hurt too. I clutched at the grill over the opening and hauled myself onto my feet, fighting off the dizziness that threatened to bring me down again. Peering out into the dimness beyond my cell, everything seemed darkness and shadows before resolving into a low, narrow corridor which curved to the left. That was the source of the feeble glow that penetrated into my cell, the mere reflection of a torch or lamp placed beyond the curve in the wall.

There was movement across the way. The shadows resolved themselves into a door like the one to which I clung, complete to the square grilled opening. Something pale was moving behind the grill. The vague outline of a face. From the voice, I guessed the man might have been fifty or so.

I shifted my stance, and groaned again.

"Prince Arn, are you all right?"

I was entombed in the most sinister dungeon on the continent by my worst enemy, my woman was in the hands of a sadist, and I had just been beaten half to death. Was I all right?

"I'm not sure. Let me . . . think about it."

Muted laughter filled the silence, and then faded away. "Thank you, Prince Arn. It's been many days since I've laughed. There has not been much good news down here, I'm afraid. Not much of any news, if truth be told. It will be pleasant to have someone to talk to. A man could go crazy in these cells. A year or two of darkness and silence would do that—but I know General Murphy does not keep his prisoners long, so I probably shouldn't worry about it in my case. But in yours—I must admit he planned to make you the exception. Or so he implied to us in his musings."

People keep telling me more than I want to hear. "Are there many others here?"

"In this block of cells? No, just you and I. There are other prisoners. There are always prisoners, but they're in other cell blocks. This is Murphy's most secure block, for his special guests. You and I qualify. We're quite honored, don't you think?"

"Who are you?"

"Who am I? I am a fool. A traitor. A disgrace. But that describes what I am, more than who I am. My name is Gregor Pi-Ling. Does that mean anything to you?"

I thought about it. I had heard the name somewhere, but—

"Your Paul Kendall knows me very well."

I had the clue I needed. The slight overlay of accent became clear. "Gregor Pi-Ling. You are the Pacifican advisor to General Murphy."

"Very good. Your wits are returning to you."

I paused, ordering my thoughts. "What are you doing down here?"

I could hear the shuffling of his feet on the dank stone floor. "It seems I fell out of General Murphy's favor. He feared I might be plotting his death, a fear stoked by the whispering tongues of others in the castle. There is no shortage of intrigue here, and I, the master of intrigue, found myself outdone. He was right, though. I was plotting his end. Of course, all would have turned out differently had we not been defeated in Kenesee, but for that I can blame no one but myself."

If he thought I was going to indulge him in his remorse, he was sadly mistaken. I would gladly have strangled him had we been in the same cell. "Mr. Kendall said that you started this war—you and the Pacificans from Virginia and the Isles."

"Did he?" Pi-Ling asked. "Paul always could ferret out the truth, same as his father. It cost him an arm, I know. Is he all right?"

"I presume so. He's been gone for several months. I don't know where."

"I hope he's well. I can imagine a few places he might be. Doing his job, no doubt. He always was most loyal to the Codes. Dogmatic and committed to each page and line, just like Mikofsky over in Arkan. Stubborn ideologues who couldn't see the future. Or so I thought in my pride." He fell silent a moment, and then spoke. "Do you know how the war began, Prince Arn? Do you know *why* it was fought?"

The man wanted to talk. I would let him talk. "Tell me."

"I started it," he responded, the resignation and regret mixed with self-indulgent pride. "Yes, it was my fault, my responsibility. I had always dreamed of the future, a future I would never live to see, of course, where the technology of the Old World would reappear and spread across the continent, bringing us to a new golden era for mankind that would eliminate slavery and poverty and disease. The idea was seductive to one with my idealism and vision, especially when mired in the reality of Texan. You see, not all Pacificans are as fortunate as Paul Kendall. Not all of us are assigned to prosperous countries with enlightened rulers. Not all of us can give advice and make suggestions with impunity, secure in the knowledge that their good king will treat those suggestions with good will and good sense."

Pi-Ling was waiting for some comment before going on, and so I provided it. "I see. You betrayed General Murphy, and that is why you call yourself traitor."

"Not at all," he protested. "You misunderstand me. I feel no loyalty to General Murphy. My loyalties were to Pacifica, and the ideal of the Codes which it had promulgated. That is what I betrayed. It is to my own countrymen that I am a traitor, not this petty tyrant Murphy."

"Go on," I urged him, becoming interested in spite of myself.

There was a glimmer of satisfaction in his voice as he continued. Satisfaction not in what he could say, but in having an interested listener. "Pacifica has done a great thing for the world, bringing the six nations into being, guiding their development, helping their population grow, offering knowledge for their prosperity, and limiting destructive forms of technological development. It has not been easy. It has taken men willing to dedicate their lives to an ideal.

"And yet, even an idealistic man may be led astray—by his own pride, as well as by other men. I began to think that our leaders in Pacifica were perhaps too conservative, too slow in their philosophy. Those of us at work among the nations of North America certainly knew more about conditions than those safely isolated in Pacifica. We should be making the decisions, or so I told myself. Perhaps more drastic action would bring about a greater good.

"A united continent would certainly hold great benefit. It would eliminate the sporadic wars between individual nations. It would provide the opportunity to eliminate evils particular to one nation or another, such as slavery and religious intolerance. It would moderate the power and actions of the more tyrannical leaders, such as Murphy. Yes, there were very real advantages to uniting the six nations.

"Thus armed with pride and intellect, years ago I went to a gathering of the Pacifican advisors and carefully—very carefully—raised the issue of unification with each of them in turn. My counterparts, Raashi in Virginia and Hashimoto in the Isles, were both mildly intrigued by the idea, and so I found opportunity to invite them to Texan for sport and education. The subject of unification just happened to come up somehow, and, well, you can imagine the rest.

"It took several years, actually, to bring my countrymen from skepticism to enthusiasm, but I was able to do it. And then we started to influence the leaders we advised, pointing out the advantages of unity, but always cushioning the advantages in terms of personal gain for themselves. And all that time, Kendall in Kenesee and Mikofsky in Arkan and Habutu in Mexico were unaware of what we were doing.

"I was quite full of myself by that time, and blissfully assumed that once set upon the path, advisors and leaders would all follow me complacently as I led the way to a new order. But Governor Rodes and General Murphy are not men to be led around by the nose, and soon they began hatching their own plans. I had not planned to bring back powder weapons, but that was one of their first concerns. I did what I could, but found my counterparts in Texan and Virginia going along with the rulers. The wagon I'd laboriously pushed uphill was finally rolling down the far slope, but I could no longer keep up with it. In time, I watched the mantle of leadership gradually slip from my shoulders and onto those of Governor Rodes. Quite a formidable man."

I listened, fascinated. Kendall had never given us so much detail. "Did you say anything to them?"

"Say anything? What was I to say? I had started it all. Besides, they argued, if we toss out one part of the Codes, why not toss them all? There was a logic to their arguments, and I found myself going along with them. For I had lied to myself. My pride saw me as a leader of men, but I am only a follower. I had not the strength of will to resist the others, and went along with their plans. I didn't like their plans, but I was in too deep to get out. You can understand that, can't you?"

I moved ever so slowly, trying to loosen the bruised and tightened muscles of my body. "And so it came to war."

The white face blurred as he shook his head. "I didn't want war. I never expected that. I thought at the worst, we could bluff the other countries into joining the Alliance. It worked with Patron Esteves in Mexico. His economy was weak, and his people not happy. He feared for his position, and we guaranteed him his rulership. It worked with King Herrick in Arkan. He was uncertain, and frightened by our strength and our will. He saw no chance against the combined strength of four nations. And finally, when the five rulers had agreed to joint action, we sent emissaries to Kenesee. We thought none could defy the five nations of the Alliance. I was reluctant now, but thought that perhaps a greater good could still be accomplished."

Pi-Ling fell silent, perhaps mulling over his own words.

I remembered something. "You—you had your counterparts killed. Mikofsky in Arkan died so suddenly, depriving King Herrick of good advice. And Habutu had to flee Mexico to escape assassination."

"So, you know about that, do you? Kendall told you that much, then. I was against such things. I have killed. I know what it is to have blood on my hands. But I had never killed a countryman. Yet Rodes and Murphy and my counterparts thought it was important to remove the Pacifican advisors from the equation. I think they had grown frightened by what they were doing, and to deny their fear they grew arrogant and ruthless. It was then that I spoke out against this war, and began plotting ways to stop General Murphy."

This villain made things too simple. I wondered whether to believe him. "You planned a rebellion?"

"A rebellion? That is not the way of Pacificans. We advise. We cajole. We persuade. We reason. And when those tools do not work, there is one more."

"One more?" I asked.

"Oh, come now, Prince Arn. Surely you are not that naive. Do you think our elimination of Mikofsky was something new for us? When nothing else works, there is always the last option. We are quite subtle about it, you know. Perhaps an overdose of a healer's drug. Or outright poison, if necessary. In need, we have turned to more violent means. On most occasions, poison will do quite nicely.

"I can guess what you're thinking. Murderer. Assassin. But we do not think of it as such. Rather our victims are casualties. And better one casualty now than a hundred later. The Codes are not perfect, but they have limited the evils of mankind. I forgot that, for awhile."

I had listened in disbelief. "You're assassins? You expect me to believe that Jason Kendall—that Paul Kendall—are assassins? I know them. They cannot be."

I could not see it, but I imagine that Pi-Ling shrugged. "That is the way we have preserved the Codes. Assassination. We are trained for it. Someone threatens a violation, and suddenly he is found dead. There was none better than Jason Kendall. He was a doctor, and who better to know the fastest way to end a life? I was quite surprised when he retired and returned to healing. I could not fathom how he could leave the halls of power. Now, I understand."

My mind churned the information. "It seems . . . so unlikely."

"Unlikely, perhaps. But not impossible. Jason was excellent, you know. In the old days, when we had a particularly difficult case, I'd call for Jason's help. Paul is not as good as his father. I prefer calling Raashi from Virginia to help me when there is need."

I wanted to disbelieve what I was hearing, and yet deep down . . . I knew. It was known that those who violated the Codes would eventually meet an ill fate, as had happened to Professor Jameson when I was a boy. At that time, I had assumed High Wizard Graven was responsible. My brother was not so sure of that, and had long suspected that Kendall had a hand in the demise of the violators. Pi-Ling's narration, unfortunately, rang true.

I could manage but a word. "Why?"

"Why? Why do we do this? For the great experiment, of

course. The great plan. The goal of Pacifica, to bring peace and prosperity to the continent. Why else would we do such things?"

"Peace? Prosperity? Is that what you've brought?"

He blinked. "Not perfectly. But we tried. The experiment wasn't over, the plan was not complete. At least, not until my pride led us to disaster. Strange, I can see my faults and mistakes so clearly now. Sometimes I wish I felt more remorse."

"Why didn't you use your—your talents to kill General Murphy? Why let him go on this way?"

"Ahh, you've come to the crux of it all, you know. I should have. I should have. I can see that now. But it is one thing to eliminate underlings. It is quite another to eliminate rulers. Our philosophy does not go quite so far. As I've said, elimination is the last alternative, not the first. By the time I saw the necessity for such action, General Murphy had recognized the threat, and—well, here I am."

I shook my head. "All the pain and suffering. All the death. Just because you wanted to—to speed things up."

"I suppose, in a manner of speaking, that you're—"

There was the rasp of a rusty bolt being thrown. Pi-Ling went silent immediately, and the milky blur of his face faded back from the opening into the darkness of his cell. From down the corridor a light approached, and the footsteps of men. I watched as they came up, stopping before my cell. There was Senior Aide Chalmers, a red-jacketed officer with a pair of guardos in similar attire, and two men, one big and one small, each of whom carried a ring of keys on his belt that jingled as he walked. Jailers always look like jailers.

"Here we are sir," said the big jailer. "That's him, Prince Scar."

I peered out, squinting in the brightness of the lantern a guardo carried. I put on my best surly voice. "Senior Aide Chalmers. What a delight to see you again."

The jailers brightened. "Shall we beat him for you, sir? That's the rules. If a prisoner talks, we get to beat him."

Chalmers looked amused. "No, not this time. He has been well beaten already. I think General Murphy will have other uses for Prince Scar."

"Yes, sir." The jailer sorted through his collection of keys, chose one, and inserted it into the keyhole. It turned with a rasp. Apparently, no one ever oiled anything down here. Or maybe they did, and it just didn't make any difference. The door swung inward, and I backed painfully into a corner. The way I felt, I should be able to fight them off for, oh, two, maybe three seconds.

"Come out, Prince Arn," Chalmers invited.

There really was no choice. I limped out of the cell and stood before them.

"You may remove his leg irons."

The jailer hesitated. "Are you sure, sir? I mean, orders are to keep them in shackles at all times."

"Quite right," Chalmers agreed. "But General Murphy ordered me to have him ready to ride. A bit hard to do with the leg irons, no?"

The jailer chuckled. "You have a point, sir. You have a point. All right, Fred, take 'em off." The small jailer removed the leg irons with yet another key. It didn't make escape any more likely, since I'd have trouble keeping up with a fast turtle. The wrist cuffs came off too.

The officer with the lantern led the way up the corridor, while the guardos took me by either arm and helped me follow, crowding in upon me from either side in the narrow passageway. Then we came to stone steps, and the two guardos as good as carried me up, for there was no other way I could have mounted the stair in my condition. We went up one level, and then another, and a third before finally emerging into what appeared to be the ground floor of a tower. We passed through a door and into the lamplit corner of a large, central courtyard surrounded by the castle and its outer walls. The cobwebs cleared from my mind, at least temporarily.

There were saddled horses clustered nearby, with four more guardos waiting beside them. They carried me to one horse, and stepped back so that I had to stand on my own feet beside it. I grabbed at the saddle and prevented myself from sliding to the ground.

What fate awaited me at the end of this journey? It could not be good. "Unless you're rescuing me, why should I get on this horse?"

Senior Aide Chalmers stepped close and spoke softly. "Because we are rescuing you."

I groaned. "You are cruel, Chalmers. Crueler than you know."

"It's true. I swear it. You'll have to mount, Prince Arn."

A rescue. Hah. I laughed at him. "I can barely stand. How am I supposed to get up there?"

"You have to," he whispered. "It's your only hope. And ours. We have to leave now, or all our lives are forfeit. We ride to Tyler."

"Ride to—Tyler?"

The guard officer came near, his voice low but urgent. "Good God, what's wrong? Shall we lift him up?"

"If need be," Chalmers said to the officer. Then he looked at me closely. "We ride to Tyler. Or wherever you tell us. But we have to go now."

The deadly earnestness in his voice could not be faked—or else he was the finest actor on the continent. "It's true?"

"Yes, it's true. Please believe us, Prince Arn. Every minute is precious, and I am frightened as I have never been in my life. To be found out now is death. Or worse."

I accepted his words at last, but realized I could not go. "No," I said firmly. "Not without Angela."

The officer rolled his eyes. Chalmers put a hand upon my arm, his voice calm but resolute. "We can't take her. We can't get to her. Don't you understand that? It was risky enough getting to you. There is no one else to help us here in the castle. And we could be discovered at any time. Our bridges are burnt now. Please, Prince Arn, go with us. Together we can defeat Murphy and return to save your woman. If you stay here, she and all of us are doomed."

He was right, of course. Reason, sanity, common sense. To stay would be foolish. And yet. . . . I looked up at the castle stretching above me. Somewhere within, Angela was at Bartholomew's mercy. Somewhere within, perhaps only a few dozen feet away, she waited for me to rescue her. And I could do nothing. Not now. Not here. To go was the only thing to do. But it didn't help the way I felt.

"Help me . . . to mount."

They put a foot in the stirrup, and with hands pushing me up from beneath I found myself mounted, though hunched over the horse's neck.

"Can you ride, Prince Arn?" the officer asked.

I took the reins and drew myself erect. "I will ride." I looked again at the castle walls. "And I will come back."

Relief spread across Chalmers' face. "Good. Good. So it shall be." He and the others mounted their steeds, and we proceeded at a walk, the hooves echoing loudly upon the stones of the courtyard. The gatekeepers nodded at our little party, unaware of the ruse. Under a raised portcullis we went, through a tunnel, under another portcullis, and then across the drawbridge and into the town. We passed the town plazas, shadowed and quiet now in the night, came to the east gate, and bid the gatekeeper open for us. He would think twice before questioning Murphy's senior aide and a squad of guardos. We cleared the gate and broke into a trot, Chalmers and the officer on either side of me, and each extending an arm as I swayed in the saddle.

We had a long way to go, and our escape was not yet assured.

But at least there was hope.

8

Returned to the Board

We rode through the hours of darkness, our way discernible in the light of a moon that was almost full, but almost lost beneath the trees that so often marked the woods through which we passed. The darkness at last brought us to a halt when the moon went behind a cloud.

For me it had been a nightmarish journey, our progress a combination of fear and pain as we rode, moving from trot to walk to canter depending upon the quality of light and the state of the horses. The soreness in my body was such that I had to clench my teeth to keep from crying out. I should have been in bed, ministered to by doctors and healers, not pounding down foreign lanes in the darkness. Only my desire to save Angela kept me in the saddle.

The moon reappeared and we started forward again, only to stop not ten minutes later at a crossroads. Well, not really a crossroads, but merely the point at which a cow path intersected the old crete highway.

The guardos officer—a captain by the name of Metaxis, I had found out—stared along the direction of the cowpath. "Corporal Dominic, is this it? Is this the side road we need to take?"

Corporal Dominic shook his head slowly. "I'm not sure, sir."

Captain Metaxis swore. "What do you mean, you're not sure? You're from around Petersville, aren't you?"

"Yes, sir."

"Well, then?"

Dominic hesitated. "I only took the path once, Captain. And that was in daylight. I'm not sure this is it."

Senior Aide Chalmers straightened in the saddle, and with his face turned up to the moon I could see his shadowy features wince. He didn't find hours in the saddle any fun either, yet his voice was patient. "What shall we do now, Captain?"

Metaxis snorted. "We'll send out scouts. It'll cost us a bit of time, but we're getting close to the horse guardos. Dominic, go and figure out whether this is the path. Goldman, take a man and go forward along the main road up to that rise ahead. We'll wait for you here." The scouts started their horses off at a quiet walk. "Nothing ever comes easy. How are you holding up, Prince Arn?"

"Half of me is dead, the other half is dying."

There were chuckles from the guardos. "Well, if he can still joke about it, he can't be too bad off."

People keep thinking I joke about such things.

Amid the daze in which I seemed to exist during this ride, there were moments of clarity. My thoughts cleared enough to think of a question. "Aide Chalmers," I said, slowly, "what has your role been in all this?"

"Puzzled, Prince Arn? Well, I can't blame you. It's not a long story. I worked as a border inspector in Whitesboro. But I liked books and learning and organizing things. So I sent letters to Dallas with suggestions for improvements. They appointed me to General Murphy's staff. Quite a step up for the son of a miller.

"I considered myself quite fortunate, until I discovered that the corruption in our system flowed downward from the highest levels. My first tour of the dungeons was a revelation. But I closed my eyes as much as I could. I put up with the evil, and kept my mouth shut. So I am guilty, too.

"The final straw was last year during the war, watching our men bundle off your women and children to slave pens. After our defeat and escape back to Texan, I contacted Landholder Mason, in whom I had seen signs of disenchantment. Things developed from there. I played the role of loyal aide to General Murphy, while providing information and advice to the Landholders. General Murphy had spies reporting that a rebellion was brewing, but lacked specifics. I volunteered to try and find the traitors, and pretend I was sympathetic to their cause. In this way, I could control what Murphy found out. It was a difficult task, reassuring Murphy that the so-called 'rebellion' was merely the grumblings of ineffectual, old men.

"Then Murphy had an idea of enticing you to Texan in order to capture you and use you as a bargaining chip. The support of Kenesee was something I had not considered up to that point, but the value of your participation became immediately obvious. So, in compliance with General Murphy's plot, I persuaded Landholder Mason to accompany me and we visited you in Kingsport. I was scared, I must admit. I'd seen Murphy's ruthlessness, and assumed others might be as just as bad."

I did not like what I heard. "So, you invited me to come to Texan, knowing that Murphy would be looking for me?"

Chalmers shrugged. "What choice did I have? The landholders would not have thrown their support to the rebellion. I told Murphy you agreed and would be coming, though where and when was unknown. I led him to expect you in midsummer, probably by ship at one of our ports. I assumed you would figure out something more clever than that. And you did."

I grunted. "It sounds complicated."

"It is—or was. I am not good at such things. I used to have more hair."

Metaxis stirred. I suspected he had grin on his face. "Given in a good cause."

Chalmers continued. "You were captured, and my heart sank. I played my role as loyal aide as well as I might, waiting. When General Murphy decided to pursue your party to Tyler with the horse guardos, I saw our chance. Your rescue was our only hope. Captain Metaxis agreed. And that is the tale. I'm just sorry that Texan has to depend on such as I for its salvation."

So. By Chalmers' reasoning, it was proper to put me at risk, even if Murphy was expecting me. But I didn't like it. Not at all. Fortunately for him, I was too tired to be angry.

Perhaps a half hour later, we heard horses coming from the highway ahead, and the two guardos reined in. "Sir, we spotted their encampment from the rise. Standard security. We were a couple hundred yards from the nearest outpost. I counted more than two-score campfires, at least, so the whole regiment must be there."

"Then we have no choice," Metaxis responded, and led us off the road and up the cow path, where the other two guardos were just returning. Corporal Dominic was still uncertain about the path, but it was clear for part of the way, at least, and headed eastward in the right direction.

We followed the path as it descended into a hollow that opened out into marshy ground, above which a cool mist hung. It was a slow walk through the mist for perhaps an hour, passing two or three peaceful farms before noting, through an open meadow, the glow which began to tell on the horizon. Dawn. And we might not yet be past the guardos' encampment. We quickened to a trot, and in a few more minutes the cow path rose steeply and rejoined the highway. We climbed the grade, and emerged once again upon the road, the hooves of our mounts ringing loudly to our ears in the morning's first light. A hundred yards behind us, a company of guardos were spread across a field, lazily rolling up their bedrolls or saddling their horses. Many turned to see who had appeared on the road ahead of them.

"Damn!" said Metaxis, giving the guardos company a casual wave of greeting before turning and leading us away at the walk, lengthening the distance between us ever so slowly.

"Everyone stay calm," Metaxis ordered in a voice that provided the example. ''We'll bluff them a bit longer and gain a few hundred yards.''

And so we did, never breaking our steady pace as a single guardo from the encampment cantered up beside us and saluted. ''Good morning, Captain. Lieutenant Reardon, Fourth Company, sent me forward to ask which company is taking over the point for our march.''

Metaxis returned the guardo's salute. ''Good morning, private. We're the advance element of the Seventh Company, to answer your question.''

''The Seventh, sir?'' the private asked without guile, more to himself that to us. ''I thought the Seventh was left at the castle.''

This private thought too much.

Metaxis raised an eyebrow at such speculation. ''Well, you thought wrong, unfortunately. We weren't so lucky. The main body of my company will be coming up presently. The General told me to take point, and I'm taking point.''

The private nodded, and glanced at me.

''Our guide,'' explained Metaxis. ''A local man. He's been sick.''

''No wonder, then. Very good, sir.'' The private was about to turn back, hesitated, and then reluctantly kept his pace beside us and presented another question. ''I almost forgot. Have to ask you for the password of the day, sir. Orders from Lieutenant Reardon.''

''Hmpfh. I don't have time for such nonsense right now, boy. You tell your lieutenant that.'' With those words, Metaxis dismissed him with a wave of his hand.

Still not believing anything could be amiss, the private saluted and returned to his camp.

The captain snorted. ''Well, if Lieutenant Reardon is worth his salt, he'll come after us to find out why I wouldn't give the password.''

''Shouldn't we move a bit faster then?'' Senior Aide Chalmers asked.

Metaxis patted the neck of his mount. ''Let's wait to see.'' Various stretches of the road were covered with a thin layer of fine dust that arose with each hoof that pounded down upon it on the road. We passed through one such stretch, and then looked back to see if anyone else should travel through it.

Soon enough, the faint haze of a dust cloud rose up above the bushes from the spot.

Unfortunately, Lieutenant Reardon *was* worth his salt. At a slight rise we turned in the saddle and studied the road behind us. There they were, perhaps two hundred yards back. It looked like the private's entire company was following at the trot, parts of the column coming into view at a spot free of vegetation, and then disappearing at more heavily foliated parts of the road. We took our own mounts to the trot. Eventually Lieutenant Reardon realized our pace, and moved up to a canter. We went into a canter too.

"Well, they're not closing the distance," Chalmers noted optimistically, shouting to be heard over the hoofs on the crete.

"Not yet," Metaxis shouted back. "But our horses have been going all night, while their mounts are rested. We can't keep this up all day."

The chase went on for a while, Lieutenant Reardon and his men certainly realizing things were not as they should be with the horsemen they were pursuing. The horses were working up a good lather in the early morning's heat.

Chalmers looked at the guardos captain. "You know what has to be done?"

Captain Metaxis did not hesitate. "I'm waiting for a likely spot."

Our little column cantered into a shallow dip where a small stream only a few inches deep covered the road, and then up a gentle slope. Woods and dense brush came within a yard or two of the road on either side. Metaxis pointed a finger at me.

"You! Scar!"

Well, he had my attention. The tone of his next words made clear that they were a command—or perhaps a curse.

"Save my country."

Chalmers looked across me at the captain. "Good-bye, my friend."

Metaxis gave a salute, and at the top of the slight rise held up his hand, gradually slowing his little force to a walk while Chalmers grabbed my bridle and forced our horses onward. I glanced behind. The half dozen guardos had halted, wheeled to the rear, and now formed a short line across the road. Their lances went down to the horizontal position, and then they charged, and were lost to our sight.

We rode on, the senior aide clenching his teeth and leading me on with dogged purpose, using the precious minutes the captain and his squad had bought us. But it was clear that our respite was temporary. The day was turning oppressively muggy and hot, and the horses were heavily lathered now, pushed too hard for too long. We might spur them on a few more miles, and then they would go down.

Chalmers looked behind us. Yes there, well behind us, the glitter of lance points in the sun, and the flash of shield colors. They were still coming. Apparently Metaxis and his brave half dozen had been unable to slaughter Reardon's hundred.

Far ahead, I saw a faint haze of dust above the road, but my mind was too dulled to think about its cause.

Apparently, Chalmers had seen it too. "We've got to get off the road," Chalmers shouted. He pointed at a tiny stream which meandered under a plank bridge, and turned his horse, jumping the animal across the tiny waterway, galloping across a meadow and toward a copse of trees. I followed dutifully, my mind clouded, caught in an unending painful daze. Actually, Chalmers's plan was the best of a bad lot. We couldn't outrun Murphy's guardos, and it would be hard to lose them. But if we could hide a while, we could rest the horses and then go cross country. Where we had left the road made it hard to see our tracks. All we needed was another minute to reach the trees unseen. A minute.

But we didn't have a minute.

The guardos company that followed us came thundering up the road in a column of twos, spotted us, and cut across the field as we halted in the copse of trees. Our horses were trembling, unsteady on their feet. Mine had almost gone down in the uncertain footing of the meadow.

Chalmers peered around us desperately, seeking some magical portal to whisk us away from our fate. Besides the guardos that followed us, we could now see the glitter of more lance points, and a glimpse of tiny figures coming up the road from the east. And it finally registered in my befuddled mind what it meant. More enemy.

Just what we needed.

Chalmers's face was red, sweat pouring from him. "Damn."

A canteen hung from my saddle horn. I drank and splashed

water on my face, grinning foolishly. The water felt good, and it was all so ridiculous. "I take it you don't have an alternative plan."

He drew the cavalry saber from my saddle scabbard and handed it to me. That would teach me to try joking. He took out his own and brought it to the position of shoulder carry.

"Well, Prince Arn, it's Murphy's dungeons—or death. Which shall it be?"

Chalmers was made of sturdier stuff than I had thought. So much for appearances.

I shook my head to clear it, and studied the situation. Exhausted horses. An overweight clerk and a cowardly prince who could barely swing a sword, against a Texan guardos company. If that weren't enough, they had their comrades coming to help, the first of those worthies coming on hard.

I set that against Murphy's dungeon, and remembered what awaited me. Yes, if we fled now they would run us down, and taking us alive would be easy. But head on, they'd be forced to use their lances. Slowly, I brought up my own saber to shoulder carry and nodded to him. "After you, Mr. Chalmers."

"To glory it is, Prince Arn."

I would never forgive Robert for doing this to me.

Together, Chalmers and I spurred our horses into a reluctant pace that might charitably be called a gallop, and charged back at Murphy's men.

Admittedly, my reputation as a warrior—undeserved though it be—might put caution into the boldest enemy. But what happened next left Chalmers and I sharing wide-eyed glances even as we loped ponderously towards the foe. Their leader put up his arm, and the column slid to a stop in the midst of the field.

Our amazement found its answer. Another arm signal, and the horsemen turned to the left, forming a two-deep line facing . . . facing the horsemen whose dust cloud we had seen ahead! The horsemen stormed off the road and into the meadow, bearing straight for the Texans. What mistake was this? I stared at them more closely, and at last I saw. Black uniforms. Kenesee Guards. They lowered lances and charged, their column widening into a wedge as they thundered forward.

In response, the horse guardos charged too, setting Texan

red against Kenesee black, and the guards of Kenesee and the guardos of Texan met with the scrunch of lance on shield, and then the meaty thud of horse against horse. Lances splintered, shields were riven, riders went flying from saddles, horses went down, and the field fragmented into scores of individual battles as red and black sought each other out, horses rearing and kicking and whirling about the field as their men hacked and thrust.

Chalmers and I had let our horses slow to a trot, and then to a walk, and finally to a halt, so that we waited next to each other upon our trembling mounts, watching the mayhem sweep and swirl around us, the Texans seeming to ignore their quarry while engaged with such serious opponents.

Man for man, the combat was well matched, but the Kenesee guards had a numerical advantage of twenty or thirty men, and numbers told in the end. A horn sounded, and the Texans turned and fled, Kenesee guards hot on their tail.

The danger of wild horses and flaying weapons removed from the vicinity, I dismounted, stood for a moment upon shaky legs, and then slid down and sat on the ground next to my horse. Chalmers came and kneeled beside me.

He looked about disbelievingly. "They said you were lucky, but who could imagine this? It's like one of the old tales of Sir John Wayne."

I blinked. "Who?"

Two of our rescuers rode up and one leaped off and knelt beside us. Sergeant Jenkins, wearing the civilian clothes I'd seen him in last. "Prince Arn! Thank God." A pause. "You look terrible."

The man still on his horse gave a worried smile. It was Sergeant Nielson, the commander of the guards that Robert had obviously sent. "Good to see you, sir. You had us worried. Take care of him, Jenkins. I have to rein in the men, or they'll try to go all the way to Dallas."

"You see, Nielson? You see?" Jenkins turned from the other sergeant to Chalmers, shaking his head. "When I saw what was happening, I told him it had to be Prince Arn. Who else would be crazy enough to attack a company of Texan Horse Guardos?"

"Who, indeed?" I replied. After which I lay back, closed my eyes and let their voices fade away.

* * *

It was some time before our men returned from their pursuit, and I was awake again. Chalmers notified me. ''He's alive, you know.''

''Who?''

''Captain Metaxis. He took a bad leg wound from a lance, and was unhorsed, but the guardos were in a hurry to follow us, and didn't stop to round up the wounded. And your royal guards didn't give them time on the chase back. Sergeant Nielson found where Metaxis had made his stand. Metaxis and two others were still alive.''

''Can he ride?''

''As well as you, considering the state you're both in. How are you now?''

''I need rest.''

But there was little enough time for that, since General Murphy's Horse Guardos Regiment would soon be coming to reinforce its point company. We needed to get back to Tyler. The combat in the meadow had cost us over a score of men killed and wounded, and we were far ahead of any supports.

A splash of cold water and new mounts—a good score were available after the spirited melee in the field; they grazed contentedly or drank at the stream, not at all disturbed by the slaughter around them—served to put us on the road again, and we trotted eastward. That evening we reached the village of Wyndham, perhaps thirty miles or so west of Tyler, and found the Kenesee Fifth Infantry Regiment setting up camp after a full day of marching to our aid. The unit's commander, Colonel Rashmid, gave me his tent and put the regiment on full alert lest the horse guardos threaten. Texan outriders and scouts investigated, but the main body held back, having no desire to challenge the long spears and superior numbers we could field.

At last we could rest, no longer afraid of the pursuit. I slept around the clock and finally woke feeling half-human. The recuperative powers of youth are extraordinary only when viewed from the middle or elder years. Instead of being grateful for my recovery, I grumbled about the aches and pains that remained.

Bartholomew's attentions had been skillful in giving me pain, but the instructions of his master had prevented him from doing permanent injury. The blows to tender parts—the kidneys, the stomach, the privates—had shown a carefully calculated restraint. The harder blows to joint and limb and muscle and tendon had left me black and blue under shirt and trousers, but the bruises would fade within a few weeks. With twenty-four hours' sleep I regained most of my old strength, though soreness would prevent me from free movement for another fortnight.

One thing I could do was shave off my beard, and I did. Colonel Rashmid's aide performed the rite in front of the colonel's tent using his tiny metal washbasin. My scar emerged from beneath the shaving soap, assuring Texan and Kenesee troops alike that Prince Scar was there to lead them. Also, it would help them know who they should be protecting. The breeze was pleasantly cool on my bare chin, though I missed having the whiskers to stroke while I smoked my pipe.

Colonel Rashmid sent a messenger ahead warning of our arrival, and at Tyler I found not a quiet greeting by my friends, but a formal military parade. Either side of the road was lined with a double rank of Kenesee infantry—Colonel Daniels's Sixth Infantry Regiment—standing at attention, which did not prevent them from bursting out into cheers as we rode past. They just never learned.

Colonel Daniels fell in next to Colonel Rashmid as we rode between the ranks, the two of them encouraging the men in their display. Robert had sent me my old Fifth and Sixth Regiments, the two finest infantry units in the Army of Kenesee. Not that I couldn't use them.

In Tyler I met Murdock and my companions, all lined up in front of the town hall, waiting for me. Murdock stood before them, a look of immense relief upon his face. Behind him, Megan and Beth stood next to one another, and I was surprised to see Beth turn and hug Megan firmly when she saw Jenkins safe and sound at the front of his squadron, and as amazing, Megan hugged her back just as firmly. Beside them, Kren stood with his hood pulled back, revealing his hairy countenance in all its splendor, his face split with an immense grin. Lorich held little Sabrena's hand, the girl looking on soberly while Lorich shifted weight from one foot to another with excitement. It was not a bad reunion, though marred by Angela's absence.

And then I left them to have a bath and be attended by Murdock and Jason Kendall.

"How many times do I have to do this with you?" Jason complained, opening his healer's bag. He examined me minutely, the sweat forming on his forehead in the heat of day and making his spectacles slide down near the end of his nose. He pushed the spectacles back up and shook his head. "The bruises look terrible, and they probably hurt like blazes—"

"They do."

"—and that serves you right for interrupting me. But I can't find anything broken or torn. You'll recover."

"Thank you, Jason."

"Don't thank me. I didn't have any choice about coming. I'm here, so I'll do my job. Just try to avoid slaughtering whole armies again. Can you do that?"

"I'll try."

"Hmpfh. Not likely."

"Perhaps not. But will you join us for lunch."

"You're getting together with your companions? Well, I'd like to, but I promised to lunch with some of the Texan healers in Tyler. Besides, Murdock will be there, and he'll want to tell stories, and I've heard them all. I'd fall asleep in the middle of a tale. Then again, most of you will probably fall asleep, too. . . ."

He was closing up his bag when we left him.

"He's been grumpy ever since he left Kenesee," Murdock chuckled. "And he has cause. Which reminds me." He handed me an envelope as we entered the town hall's empty meeting room. It contained a long table and chairs for perhaps a score, windows open for any cooling breezes from the sea that might slip over the town walls, and paintings of various quality upon the walls. The table was set, though no food had yet been laid out. Preparations for our lunch already made. I seated myself in the chair at the head of the table while Murdock stared out a window, his hands clasped behind him.

The envelope contained formal orders and a letter from Robert that Colonel Daniels had brought with him. Both documents had already been opened and read by Murdock, as was proper in my absence. I ignored the broken seals and read the pages of the letter with eager eyes. It was in Robert's own handwriting.

May 9th, 2654
The King's Castle
Kingsport, Kenesee

Dear Arn,

Now it is my turn to write the letters, it seems, sitting here at Father's desk and moving the pieces about the board just as he did. A pity there are so few pieces now. A pity he is not here to move them. The waiting has been hard—harder than any battle, I must tell you. But now it is near an end, and if you are still alive to read this, we can go forward with our plan.

I trust the women are well. I had my doubts about sending them to you, but since the high wizard advised it, I could not deny him. Still, O'Dowd has been worried sick that his sight was not true, and that he would be responsible for ill tidings. The responsibility, of course, is not his. It is mine. I wish it were not so.

Governor Rodes is up to his tricks again. He has been assembling his forces, and I suspect he is waiting for the right moment to strike. I trust it will be when he discovers I am weakening the Army of Kenesee by sending you two infantry regiments, as well as one of cavalry. Also, I'm sending you five squadrons of guards commanded by the senior squadron leader, Sergeant Nielson. Like Sergeant Major Nakasone, he is steady and dependable. I will rest easier knowing you have some royal guards around. They do come in handy at times, though they are few enough now, God help us. I'm sending you fully half their total number, and yet that is still less than a hundred and fifty.

I will assemble the other regiments when your forces sail, and prepare for anything Rodes might attempt. Hopefully this matter will be over quickly, and the men can get back to the harvest. Our grain reserves are down, though the fishing fleets have had great success this spring.

Formal orders accompany this letter. Colonel Daniels is in charge of the landing force. He will place himself under your command when you arrive, or under Wizard

Murdock in your absence. If neither of you appear within a fortnight, he will reembark his troops and return to Kenesee.

I'm sorry, Arn, but that is the reality of it. With secure borders, nothing could stop me from marching to your aid with every man in the Army of Kenesee. With Governor Rodes threatening in the east, I dare not take that risk. I have agonized long over that decision, but realize there can be no other. In such contingency, you will never read this letter, for you will be dead, or imprisoned in General Murphy's dungeon. But I felt compelled to explain my reasons—to myself, if not to you.

I do not think such will be the case. You have overcome far greater odds. With your abilities and Murdock at your side, I do not think anything can defeat you. That has been my comfort in these long days of waiting.

Captain Grayson has kept me informed of your progress, and his reports have brought both relief from worry and hope for the ultimate success of your mission. If you prevail, we will deal with Governor Rodes and the Virginians. And then, who knows. I have been thinking much about what we discussed before you departed. Perhaps the Alliance was not far wrong in its goal of uniting the six nations, though their leadership and their methods besmirched that goal. Perhaps with a new vision by those willing to lose rather than gain, it might be done. Perhaps this is the time for the six to form a greater nation. We shall see.

That is all for now. When you defeat General Murphy, occupy Dallas and report all to me. Administer the country as you will and wait for my orders.

I look forward to hearing of your victory. Stay well.

Your brother,
Robert

P.S. Oh, yes. I've persuaded Jason Kendall—the healer—to go along with the expedition. I'll feel better if I know he's there with you, just in case. However, his opinion of me may not be quite as benevolent as it was. I left him little choice in the matter, and he grumbled as loudly as old Graven ever did. I pray you will not need his services.

I looked over the orders quickly. They were merely a formal rendering of what Robert had already told me. I folded both documents back into the envelope.

Murdock had waited patiently while I read. "Quite bold of King Robert, wouldn't you say? In the face of the Easterners he sends you the two largest and best infantry regiments in Kenesee. I think he may be tempting Governor Rodes to attack."

He might, indeed. If so, did he realize it? In any case, now I had to worry about Kenesee as well as Texan.

"A dangerous game, he plays," the wizard observed. "But at least one of his pieces is back on the board."

"Yes," I agreed.

And the piece much preferred it to the box.

9

Plans and Decisions

Murdock expected a smile, so I gave him one. "Have things gone well?"

The wizard left the window and settled into a chair next to me. "As well as could be expected, considering that our leader was held hostage by the enemy. Colonel Daniels landed his infantry three days ago, and the cavalry regiment disembarked yesterday. The mayor of Tyler did not go to the Gathering in Dallas, nor did the local regimental commander, but both had agreed with Landholder Fields about the need to get rid of Murphy, and planned accordingly. The mayor had been told we might come, and to welcome us. He did so, though there was some grumbling among the citizenry. The regimental commander put out the call to his regiment, and the companies are assembling now.

"Of the other forces, we won't know how many will join us until they're here—assuming they can get here, with Murphy astride the roads at Dallas. It'll be two weeks before all the Texan regiments of rebellion reach us, at best, and from what I've seen on the drill field of a few companies, I fear the infantry regiments of the rebellion will not be what we might have hoped for. Our consolation is that Murphy's loyalist regiments should be no better. The Texans are dispirited, and not anxious to fight against their countrymen. Murphy's loyalists are not too happy with him, and the rebels are not too happy to have Kenesee soldiers on their soil."

I snorted. "My sincere condolences to the Texan rebels for putting up with us."

"Yet there are Texans of honor and courage."

I thought of Chalmers. And Metaxis. "Yes. A few. Hopefully, they will be enough. Well, until the others get here, tell me what's been happening in my absence."

"You want to know everything?"

"Leave something for the others to say, or the women will be disappointed."

The wizard limited his narration to a brief overview of events. I heard of their successful escape from Dallas. Landholder Fields had been true to his word. A dozen of his personal troops had met them at the village of Red Tavern and provided fine mounts for all. Abandoning the wagons, Murdock, Jenkins, Lorich, Megan, Beth, and Kren—the beastman with Sabrena seated before him on the saddle—had ridden with Fields and his troops, easily passing through checkpoints and towns.

They arrived in Tyler to find Kenesee infantry aboard newly-anchored ships in the bay, waiting their turn to disembark. The landing had gone smoothly, though the town had responded with alarm until the mayor had reassured the citizens of our true purpose and declared the town for the rebellion. All loyalists who cared to leave were permitted to, but there were only a few dozen of those who felt so strongly.

Wizard Murdock had taken command of the Kenesee forces in my absence, and with Colonel Daniels the wizard had organized the effort with his usual efficiency. Only my absence had put them into doubt as to the best course of action, and they had pondered a direct march upon Dallas, foolish as that might be.

Murdock ended his story as footsteps were heard down the hall. Wizard Lorich stuck his head in and burst out with a smile. ''Prince Arn! Master! It's so good to see you both together again. Prince Arn, I prayed for you. For you, and Angela both. I—''

He was prodded forward by those gathering in the hallway behind him. We heard the voice of Jenkins. ''Mr. Lorich, if you will stop talking for a minute, maybe the rest of us can get in the room, too.''

''Sergeant Jenkins! Sorry. I was so happy to see Prince Arn with my master.''

Jenkins and Lorich stood aside for the others.

Next to enter were Kren and Beth, the beastman formally escorting the ex-courtesan as if she were a great lady—and who was to say she was not—followed by Colonels Daniels, Rashmid, and Smith of the Tenth Cavalry Regiment. Then came Sergeant Nielson, my guard commander, and at the last Sergeant Jenkins, dressed like his commanding officer in the familiar black with three yellow sergeant stripes on his sleeves, but giving Nielson every respect.

All took their seats and waited expectantly.

''Where is Lady Megan?'' asked Lorich, looking around the table.

''Mr. Kendall has arrived just this hour,'' Beth informed us all. There were exclamations of surprised satisfaction at the news, and Beth waited till the noise abated. ''Lady Megan and Mr. Kendall will be . . . delayed.''

I cleared my throat.

''It is good—very good—to see you all again.'' There were smiles and nods of agreement. ''I will be meeting with the Texans after this to discuss planning, but wanted first to share information with you, find out how you fared, and most of all, to gain your advice. I presume that would be acceptable to all? Good.''

And then the Texan servants—accompanied by a half-dozen watchful Kenesee guards, which didn't deter the two sergeants from standing on either side of me while the Texans were present—arrived bearing platters, bowls, and pitchers. My mouth started to water. There were sides of broiled fish in butter sauce, roasted potatoes and beets, greens in a salad with oil and vinegar, cheeses and bread, and melons for dessert. The pitchers offered beer and wine.

Well, at least I'd regained my appetite. That was a healthy sign. I filled my plate, topped off my mug with beer, thrust my fork into the mound of food, opened my mouth and—

The others waited, watching me expectantly.

"Is . . . something wrong?"

Beth was all sweetness. "We thought you might want to tell us what happened to you after we parted."

I looked down at the fish on my fork. "Before we eat?"

"Oh no," Kren corrected me. "We'll eat while you talk."

I laid down the fork. The inevitable cannot be denied. They would hound me until I told them all. And so I started. I told them of how Angela and I were captured, of our time in the dungeon, of Bartholomew taking Angela for his amusement.

"We mustn't lose hope," Beth stated. "Angela is a level-headed girl. She'll find ways to keep herself safe until General Murphy is defeated."

"You don't know Bartholomew," I retorted sharply, and then caught myself. "But your words are appreciated." I glossed over my own torture—though Kren and Murdock each looked at me with a lifted eyebrow—and described my escape from Castle Corral thanks to Aide Chalmers and Captain Metaxis, ending with a more detailed account of the two Texans' bravery.

"Fine men, it appears," Kren stated.

"The hope of Texan," Murdock concurred. "I've talked to Aide Chalmers. His soft manner hides metal."

"We could use more like them," I agreed. "But now, tell me how you fared after we parted in Dallas."

My companions with me through Arkan and Texan looked at each other, then at Murdock, who remained silent for once, smiling back at the others pleasantly between bites. Kren noted Murdock's preoccupation, and leaned forward to play the spokesman. "Things went smoothly for us, though we feared the worst for you. Sergeant Jenkins and Beth met us outside the east gate, and we immediately departed on the road to Tyler. Landholder Fields was waiting for us at Red Tavern with a dozen of his men. We abandoned the wagons, took saddle horses he provided, and rode east. We made good time, passed through watch posts and met officials without question, and arrived at Tyler after two days. Your regiments were offshore waiting to land, and contact had been established with the Texan rebels. Wizard Murdock took command in your absence. The only thing marring our return to a safe haven was the absence of you and Angela. We worried mightily.''

Captain Daniels nodded, the light reflecting off the sweat of his forehead. His hair was receding, and he looked as he might in his tailor shop at home working over a piece of cloth in the hot summer air of Loren. ''They did. Sergeant Jenkins was adamant that we send the guards after you, Prince Arn. I was doubtful. They were our only cavalry then, and I feared they might be lost. But Wizard Murdock did not hesitate in giving the order. Their boldness was the reason you are here today. I opted for caution, and was wrong. Thank God that wiser heads prevailed.''

''All have played their parts well,'' Murdock corrected him. ''I suspected that there might be a chance of escape for Arn, knowing there were still friends on General Murphy's staff. Colonel Daniels was not aware of this situation, and advised according to his information.''

''Very good,'' I stated. ''And now, if the colonel could give us an account of his journey and order of battle?''

Daniels made the report short. The Fifth and Sixth Regiments and the King's Royal Guards sailed from Kingsport on May 10th, and the Tenth Cavalry Regiment from Wickliffe on May 11th. The infantry and guards arrived on May 15th, as planned, their transports accompanied by most of the ships left in the Royal Navy. They had caught the Texan Navy in port, and overwhelmed them with numbers before the Texans warships could sail. The ships carrying the cavalry ran into an unexpected calm and arrived several days late. A goodly portion of the men had experienced some seasickness, but most recovered immediately after setting foot ashore. Supply ships were even now being unloaded at the Tyler docks, bringing food for the men and feed for the horses.

Daniels continued. ''Our order of battle is better than I had expected even three months ago. Some of the wounded have recovered and returned to ranks, and some of those in the militia turned eighteen and transferred into regiments. The Fifth Infantry Regiment numbers almost seven hundred, and the Sixth over nine hundred. The Tenth Cavalry Regiment is at full strength, almost five hundred men and mounts, and the horses have had a day to recover from their shipboard experience. King Robert insisted that Prince Arn have at least one good regiment of Kenesee cavalry at his command. He's sent you the best troops in the Army, sir. I warned him against that, given the threat from the Easterners, but he would have no argument. Perhaps he thinks the beastmen will help again.''

Kren shook his head. ''He knows they will not. The Council has apologized to Virginia, and is now sworn to neutrality. The Army of the Beastwood will not cross its borders again. Governor Rodes is free to act, and Robert knows it.''

''And our units—are they ready for action?'' I asked the colonel.

Daniels had a satisfied grin. ''Our numbers may be fewer than last year, but man for man, I'll put the infantry against any troops on the continent.''

''And the cavalry?''

''Robert wanted you to have one unit of cavalry you could depend on. Another day, and the horses should be ready for hard service. They aren't royal guards, but they'll match any line unit of mounted.''

I mulled it all over. ''So. What should we do now?''

They looked at each other, and finally to Murdock. ''That,'' he stated reluctantly, ''will depend on the Texans.''

The servants cleared the table while we chatted of innocent matters, and then my companions each discreetly took leave, until I was left waiting with Murdock and Daniels, while Jenkins and Nielson stood at rest position behind me in anticipation of our Texan comrades.

Footsteps were heard in the hall, but it was not the Texans yet.

''Mr. Kendall!'' I greeted the advisor, shaking his one hand with both of mine. ''We heard you'd arrived.''

''Hello, Arn.'' He shook hands all around and took a seat. ''It's good to see you. I told you to expect me. But I didn't expect to find Megan here. I'll need to have a talk with the

High Wizard about this when we get home. But you have a meeting with the Texans coming up. Should I stay?"

"Of course," said Murdock. "I just wish we had more time. I think they're coming."

We held our questions for each other as more footsteps were heard and, punctual folk, the Texans came just as the town clock struck the hour. Entering were Landholder Fields, Mayor Charles Dobson of Tyler, Colonel Meyers, the commander of Tyler's Seventeenth Infantry Regiment, and last, after standing politely aside for the others, came Senior Aide Chalmers. He looked much better for a night's sleep. We exchanged greetings and sat, this time with Murdock, Kendall, and Daniels on one side of the table; Fields sat with Dobson and Meyers and Chalmers on the other. A diplomatic nicety: We faced each other as equals in the joint venture against General Murphy.

I gestured to the guardsmen behind me. "Thank you, Sergeant Nielson."

"Yes, sir." He and Jenkins strode out and shut the door behind them. To have left them with us would have been an insult to the Texans.

I presented the same question to them that I'd asked my companions earlier. "So. What should we do now?"

Landholder Fields coughed and snorted, his eyes peering at me from under heavy lids, as if trying to reach some judgment. "Prince Arn, I understand your woman is in Castle Corral."

I nodded. "That is correct. A young woman named Angela. She was taken prisoner when I was, but we could not rescue her when we made our escape. Angela is very . . . close to me."

The landholder chewed some unknown cud while still staring, still judging. "And so you think we should march out to Dallas and storm Corral."

His tone was challenging, and a bit scornful. Murdock made to speak, but I waved him to silence. "That is my desire, but not my intention."

"No? Then what is your intention?"

"To stay here and await the assembly of the Texan regiments. To allow General Murphy to march to us, as he must if he wishes to quash the rebellion. To meet him on ground of our choosing, and defeat him there."

"Is that so?" The landholder raised his eyebrows. "Well, it sounds like a good plan to me. You'll do, Prince Arn. You'll do."

"Your acceptance is appreciated," I intoned politely, though I could gladly have broken a pot over the old man's head.

"You'll command the forces," he stated evenly, chewing away.

"The Kenesee forces," I clarified.

He chewed his lips. "All the forces."

"The other Landholders have not yet agreed to that," Murdock observed.

"No. But they will, when they get here. It has to be. The men need to know a winner is in charge."

Well, it made sense. I didn't like it, but it made sense.

The landholder continued. "Wizard Murdock or whomever you want can lead the troops of Kenesee. And Senior Aide Chalmers will lead the Texans."

Chalmers jerked back and stared at the landholder. "With all due respect, Mr. Fields, I don't think—"

"You don't think what? Who else should lead our forces? One of the other landholders? Not if I have any say about it. I don't want one of them getting control. A regimental commander? Perhaps. Perhaps not. None of them are known beyond their own regiment."

"And neither am I," Chalmers protested. "I'm just a functionary. If anything, the people will associate me with Murphy, and all that he stands for."

"No more than the rest of us," the landholder continued placidly, his answers unvarying.

"I am not a military commander."

"But you know how Murphy thinks."

And so it went. In the end, Chalmers gave up and accepted the role of commander of all Texan forces under the great and exalted Prince Scar. Murdock would be the other commander, leading the Kenesee regiments.

But it was Chalmers who was left shaking his head in disbelief. "I do not want this position," he stated, no hint of self-deception evident. I had no reason to disbelieve his protests, for I wanted to be in charge as little as he. Fat lot of good it did us.

Chalmers continued. "I do it only because the Landholder thinks it will be best for our cause. Prince Arn, I fear we will have to ride together again. I pledge to you my cooperation and commitment to our cause."

It was only later, as we all left the meeting room and proceeded down the hallway, that I heard Landholder Fields share his motives with Mayor Dobson. I was at the front of the little procession making its way down the stairs, while the two Texans hung back, far to the rear, whispering.

"Why did you support Chalmers for commander?" the mayor asked.

"Why? You haven't seen it yet? Think, man. The other landholders could stomach my leadership as little as I would stomach theirs. Our jealousies are too great. The colonels and mayors all have loyalties to one landholder or another. Whichever of us held command would grow too powerful. We need someone who is on no side, yet will remain . . . *pliable*, shall we say? Our Senior Aide Chalmers is a clerk. He can be controlled."

The forces of the rebellion were not yet assembled, and already there was intrigue and jealousy afoot. This was not unexpected, of course. I am only too aware—and subject—to the same follies and weaknesses of mankind. If I have any redeeming quality, it is that I recognize such faults in myself, and realize my own unsuitability for the roles into which I am thrust. I am ill-suited for wielding power.

Other men do not seem to suffer from such thoughts. From such sly maneuvering and greedy calculation and selfish grasping as I had seen and heard was supposed to come a new hope for Texan. It was enough to make one doubt the effort.

I shared my concerns with Paul Kendall later that night in my chamber. The others had retired to their rooms, but Paul had seen the light of my lamp from the crack beneath the door, and asked if I'd like to have a last drink. I hesitated for the briefest moment, and then invited him in, checking to see that my guards were well placed and tended. We sat at a round table in a corner of the room, and with his left hand—his only hand—he poured mugs of warm beer from the pitcher. The sight of his armless sleeve set me to brooding upon all we had faced, and all we had yet to face. We sat in silence a moment, and then I told him of what I had heard in the passageway.

He rolled his mug so that the beer swirled inside, and stared at the patterns of foam amidst the amber liquid. "From what you've told me, I think our landholders may be in for a surprise. Even a clerk can have courage, and audacity, and a will of his own. It will be interesting to watch."

"It was sad," I commented, easing off my boots.

"Sad?" he rejoined. "I dare say it was. Most affairs of men are sad things. The best of governments are imperfect, the wisest of laws unfair, the most generous of peoples small-minded and fearful and self-absorbed. The imperfections of society are but manifestations of the human condition, our institutions and organizations reflecting the failures and glories of mankind.

"And from that arise both our despair and our hope. For all our tragedies and failings, yet Man goes on, surprising us with qualities and virtues that redeem him in his own eyes and in the eyes of God."

I stared into my own mug. "Do you really think so?"

"No. But it sounds good, doesn't it?" He laughed at the look on my face. "All right. So I do believe it. And that's why I believe in the Codes."

"How so?"

"You must recognize Man's capacity for evil before you can deal with it. But do not blind yourself to his capacity for good. The ancients destroyed themselves in great numbers even before the Cataclysm cleansed the earth. Gigantic bombs, powerful warships, powder weapons—their capacity for killing soldiers and citizens alike was great and often indiscriminate. Battles lasted months, wars dragged on for years, women and children suffered and died, men were consumed. Losing societies collapsed. While one section of the globe lived a decade in peace, another might be torn apart in an unending war."

I thought about what it would mean to be at war for year after year, to have the horror we had lived through continue without end—

"Do you see, Arn? That's what the Codes prevent. Has our war been horrible? Yes. Did it cause great loss of life? Yes. But it was over in a few months. A battle or two, and the matter was decided. There was no destruction of our economy, no demolition of roads and bridges, no countryside turned into a wasteland that would take a generation to recover. Most citizens did not directly suffer from the war.

"Wait, I know your objections. Yes, there are widows and orphans everywhere. Yes, there were horrors suffered by some citizens. Don't you and I know it only too well? I am not denying it. God help me, I cannot do that. But except for Lexington and the villages razed by the Texans, the citizens could return to their villages and towns to pick up life as it had been before. The Codes were not meant to prevent war. That would be a vain effort, denying man's capacity for evil. But they limited the nature of warfare and the weapons of war. They limited the scope of the war, and saved us from even greater horrors."

"And yet," I stated, looking at him steadily, "were not the Codes the base cause of the war which we have just fought?"

His sincere look faded into puzzlement, and then caution. "What do you mean by that, Arn?"

I could see the sheen upon his high forehead gleaming in the light as he considered me. I took a last drink and set down the empty mug. "Gregor Pi-Ling, Pacifican Advisor to General Murphy, is a prisoner in the dungeons of Castle Corral. I spoke to him."

Kendall was thoughtful. "You didn't mention that."

"I thought it best not to."

"I see. Perhaps you are right. What did he tell you?"

"Much that we already knew. His role, and the roles of the other Pacificans. His impatience with the Codes, his pride, and his downfall."

Kendall sighed. "Which just proves what I said. Even the keepers of the rule succumb to their faults. All the more reason for the Codes."

"Perhaps you are right."

"The worst in man will drive us to ruin. This war has reinforced my belief in the Codes. Oh, not every little rule and stricture, Arn. We violated those ourselves, at Lexington. But in its essence, in its purpose, in its control of our technological development. Can you imagine what Murphy and Rhodes might have done as victors? Look at what Murphy is doing right now. A regiment of muskets! We have to end this, Arn. We have to do away with Murphy and his powder weapons.

We have to reestablish the stability of the six nations. Otherwise, there'll be no hope of ever getting the genie back in the bottle."

"What if it's already too late?" I countered.

"It's not too late. It can't be."

"What would you do," I tossed out offhandedly, "if Robert were to unite the nations under the leadership of Kenesee?"

Kendall sat back in his chair. "Is this idle speculation, or—"

"Your colleague Pi-Ling shared with me the method by which Pacificans have enforced the Codes."

"He did?"

"They had a great deal of respect for your father. And for you, too."

Kendall nodded. "So, you know."

"Pi-Ling said you were good at your job. Not as good as your father Jason was, but good."

"I am," Kendall agreed, putting his elbow upon the table and resting his chin in the palm of his hand. "God help me, I am."

"Professor Jameson, one of my old tutors. That was you?"

"Professor Jameson and his steam engine. His 'toy.' Yes, I did it. It wasn't hard. There are many ways to kill a man if one knows the right ingredients, the right items. But Jameson wasn't the only one, Arn. There were a dozen others scattered across the length and breadth of Kenesee and even in the other nations."

"So Graven was right about the Pacificans."

"Right? That we had a greater loyalty beyond the nations we advised? Yes. But the loyalty was to an idea, not to a country. And the idea was for the good of those nations—all of them. For that I will make no apology. For the deaths of those men who violated the Codes—that blame I take, and I'll face God with them on my soul. Yet I think He'll understand what I was doing. For I was fighting a war and they were casualties, just as surely as those men you've killed on the battlefield."

I was silent, pondering all he had said.

He slapped his hand on his thigh and stood. "It's late, and Megan will be waiting up for me. Arn, I hope this will not change our relationship. You've had my trust and friendship through the years. You have it still."

"Yes, of course," I spoke without thinking. "And you have—" I stopped and looked at him. I thought of Robert's letter. "—and you have mine. But Paul . . ."

"Yes, Arn?"

"If it should ever come to that, I will stand with my brother."

He paused, an air of weariness upon him. "I know that, Arn. I know that."

10

The Battle of Tyler

The rebel Texan regiments trickled in over the next two weeks, coming from inland to the Coast Road, and then marching up or down the coast to reach us. It was a maddeningly slow process because Dallas and General Murphy sat at the center of the road net. Those sympathetic to our cause often had to find routes other than the old roads, paths subject to the dust and mud and vagaries of weather that dominated any unpaved way.

Yet Murphy never had such an edge in regiments or troops that he could take advantage of his central position and move against us before final assembly. His intelligence was too uncertain—as was ours—and the balance too fine. His own troops were coming in slowly, too, and to lunge with them after one rebel regiment or another would put him off balance, and risk my advance upon Dallas while he dangled far from that strategic point. It was for none but the boldest to risk such a premature move. And he had learned the price of boldness in Kenesee.

Some of the regiments came in quite exhausted after their march, and a few had harrowing—or comical, depending upon the viewpoint—experiences. One of the rebellious cavalry regiments even bumped into a loyal infantry regiment going the opposite direction. The two commanders exchanged greetings, discussed the situation, and then marched their units past each other on the road to continue on their way. Not a weapon was drawn, not an insult heard. Rebellion is a strange beast.

General Murphy did move at last, of course. And all things considered, quite smartly, too. For once assembly was done, every day that he allowed us to stand unchallenged gave the rebellion greater credence to those who might be undecided. We heard of his movement on the evening of June 5th, and the next morning our own forces set out westward. The march was not a long one, for within a dozen miles of Tyler we reached the site we had already chosen for battle. It was just after noon.

I endured the ride without undue problem. Two weeks and more had seen my body well on the way to recovery. I still ached in my joints. Perhaps I would always have some pain, a permanent memory of my time in the dungeon of Castle Corral. But I could ride, and swing a sword, and pull the string of a bow. If General Murphy were on the battlefield and sought me out, I would be ready. Not that I intended to duel him man to man. He might be a superior swordsman, or get in a lucky blow. I had learned duty, not heroics.

Still, for the first time in my life I found myself anxious to commence battle. No, I was not filled with any bloodlust. Yet there was only one way to rescue Angela, and that lay in defeating Murphy. The sooner, the better.

Our position was adjacent to the road in a flat, open clearing that stretched out northward around a wooded copse, fields of cotton, wheat, and sweet potatoes, and a peach orchard. Bounded on all sides by pine forest, the clearing was shaped like a funnel, the road threading along one edge. The field of battle was cut by a shallow stream that offered water to the army, but presented little obstacle to man or horse. The orchard and plowed fields stood north of a cabin belonging to an old farmer. We appropriated his cabin for my quarters, chickens and pigs roaming about the muddy yard outside the door. The farmer squawked loudly about the appropriation until someone put a few coins in his hand, and then he hitched two oxen up to a cart and tottered off on the road toward Tyler, his wife berating him for accepting so little.

In the heat of the day, our units marched up after us and took position at what would be the narrower end of the funnel, settling into bivouac and building campfires to cook a meal. In the late afternoon we saw the glint of sun on speartips far down the road. Then the outriders appeared, and the scouts, and the first unit of cavalry. We watched carefully for any opportunities to strike his approach march, but General Murphy was not to be surprised.

Murphy's sweating loyalists came up the road and deployed far back from us at the wide end of the field, the cavalry spreading out across the open ground, the infantry taking position in the woods that formed the edge of the meadow at that point. It was not possible to fall upon Murphy while he deployed—not and accomplish anything decisive. His cavalry could fall back along the road, his infantry could receive our attack from the protection of the woods. And disaster might befall us trying to maneuver among the trees, just as certainly as it might befall them. Nothing to be gained there, unfortunately. The thought occurred to me that John Black, had he been at my side, would have found a way to finish them there and then; but General Black was not at my side. Nor would he ever be again. Yes, he would have found a way—a flank march through the woods, or a ruse, or a deployment to entice Murphy to disaster. But not Prince Arn of Kenesee. My one lucky stroke had been at Lexington. I could not expect another, nor could I see one. There was no easy solution.

We watched Murphy's careful entrance onto the field from the middle of our position. Commander Chalmers and his staff stood to my right, while Murdock and his staff stood to my left. We had discussed the appropriate rank and title for Chalmers before choosing "commander" as his designation, though some of the haughtier leaders in the Texan forces scornfully referred to him as "Clerk Chalmers."

We took the opportunity to review our plans.

"Commander Chalmers," Murdock began, recognizing the need of the moment, "could you give us the final count of your forces again?"

Chalmers gestured to the leader of his personal guards. Captain Metaxis awkwardly stepped forward with ledger in hand, his right leg bound and braced, his red jacket gone and replaced by the tan uniform of the Texan Army. He should have been in bed, but apparently was as difficult to reason with as a toothache.

Metaxis opened the book. "The final count gives us five regiments of Texan infantry and four of cavalry. The largest infantry regiment numbers over eight hundred, and the weakest just under six hundred. The cavalry regiments all number at least three hundred men. Total Rebel strength on our side is around three thousand, five hundred infantry, and just under thirteen hundred cavalry."

The numbers reminded me of the gloomy tally we'd made the night after the Battle of Yellow Fields. So few. Well, it was to be expected. Texan's finest units had been destroyed during last summer's campaign. These were but half the regiments that Texan could still muster. The others were marching into sight on the other side of the battlefield. And the size of the units told that many men had never answered the rolls. Many preferred to sit out the uncertainty and wait for a winner to whom they could declare loyalty.

From such stalwart fence sitters come great moments in history.

Murdock did mental arithmetic. "And of Kenesee regiments we have two infantry regiments totaling fifteen hundred infantry, and a cavalry regiment of almost five hundred men, plus a hundred and some royal guards. So the total forces of the rebellion number five thousand infantry and one thousand, nine hundred cavalry. Or six thousand, nine hundred in all. Now, what is the estimate for General Murphy's force?"

Metaxis moved his finger down the ledger. "Given the reports of our spies and scouts, it looks as if all the remaining regiments of Texan have joined General Murphy except for Colonel Bertrand's Twenty-Second Infantry Regiment in Whitesboro. Colonel Bertrand has declared that he will not take the last field regiment from the frontier in the face of the plains tribes. A good excuse in itself, though his real concern might be to hold himself aloof of the conflict so that he might cheer on the winner—whomever that might be."

"Just the numbers, Captain," Chalmers reproved him gently.

Metaxis shrugged. "General Murphy has five infantry regiments and six cavalry, plus the two large Presidential Guardos Regiments. A couple of their cavalry regiments are quite good, hardened from campaigning on the border against the plains tribes. Otherwise, their line units have suffered desertions, as have ours. The best estimate is that General Murphy has four thousand, six hundred infantry and two thousand, seven hundred cavalry. A total of seven thousand, three hundred."

"Almost the same number as ours!" burst out Lorich.

"How about that," Sergeant Jenkins observed brightly. "We finally get to fight a battle at even odds."

Now that was promising. I had been afraid we'd be heavily outnumbered again. "About time."

Metaxis tucked away the ledger. "Yes, the armies are well matched. Of course, Murphy's foot guardos have muskets, but Prince Scar will think of a way to overcome those."

I turned to say something to him, and thought better of it. "Indeed."

Drums and horns sounded, and Murphy's infantry stepped out of the forest and into the open field. From the distance, the regiments looked like carefully arranged squares, the tips of their throwing spears gleaming in the sun like thousands of tiny mirrors. The men strode forward a hundred yards, halted, and began to encamp. There was still two-thirds of a mile between our forces.

"Is it necessary to review our strategy?" I asked Commander Chalmers.

"I believe we're clear on that, Prince Arn. We've taken position here because the open field narrows. General Murphy will have little room to deploy the superior numbers of his cavalry."

"Very good," I approved. "Please go on."

"Unless the General gives us some opening to exploit, we'll receive his attack with our Texan infantry, holding the Kenesee regiments back to commit at the moment of opportunity."

It was a sound plan, simple and straightforward, taking advantage of our strengths while compensating for our weaknesses. What surprised me was that the plan was my own, given the nod of approval from Murdock, the Kenesee colonels, and Commander Chalmers. But when our "moment of opportunity" might come, I could not be sure. Most likely, we'd put the Fifth and Sixth Regiments in on the right flank in a fierce counterattack, break the Texan line, and then roll them up.

We watched the loyalists until we were sure they were actually bivouacking and not just trying a ruse. Scouts came in and reported that the enemy were sending out heavy security detachments in all directions, as we could see by the line of pickets that advanced to midfield before halting warily. There would be little chance of surprising them by a flanking maneuver.

I thought of something. "Is our own security in place?" I had ordered it. But it's one thing to have something ordered, and another to have it done.

"I relayed your order to my regimental commanders," Commander Chalmers assured me. "But I'll go and make the rounds to see that it's been done."

I was about to let him go, and then stopped. General Black and King Reuel had always instilled in Robert and me the need to check things out for ourselves. "I'll go with you."

We rounded the compass, and it was a good thing we did. The colonel on the right flank had not received his orders, and had put out only local security. A Texan cavalry colonel covering our rear had thought it unnecessary to guard the back of the army, and had ignored the order from the presumptuous clerk Chalmers. He was relieved of command for willful disobedience, and avoided my order to hang only because Chalmers and Captain Metaxis and Murdock warned that such punishment might have a bad effect upon the army's morale. Where there *was* adequate security, we found the sentries drifting toward the loyalist picket line and chatting with their opponents as if on a picnic. That was soon ended by our order, with grumbles from the sentries on both sides of the field.

There was one last precaution. "Wizard Murdock, is there any other danger we should be aware of?"

Murdock shook his head. "Their regimental wizards are putting up static, as are ours. But there have been occasional lapses in the loyalist static, and during those times I've had no sense of any other threat. Unless another force hides in the woods behind what we see—and our scouts tell us there is none—or comes toward us from more than a day's march away, our only concern is the army before us."

"You're sure?" Chalmers asked the wizard.

"My Master is always sure," Lorich replied.

Murdock eyed the young wizard. "Hopefully, my apprentice will be as sure when his moment comes."

Lorich wilted. "Yes, Master. I'll try. But I've got to be close."

"Well, wait your chance, and don't do anything foolish. Stay close to me in battle."

After our tour, a table from the farmer's cabin was dragged out into the grass beside the road, and a half dozen of us ate dinner in the relative coolness of the late afternoon. The pigs and chickens around the cabin had all disappeared, while coincidentally the smell of cooking fowl and pork spread across the campsites of the Texan regiments. The Kenesee troops knew better than to forage, but such strict conduct was not to be expected from the Texans. They had much practice at taking, after all.

Our dinner was a not uncheerful affair of roasted chicken, hardbread, cheeses and milk. I found I had a decent appetite, and ate freely, only regretting it when my stomach belatedly assumed the familiar knot of anxiety and fear that preceded danger.

We leaned back from the table afterwards, those who chewed pipeweed stuffing wads of tobacco into their mouths, while the smokers filled their pipes and lit up with quiet satisfaction. It was a gentle summer evening, the heat of day breaking as the shadows of the trees grew longer, the sunset late and lovely, the air filled only with the evening song of birds twittering among the trees, and the chirrup of spring crickets in the grass.

Songs broke out amongst the troops, and then the men quieted, for across the field we heard General Murphy's men singing too. From the loyalists a song started off sweet but faint, then grew stronger as their entire camp took up the melody. And then from around us our own Texans joined in to serenade the Kenesee regiments, and the two Texan armies together sang the ancient song, and "Red River Valley" drifted into the sky.

The Texans could sing. I'll give them that.

I listened for a while, and then turned to Murdock, and our eyes met. "Arn. Your plan. . . ."

I saved him the trouble. "It won't work."

He nodded in agreement, perturbed. "I'm afraid not."

Chalmers's head swiveled between us. "What do you mean? Why won't the plan work."

"Listen to them," Murdock flung his arm out in a broad sweep. "Murphy's men and yours. Texans all. They don't want to fight—or at least, they don't want to fight their own countrymen. They're unsure who really has the right in this whole thing, and they're wondering why they should risk death for a cause they have little stake in. Yes, Commander, your troops want to be rid of Murphy. But they may not want to be rid of him bad enough."

Chalmers surveyed the field. "I see. So—my men won't fight."

Murdock looked across the field. "Oh, they'll fight. For each other, if nothing else. But their hearts won't be in it. How hard they'll fight, and how long—that's the problem. Murphy's men are just as unsure about this whole thing. Opposing regiments that pass each other peaceably on the road; sentries that chat with the enemy; armies that sing the same song—the men are reluctant, the armies brittle. Our plan is too dangerous. It asks too much of our Texan troops. Either side might collapse in the moment of crisis, and there's no way of knowing which will go first.

Chalmers looked relieved. "All we need, then, is a new plan."

"That's all," Murdock agreed. "A new plan."

Even as the black of night faded into a lighter darkness, we knew the morning would dawn hot and thick, the air pungent in our nostrils with the sweat of almost seven thousand men about to go into battle, most of them for the first time. Our army was already rising, men tossing wood onto fires, wandering off to the latrines dug in the woods, cooking breakfast and preparing for war in the long shadows formed by the trees as the sun peeked over the horizon.

Our Texans were subdued, talking in low voices over bread and bacon and coffee, staring into their campfires and trying to ignore the hundreds of fires that twinkled on the other side of the field and faded with the coming dawn. They spoke of mosquito bites and ticks and rocks under their blankets and stiff necks and tired feet and what they would do when they returned home. And only when no one was looking would they cast a furtive eye across meadow and orchard and plowed furrows at the milling thousands of Murphy's army. His men stretched out across the slightest of rises, just a few feet in height, which rose like an island above a sea of thin mist, the cloudy whiteness clinging to ground that lay between us.

Ah, yes. Another morning. Another chance to die. How exciting.

I stood, Murdock and Kren on either side, staring off across the clearing, while Lorich hovered just behind. With him would be Sergeant Jenkins, casting a watchful eye on us. A dozen yards behind Jenkins, the squadrons of royal guards quickly readied themselves under Nielson's orders, breaking camp with a quiet efficiency that made the Texans hurry their own preparations.

"A quiet night," I commented for lack of anything better to say. I avoided breakfast, of course.

Kren nodded. "No surprises. Security was out good and proper on both sides, and Murphy held tight."

"Why shouldn't he?" I asked gloomily "He may have the winning hand."

"Ahhh," Murdock exclaimed. "Now that's the Arn I know. Never cheerier than before a battle."

"Have you seen our Texan comrades?" Kren whispered. "They're subdued. One good blow, and the whole mass of them will break and run."

Jenkins cleared his throat. "Aye, sir. That they might. But then again, who's to say that Murphy's regiments are any better?"

And that of course, was what we had to hope. The destruction of the Texan army in Kenesee the previous year had shattered the morale of the Texan nation and saddled its people with a bitter and humiliating defeat as well as a tragic loss of their best men and most highly-trained leaders. If our analysis was correct, neither side would have an advantage here. Loyalists and Rebels alike would have colonels with little battlefield experience.

The issue could well be decided by the Kenesee units. They were all battle-tested, the infantry probably the finest on the continent. Against them, Murphy could put his foot guardos and horse guardos. Probably just about a draw, overall—until you factored in the wild card. Muskets, and a form of warfare not seen for over three hundred years.

It took a goodly while to deploy the army. The plan of deployment was changed during the night, and each regiment had to shift forward or back, left or right according to its new position. But General Murphy seemed to need as much time as we did to deploy properly. Maybe he had changed his plans too.

We anticipated Murphy advancing upon us. Just as he had taken the strategic offensive, he would have to take the tactical offensive, for we could sit here facing him as long as he was willing. With each day his troops would wonder why he did not attack, and doubt even more, while our men took heart at his hesitation. Likewise, given Murphy's advantage in missile power provided by the muskets, we could not afford to sit in place and allow him to close to musket range and blast us from a distance. *We* needed to take the offensive when the enemy approached, and to use our elite troops to best effect, closing quickly and breaking their line once and for all, while minimizing the stress of combat upon our Texan units.

To this end, our own forces were deployed in a large, blunt wedge pointed toward the center of the enemy line, each flank of the wedge reaching to the woodlines on either side. At the apex of the wedge stood the Sixth Regiment in two lines, each line five men deep. The Fifth regiment, in two columns of companies, was deployed behind the Sixth, and behind the Fifth were two cavalry regiments, the Kenesee Tenth Cavalry Regiment, and the Texan Ninth. The Ninth was supposedly the best horse regiment the rebels had. On either flank of the Sixth were the regiments of Texan infantry, each regiment's front straight and correct, but the position of each regiment echeloned back twenty yards from the one before it. Regiments of horse hung behind the trailing regiments of the wedge, ready to swing out and guard the flanks from enemy cavalry should an opening appear. If all went well, they could exploit the hole punched by the Sixth Regiment and complete the route of Murphy's army.

If all went well.

Sergeant Jenkins eyed me. "You're looking a little pale, sir."

"Am I?"

"Yes, sir. There's a copse of bushes right over there, if you've a need."

"Perhaps that would be best." I dismounted, the Texan colonels giving each other puzzled looks. Trying to control the acrobatics performed by my stomach, I strode into the brush with as much dignity as I could muster, and when none could see, leaned over and was thoroughly sick. I was getting used to this sort of thing, and was quite neat about it. Almost none splattered on me.

Wiping my mouth with a kerchief, I sauntered out casually and mounted. "Thank you, Sergeant."

"You're welcome, sir."

Murdock grinned. "It's been almost a year. I'd forgotten."

"Good heavens, sir," the sergeant admonished Murdock. "It *is* important we maintain the traditions."

I added Jenkins to my list of people to have a little talk with—when all this was over.

Murdock leaned forward, his elbow on the pommel of his saddle, squinting at the enemy line. "I'm afraid General Murphy may have arrived at the same tactic we have—the weight of attack in the center. Take a look. The crested helms and red jackets. Guardos, no?"

I took out my pipe, stuffed the bowl half full with tobacco. And then, from the tiny pouch Jenkins had procured for me upon my order, sprinkled some yellow powder over the tobacco. I struck a match and lit up.

Murdock sniffed the air and looked at me. "Careful, Arn. I wish you wouldn't."

I puffed away. "Your advice is appreciated."

"Remember. This is the second time."

The beastman Kren stroked his cheeks. "Foot guardos three deep, and almost three hundred men in the first rank. I think we know where their muskets are now."

Flags and banners were unfurled above General Murphy's ranks.

Jenkins squinted. "I guess we'll find out for sure soon."

Across the field, bowmen took position as skirmishers before the formed troops. Horns and drums and bugles sounded, and the loyalists started forward. Not everyone, at first. The guardos in the center, and a dozen heartbeats later, the regiments to either side.

Kren laughed. "General Murphy is using a wedge formation. Now, where have I seen that before?"

Wedge against wedge. Elite Texan guardos against elite Kenesee infantry. And that would determine it.

We mounted.

Murdock gestured at the guardos. "Three deep is a thin line—especially against cavalry."

I studied the situation. Murdock was right. General Murphy's entire army was moving now, their deployment a mirror image of our own, marching across the wide meadow and towards the narrow mouth of the funnel where we waited. As they came, their cavalry companies on the outermost flanks had to swing in and take position behind other units to avoid the forest. That part of our planning was going well. There was some confusion evident during those maneuvers, but the horsemen seemed to overcome that readily enough.

Behind their skirmishers they kept coming at the steady pace of an infantryman in close formation, their army regiments with shields up, their throwing spears held vertically. The trick was to make sure they were far enough down the funnel to negate their cavalry, yet far enough away for our own units to find their stride before charging. I conferred with Daniels. Yes, two hundred yards would do it.

Our own bowmen trotted out to form a skirmish line front of their regiments. The moment came. I nodded to Chalmers and Daniels. Our own horns and drums sounded, voice commands rang out, and our army started forward. One or two of the Texan regiments on the right were slow getting off, but they lost only a few yards before falling into the pace.

There was the swish of feet through tall grass and wheat, and then the rustle of leaves from the cotton and potato plants. Complementing this was the sound of horses' hooves, the rattle and rasp and creak of leather and wood and metal as soldiers and horses went forward, the sounds clear in the heavy air. Yet while officers called out encouragingly, the men were, for the most part, silent. The grim work was upon them.

I had already planned this with Chalmers. "The center of their line. Break it."

I needed to say no more. He gave a signal, and the colonel

of the Texan Ninth brought his horses forward at the canter, and they passed around either flank of the Kenesee infantry regiments in columns of four, lowering their lances and going straight into the charge without deploying further. The foot guardos, after all, did not even have throwing spears to fend off the horsemen. Perhaps this would do it.

I could make out General Murphy now, following behind his red-jacketed infantry guardos, a dozen of his staff and their aides around him awaiting his orders, a few squads of red-jacketed horse guardos following. Upon his face I could almost make out the arrogant sneer that he must have worn, ready to unleash the forbidden weapons upon our troops, and shatter the rebel army with a half dozen volleys. He looked forward to finally getting his hands again on this unlikely prince who had so upset his plans.

Worst of all, it could happen. Which way would the fates decide?

The skirmishers of both sides faded back to find safety behind the formed troops. Our infantry kept marching behind the cavalry. The Ninth gained speed and thundered toward the enemy, their lances lowered to the horizontal. Murphy's guardos halted, orders rang out and a command was given. The muskets were put to shoulders. Only twenty yards separated the charging horsemen from the line of infantry. A thousand muskets blossomed clouds of white smoke, and immediately an awful crackling noise pounded at our eardrums. All the infantry on the field came to a sudden halt.

"Good God in Heaven," Kren exclaimed.

I puffed harder.

Our charging cavalry slid to a stop in a jumble, scores of horses and riders going down and coming to rest only a few paces from the enemy line. The surviving animals went crazy, backing off and bucking and breaking for the rear of their own accord. The regiment broke into fragments, clusters of wild-eyed horses streaming past us to get away from the hellish noise and sulfurous fire which they had never experienced before. Perhaps horses could be trained to tolerate the unholy blasts of the muskets. For now, none could stay against the hell fire. Our own mounts, farther away though we were, had to be reined in and reassured, some with great difficulty. So much for the cavalry.

Nor was it just the horses that were affected. The infantry of both armies stood in place, halted of their own accord, seeing and hearing a form of warfare that stunned them with its noise and smoke and death.

There was wavering in the ranks of our Texans. I heard Steward Montrose, one voice among many. "Steady, men. STEADY!"

The smoke dissipated, and through the thinning tendrils we could see Murphy's guardos standing in place, but busy doing something.

Reloading. They were reloading.

The smell of sulfur drifted across the field.

Colonel Daniels, with his Kenesee Sixth Regiment, took in the situation quickly. The Sixth was halted, standing no more than seventy yards from the guardos. He stepped in front of the regiment. His voice rang out, and the regiment started forward again.

The guardos aimed their muskets, and another blast of noise rang out as smoke billowed. Blood spattered in the ranks of the Sixth. Several heads seemed to explode. The tips of the long spears stirred as if there were a wind blowing through grass, and the Kenesee infantry came to a halt again, stung. A hundred men at least, perhaps two hundred, must have gone down with that single volley. Incredible. Colonel Daniels had been hit too, for his sword drooped and he held his stomach as he sagged against another man, who lowered him to the ground.

There was disorder in the ranks of our Texans nearest the Sixth Regiment as they took a few musket balls and recoiled from the massacre before them. It was frightening to stand before this strange hellfire and die by unseen missiles that could blow a head apart. Even the stalwarts of the Sixth were stunned by the violence of the new weapons. Another volley or two, and the regiment would be shattered.

We were coming to the key moment, the moment of decision, the climax of the battle.

It grew warm, very warm, and then all of existence had a terrible lucidity. Time seemed to slow, and I had all the moments I needed to study dispositions and ponder a solution. The pieces were on the board. Which piece should I move next? And then the answer came to me like a vision. I knew what needed to be done. The guardos must be distracted, their aim made high and wasted. The duty was clear.

I took a deep breath, and the vision receded.

"Murdock, Chalmers, stay here." I stuffed my pipe into a pocket and galloped up to the front of the Sixth. The men saw me and cheered. Across the intervening yards the guardos watched too, even while they reloaded their weapons. Murphy, a tiny figure on horseback in the distance behind his guards, pointed at me and shouted hurried orders to his officers. He was still too far back for Lorich to give him a squeeze. A pity.

I was not dismounting. It was essential I stay on horseback. I drew my sword and held it aloft.

"SIXTH REGIMENT!"

The line straightened and spears angled forward and steady, waiting. Colonel Daniels, seated in the grass and holding his belly with one hand, looked and raised his sword in salute. Their glorious Prince Scar was leading them now.

"FOR JOHN BLACK."

"FOR JOHN BLACK!" thundered back from hundreds of throats.

No time for further niceties. "CHARGE!"

With a yell they surged forward.

A motion to my right. It was Chalmers, who had reined in beside me. Farther back, Murdock and Kendall and the rest of my guards were spurring forward to join us. No one ever obeys my orders.

"You fool," I berated Chalmers. "Don't you understand? I'm the target."

And then the guardos fired again, and the air was filled with a buzzing noise left and right, as if bees, dozens of bees, were flying past my ears. Chalmers' chest spouted blood and he tumbled from his horse just before his mount fell dead. My horse reared, hooves cutting the air, and then went over backwards, pierced by a half dozen musket balls.

I lay on my back on the ground, staring at the sky. Clouds drifted slowly across the brilliant blue in great cottony piles. It really was a very pretty day.

A head thrust into sight, the face of Jenkins staring down at me with concern. From the edges of my vision I saw blurry figures approaching, and heard their voices. "Is he dead?"

Jenkins inspected me up and down. ''I don't see any wounds. Sir, are you all right?''

''The sky is very pretty.''

''He's cracked his head.''

I blinked. ''Have we lost?''

''Lost?'' Jenkins chortled. ''No, we're winning.''

''Help me up.''

Murdock's face appeared. ''You never fail to surprise me, Arn. That was a foolhardy thing to do, my boy. Here you are, up we go. Are you dizzy? No? Just rest.''

The area around me was a charnel ground of horses and men sprawled over the grass. Several of the horses stirred, trying to rise and failing, while wounded screamed or groaned aloud. Nearby, Chalmers lay upon the ground, a staff doctor already at work over him. And Kendall was bleeding from the leg.

''Their third volley wasn't as effective,'' Kren offered. ''I think maybe they aimed high. The Sixth went in, and the Fifth followed.''

Indeed, the battle was won, or was being won. It unfolded exactly as I had imagined it in my moment of clarity. Many of the guardos had aimed high, at Chalmers and me on horseback, rather than at the infantry. The Sixth had absorbed more punishment from the last volley, but not enough to stop it. The foot guardos had seen the deadly Kenesee spearpoints getting closer, and realized there was no time to reload. Apparently, they did not have bayonets, though I doubt if those would have done them much good. To their credit—or their stupidity—they'd tried to draw swords and stand firm. Shieldless against long spears, they did not stand long. A moment, and then the guardos—what remained of them—were running away.

The Sixth and Fifth prepared to charge the flanks of the other regiments, but the Loyalist line regiments did not need other encouragement. Those nearest the Kenesee regiments broke and ran, so that the center of the Loyalist line was gone. The infantry regiments further to the flanks simply laid down their weapons and surrendered *en masse*. Even the Loyalist cavalry drew back, halted, and dismounted, waiting to be taken prisoner. They did not appear to be terribly unhappy about the outcome.

Murphy's horse guardos were another matter. They had been held back in reserve, and Murphy and his staff rode back now to join them and make their escape.

Their escape.

"A horse! Get me a horse." I saw one standing riderless, and leaped upon him without benefit of stirrup, a jump greater than I had ever done. Jenkins and the others were hurriedly mounting while I found Sergeant Nielson and the royal guards. I pointed at the horse guardos. "Take them."

Sergeant Nielson was dubious. "Attack the whole regiment, sir? With a hundred men?"

Well, I couldn't blame him. "Try to flank them. I'll send you help."

They started forward, deploying into line as they went.

I raced over to the colonel of the nearest rebel cavalry regiment, my party trailing behind me. "Attack the horse guardos."

The Texan colonel eyed me primly. "I take orders from Commander Chalmers. Not from you."

I smashed the pommel of my sword into the side of his face and he tumbled from his mount, flopping to the ground with a satisfactory clunk while his subordinates' eyes widened in disbelief. "Now, who's next in command?"

"Is he always like this?" Metaxis asked from behind.

An officer stood in his stirrups. "Sir!"

"You heard the order? Do it."

"Yes, sir." He had the regiment moving within seconds.

Education is a matter of example.

The next cavalry regiment was more cooperative. "We can't let the guardos get away. Advance down the road and seal it off so they can't retreat."

My whole purpose was to keep the guardos busy and cut off Murphy's escape. Yes, I might have raced off after him directly—and found myself battling eight hundred of his guardos. Fine for the ballads, but not so good for survival.

Furious with the collapse of his army and preoccupied with the force attacking him in front, Murphy didn't pay attention to the road until it was too late. Only a few scattered horsemen escaped by that route. Cursing as he saw the road closed behind him and his last unit outflanked, Murphy and his staff rode off into the forest. His guardos put up a token resistance to give him time, and then—those who didn't surrender outright—dispersed and followed.

It was not yet midmorning.

Any other time, and I would have launched the pursuit of Murphy with grim satisfaction. But I had different things on my mind. "Murdock, stay here and take care of things. Don't let Murphy get away. I'll take the royal guards and the Tenth and Lorich. And Metaxis. He might be helpful."

Murdock knew my mind. "Dallas?"

I called out behind me as I spurred away.

"Follow as quickly as you can with the army."

11

Castle Corral

We rode hard, though not so hard as to wear out the horses and leave us vulnerable to a fresh enemy. I was anxious, but not unbalanced by my anxiety. What needed doing needed to be done well. And so we rode back up the road to Dallas, not a single obstacle in our path before the east gates of the town. But those were challenge enough.

We arrived to find the great wooden portals firmly closed against us, the bells of the churches finally quiet after giving loud warning of our approach, and the defenders clustered upon the battlements of the walls. Not more than a thousand ill-trained conscripts they were, perhaps, but against fewer numbers without siege equipment, they would stymie an attacker quite nicely. Diplomacy was the only hope of a quick entrance into the town.

Our forces were deployed in the cotton fields facing the gate, five hundred cavalry of the Tenth to the rear at the extreme bow range of the defenders, and in front of them more than a hundred royal guards in dress line. They all had the unmistakable look of hardened veterans, and the coating of dust on their uniforms only added to that appearance. Before them my staff and I clustered just in front of the gates, all too aware of the archers on the wall. In my hand I held my pipe, the bowl half-filled, but unlit.

The mayor of Dallas, a pudgy man whose face glistened with sweat, looked down from the walls with dismay. "What's that you say?"

Captain Metaxis sighed. "The mayor is hard of hearing. Gets worse every year."

"Are megaphones prohibited by the Codes?" Kren asked.

"Listen well this time," Metaxis shouted up.

But the mayor had been shouldered aside by another man, who took his place on the battlements with two dozen guardos. Sheriff Matthew Bartholomew looked upon us as if surveying a trash heap, his tone mocking. "That voice sounds familiar. Can it be Captain Metaxis?"

"Yes, Mr. Bartholomew."

"So I see. Well, Traitor Metaxis. Do tell us again."

Captain Metaxis stifled a curse. "I said General Murphy's loyalist army has been defeated by the Army of Rebellion. Murphy's army was captured intact, right on the battlefield. By now, General Murphy himself is probably captured."

Bartholomew looked over our ranks. "So you say. And how many men does this Army of Rebellion number?"

"Almost seven thousand horse and foot," the captain shared. "Maybe more, now. Some of the loyalist units may have joined us."

"Lies and untruths," Bartholomew stated. "You've avoided battle with the General and swung around his rear to try and take Dallas by ruse. Is this your doing, Prince Arn? Anxious to see your little flower again? She is sweet, I must admit. Well, your ruse won't work. It was only by the treachery of a trusted subordinate that you escaped our hospitality. Treachery and lies. In open battle, your true colors would be seen. When General Murphy returns victorious, we'll put you back where you belong, if you live that long. Archers!"

"Prince Arn?"

"Not *now*, Lorich."

I wheeled my horse and led—if truth be told—a most hurried and undignified retreat as arrows fell among us. The aim was not good. Bartholomew's command to the archers must have surprised the doubtful bowmen, who might have caused us some damage had they been ready. Or, their inaccuracy may have been due to the volley of arrows the royal guards provided from horseback as covering fire. From a safe range we halted and gazed at the battlements. Bartholomew was already gone.

"Too bad," Metaxis sighed. "He can't have more than two companies of guardos left in the castle. Two hundred men, at most."

"Prince Arn?"

I grimaced. "Yes, Lorich?"

"It's too late now, but if you'd wanted, I could have—"

I held up my hand in a clenched fist to silence him, though my anger was with myself. Lorich's power. Of course. The range was long, probably too long, but it should have been tried. Lorich might have squeezed Bartholomew. But I had not thought the sheriff would be there, and Lorich could not know my will. I cursed my own stupidity.

Minutes passed. Jenkins and Kren exchanged glances.

"What now?" Kren asked me.

What indeed? I was out of ideas.

Fortunately, I never needed to provide an answer to Kren's question. A small white flag—perhaps someone's kerchief—was hung over the battlements. We looked at each other.

"A trick," Kren ventured.

"Possibly," Metaxis agreed, "but there's only one way to find out."

We rode forward to the gate.

The pudgy mayor was arguing with a companion, and then there was a commotion and the mayor disappeared from view. A helmeted guardos officer peered down at us. "Captain Metaxis? It's Major Gardner. Mr. Bartholomew has gone back to the castle."

"Aye, sir?"

"We had riders coming in from the east before you arrived, and they've told their tale. So is it true? Has General Murphy been defeated?"

"True. Every word of it."

I lit a match and applied it to the tobacco. I must have

looked the cool one to those watching me. My hand wasn't even trembling. Sometimes I surprise myself.

Kren wrinkled his nose. "Prince Arn. Again?"

Lorich could not restrain himself. "Sir! Wizard Murdock warned you. This is the third time!"

The major on the wall looked at his comrades, then back at Metaxis. "Do you swear by God and the salvation of your soul that what you have stated is the truth?"

Metaxis nodded. "By my God and on my soul, I do so swear. We have come ahead of the army to rescue those held in the dungeon of Corral. Beside me is Prince Arn—Prince Scar—of Kenesee. Look at his face if you doubt. Bartholomew knew him for who he is."

Puffing vigorously and leering up at them, I turned my face to profile so they could catch the proof in all its glory.

"You see?" Metaxis continued. "It is he. And here are his royal guards, and a regiment of Kenesee horsemen. Would General Murphy have allowed such a force to slip around his rear? He controlled the road. How might we have come?"

There was more, but finally they were convinced. "What will happen if we open the gates?" the major asked.

"The people of the town may go about their business without interference. The defenders and guardos will be dismissed from service and may go their way once they swear the oath of a year and a day. The Army of Rebellion seeks no retribution. We are not conquerors, but liberators. Prince Arn has agreed, and guarantees it."

Actually, many of the red jackets deserved more than just dismissal from service. Many of them were brutal and cruel, and had willingly followed Jack Murphy in all his tyrannous acts. A Captain Metaxis was a rarity, a sensitive man of conscience who could no longer justify to himself what he saw and was asked to do. But I wanted into the town and Castle Corral quickly. If that meant pardoning some of the guilty, then so be it.

"And if we refuse?"

"In Kenesee, there was a town named Lexington. . . ."

There was more commotion on the wall.

The major again. "We would have Prince Arn swear to those terms. Upon his soul."

Upon my soul? That would be a worthless oath, indeed. My

soul was already damned. I refrained from laughing. Yet, soul or not, they were right to ask for my promise. I would not violate that, regardless of what I swore upon.

"Except for Bartholomew, I swear to the terms as stated. Upon my soul."

"Wait a moment. We're opening the gates."

"It could still be a trick," Kren warned.

"Trick or not," I smirked as the gates swung wide, "we're going through."

I led them in at a goodly pace, puffing away, the pipe clenched firmly in my teeth. Behind rode Kren, Lorich, Metaxis, Jenkins, and the royal guards. Following came the Tenth. We clattered through the town, women and children staring in wonder from doorways and windows. We pounded up several streets I recognized, past the town hall and market plaza, and on to the wide, paved way that ran along the ramparts of Castle Corral.

The castle's gate was still open.

There were yells of surprise and alarm from the castle walls, and a trumpet blew warning.

I spurred my horse and we raced under the gate tower, through the tunnel, and into the courtyard of Corral. Behind me came my comrades and the royal guards. In the corner was a cluster of horses being prepared for riders, large saddlebags attached to their sides. Had Bartholomew been preparing to flee?

From out of doors and towers came a dozen, a score, and then half a hundred men in response to the alarm. No, not a trap. At least, not a planned one. They stopped a moment, stunned at our arrival, and then gripped their weapons and came on. Behind us, there was a ratcheting sound and a clanking of chain as a portcullis over the gate slammed down, isolating us from the men of the Tenth. Inside, perhaps four score of royal guards were reining to a halt. There was no room to charge, and guardos were coming from every direction. The royal guards threw down their lances, drew swords, and piled into the enemy.

I ignored the confusion behind me, spurring straight for the open door to the castle proper. The two guardos at the door began to swing the leaves shut, saw me coming, and turned to defend themselves. I smashed one up against the wall with my horse, leaped from the saddle, and cut the other down. Then I took the pipe from my mouth and pocketed it. "Follow me," I ordered, and went in.

A main corridor. Doors, passageways, two sets of stairs.

My comrades were just entering, Metaxis limping painfully, with Jenkins's men right behind. They moved so slowly.

"Metaxis! Where?"

He pointed. "Up the stairs. To the right."

I took the stairs three at a time, turned to the right, and was attacked by a half dozen guardos with spears and swords. I flailed my sword at them, backed away as they followed, then leapt on the first and smashed the pommel of my sword into his face. I heard teeth break. He went down.

The second thrust his spear at me. I stepped aside, grabbed it and pulled him onto my sword point. His mouth opened wide. I pushed him off with a knee and parried a spear thrust from the third.

Everyone was moving slowly.

Except me.

A sword stroke, and the man's spear was in two pieces. Alas, so was my sword. I thrust the shard into his chest below the breastbone. Far ahead in the passageway, a door opened and Bartholomew emerged, pulling an unwilling figure behind him.

"Angela!"

Another guardos was in my way. I picked him up and threw him against a wall. He crumpled. The remaining two Texans backed away from me and ran down the passageway after Bartholomew. I picked up a spear and followed. Behind me, my friends reached the top of the stairs and I could hear their voices echo down the passage.

"Good Lord," said Lorich.

"I don't believe it," said Kren.

"Just like Sir John Wayne," exclaimed Metaxis.

"After him!" said Sergeant Jenkins.

For some reason, I could not seem to catch the slow-moving guardos who ran away from me. My knee wasn't working right. Blood covered the pant leg. I kept going, the footsteps of my friends growing louder behind me. The passage widened out into a central hall. More doors, and at the far end circular steps leading up and down. Fresh guardos bubbled down from the stairs and came for me. Ten, twenty—the odds were becoming a little steep. Jenkins and Kren leaped to my side, and a dozen of my guards. It was a soldier's fight, for most of the fighters were evenly matched, and there were many parried thrusts. But their numbers, their numbers. There must have been forty at least, pushing to the sides, trying to flank and stretch us.

I jabbed the spear into one, and watched while another brought his sword around to chop through my shoulder. The sword bearer stopped, shivered, and stiffened, dropping like a board. Lorich? Yes, Lorich. Then the young wizard was busy keeping himself alive, stumbling back from a guardos with a short spear who thrust at him between the front line of combatants.

The fight went on, but the enemy's strokes were not so slow now, and mine were not so quick. The opiate was wearing off, or I was wearing out, or perhaps both. One of the royal guards went down, and another, and we were being forced back. The unequal struggle could not go on for long.

And then it was our turn. Sergeant Nielson and royal guards stormed up from the stairs ahead, and more appeared from the passage behind. The fighting grew intense, the numbers making for close quarters and hand-to-hand struggles before a voice rang out above the clatter of battle.

Metaxis. "Guardos! Down your swords!"

The strokes grew less fierce, thrusts became tentative, there were more parries than attacks. And then they lowered their weapons, suspicious and yet realizing that it was over for them, one way or another. Royal guards moved quickly, disarming them before anyone else arrived to change the equation.

Lorich held his head, but was still on his feet, aware of what went on around him. How much did he have left in him?

Sergeant Nielson stared at my leg. "You're bleeding to death, Prince Arn."

"Not now."

"We managed to open the portcullis," Nielson babbled on. "The Tenth came in, and that did it. I left them to mop up, and brought the guards after you. Just in time, it looks like. Tough, these guardos."

I grabbed Metaxis, who had trailed behind the others but arrived with Nielson. "Which way?"

"Up. It has to be up."

I let Sergeant Nielson and the guards take the lead, for I could no longer keep pace. Thank God the guardos hadn't opted to defend from these stairs. The curving steps were steep, and my leg was worse now as we went round and round the tiny passage. Blood squished in my boot. We came to a round landing, and daylight streamed in from an open doorway. I stepped through and onto the western wall of the castle.

And there ahead of us, perched atop the crenellated battlements just a few inches from its edge, Bartholomew stood defiantly, Angela clutched in his arm while his other hand held a dagger to her throat. Remarkably, she looked unharmed, though her hands were bound behind her and a gag was stuffed into her mouth, held there by a rope. Her eyes were wide.

There were a few guardos still scattered about, but they lowered their weapons as guards continued to surge onto the wall walk and Metaxis gave the order. They were taken, and quickly there was only Bartholomew left, holding his hostage and watching the drama unfold.

Lorich came to my side, his face furrowed with such pain that he put a hand to the side of his head, as if to keep his brain from throbbing through the skull. He whispered to me. "I can do it, Prince Arn. I can do one more."

And perhaps he could. But the way Bartholomew clutched Angela, his death spasm might lock her in his grip, and she could well be taken over the wall with him.

"No," I whispered back. "Don't try."

"Well, well, well," Bartholomew said. "The young prince come to rescue his woman. This will make quite a tale, won't it?"

I waved the others back, took a few steps forward, and glanced over the side. The ground fell away on this side of the castle. The fall would be seventy feet at least, ending on the pile of rocks and boulders below. I felt dizzy, and looked away from the rocks.

Angela's eyes were glued to mine, but there was no terror in them.

I laid down the spear and folded my arms across my chest.

The opiate had not worn off completely. The words came easily. "We seem to be at an impasse."

Bartholomew laughed. "I suppose you might say that. I really thought I'd be able to get away before you took the town. Horses were being readied, and I could have left by the south gate. I knew I couldn't trust the townspeople to defend the gates. I just didn't expect the guardos I left there to turn so quickly. I should have realized. I had the example of Metaxis. But that was my mistake, and so here we are. Do you have any ideas?"

"The woman is unharmed?"

"Your little flower? Oh, she is, on the whole. I was rather taken, you know. She has something about her. I quite surprised myself. And there was a certain appeal to having the woman of a prince. An opportunity to gloat, and all that. It was tantalizing to keep her well, to keep her hoping, to keep you hoping, to know that at any time I could—well, I shall not have the chance now, shall I? You've spoiled that. All I will have is memories of those afternoons and nights together. What do you say about that, my dear?"

He caressed her neck with the back of his hand, the blade of his dagger floating in the air before her eyes. "I did enjoy the more usual forms of recreation with her. I want you to know that. It was quite a change for me. Nice, but rather dull, you know? I think she was falling in love with me. Weren't you, my dear?"

She shook her head back and forth in denial, and squirmed in his grasp. I don't think "love" was quite the term.

I measured my words carefully. "You can go free. I give you my word. My promise. Just let her go."

Bartholomew tilted his head. "Your promise? Your word? It's said that you take your word very seriously. That you never break an oath."

"It's true. I will let you go, and none will pursue."

"That's very tempting. Very tempting, indeed. I would like to believe you, but I can't. No one keeps their word. A promise is nothing. An oath merely a curse. No, Prince Scar. I will not accept your promise."

"Then what can I offer?"

He looked about. There were a half dozen guardsmen who had found bows, and now waited with nocked shafts. A word, and Bartholomew would be pierced with arrows. And so would Angela. Dozens of other guards still stood about, waiting to spring to my defense. At any other time, their presence would have been reassuring.

Bartholomew considered. "An exchange might work."

Angela stopped squirming, looked up at Bartholomew, and back at me.

"An exchange?"

"A more valuable hostage. You, Prince Scar."

Angela desperately shook her head no.

"That could be done." I swayed, and had to lean against the hard stone of the battlement. "But you have to let her go first."

"Oh, no. Not first. After. I will let her go when I have you in my grasp."

Bartholomew would have me, then. With me, his plan of escape might actually work. Out the castle, out the town, and into the countryside on fresh horses with extra mounts for good measure. Yes, he might get away with it. And when he was a day's ride away, what would he do with Prince Scar? Release him? Not likely.

I did not hesitate in answering his terms. "All right."

Bartholomew grinned.

Angela's eyes widened, and then narrowed. I had seen that calculating look before. She had figured out what events were going to transpire, just as I had. She understood what the end of the story would be. And now she was determining what to do. The opiate must have weakened considerably, for at that moment I grew truly frightened.

The little fool was going to try something.

I puzzled how to warn her. How to warn *him*. But there was no time. She went limp against Bartholomew, slipping down a bit in his grasp, and suddenly drove upward and back, hard against him, driving him back towards the edge of the stone battlement. She was trying to save me by pushing him off the battlements to his death—and hers. The huge Texan was momentarily off balance, his arm still securely around Angela, and my heart stopped as he teetered on the edge. But she could not offset his size and strength. He recovered, and grasped her more tightly, the knife against the skin of her neck now.

"Well, little flower, why did you do—ahh, it was your Prince Scar, wasn't it? You do love him more than me. And so you would kill us both to save him." Could there be an honest note of revelation and disappointment mixed with the irritation in his voice? Could he be so self-deluded? He nicked her skin with the knife, and drops of blood dripped down her neck as he whispered into her ear. "You see? You see what I could have done to you, and didn't? Do you understand? The slow death. That's what's to be feared. The slow death, not the quick one. And I spared you that fate. I would have expected more gratitude." He paused, pondering events. "Well, we had so little time together, I'm sure that's it. A few more days with me, and your brave hero would not mean so much. Be still."

He eyed the guards, letting them know he was watching and ready. "And now Prince Scar, if you'll have someone bind you securely, you can come up here and—"

I had taken a step toward him, and for the first time he noticed my leg.

"A wound, Prince Scar? And bleeding quite freely, from the looks of it. Well, that rather finishes it, I should guess. Surprising, that I didn't notice it before. I'm usually very good about noticing such things, though the last hour has been somewhat busier than normal, which could account for it."

"The wound doesn't matter. Sergeant Jenkins, tie me."

Bartholomew shook his head. "Prince Scar, Prince Scar. You don't understand. You're the only one who could get me out of here. The only hostage whose value would prevent your guards from trying something here, or in the passageways, or the courtyards, or the town. But look at you. You're no good to me like that. Soon you'll pass out from loss of blood. How can I drag around a wounded man? I'm afraid your guards would be on me in a moment, and then you would have me. No, I'm afraid that was a very unfortunate wound. It changes everything."

I leaned against the battlements again. Spots were beginning to hamper my vision.

Metaxis stepped up and steadied me with a hand. "Mr. Bartholomew, come down. You have our word. You won't be harmed. And if Prince Arn wishes, we will let you go. Please."

"On your word, Metaxis?" he said with scorn. "On your word?"

"No, not my word. On the word of Prince Arn of Kenesee."

I felt so weak now. As weak as I had felt strong.

Angela struggled uselessly in the arms of the sheriff.

Bartholomew considered us for a long moment. He surveyed the battlements, the castle, the town and countryside, looked down at the rocks below, and finally, up at the sky. He sighed. "No, I'm afraid not." His grip on Angela tightened.

"Please, sir," Metaxis pleaded. "Do not do this thing."

"I have no other choice," Bartholomew replied with finality. "The quick death. Say good-bye, Angela."

She looked at him in understanding, and struggled against his overwhelming strength.

I roused myself for a lunge, but my body betrayed me. I had barely the strength to stand.

Bartholomew swept her up in his arms, and Angela's eyes met mine, but what message they held, I could not tell.

He smiled at us all, laughed with hopelessness, and stepped off into the air.

12

Aftermath

The ceiling was interesting, made of oak planks supported by foot-thick crossbeams. The wood, stained dark, was strong and hard and had a permanence about it that was most appealing. I traced the grain in the wood, following it up and down the beams until there was not a sliver I had missed. Some tiny thing moved into my vision. Spiders had begun leaving webs in the angles, and one hung suspended in the air, dangling by an invisible thread, thus defying gravity and preventing it from—

I turned over and buried my head in the pillow, my cheek rubbing against the cloth with a scratchy sound. The bristles of a new beard had sprouted. When had that happened? When was the last time I had shaved? Three days? Four? Something like that. I remembered that it was right after I'd bathed. Lord, hadn't I bathed since then? Did that account for the smell I detected? Did it arise from me, a sprawled body made ripe in the heat of the Texan summer? And perhaps that accounted for the sour taste in my mouth, and the coating over my teeth. When had I brushed my teeth last?

There was a knock on the door. I ignored it. There were voices from the other side.

Kren. "Is he all right?"

Murdock. "It's been getting worse. At least before, he was keeping up appearances. For the last few days, all he's done is lie in bed, or walk around the floor in a daze. And every few hours, out comes that damn pipe. He's hardly eaten in the last three days."

Kren's voice grew even more concerned. "He hasn't eaten? Lord, this is serious. Maybe we should send for Jason the Healer."

"Perhaps," Murdock responded, thoughtfully. "I'll talk to Arn one last time. Reason doesn't work. Maybe angry commands will."

"Good luck, then. I'll go and send in the servants.

Another knock, and then the door opened. I had forgotten to lock it.

The wizard bustled in. "Ahh, there you are, Arn. I thought I'd find you here."

Where else was he to find me?

I lifted my head to look at him. Murdock studied me. "Court's starting shortly."

I lowered my head to the pillow. "You handle it."

"I can administer, but only with Prince Scar there to give my decisions weight. Otherwise, nothing will be done. You know that."

I turned over. A parade of servants was bustling through with buckets of steaming water for the tub in the corner, royal guards watching them carefully. Murdock spoke for the benefit of all ears. "Excellent. Just the thing for Prince Arn. He'll get over his cold all the better after a good soak." The tub was filled, and the servants departed with their guards.

A cold. Hah.

"Must I come?" I asked, my thoughts turning already to my pipe.

"When Commander Chalmers recovers from his wounds, he can take over. Till then, it would be for the best. For them—and for you."

"I'm tired."

"Arn, it's been three weeks."

"I'm wounded."

"Bah. Your knee is coming along nicely."

"I lost a lot of blood."

"Not all of it."

"Jason the Healer should be here to take care of me."

"The doctors here are competent. They kept you alive. Jason is still at Tyler with the wounded. I would have sent for him, was there need."

I covered my eyes with an arm. "I'm still tired."

"Arn, you haven't—"

"No, not today. Not yet." I'd been turning to the opiate rather—steadily, shall we say? At first, its effect was familiar. Strength, courage, energy, optimism, a sense of security, a blissful glaze over tragedy and loss. By the end of the first week of use, the strength was gone, the courage evaporated, the energy vanished. Taking their place were the traditional effects of the opiates. The dulled senses, the dreamy somnolence, the blissful soothing of pain inside and out, and a stupefied sense of idle well-being and peace.

Murdock frowned. "You can't use it anymore."

"I know."

"It will damn you and destroy you."

"I'm already damned."

And that was one comment too many. Murdock pulled back the sheet, his voice stern. "Arn, get out of bed. General Murphy will come before you today. And the landholders. You've forgotten."

I *had* forgotten. Even Murphy, I had forgotten. My mind told me that was bad, to forget Murphy just because of the opiate. My body told me I was ready for another pipeful.

Hatred overcame anguish. "For him, I will come."

My room was in the presidential chambers, a pleasant wing

of the castle that received the best Dallas breezes and the most light. Once it was rid of bodies and the blood was mopped up, it made quite respectable quarters for a resting prince. Far more opulent than the austerity of the King's Castle in Kingsport. Murdock waited while I got into the bath, washed, dawdled in the warmth of the steaming water, and finally got out feeling somewhat better. Murdock handed me a large, thick towel and I dried, after which I shaved from an ornate ceramic bowl with a fancy mirror above it, and then brushed my teeth.

The wizard was troubled. "Have you decided what to do with him?"

Him. General Murphy. He had been found the afternoon of the battle hiding in a place befitting him. An outhouse.

"I still don't know," I replied dumbly, trying to splash the fuzziness from my mind as I splashed the shaving soap from my face. At least I was thinking a bit more clearly as I put on a clean shirt and dress coat.

Sergeant Jenkins stood with two royal guards at my door. I took up my cane. We followed as Jenkins took the lead down a stairway and showed us into a small anteroom, another door on the far wall leading into the presidential reception hall. A table and comfortable chairs filled the small space, and I imagined Murphy waiting here while the audience gathered so he could enter the teeming reception hall last of all. We sat.

Murdock glanced at some papers on the table, and then shuffled them together. "You have to decide now. We've discussed this before—you remember that, don't you?"

"Before? Uhh—yes, of course I remember."

He looked skeptical. "Well, you'd better decide what you're going to do with him."

"I will," I protested, and my answer would have been curt had the opiate not mellowed the sharpness out of me for the moment.

I'd explained it all to the wizard . . . I think. My impulse was to give Murphy a slow death. I had seen the instruments of torture in his dungeon. I knew we could make him linger in agony for many long days before the final act. Certainly, such an end would be just, given what he'd allowed to transpire in that hellhole. But it wasn't justice that I sought. It was revenge. Bartholomew was gone from my grasp. Murphy was still available.

But then the scene would come to me of two small boys disguised as commoners in the streets of Kingsport. And Robert's words. "*Promise me you will forsake revenge, and only challenge wrongdoers in an honorable way.*" And my words, foolishly given. "*Yes, Robert. I promise.*"

What to do? The opiate dulled my feelings into an outward mellowness, but the malice and hatred still burned within me. Perhaps I could forsake the torture and just give Murphy a quick execution. Would that judgment be free of revenge? He had earned death, certainly. Then again, so had I. But though I stood condemned before Heaven, God had not yet conducted the execution. No doubt Murphy would have seen it as quite unfair—and been right. How could I be sure my sentence of him was not tinged with the rage that waited for the opiate to wear off? Could any sentence I passed be free of revenge? It was a dilemma I had not yet solved.

We sat in silence, Murdock doubtless pondering my indecisiveness. The knock on the door we had come through brought me back to the present. Jenkins stepped in with a message pouch. "Messages from the King and from Jason." He handed it over and discreetly left, not revealing a bit of the curiosity that must have assailed him—and the rest of our men—about what was happening back home. I unlaced the pouch and removed two envelopes, one of fine leather that bore the royal seal of Kenesee, and another of common usage. Inside the first were several pages of script—a letter in Robert's own hand.

I looked at the top page, but the words were blurry. At arm's length or close to my squinting eyes, the letters wavered even as I tried to fix them on the page. I could make out a word here and there, but that was all. Still it was better than yesterday, when I'd tried reading a report from the colonels immediately after smoking my pipe. The opiate had many effects to surprise the new user.

"My eyes are tired. Perhaps you could. . . ."

Murdock frowned and took the pages.

June 23rd, 2654
Governor's Fortress,
New Richmond, Virginia

"Good God!" I moaned. "Robert's been captured and a prisoner in Virginia. The army must have been defeated. All is lost!"

Murdock lifted his eyes from the page. "If a certain young prince would stop leaping to conclusions, maybe we could find out what the letter says."

"Sorry."

"Shall we try again? Good. Now be quiet until I've finished." Murdock really was turning into quite a grouch. He continued reading.

Dear Arn,

I received the letter from Wizard Murdock two days ago, but have had no chance to reply before this. Your victory at Tyler brought me great joy. I anxiously awaited news that your mission had ended in success. You and your men have earned great glory, and Texan has been freed of a great evil. If you catch General Murphy, do with him as you will in accord with the laws of justice.

And now, for my news. Forgive me if I pass from the subject of your deeds. I do not make light of what you do in Texan. The Kenesee victory deserves much attention, and indeed I have thought long about what you have accomplished in Texan, and what can be done based upon your success. However, events up here have been just as momentous. Fortune has smiled upon Kenesee again. We took New Richmond today, and I write this from Governor Rodes's fortress. Tonight I shall sleep in his room. He is a prisoner here, under lock and key and guarded by a full company of Kenesee infantry. In my euphoria, I can barely believe what has been done.

Our story is marvelously simple. As we feared, Governor Rodes marched as soon as he knew I was sending you regiments. I met the Army of Virginia at Mooresville with most of our forces, and then fell back before him. His force was the larger, of course. Though Rodes moved quickly, his men were hesitant, having neither enthusiasm nor resolve to steady the ranks. Who can blame them, given what you did to their army last summer?

We gave battle at Greenville. Our cavalry proved decisive, flanking the Easterners. We forced them to retire from the field, and they lost perhaps a fifth of their number in casualties and prisoners. We pursued them vigorously all the way back to Mooresville, where Virginian discipline collapsed. After that, it was a matter of sweeping up the fugitives. We harried the remnants up the Coast Road all the way to New Richmond, and took the town by a surprise assault upon the gates at dawn.

And that is the tale. The men performed magnificently, and there is glory enough for all.

For myself, I must tell you that I feel a great weight has been lifted from my shoulders. My mistake at Yellow Fields can never be forgotten, but the guilt that tormented me for that tragedy has been greatly eased by our success here. With inferior numbers I have fought and won a military campaign against a capable enemy, and that is balm, indeed. Sleep will come easily at last.

By the way, a foundry was discovered here with three cannon in it. Yes, and powder and ball, too, in a nearby warehouse. The cannon resembled the type used in the eighteenth and nineteenth centuries. The barrels were pitted, and one had split open upon testing, apparently. Our smiths report that these three were badly cast, but that new molds were found that would have soon been prepared for casting. A few more months, and they would have had a battery of such weapons. And then what might they have done to our fine men of Kenesee?

I am tired, and must sleep soon. And yet the opportunity! Arn, the opportunity! We dominate the six nations. The leaders will follow our guidance. We must take advantage of this period of flux. Perhaps it is time for a new alliance—or perhaps beyond an alliance. I have much to think about. And we must talk.

I will write again soon. For now, extend my congratulations to your entire command. Kenesee has never seen finer men. Keep yourself well, and keep me informed.

Your brother,
Robert

P.S. Those muskets you captured. Rather than destroying them immediately, I think it would be better if you brought them back to Kenesee.

Murdock and I looked at each other. His lips curled upward, a broad smile formed, and then he leaned back in his chair and sighed. "Virginia conquered. Rodes vanquished. Oh, this is good news. Good news."

"Yes, it is."

"Arn, you're smiling! No, don't let it fade. We have much cause to rejoice. We have had tragedy in great handfuls. If our sacrifices have been blessed with victory, then it gives them all the more meaning."

I laid a hand upon his arm. "I do rejoice. Truly. But it—it's too soon for me. Do you understand? Too soon."

He stared at my face. "Perhaps. Well, time heals all wounds. We will give it a bit longer before calling you to task."

"To task? That's all I do."

"Well, you have another task today, and a pleasant one announcing this news and—all right, don't make that face, I'll do the announcement."

"Thank you, Wizard Murdock. What's in the second envelope?"

Murdock read the front and then broke the seal. "It's from Jason in Tyler." The letter consisted of a single page, and there were but few lines upon it. Murdock scanned it through in a moment, grimaced, and read the words.

June 30th, 2654
Tyler, Texan
To: Prince Arn and Wizard Murdock.

Commander Chalmers is doing well, and should recover from his wound without difficulty. He will be ready for duties within a month. And my son's leg wound is not serious.

But Colonel Daniels died early this morning of peritonitis, a condition common to wounds of the abdomen. I am sorry.

Jason Kendall
Healer

Colonel Daniels, the modest tailor from Loren who had led the archer company at the Rift Gates, and commanded the Sixth Regiment during the War Against the Alliance. John Black had considered him one of the ablest leaders in the army. I had planned to recommend him for promotion to general.

Another trusted man gone. The shock of yet one more loss swept the fuzziness from my mind, and I thought clearly for the first time in days.

''Wizard Murdock.''

''Yes, Arn?''

''You will render the judgment on General Murphy. Your decision will be mine.''

He looked doubtful.

''Please,'' I added.

Murdock slowly folded the messages and put them back into their envelopes. ''Perhaps that will be for the best, after all.''

Sergeant Jenkins knocked and entered. ''Everyone's assembled, sir. They're all waiting.'' He caught our expressions and hesitated. ''Things aren't well at home?''

Murdock stood. ''Things are very well, as you'll hear. But Colonel Daniels is dead.''

Jenkins absorbed the news. ''Damn. He was one of the good ones. A fine officer. I'm sorry.''

''So are we,'' I agreed, standing up slowly. ''So are we.''

In General Murphy's better days, the rectangular reception hall had been devoid of furniture except for the Great Chair. Placed in the middle of one wall, the great chair was a large and impressive construct of metal and wood, thickly padded on seat back and bottom. It stood upon a finely-polished wooden platform with three steps running all around its front and sides. Actually, such a stepped platform was much more convenient than the single-level dais holding Robert's throne in Kingsport. I would have to tell him about it.

A throne by any other name. . . .

Changes had been made to the reception hall. We had arranged the front of the chamber with benches for those awaiting their audience. Most of the benches were filled now, over a dozen great landholders and mayors and colonels seated in the front rows and expecting audience, as well as two score lesser folk occupying the benches behind and hoping to offer their petitions.

To either side of the platform stood a dozen black-uniformed royal guards, shieldless, but with swords out in the rest position while they alertly watched the audience. They could move quickly to intercept any threat to their precious Prince Scar. Along the walls stood some forty infantry from the Sixth Regiment with sheathed swords and another forty from the Texan Fourteenth Regiment.

The Army of Rebellion had arrived at Dallas a few days after our successful entry into the town, Murdock in charge as acting commander-in-chief since both Commander Chalmers and I had been absent. The Loyalist Texans had been paroled with the oath of a year and a day, except for certain Loyalist leaders known for their devotion to Murphy, or accused of heinous crimes in his service. Murdock turned command of the army back to me, and I sent all but two Texan regiments back to their home towns to stand down. The Kenesee regiments were camped outside the city gates with the Texans, but four companies from the Sixth Regiment took up quarters in Castle Corral itself. There were more than enough barracks for them. General Murphy had always liked to have plenty of guardos nearby.

The chatter in the room subsided when the anteroom door opened. The supplicants rose as I entered and painfully climbed the three short steps of the platform. They sat only after I'd taken my place upon the great chair. It really wasn't very comfortable. Too wide and deep, the seat made me feel as if I were slouching if I rested against the back. I seated myself upon the front edge, placed an elbow on the high arm of the chair, and rested my chin in the palm of my hand. I heard the faint creak of wood as Sergeant Jenkins and Sergeant Nielson took station immediately to the left and right of the chair. There, everything that could be done had been done. A nod.

Murdock took his place on the first step and checked the stack of papers he had brought from the antechamber. "Good morning, good people of Texan. Before business, an announcement." He informed them of Robert's victory in Kenesee and triumph at New Richmond. Our troops broke out into cheers, while the Texans looked at each other and wondered what this news would mean for them.

Murdock finished the announcement. "And now, the first order of business today is the judgment of General Jack Murphy, former President of Texan. Bring in the prisoner."

The audience turned their heads to the doors at the back expectantly, chattering until the door opened.

Murphy was led in, shackled and chained. He had been allowed to wash and shave and dress in the clothes of his choice retrieved from the wardrobe in his former bedchamber. He wore a coat of green over a white shirt, with black pants and boots, and a ceremonial sash at his waist. His long hair was plastered wetly to his skull and bound into a ponytail, a new look for the curly-headed tyrant. He was swarthy and rough-featured, his thick, powerful form erect, his stride limited only by the length of the irons that bound him.

For a moment he looked almost dashing as he walked between his four guards, head erect and proud. Except that his eyes darted left and right, furtive and suspicious, putting everyone under his gaze, while the sneer on his lips was for all who walked unfettered. Yes, he did look as much the liar and petty tyrant as he had at the parlay before the Battle of Lexington. Only his fierce defiance served him well, lending an air of confidence that was compelling to watch. No wonder he had held such sway for so long.

His guards forced him to halt before me. "Well, Prince Arn, we meet again," he snarled, and then let forth a stream of oaths and curses directed at me and my kin that raised the eyebrows of even the most experienced soldiers.

It was not really the way to garner mercy, but then, perhaps mercy was not what he sought. Or perhaps bluster was all that was left to keep him from collapsing. I know that in his place, I would have been upon my knees wailing for mercy, beseeching my captors their forgiveness.

Murdock waited impassively, until Murphy tired and fell silent. "If you are done, we will proceed." Not a word more from the general. "You are here to be judged. The responsibility for judging you has been delegated to me. I alone will render judgment. Likewise, I alone will determine your punishment. Do you understand? Good. Your actions are well known, but judgment has not yet been made. This hearing is the one and only opportunity you shall have to plead your case. Do you wish to say anything in your defense?"

He sneered. "I will not plead for anything before this rabble. Kenesee has played upon the trust of my people and divided them, leading my followers astray. Soon you will betray that trust. Foreign domination. That's what my people will suffer now. I say no more."

"Your argument is noted," Murdock intoned. "Will anyone speak on behalf of General Murphy?"

There was silence, and the room was still. None moved, fearful of attracting attention.

"No one? So be it. None will speak for you, General. Do you have any words before judgment is made? This is your last chance to speak."

General Murphy drew himself erect, and I thought he was about to shake his head no. That would have given him a touch of dignity that might be remembered in the histories. But his resolve to be silent could not be maintained. He looked directly at me, and a glint came into his eye, and the malice of the man won out over his common sense. "Just this. One of my followers was loyal to the last. Bartholomew did not surrender. Instead, he took that girl of yours with him. And that thought will give me much comfort, Prince Arn. Much comfort, indeed."

There were gasps from the audience, and all looked to see the effect of the words upon me. But they could read nothing in my features. Few ever could.

Murdock's voice was flat. "General Murphy, you are judged guilty of crimes too numerous to list. Crimes against the Codes, crimes against Kenesee, crimes against your own people, and against the poor wretches you've tormented in your dungeon."

The audience nodded in agreement as the wizard spoke. No surprises so far. They leaned forward attentively, savoring the moment as they waited to hear the sentence. "For your crimes, I sentence you to hang. Sentence is to be carried out immediately."

Murphy began to laugh. Perhaps he was relieved. They took him away, his laughter fading away as the doors were shut behind him But for me, his laughter would never fade from my memory.

Murdock took a deep breath. "Perhaps Prince Arn would like a short recess—"

"No recess. Proceed to the next order of business, please."

Murdock looked at me, and nodded in compliance. "The judgment and sentencing of General Murphy's counselor, Gregor Pi-Ling, originally of Pacifica." We had released most of the poor wretches in the dungeons, who were, almost to a man, merely "traitors" rather than criminals. A few we had kept.

"Prince Arn will render judgment in this case."

Pi-Ling was brought in chained but not shackled, unaccustomed to the light and squinting at the sunshine pouring in through square windows. He had only two guards, though given his physical condition after months in a dark cell, a child would probably have been able to subdue him.

We went through the process, Pi-Ling having his chance to talk. "I've betrayed my trust to Pacifica, and to my adopted nation, Texan. I have failed them both. I realize my error, and regret the suffering my pride and arrogance have caused. I am willing to accept judgment, but ask that mercy be considered in my case. I ask for mercy *not* because I deserve mercy, but rather that I may use my talents to help rectify the wrong I have done."

Not a bad defense, all things considered. Only Kendall spoke up for him, and his comments dealt only with an unlikelihood. "If you presume not to punish Pi-Ling, I ask that you turn him over to me that I might take him back to Pacifica, where his own people will bring him to task for his crimes."

I pronounced my finding. "Pi-Ling, you are judged guilty of crimes too numerous to list here. Your guilt is proven. For your punishment—"

All waited upon my word. Pi-Ling listened hopefully.

"—you are to be hanged. Sentence to be carried out immediately. Take him away."

The Pacifican was still for a long moment, only the features of his face betraying his dismay. And then he accepted the inevitable, bowing politely, turning, and striding out with only the least uncertainty in his step. Every head followed him out.

Murdock gave me a disapproving look. He had tried to convince me earlier that a repentant Pi-Ling might be of some use. I was having none of it.

"Next."

"The Great Landholders of Texan, Prince Arn. You have set a schedule for freeing the slaves, and they have grievance."

Actually, Murdock had set the schedule, and I'd merely nodded approval during one of my more intense bouts with the opiate pipe.

There were six Great Landholders present, all of whom had supported the rebellion. Four, including Fields, were silent, making guarded protest simply by being there. But Lyle Parsons of New Harbor and another were firebrands, arguing how unfair it was to take their property and abolish their economic institutions. No amount of compensation, let alone what was offered, could ever make them give up their property. The two declared that while others might bow to my ruling, they would never submit to tyranny of this sort. They had the courage of their convictions, and I admired them for it.

I told them so. "I admire your resolve and courage."

The two smiled at each other.

"And you are sure your stance is unalterable?"

"Aye," they answered together.

Well, now. I thought about it. Such resistance to the new government—whether me or Chalmers or someone else—could not really be tolerated. Yet, drastic action might create resentment among the Texans, and foment the beginnings of a new rebellion. I did not want to cause further headaches for myself. Then again, in less than a month it would be Chalmers who would have to put up with the headaches, not me. And I remembered the slave pen and the auctions.

"Sergeant Nielson, assign a detail. Take these two out and hang them."

There was a collective gasp, followed by silence. Sergeant Nielson pointed, and four royal guards started toward the landholders.

Murdock rolled his eyes. "Arn. . . ."

Metaxis mumbled to Kren. "He's always ready with the rope, isn't he?"

The beastman shrugged. "Well, not *always.*"

Old Landholder Fields stood and stepped forward, quickly joined by Parsons's steward, James Montrose. Fields hesitated, his courage perhaps balanced by his fear as my attention swung to him, and Montrose spoke first instead. "Prince Arn. May we have one moment with the offenders?"

Ahhh. As I had hoped. I gave a carefully reluctant nod.

The two men stepped close to the condemned, and urgent conversation began. Soon the other landholders joined the conversation, all forming a tight circle from which frantic whispers leaked across the room. They shot anxious glances at me, and eyed the guards who waited nearby.

I gave them a minute or two before speaking. "Enough of this. Have you anything to say?"

The circle was instantly silent. Montrose stepped forward. "Prince Arn, the Great Landholders have pressed their comrades to see reason. And they have agreed. For the friendship of Texan and Kenesee, and the future of our new government, I ask that you pardon the condemned for their hasty and ill-judged resistance."

That was more like it. I grinned wickedly at the landholders. "And what do the rest of you think of our plan for the slaves?"

One gulped. "After further consideration, I believe it is workable, Prince Arn."

"Oh, yes," said another quickly. "Workable."

I leaned forward eagerly. "Are there any objections to it?"

"Objections?" "No objections." "None at all, Prince Arn."

"Very good," I exclaimed. "And is the compensation for each slave adequate?"

"Most adequate." "Generous." "Extremely fair."

Almost there. I stared haughtily at the two firebrands. "And do the condemned agree to the freeing of the slaves?"

Parsons swallowed, looked at his companion, and the two nodded reluctantly. "We agree."

"Excellent. You are pardoned."

A few hangings solve many problems.

I grinned at Murdock. "Who's next?"

The people on the benches looked at each other, and made for the door.

The audience over, I had to listen to Murdock's voice all the way back to my room. "Arn, that was a dangerous ploy. You hang Gregor Pi-Ling against my advice. All right, that's a judgment call. But to threaten the landholders could be dangerous. We need their trust, not their fear."

"You wanted to abolish slavery, we've abolished slavery."

"There are ways of doing these things, Arn. There is consistency. There is persuasion."

"I've persuaded them." I laid down on my bed. Someone had changed the sheets.

"And what if no one had spoken up for them?"

"Well, I am the Hanging Prince, after all."

"Still, that was a dangerous game. Firebrands often enjoy martyrdom."

"I'm tired, Wizard Murdock." I wanted him to leave me so I could get out my pipe.

Murdock threw his papers on the desk. "Tired? Oh, no you don't. Get up. Up." He took me by the arm. "You've had three weeks of opiate to dull your pain. And that's the end. You come with me."

I could not resist the force of his personality. Perhaps I did not want to. "Where are we going?"

I was afraid I knew.

He prodded me up the circular stone stairs from behind, my progress slow and awkward even with a cane, for my leg was stiff; then across the tower room, and out into the sunlight that shone upon the battlements. The battlements. It was a hot and sunny day, just like—

"Murdock, I want to go back down."

"I know you do. I know what you want. That's why I brought you up here. You haven't been up here since that day, have you? Three weeks, and all you've done is lie in your bed or sit listlessly through audiences. Well, it stops now. You can't wallow in sorrow any more. Angela's gone. You face it, and you go on."

"I'm tired."

He pulled me over to the edge, just where Bartholomew had stood with Angela. "Now, you look down."

"No."

"Look down, Arn. You must do this. It will help."

"It will?"

"I think so. At least, you've got to try. Look down, now."

My eyes were on the stonework. She had stood there, right there, less than a month before. And then, gone. I lifted my gaze, and reluctantly let it travel across the stone, to the sharp edge, and then over. I leaned out. Below, the rocks and boulders still waited implacably for anyone else who might seek their answer. There was a stain upon them. I'd heard the rocks had been washed, but still, there was a stain.

I groaned and looked away. From the tower above the west gate hung two tiny figures, each swaying gently in the breeze.

I put my face in my hands, then searched in my pocket.

"I want my pipe."

Murdock's arm went around me. "The pipe, you can have. And the tobacco. But not the yellow powder. Not the opiate."

"But that's what I need." I found the small pouch.

Murdock took away his arm. "Then you must make a choice, Arn."

I held the pouch with both hands wrapped around it. "What choice?"

"The opiate . . . or my friendship."

That stopped me. "You wouldn't go."

"Oh, but I will. I'll have to. You see, I've lost friends, too. So many that I can't bear to lose another. And that's what will happen if you succumb to the opiate. You'll be gone, and my friend Arn will just be a memory, for in his place will be a slave, chained more securely than any working the fields of Texan. I don't think I could bear to see that. Better you were dead."

I studied the pouch. "You want me to stop."

"Yes. Just that."

"I don't think I can."

"The choice is yours. And if my threat is not enough, consider. What example do you set for Lorich, and the others? What path should they follow when adversity strikes them, too? Is that how Lorich should soothe his loneliness? Think, Arn. And if that is not enough, what of Angela? What would she want you to do?"

Angela.

And then the reality of it thundered in upon me, and the truth of it was there for the first time. My chest felt as if it would burst. My face twisted. Murdock opened his arms, and I buried my head in his shoulder. He held me while I sobbed, waited patiently for the tears to end. "She's gone, Murdock. Gone."

"I know Arn."

I lifted my head. "I couldn't rescue her. It's not like the ballads."

"No, it never is." After a time, he held me at arm's length and brushed my hair back into place with his hand before stepping away. "And now you must choose. Despair, and the opiate. Or hope, and life—in all its joy and pain."

"Will you stay with me? If—if I stop?"

"If you stop."

He had me. He and Lorich and Angela. Each argument, alone, might not have worked. But together. . . .

I opened the pouch, held it out over the edge, hesitated, hesitated again, and finally made up my mind. I slowly turned it over. Yellow powder spilled out, was caught by the breeze, and blown away, disappearing almost as if it had never existed.

Murdock's face was not unkind. "The next three or four days will be hard for you. A torture of a different kind. Are you ready for that?"

"Each day is already hard."

He sighed. "Some things are harder. Not many, but some."

We wandered around the length of the battlements and stopped above the central courtyard, simply because of the activity there. Down below, the castle folk were going about their business. Drawn up in front of the castle's doors, two wagons had just arrived under guard of a squadron of cavalry. The tarpaulins covering the wagon were thrown back, revealing their cargo. Muskets. Hundreds of muskets. The muskets of Murphy's guardos, collected off the battlefield of Tyler and brought for safekeeping to the castle. And now, they would have to be sent right back to Tyler for shipment to Kenesee, in accord with Robert's suggestion.

Murdock watched the activity for only a moment. "Let's go back down now. We can talk about it with mugs of beer, and maybe even a little tobacco for you, if you want. We'll rest, chat, and decide what to do. Staying busy will help. There's Robert's letter. We'll have to answer him soon. He'll be wondering. And the slave business will have to be taken care of. And then, there's . . ."

My leg ached terribly, an insistent pain as the wound healed. And then it came to me as I watched the soldiers move the weapons, springing full-blown in my mind as I felt the pain in my leg echoing the pain in my heart. So many had been hurt in the last two years. So many soldiers killed, so many widows left, so many orphans made. War had ruled.

I knew what I must do. "Murdock? I've thought of something. An order."

"What, Arn?"

"The muskets. The muskets we captured."

"Yes?"

"Destroy them."

About the Author

RON SARTI was an administrator in higher education before he began writing full time. He is a Vietnam veteran, and uses his knowledge of military history in his writing. Ron lives in Dayton, Ohio, with his wife and two children.

Ron welcomes mail from readers. He can be reached online at ron7172@aol.com, or by postal mail at: Box 41222, Dayton, Ohio 45441-0222.